M000306676

Luisa

Luisa

A Vivid and Inspirational Story
Based on a True-Life Puerto Rican Girl

NORMA I. GARCÍA PETTIT

Charleston, SC
www.PalmettoPublishing.com

Luisa

Copyright © 2021 by Norma I. García Pettit

All rights reserved.

No portion of this book may be reproduced, stored in a retrieval system, or transmitted in any form by any means—electronic, mechanical, photocopy, recording, or other—except for brief quotations in printed reviews, without prior permission of the author.

First Edition

Hardcover ISBN: 978-1-68515-489-9
Paperback ISBN: 978-1-68515-490-5

Author's Note

In Puerto Rico the Spanish tradition of using two surnames is used. The paternal surname comes first followed by the maternal surname. For example, a man might be named Juan Manuel López Irizarry and be married to María de los Santos Maldonado Torres. Their daughter, Ana María López Maldonado, received her father's first surname (López) and her mother's first surname (Maldonado). In the case of my protagonist, Luisa Torres Torres, both her father and her mother had the same surname.

It is important to note that, historically, middle names do not exist in Puerto Rico. In the above samples, Juan Manuel is his full given name and his wife's full given name is María de los Santos. That being said, nicknames are common; Juan Manuel may be known as Juan, Juanito, Manuel, Manolo, or even something referring to his physical appearance, such as *El Flaco* (the skinny one). María de los Santos might be called María, Mari, Santos or Santa. *Don* (for a man) and *Doña* (for a woman) are sometimes used before an adult's first name to show respect.

When women marry, they do not take their husband's surname. You will see that throughout this book; Luisa's sister Petra married Juan José Collado, but she did not become Petra Collado. She remained Petra Torres Torres. To indicate their marital status, women often add "de" and their husband's surname after their surname. Thus, Petra could have gone by Petra Torres de Collado.

Who was Luisa Torres Torres? She was my maternal great-grandmother. I neither met her nor have a photograph of her. As an avid genealogist, however, I have the names, dates and events that surrounded her life. That data formed the outline for this work of fiction in which I have created a story as I imagined it could have happened. Someday, when I meet Luisa in heaven, she may stand before me with one hand saucily on her hip and ask, "Is that how you pictured me?" I will nod and say, "Yes, that's exactly how I imagined you."

*This book is dedicated to the memory of my parents
Oscar Cruz García and Ana López Maldonado
and to all of my ancestors whose personal stories
have impacted my life.*

*A huge thank you goes to my friend, Kim Reyes,
for all of her tireless help in proofreading and refining my writing.
Thanks also go to Cheri Walswick, Liz Ulmer, Ruben Quiñones,
Tory Serrao, and Wilfredo Quiñones for their input.
I am most grateful to my husband, Randy Pettit,
for encouraging me to fulfill my lifelong dream and for his
unwavering faith in my ability to do so.*

*Luisa Torres was my maternal great-grandmother. Born in June
of 1848, she was raised in the mountains of Adjuntas, Puerto
Rico. In this fiction book I have added flesh and personality to
Luisa and the people that were in her life between January 1867
and May 1870. Most of the names and dates were taken from
my genealogical research, although a few of them were changed by
necessity and several of the characters were my invention.*

*Please note that in the back of the book there is a glossary of the
Spanish words and phrases sprinkled throughout this story.*

Table of Contents

Chapter 1

Preparations

January 13, 1867

The rhythmical sound of the hand-cranked coffee grinder was the first thing that eighteen-year-old Luisa Torres heard as she awoke in the early morning. Unwilling to leave the comfort of her warm bed, she snuggled under her light blanket, hoping to slip back to sleep. Then the rooster crowed gustily, right beneath her window, shattering the remnants of her drowsiness. She opened one eye and saw that Petra's side of the bed was already empty. What was it about today that had gotten her older sister up before the rooster even crowed? Oh! It was the day before Petra's wedding, and there was much to do in preparation. With a low, complaining moan, she threw back the blanket and reached for her sandals. The winter mornings were chilly up in the mountains of Adjuntas, Puerto Rico, despite it being a tropical Caribbean island. Luisa hurried to dress in her everyday ankle length brown cotton skirt and white blouse.

Speaking softly to the younger sister sleeping in the cot against the other wall, Luisa said, "Get up, Pilar. Petra has already risen. She is going to need our help today." She jiggled Pilar's foot for emphasis, and unlocked and opened the wooden shutter from their one window, letting in the early morning light. The rooster crowed again, sounding even louder through the glass-less window opening. Now that she was fully awake, she could hear the murmur of voices coming from the kitchen. A curtain instead of a door closed off their room and the plank walls did not go all the way up to the tin roof of the house. Even though the conversation was not distinct, Luisa knew it was Chenta and Petra talking as they prepared breakfast for the family. She brushed her brown hair quickly and plaited it into one long braid down her back.

Petra bustled about the small kitchen, setting bread and steaming cups of coffee in mismatched cups on the table. A little taller than Luisa and with a darker complexion, twenty-year-old Petra seemed practically to dance as she stepped lightly from the stove to the table. She was wearing a flowered dress that seemed to match her buoyant mood, and her ebony hair was coiled into a tight bun at the nape of her neck.

Two eggs sizzled in the frying pan on the wood burning stove. Ricardo must have his breakfast before all the others so that he could get an early start on his long day of labor on their small farm. He cultivated coffee beans, oranges, grapefruit, papayas, bananas, plantains, avocados, and the staple of the *jibaro* diet, *vianda*—an assortment of tubers such as yucca, taro, celery root, malanga, and sweet potatoes. He worked hard to provide for his family, and they were actually better off than a lot of other mountain families. They had a farm wagon and a team of horses, two goats, a flock of chickens, and two pigs. They used to have three pigs, but one had recently been butchered because of the approaching wedding.

In his late forties, of medium height and build, Ricardo sported a mustache and curly brown hair that tended to get bushy unless cut short. His work on the farm kept him lean and fit.

Ricardo ate his breakfast in contemplative silence, seeming to block out the feminine chatter that Luisa had joined upon entering the kitchen. Serious by nature, but not ill-tempered, Ricardo was a man of few words, anyway. Perhaps he was musing about his work plans for the day, or maybe he was avoiding the conversation that revolved around Petra's big day, for whatever reason. He had to admit to himself that he had mixed emotions about it. Not that he had any qualms about his future son-in-law, who had actually been working for him for a few years, nor did he desire to suppress his daughter's happiness or her right to her own home and future family. It was just bittersweet, that's all.

Rising from his chair, he picked up his straw hat and stepped out the kitchen door to a chorus of "*Bendición, Papá*," from Petra and Luisa as well as Pilar, who had appeared just in time to see her father leaving. It was customary to ask for a parent's blessing when they were arriving or leaving the house. "God bless you, daughters," responded Ricardo. "*Adiós,* Chenta. I'll see you at noon."

Vicenta Torres, or Chenta as she was usually called, was some fifteen years younger than her husband. She and Ricardo had both already lost their first spouses, and while she had been childless, Ricardo had been left with eight motherless children.

When Ricardo, a distant cousin, had approached her with his proposal, Chenta had considered it carefully. It had not been an easy decision for Chenta to agree to marry a man with such a large family and take over the responsibility of raising another woman's children. Ricardo's first wife, Ildefonsa, had been much loved and deeply missed by all. Would the children accept her, or would they cringe at the thought of her occupying their mother's place in their father's bed? Would they listen to her advice and respect her authority in the home? At least Chenta had been familiar with the whole family, having lived in the same mountain community of Juan González, and socializing with them on numerous occasions throughout the years. In all the years that Chenta had known Ricardo, she had never seen him angry or drunk. He was a hardworking man and had a house and land. She could do far worse, and he *was* interested in her.

After a brief courtship, Ricardo and Chenta were married by the priest, and Chenta had moved in. The two oldest girls, Rosa and Sebastiana, gratefully surrendered much of the care of their younger siblings into Chenta's capable hands. Short and a little plump, Chenta wore her long, dark hair slicked back into a tight bun. She was always busy doing what needed to be done around the house and tending to the children's needs. Her presence had soon become not just accepted but welcomed by everyone in the family.

Rosa and Sebastiana had eventually established homes of their own. In fact, three years after Ricardo and Chenta had married, Rosa had married Chenta's younger brother, Domingo, further connecting the two families. They lived in Juan González but not within walking distance. Sebastiana had been married to Juan Francisco Laboy for almost a year now, and they had moved to his hometown of Ponce. The Torres family had not seen Sebastiana and her husband since then. And now Petra was about to be wed! She and her *novio*, Juan José Collado, were looking forward to moving into their own cabin located on another part of Ricardo's property, away from the crowded conditions of her family home. Petra voiced it out loud with a sigh.

"One more busy morning here, and then I will move to the quiet and tranquility of my new home." Petra's eyes were shining with anticipation.

"Yes, but it won't be long until you start filling up your cabin with baby after baby," teased Luisa.

"No. I don't want to have a lot of children. Probably just one or two will be fine," asserted Petra, with a shake of her head.

"You will have the children that God gives you," said Chenta.

"Well, hopefully not for a while. I could use a break." She said this with a little grimace and a sheepish glance in Chenta's direction. In the seven years since Chenta had married Ricardo, she had already given birth to four babies. Tragically, one of the children from the first family, Mario, had died from a fever five years ago, but there was still a house full of younger siblings that Petra had been helping to care for.

"Será cuando Dios quiera y si Dios quiere." It will be when God wills it and if God wills it. Chenta's words were matter of fact. She had a quiet and unshakable faith in God's sovereignty.

It wasn't long before the home was abuzz with activity. As the still sleepy-eyed younger children shuffled into the now cramped kitchen and were hustled out to the porch by Chenta to wash their faces and get a comb run through their hair, Luisa was again filled with a feeling of appreciation for her stepmother.

Petra assisted Chenta in getting the little ones fed, while Luisa began the process of washing the dishes. The kitchen sink hung from outside the kitchen window, far enough down that the wooden shutters could still be closed at night to keep unwanted critters from entering. Luisa heated up water and poured it into a small dishpan, then added soap. Another dishpan held fresh water for rinsing. They would need to fetch a lot more water today to cover all the bathing, cooking, and cleaning needs for tomorrow's celebration.

After breakfast, and after the chickens and pigs were fed, Pilar supervised the making of the beds. Ramón ("Moncho"), 10, and Juan Jacinto ("Juanito"), 6, shared a twin bed, and in the same room Vicenta, 4, and Bonifacia, 2, shared another. Baby Juan Antonio Abad ("Toño"), only one year old, slept in a crib in his parents' room. Chenta took care of straightening up her own room. None of the children except the baby were allowed past the curtain that hung in the doorway.

Luisa gathered up the assortment of empty cracker tins, buckets and jugs used for hauling water, and she set out with Pilar, Moncho and Juanito. They hiked along the path that went winding uphill through the lush, tropical vegetation to an area where the unpolluted spring water ran clear and cold. "Let's catch our breath before collecting the water and heading back down," suggested Luisa. She and Pilar found some huge *yagrumo* leaves to sit on. Luisa thought that the *yagrumo* was an interesting tree. It was tall, for one thing, often growing to sixty feet in height. Its leaves were dark green on top and pale underneath. When the leaves turned upside down, showcasing their silvery undersides, it was an indication that rain was imminent. Furthermore, its enormous leaves that littered the ground could function as umbrellas in an impromptu rainstorm or as protection when one was sitting on the ground, as the girls were now doing.

Moncho and Juanito were still full of energy and chased each other around on bare feet. They knew better than to dip their toes into the water, though. The upstream water had to be maintained clean for their drinking and cooking needs.

The freshness of the morning was already giving way to the effects of the warm sun filtering through the canopy of trees, but the chirping of the birds and the gurgling of the water along the rocky stream were relaxing. Luisa closed her eyes and breathed in the fragrant mountain air. She would have been content to stay there all morning. Maybe next week things would be less hectic and she would have a chance to enjoy the surroundings that she so loved.

"So, what work do we have to do today besides this?" asked Pilar.

"Well, first I want to make sure that our clothes are ready for tomorrow. Is your best dress clean and ironed?"

At a shake from Pilar's head, Luisa continued. "Then that's the first thing we will do when we get back to the house. I will check to see that everyone else has their clothes ready, and I will wash what needs to be done. You and these two boys might as well go with me so that they can bathe and you can wash your hair in the creek."

That being decided, the four of them filled their various containers and trudged back down the hillside to their home with the water. They walked single file along the narrow mountain trail, stepping to the joyful tune of the *ruiseñor*, the Puerto Rican nightingale. Luisa loved to be serenaded by the *ruiseñor*, and she generally stopped whatever she was doing to listen to the songbird's beautiful melody. Today there was no time to stop, but at least it made the trek down the hill more enjoyable. When they deposited the containers in a corner of the wooden floor of the kitchen, Luisa noticed a large burlap bag full of root foods.

"Sebastián brought that by a little while ago," said Chenta.

"What? And he's already gone? I didn't get a chance to see him?" As her only older brother, six years her senior, Sebastián was one of Luisa's favorite people.

"He will be back tomorrow. You will see him then."

Luisa doubted that she would get to spend much quality time with Sebastián during the wedding celebration. She'd probably be too busy refilling people's plates and supervising her younger siblings. In fact, maybe she should put Pilar in charge of the little children. At eleven years old, she was now going to be the second oldest child in the house. It was time to pass on some of the duties of bossing around the younger family members. Moncho, being only one year younger than Pilar, probably wouldn't be too agreeable to her supervising him, and Juanito followed Moncho around like a mischievous little shadow. Luisa could see the difficulties that Pilar would have with those two, but at least she would be a big help in caring for Vicenta, Bonifacia and Toño. If Mario, her sweet, fun-loving brother, had still been alive he would have been fifteen and would have been a great help with the younger boys. But Mario was gone now. Luisa's heart still constricted with sadness over the memory.

Shaking off her brooding, Luisa gathered up the clothes and supplies for washing, rounded up Moncho, Juanito and Pilar, and headed down to the lower area of the creek which was designated for bathing and doing laundry. She had her favorite rock which was perfect for sitting on and the rock next to it which was ideal for scrubbing the extra soiled parts of clothing. Ricardo's clothes could get very grimy from his work on the farm, but today Luisa was only washing those better items of clothing that they intended to wear tomorrow. She kicked off her sandals and gathered up her skirt from back to front between her slender legs, tucking the hem into her waistband. Wading into the creek, she perched herself on the flat rock to get to work. Pilar and the boys were already in the creek, and Pilar was bent over, initiating the process of washing her hair. Luisa was glad that Pilar was old enough to take care of herself now. She was growing so fast! It would not be long until she was a *señorita*. Luisa vowed to herself to have a little talk with the girl soon, to make sure she was aware of the changes to expect in her transition into womanhood.

The laundry task completed and the children bathed and happy from their splashing in the creek, they returned to the house. Pilar helped Luisa carry the clothes heavy with water up the path. Luisa began shaking out the articles of clothing and spreading them to dry on the bushes that surrounded the *batey*, the open, flat yard in front of the house. Looking about her as she hung the wet clothing, Luisa saw that the *batey* needed sweeping, but it would have to wait until after the clothes dried and were removed from the bushes, or they would only get dirty again. The sun was shining bright and warm now; it would not take long for the laundry to dry.

On the porch, Chenta and Petra sat washing and peeling the *vianda* that Sebastián had brought over. They would later cut it up and leave it soaking until tomorrow. It would be boiled to compliment the roast pork, rice, and beans that were to be served to the guests. Three slats of wood across the open door-way of the house kept little Toño from escaping. For the moment, he was happily playing with a spoon and some tin cups, making a harmless racket. But now that he was pulling himself up and toddling around, it was only a matter of time before he tried to escape. Bonifacia, or *la nena* (the little girl) as she was most often called, was also playing with Toño. She was a pretty tot with an abundant mop of curly brown hair. Chenta kept a watchful eye on both of them as she worked. Vicenta had the freedom of playing in the *batey,* and she eagerly wanted to help Luisa hang the laundry. Luisa washed her little hands first and then allowed the small child to help. *She might as well start learning now how things have to be done*, thought Luisa.

"We hang the whiter clothes where they get the full sun, Vicenta," she explained, patiently. "The darker colored clothing goes on the bushes shaded by the house so that they won't fade so much. They will still get dry even though the sun is not beating on them."

Chenta boiled some of the *vianda* for their midday meal and served it to the children with a bit of stewed codfish. Pilar mashed a couple of pieces of the soft roots and spoon fed Toño. After tending to the needs of the younger children, and settling them down for their naps, the older females were able to relax and enjoy their own meal. Ricardo came in and was served his plate of food. He drizzled olive oil on his *vianda,* offered up a short prayer of thanks, and dug in with the appetite that hard work produces.

"So, who is going to the church tomorrow to witness my marriage?" asked Petra. "I can't imagine everyone going. It would take all day to get everyone ready and down to the plaza."

After some discussion, it was decided that only Luisa and Ricardo would go to town. The bride and groom would ride with them in the wagon. The younger children would stay home with Chenta. Pilar pouted a bit because she had really wanted to go, but she would be needed to watch her siblings while Chenta prepared the feast.

As soon as the clothes were dry, Luisa brought them inside and then gave the hard-packed dirt *batey* a careful sweeping. The iron had been set on the stove to heat up for the task of pressing all the garments, and Chenta was now heating up water for bathing the three youngest children after their nap. This all had to be done before supper. Petra and Chenta also began a big pot of chicken stew which Petra tended to while Chenta bathed the youngsters on the porch and Luisa ironed.

The ironing took a long time because as the iron cooled it had to be set back on the stove to get hot again, so Luisa did the ironing in the living room to be closer to the kitchen stove. She heard Chenta call out, "Toño, *ven acá*. Come here and let me finish drying you off." Luisa looked up from ironing her father's dress shirt in time to see baby Toño standing naked in the doorway. "There's our little Taíno Indian boy!" laughed Luisa. Toño squealed and tottered back to his mother on unsteady feet. Luisa smiled as she continued her task. The ironing was making her hot, and she envied how Toño could frolic around nude, still damp from his bath.

Realizing that more water was going to be needed to accommodate the bathing of the adults in the house plus tomorrow's cooking and drinking needs, Luisa, Pilar and the boys gathered up their containers and made another trip up to the spring-fed stream. Emptying the water into a cistern on the porch, they made one last trip for more.

Juan José showed up at suppertime and, of course, was served a bowl of the savory chicken stew. Any person that showed up at mealtime was served a plate of food; that was just customary hospitality. Children learned to eat their food as soon as they were served because if a guest arrived unexpectedly, and there was nothing left on the stove, any untouched food might get taken off of their plates to feed the guest.

After supper, Petra and Juan José disappeared down the path for some quiet conversation, handholding, and a few stolen kisses. They were both so excited to be getting married! Luisa and Pilar did the dishes while Ricardo and Chenta had their own conversation and Ricardo gave some attention to the little ones clamoring for it.

Luisa heated up water, deciding to do her bathing early in the evening while the others were occupied and the bathhouse was *un*occupied. The bathhouse was a small wooden structure just beyond the *batey*, separate from the outhouse. It was empty except for two basins that hung on the wall, a wooden bench along one wall, a short ledge for the soap, and a clothing peg. Luisa brought in her towel and a change of clothes and laid them on the bench. Taking the basins down from the wall, Luisa filled both of them with fresh water, adding hot water from the stove to both basins until the water was a comfortable temperature. The bar of soap was plopped into one of the basins. She undressed, used a tin cup to scoop up water to splash on herself, soaped up, then rinsed off with scoops of the clear water. Quickly drying off and dressing in the clean garments, Luisa emptied the basins of water, hung them back up on the wall, set the soap to dry on the ledge and gathered up her soiled items.

Outside, the air was now cool and the sky filled with stars. Luisa lingered on the porch, listening to the chorus of *coquís,* the tiny but loud frogs endemic to Puerto Rico. The doves were also cooing on the roof, evoking a peaceful environment. Juan José and Petra had returned from their walk, and he had gone on home. Petra was back inside, helping get her younger siblings ready for bed one last time. For Luisa, this was practically the first time she had been idle all day long, and she relished the tranquility of those few moments of solitude. It had been a very busy day, and tomorrow promised to be an exciting one.

Chapter 2

The Wedding

When Luisa entered the kitchen the next morning, Petra was already having her usual breakfast of bread and coffee and was heating up water on the stove to use in the bathhouse. The sisters both wore huge smiles as they greeted one another. Luisa poured herself a cup of coffee and joined Petra at the table.

"Today is the day, huh? You are getting married! Are you nervous?" asked Luisa.

"Not nervous, but anxious for everything to go well. I wish the water would hurry up and get hot. I need to get ready."

"Well, that is why I bathed last night. I didn't want to tie up the bathhouse today because you would need it more than me. Where are Chenta and *Papá*?"

"*Papá* is in the barn taking care of the animals and Chenta is in their room with Toño. He is being a little fussy this morning. Here—have some bread with your coffee. We need to be ready to go when Juan José shows up."

"It is our last time having morning coffee together," observed Luisa. "I am going to miss you. You know we have shared a bed as long as I can remember, and you are my best friend."

"I will miss you, too," replied Petra.

"No, you won't!" laughed Luisa. "You are going to be a wife and will spend all of your time with your handsome husband. But promise me that you will visit soon."

"I promise!" Petra downed the last of her coffee and gave Luisa a hug before getting up to take the hot water to the bath house. Luisa hurried to finish her coffee as well.

Back in her room, she rustled Pilar out of bed with a nudge and a "Get up, *Mamita,* you need to help Chenta with the little ones today. I'm not going to be able to help her."

Luisa made the bed that she had shared with Petra almost all her life, and then laid out the dress that she had washed and pressed the day before. Though not new, it was her best dress and had only been worn a couple of times for special occasions. *At least I do not have to worry about outgrowing my dresses anymore*, she thought. Luisa hadn't grown any taller during the last few years, and at 5'2 she was about two inches shorter than Petra. Slipping out of her nightdress and into the sky-blue cotton dress, she smoothed out the fabric and admired its pretty pattern of tiny white flowers. It would do nicely. She didn't want to look shabby accompanying her sister and father to the church in the plaza or afterwards, when family and friends came to partake of the celebration.

She was brushing her long hair when Petra came in, fresh and clean, but wearing a worn housedress. She hadn't wanted to take her wedding dress into the bathhouse. "Here, let me help you with your hair first, and then you can help me with mine," she offered.

Petra parted Luisa's hair down the middle, and coiled it along the sides of her head, using pins to secure it in place. "Do you want it hanging down loose, braided, or in a bun?" she asked.

"I think braided and then in a bun. It will be out of my way while I'm running around serving people," replied Luisa.

"You are such a blessing! When it is your turn to marry, I will come to help you," promised Petra.

"Sure you will—with three or four kids hanging onto your skirt!" laughed Luisa. "Besides, I don't know who I will marry. There isn't exactly a string of suitors coming around here asking for my hand in marriage."

"Maybe you will meet the man of your dreams today. You know what they say, *'De una boda sale otra.'" Out of one wedding comes another.*

Luisa helped Petra into her wedding dress, which had been made for her by Chenta, with Petra and Luisa's help. Chenta had done the cutting of the fabric and the sewing together of the parts, while Petra and Luisa had done the finishing—the hemming and the lace trim. The cream-colored gown, with lace-edged ruffles along the neckline, created a striking contrast with Petra's umber skin tone. It fell in gentle folds to her feet.

"Te ves bella," a misty-eyed Luisa told her sister. *You look beautiful.*

Petra opted to have a similar hairstyle as Luisa, with her dark brown hair also rolled on the sides and gathered securely in the back with pins but with the rest hanging down her back in soft curls.

"We will put a red *amapola* in your hair when we go out to wait for Juan José, and you will be all set." Luckily, the hibiscus-like flower bloomed all year long right off the *batey*.

"I also have my white lace mantilla to wear in the church," added Petra. "I don't want to put it over my head until we get there, though. It might blow off and land in the dirt. That would be a disaster!" She laughed at her own exaggeration.

Within an hour, the family was waving goodbye to Juan José, Petra, Ricardo, and Luisa as they began their descent down the mountain to the town center. Ricardo drove the team of horses with Luisa next to him, while Juan José and Petra sat directly behind them on the bench seat in the wagon bed, facing backwards. Juan José was dressed sharply in a brown suit with a new white shirt and brown tie. His mustache was nicely trimmed and his brown, wavy hair was neatly combed. His skin was tanned from working outdoors, although he was not as dark as Petra.

The horses picked their way carefully, and the little bridal party was greeted intermittently by neighbors that came out to their front porches, summoned by the sound of the hooves and the wagon wheels. Once down on the main road, they also encountered a few travelers who doffed their hats and called out a blessing to the bride and groom: *"¡Dios los bendiga!"* All along the way, they were serenaded by birds, and a gentle breeze swayed the tree branches and ferns that lined the roadway, adding to the perfection of the morning.

The Catholic church, San Joaquín, was on one side of the plaza. When they arrived, Luisa could see that other family members were already there, including her sister, Rosa and brother-in-law, Domingo. Rosa was twenty-six years old and had been married to José Domingo Torres for five years. Short and pretty, with medium brown hair and a light olive complexion, Rosa was the sister that Luisa most resembled. The big surprise was their sister, Sebastiana and her husband, Francisco, who had come from Ponce for the wedding! Rosa and Sebastiana hugged Petra and Luisa and exclaimed over Petra's gown and hair.

Ricardo, on seeing Sebastiana, exclaimed, *"¡Eh, mira quien está aquí!" Look who is here!* He embraced his daughter and shook Francisco's hand. Francisco looked dapper in a tan suit. His face was clean shaven and his dark brown hair neatly combed. Sebastiana was lovely in a long dark skirt and white blouse with her straight brown hair hanging loose down her back. She looked a lot like Petra except with lighter coloring.

"We didn't know that you were coming, Sebastiana," said Luisa, still in shock. "When did you arrive and where are you staying?"

"We got here yesterday and are staying with Rosa and Domingo," responded Sebastiana. "We were not sure that we would be able to come, but it worked out that we could, and here we are! Rosa was just as surprised as you when we showed up at her house."

Also in attendance was their maternal grandmother, Eusebia. Luisa turned to greet her with a hug and kiss and said, *"¡Bendición, Mama Sebia!"*

"Dios te bendiga, Mija." The elderly woman appeared to be so much frailer than the last time that Luisa had seen her. She looked worn out. *Well, no wonder*, thought Luisa. She knew that her grandmother had given birth to fifteen babies, several of whom had not survived infancy. Three adult daughters had also already passed away. The first was Luisa's mother, Ildefonsa,

in 1858. A year later, María Apolinaria had died, and in 1865, Marcelina. Luisa did not know how her grandmother could have withstood so much pain, but the withered little old lady was stoic and strong in her faith. She was confident that one day she would be reunited in heaven with all of her loved ones.

Taking Mama Sebia by the elbow, Luisa guided her into the church. They dipped their fingers into the receptacle containing holy water and made the sign of the cross. Luisa genuflected as she crossed the center aisle that led to the altar, and she and Mama Sebia made their way slowly to the front of the church. Mama Sebia's steps were labored, and Luisa, still holding on to the elderly woman's elbow, matched her pace to her grandmother's. They took their seats in the front row, next to Ricardo, Sebastiana and Francisco.

There was no fanfare, no music, no procession down the aisle, no bridesmaids in fancy dresses, or groomsmen standing starched and uncomfortable next to a nervous groom. It was a simple *jíbaro* wedding. Petra and Juan José stood humbly and reverently before the beloved parish priest, *Padre* Irizarry.

Rosa and Domingo stood alongside Juan José and Petra as their witnesses when *Padre* Irizarry conducted the wedding ceremony. *Will I really be doing this someday? Which of my sisters will stand with me as witness? Who will be my future husband? What will he be like and where will we live?* With an almost imperceptible shake of her head and a double blink of her eyes, Luisa brought her thoughts back to the bride and groom and the benediction that was now being given by *Padre* Irizarry. In no time at all, the blushing bride and her grinning groom were being hugged, kissed, and congratulated by the family and friends that were in the church.

By the time the guests began arriving at the house that afternoon, Ricardo and the boys had already set out a table for the bride and groom, another makeshift table for the food, and a third for the gifts. An assortment of chairs, crates, and overturned buckets dotted the perimeter of the *batey.* First to arrive was *Doña* Felipa Sandoval, Juan José's mother, who was accompanied by her daughter, Juana María and son-in-law Luciano Serrano. Sadly, Juan José's father, Manuel Collado, had passed away a few years earlier. At forty-seven years of age, *Doña* Felipa was still healthy and vivacious, and she immediately went to assist Chenta in the kitchen. Next to arrive were Domingo and Rosa, and Sebastiana and Francisco. Rosa also went right in to help out, but Sebastiana was accosted by her younger siblings who had not seen her in nearly a year. Pilar, holding Toño, was the first to embrace Sebastiana.

"Is this Toño?" exclaimed Sebastiana. "Oh, my goodness! He was just a newborn when I saw him last. And look at these little girls! Vicenta, do you remember me?"

Vicenta nodded and allowed her big sister to give her a hug, but Bonifacia hung back behind Pilar's skirt.

"*Ay, bendito, la nena* doesn't know me. *Ven acá, Mamita.* I am your sister."

"She will warm up to you soon enough," assured Pilar. "Look, here come Moncho and Juanito."

The boys bashfully allowed themselves to be hugged and exclaimed over. They were still in shock over the unexpected arrival of Sebastiana and Francisco. Sebastiana noted how much taller Moncho now was. With his curly brown hair, he was beginning to look a lot like his father. Juanito's hair was lighter and straighter. Sebastiana commented on how nice he looked in his best pants and shirt and with his hair neatly combed. The boys beamed at the compliments. After all of the greetings were exchanged, Sebastiana went into the house to see if her help was needed.

Mama Sebia was brought in a horse drawn wagon, driven by her son, Gregorio, who lived in a different *barrio* of Adjuntas. The wagon bed carried his wife, Paula, and four of his seven children. Luisa was glad to see her cousin María de la Paz, who was close to her in age. She hoped that they would have a chance to visit during the course of the afternoon. *Tío* Agustín arrived with his wife, Bartola, and their three children, Carmen, Juan, and Casimiro. *Tío* Canuto and family lived in Vegas Abajo, a barrio that was adjacent to Juan González. He came with his wife, Anastacia, and surviving children, Catalino, Andrés, and Margarita.

As the guests arrived by horseback or in horse drawn wagons, the menfolk gathered outside Ricardo's stable to tend to the horses and talk about their work, their concerns over political unrest on the island, and news in general.

Friends and neighbors also made their way to the Torres home, including several of the Maldonado clan. It was said that anyone with the Maldonado surname was related in one way or another, and there were Maldonados scattered throughout Juan González and other barrios of Adjuntas. One such family lived on the other side of the ravine and socialized frequently with Luisa's family. They were Leocadio Maldonado, a big man with a booming voice, and his slender, dark-skinned wife, Aquilina Montero. Their children were Felita, Dionicia, José, Rosa, and María. Another daughter, Gracia, was already married, and she came separately with her husband, Juan Pablo Arroyo.

All the families that arrived brought something to contribute to the wedding feast, in addition to a gift for the bride and groom.

Luisa had placed a clean tablecloth on the long food "table" made of planks supported by sawhorses. Doña Felipa and Luisa began carrying out the food that Chenta had spent all morning cooking, and Luisa's aunts hurried to help, as well. Between what Chenta had prepared and what others had brought, the table was brimming with pots of rice, beans, *vianda,* roast pork, stewed chicken, *bacalao,* bread, rice pudding and cake. By prearrangement, Rosa, Tía Marcelina, and Aquilina had brought plates, bowls, cups, and cutlery from their own homes since Chenta didn't own enough for all the guests that they anticipated having. The womenfolk were kept busy filling plates and serving guests, and soon everyone was enjoying the meal, whether sitting on a chair, an overturned bucket, or a crate. Several of the men were eating while standing up or sitting on their haunches. The small children ran around but returned to their mothers for intermittent bites of the savory food.

Pilar, taking her childcare duties to heart, gathered up the little ones to play together where she could keep an eye on them. It wouldn't do for a small child to wander down the trail to the creek, although that is exactly what some of the mid-sized boys were scheming to do. Little sister Vicenta was overjoyed at having her cousin Margarita there to play with. They were happily preparing "food" for their imaginary babies, using leaves and twigs as "ingredients," and chattering non-stop. Bonifacia wanted to play with them, too, but Vicenta protested loudly that *la nena* was messing up the meal that she and Margarita were preparing.

Tío Gregorio brought along his *bordonúa*, Leocadio his *cuatro*, and *Tío* Canuto his *tiple*. Together they made up a *jíbaro* orchestra of stringed instruments of the guitar family. Ricardo brought out his maracas which he had made himself out of hollowed out and dried gourds filled with dry roasted coffee beans. Someone else had a *güiro,* also made from a gourd, with lines scored into it. When the musician used a metal pronged *púa* on it, a scratchy rhythm was produced that got everyone's feet moving. Luisa noted that the essential elements of Puerto Rican festivities were all there: family, friends, food, and music. This might be true of every culture, but Luisa only knew the country lifestyle of her mountain community. She knew that every family there that day had experienced their share of sadness and hard times, but at that moment everyone was joyful, had full stomachs, and were enjoying the pleasures of good conversation and music. Soon the *batey* was filled with dancing couples, from old to young.

Luisa finally had a chance to sit with María de la Paz and their friends, Felita and Dionicia, and indulge in girl talk. Dionicia kept stealing glances over to where some of the young men were standing under a mango tree just off the *batey.*

"Who is that handsome man next to your brother, Sebastián?" she asked Luisa in a low voice.

Luisa turned to look, and then said, "Oh, that's my cousin Catalino. He is my uncle Canuto's oldest son. They live in Vegas Abajo."

"Oh, I remember Catalino now. I have not seen him in a long time. He sure has gotten cute, and he is looking over here, too," said Dionicia with a giggle. "I hope he asks one of us to dance."

"You mean you hope he asks *you* to dance," said María de la Paz, "He is my cousin, you know."

"That doesn't mean anything, really," observed Luisa. "My parents were cousins, and even Chenta is a distant relative of my father."

Luisa saw Catalino say something to Sebastián, and Sebastián responded by nudging him with his elbow. Then Catalino crossed the *batey* to where the girls were still whispering, and looking directly at Dionicia, he smiled and asked, *"¿Quieres bailar?"*

Without hesitation, Dionicia accepted his invitation to dance. The other girls shared knowing looks and smiles. A minute later, Sebastián came to ask Felita to dance, and Luisa and María de la Paz were left alone to share their thoughts and feelings about the day's happenings.

"Petra looks so radiant, doesn't she?" sighed Luisa. It was going to be so different without her closest sister there in the house with her, but Luisa was happy for her. Juan José was holding Petra close as they danced, and the adoring looks that they exchanged were sweet to see. They seemed to be in their own world, oblivious to the others dancing in the *batey.*

"Pacita, do you think there is someone out there for us?" asked Luisa.

"Oh, yes, absolutely!" gushed María de la Paz. "Maybe not here and now, but our day will come."

"Maybe Dionicia's day has already come. Look at them!" Luisa used her pursed lips to point in the direction of Catalino and Dionicia, who were barely moving, his hands still on her waist and hers on his shoulders. They appeared to be deep in conversation. "She's younger than I am. I hope she takes her time and does not let Catalino sweep her off her feet. He is a good person, but he is a grown man, older than Petra, and she is only sixteen."

María de la Paz looked at Luisa in astonishment. "They are only dancing and talking. You have them practically running off together already!"

Luisa laughed. "Well, that is how it usually starts. But you are right." Immediately, one of her father's sage sayings came to her mind: *Piensa para hablar y no hables para pensar. Think before speaking and don't speak to think.* Luisa realized that she had been voicing her thoughts out loud and that it was best to keep her thoughts to herself...at least for now.

The neighbors and family would eventually be heading to their homes and Luisa would be busy saying goodbye to their guests and then beginning the task of helping to clean up, but for now she would enjoy this time of celebration. Sebastián and Felita had finished their dance and he now held out his hand to his sister. Luisa was all smiles as she and her brother moved to the lively beat of *guaracha* music. What could be better than being in this moment, in this place, with so many happy people?

Chapter 3

A Trip into Town

It was a nearly a week after the wedding before Luisa and Petra saw each other again. Following the celebration, the bride and groom had loaded up Ricardo's wagon with their wedding gifts and her personal belongings and had gone on to begin their married life in their own cabin. The cabin was actually one of three small dwellings in addition to the family home, spaced out on Ricardo's ten-acre farm. Sebastián had been occupying one of them for the past two years, and now Juan José and Petra were living in the second one. The third one had been vacant since a former farm worker and his family had moved to the town of Utuado the previous summer.

Sebastiana and Francisco had a wonderful time visiting with family and friends at the wedding, but the next day they departed from Rosa's house to return to Ponce. It had been a short but sweet visit. Luisa hoped that another whole year would not go by before they all saw Sebastiana again.

On Friday, when Ricardo came home for lunch, he brought a message for Luisa from Petra by way of Juan José. After opening their gifts, Petra had expressed the desire to purchase a couple more items that she felt were necessary. Juan José had suggested that she and Luisa ride to town with him and Sebastián on Saturday when they took farm produce in to sell at the *plaza del mercado*, the farmer's market. They would have a few hours to shop at leisure in town. In the afternoon, they could drop Sebastián off at his place and Luisa at her home on their way back to their own cabin.

Luisa was ecstatic. *"¿Me das permiso, Papá?* "

Ricardo chewed on a bite of his lunch, swallowed, and took a sip of water before responding. Luisa waited hopefully. *"Sí, Mija,"* he finally said. "You have permission to go. But remember who you are. Don't be flirting with men."

"¡Papá! How can you even say that to me? You know that I would never do that!" Luisa was genuinely offended.

"No, of course you wouldn't purposely flirt with men, but *Mija*, when men see a fresh, lovely face like yours, they are going to try to talk to you, you know, to try to get close to you."

Luisa felt color rising in her cheeks. "Well, they can try all they want. I am just going to ignore them. I am only looking forward to spending a day with Petra and looking at all the pretty things in the stores. That's all."

Some of the joy of the planned outing had escaped for Luisa, but she understood that her father had only spoken out of his love and concern for her. She tried to put their conversation out of her mind as she planned what to wear the next day. There were not a lot of choices, actually. Besides her two everyday outfits for working around the house and her best dress which she wore for Petra's wedding, she had two other dresses to choose from. Either one would do, she decided, but remembering what her father had said, maybe the gray cotton dress would make her less conspicuous than the beige dress with large pink flowers.

The next morning, Luisa was up before dawn. On the days when the men took the produce to town, they had to get an early start. As it was, stopping by to pick up Luisa would make them later getting to town; she did not want to add a further delay by not being ready when they showed up. In fact, she was the first one up. She ground the coffee beans and put the fresh grounds in a pan of water on the stove. When it was boiling, she poured them through the *colador*—a cloth sack that hung from a metal frame with a handle—and into a pot. The coffee grounds stayed in the strainer and the pot was filled with fragrant black coffee. To make their customary *café con leche*, Luisa poured some black coffee into another pan, added milk and heated it up. Luisa had just finished having a cup of *café con leche* with some bread and butter, when she heard the wagon pull up.

The two sisters were happy to sit on the bench in the wagon bed directly behind Juan José and Sebastián and chat all the way. The wagon was loaded with crates of oranges, avocados, grapefruit, and papayas. The first part of the road down the mountainside was rough and bumpy, and Luisa half expected a papaya or two to go flying out of the wagon. The girls had to hold on to their seat, but it was such great fun to be together again. Once down on the main road that ran between Adjuntas and Utuado, the way was smoother, and Luisa and Petra were able to relax their grip on the bench. Sebastián guided the horses on toward the town of Adjuntas.

"So, tell me how your life is now as a married woman," prodded Luisa. She looked intently at Petra to study her expression as she responded.

"Well…" hedged Petra, looking straight ahead and choosing her words carefully. "It does take a little getting used to. I think the biggest thing is how unnatural it is to wake up in the morning next to Juan José. We have known each other for so long, but you know how protective *Papá* is, and how little opportunity we were given to be alone together. So, it is strange that after standing before the priest in the church and then having the celebration in the *batey,* suddenly it was okay to be in bed with Juan José that night." Petra giggled a little self-consciously.

"Yes, that would be strange. I cannot even imagine it." Luisa turned her questioning in a different direction. "What is it like to cook for him? Is he picky and demanding?"

"No, not at all," asserted Petra. "He seems to like my cooking, and really, he goes off to work in the morning just like Papá and comes home for lunch, then he is off again until suppertime. I have the whole day to myself. It was fun setting out or putting away the wedding gifts, but that did not take long, and I sweep the cabin every day, but that does not take long, either. The most time-consuming chore is the laundry. Since I do not have a creek close to the house for washing clothes, I have to use a tub and a washboard and haul in lots of water. But it is only laundry for two people, so that's not so bad."

"Sounds like you have extra time on your hands, Petra," observed Luisa. Then she added with a wink, "You could always come over and help take care of your little siblings."

"No, no, no," laughed Petra. "It's nice and quiet at our place, and I like it that way! You are welcome to come visit me, though.

Maybe you and Pilar can come over tomorrow for a while in the afternoon, while the little ones are napping. Surely Chenta can spare you for a few hours."

Luisa smiled. "That would be lovely. I am sure Pilar would be thrilled to make the trek to your place with me. She is growing up quickly, and I was thinking that I should have a talk with her soon because I don't think Chenta will, and I don't want her to be caught by surprise when…you know… Do you think that is something that we can do together when we are at your cabin tomorrow?"

Petra nodded. "Yes, that would be the perfect time. We will be all alone and have the privacy that we need."

Arriving at the already bustling plaza, Sebastián pulled the team alongside of it at a clear spot where they could offload and display their produce. Juan José jumped down and reached up a hand to help the girls climb down.

"Would you like us to stay and help you set up?" asked Luisa.

"No, that's men's work. You girls go off and have fun doing your shopping," her brother answered.

With a shrug and an "Okay," Luisa looped her arm through Petra's and they headed off in the direction of the general store. As they passed groups of men setting up their crates of produce, Luisa and Petra were followed by more than one set of interested eyes, but they paid them no mind. Newlywed Petra's mind and heart were only filled with thoughts and feelings for her husband and their home. Innocent Luisa was blissfully unaware of how fresh and sweet she looked in her dove gray dress, with her long braid swinging as she walked.

The general store was on the other side of the plaza. A bell on the door tinkled as the two young women entered, and they were greeted by *Doña* Juana.

"Buenos días, chicas, ¿en qué les puedo servir?" *Good morning, girls, how can I help you?*

"There are a couple of things that I need to get," said Petra, "but first we would just like to look around, if that's okay. We are not in a hurry."

"Sí, como no. Tomen su tiempo." *Yes, of course. Take your time.*

Luisa and Petra sauntered through the store, fingering cloth and imagining the dresses that they could make from them. Both were adept seamstresses, sewing one's own clothes being a necessity in the rural mountain communities of Puerto Rico. They admired the china figurines that were on display on one shelf, but neither one had any use for them nor did they have money to spend on such impractical things. Luisa paused by a table stacked with books, notebooks, and other educational supplies. None of Ricardo's children had ever been to school, and Luisa and her siblings did not know how to read or write. She would have liked to learn, but she was never given the opportunity. There wasn't even a schoolhouse in Juan González or in any of the other rural *barrios*.

There was only so much to look at in the center of the store. Most of the goods were up on shelves on three of the walls, and *Don* Pepín often had to climb up on a ladder to reach the requested item. Petra now approached the counter and told *Doña* Juana that she needed *un caldero*, a large pot. She had been given one as a wedding present from Juan José's mother, but she was in need of another one so that she could use one pot for making rice and the other one for stewing beans.

NORMA I. GARCÍA PETTIT

"So, what have you been using to cook your beans in, if you didn't have a big pot?" asked Luisa.

"I have a small pot that I used for cooking the rice and I used the *caldero* that *Doña* Felipa gave me to stew the beans. But if I have guests that I need to cook for, I am going to need a bigger pot for the rice."

Doña Juana produced a set of three *calderos* in varying sizes, and Petra chose the one that she wanted. Next, Petra asked to see coffee grinders. The one that was already there mounted on the kitchen wall in the cabin was very old and in poor condition. Petra felt that she was wearing out her arm from trying to use that old thing every morning. *Don* Pepín had to locate a coffee grinder on one of the top shelves and use his ladder to retrieve it. Petra was happy with it, so *Doña* Juana rang up the purchase while *Don* Pepín wrapped up both items in sturdy brown paper and tied a string around each package.

Luisa and Petra each picked up one of the packages, said their cordial goodbyes to the store owners, and headed back outside into the bright sunshine. They took a leisurely stroll around the plaza, stopping to look in at store windows or to see what produce and other goods were being sold at the farmer's market. Eventually, they made their way back to where Sebastián and Juan José had set up their produce to sell.

Juan José helped the girls back up into the wagon bed where they proceeded to unwrap the lunch that Petra had packed. Sebastián and Juan José took turns having their simple lunch of bread and cheese with Luisa and Petra while the other continued taking care of prospective customers. They helped themselves to fruit from the crates *para endulzar*—to "sweeten up" after their meal.

With the sun just beginning its descent toward the western mountain peaks, the foursome headed home with a lighter wagonload but still with lots of produce left to divide between the households. The first stop was to drop off Sebastián. Luisa and Petra alighted to take turns using Sebastián's outhouse while he put a small assortment of fruit into a crate for his own use. As a bachelor, he didn't need much. The bulk of the leftover fruit would go to Ricardo's house. The next stop was to drop off Luisa. Petra put together a crate of produce for her and Juan José, and then went in to visit with Chenta and her younger siblings, leaving Juan José to offload the rest of the crates onto the porch.

Luisa went directly to her room to change out of her gray dress and into one of her house dresses, and then rejoined the family. Back on the porch, the children were clamoring for *chinas,* so Luisa and Juan José obliged by peeling several oranges for them. The trick was to use a sharp knife to remove the orange peel in one continuous coil, without breaking it. Juan José was particularly adept at this, to the great admiration of Moncho and Juanito. The coils of orange peels were tossed onto the ground to see what "appeared." Sometimes they declared that the peels looked like snakes, other times like a bird's head. The children were each handed a peeled orange with the top sliced off. They squeezed the orange to suck out all of the juice while playing their orange peel game.

Later on, Vicenta, Bonifacia and Toño were taken inside for their nap, and the others stayed on the porch, enjoying the traditional mid-afternoon cup of coffee. Even Moncho and Juanito were permitted coffee with lots of milk, which thankfully, the she goat provided plenty of. The ladies reminisced about the excitement and busyness of the wedding celebration that had taken place right there in their *batey* only the week before. Petra talked about the gifts she had received: some pillowcases, aprons, towels, bed sheets, cups and plates, cooking and eating utensils, and the *caldero.* Petra was still amazed at the assortment of useful gifts that had provided almost everything that she and Juan José needed in their cabin. Ricardo had given the couple some hens and a rooster so that the newlyweds could start their own flock. The cabin had already been furnished with a bed, a table and chairs, and a wood burning stove. In the months before her wedding, Petra had sewn some curtains for the windows and the doorway to the bedroom. She was anxious to have her first guests in her little home.

"Chenta, can you spare Luisa and Pilar tomorrow afternoon after the little ones go down for their nap? I would like to have them come to my cabin for a couple of hours." Petra implored Chenta with her eyes.

Chenta gave her approval, and Pilar's whole face lit up with excitement. She never got to go anywhere. Spending an afternoon with her older sisters away from her home was such a grown-up thing to do! Luisa smiled affectionately at Pilar, knowing how much she would enjoy the outing.

Petra and Juan José went home, and Luisa, Pilar and the boys made a trip up the mountain trail to the stream for fresh water. They were back in plenty of time for Luisa to sweep and tidy up the house and to help Chenta with the cooking and the children before Ricardo came home. He liked to find things orderly and his supper ready when he walked in, exhausted from his day's labors.

All too soon, the wonderful day was drawing to a close, but there was something to look forward to tomorrow that would be another pleasant break in Luisa's daily routine. She would sleep well that night, with the *coquís* singing outside her window, memories of her day with Petra in her head, and anticipation for the morrow bringing a smile to her relaxed face.

Chapter 4

Changes

The next afternoon, as planned, Luisa and Pilar set out to visit Petra. They hiked up the mountain path, a different path that did not lead them past the stream where they fetched water. The girls carried their sandals in their hands; walking up the sometimes slippery fern-lined path was easier with bare feet, and they also didn't want their sandals to get dirty. For much of the way, they had to walk single file, but in other parts the path widened and leveled out. They were able to pause and rest in these areas, and Luisa reveled in the sights and sounds of her beloved Puerto Rican jungle land.

"*¡Escucha al pájaro carpintero!*" *Listen to the woodpecker!* "And I hear a San Pedrito, also." The little songbird's distinctive chirping echoed through the trees. Luisa peered up into the fronds of a tall Palma de Sierra, hoping to see the bright green feathers of an elusive *cotorra*, the Puerto Rican Parrot.   She had seen a parrot before, and she knew that they fed on the fruit of the palm trees, but today she was not in luck.

"Can we sit for a little while?" asked Pilar, a little plaintively.

Luisa noted the beads of perspiration on Pilar's forehead and nodded in agreement. She was a little winded herself, and sitting under the shade of a *nogal* sounded enticing. The *nogales*, walnut trees, were important for providing shade for the coffee plants on Ricardo's farm. They found *yagrumo* leaves to sit on, as they customarily did.

They sat and rested for a period of time. The sounds of the leaves being ruffled by the breeze and the songbirds and buzzing insects all combined to create a tropical orchestra. Adding to that, Pilar's never-ending story about a dream that she had the night before was causing Luisa to start feeling drowsy. A nice, hot cup of coffee was calling to her.

"Let's get moving again," she said, as she scrambled to her feet. "Petra must be waiting for us."

Along the next section of their trek, they discovered a *guamá* tree and picked pods off of it, eating the fluffy interior of some of them as they continued their hike, and saving some of them for Petra. Closer to the cabin, they snapped off a couple of small branches of another tree, the *laurel geo*, which had lovely white and yellow flowers. They wiped their feet on a patch of grass and slipped on their sandals.

Petra greeted them joyfully when they arrived, exclaiming over the *guamá* pods and the flowers, and inviting them to sit and relax while she served them coffee and crackers. She put some water in a glass jar and set the flowered branches in it. They looked pretty on the little table.

Luisa savored the flavorful coffee and admired the cabin, which Petra had tidied and scrubbed in preparation for her first visitors. The kitchen was even smaller than Chenta's, and there was only one bedroom off the main room, which doubled as living room and dining area. Their only furniture was the table with its two chairs and two rickety rocking chairs. The little unpainted cabin had no front porch, so if Petra and Juan José wanted to sit outside, they had to use the steps leading up to the front door. But the tiny house was Petra's own space—hers and Juan José's. Luisa thought that she would like to have her own home someday, maybe even one that was close to the Collado's cabin. It would be so much fun to be neighbors with Petra.

Petra dragged one of the rocking chairs closer to the table so that the three girls could sit together. Pilar was enjoying this time with her two older sisters and feeling quite grown up. She sipped at her *café con leche,* spread butter on her saltine crackers, and nibbled delicately at their edges, trying to make the treat last longer. She was content to listen in on the older girls' conversation about happenings in general without commenting much. She sobered a bit when the conversation eventually turned to the topic of growing up and becoming a woman, and she realized that her sisters were now speaking directly to her. Pilar wasn't sure that she wanted anything to change. She was thinking that she would like to stay eleven years old and carefree forever—and not have to face the inconveniences and responsibilities of womanhood. Petra and Luisa assured her that she would be fine. They would be there to help and answer any questions that she might have. Changes in life were inevitable, but once you embraced them and adapted to them, life moved on.

The sun was now dipping behind the treetops, and Luisa and Pilar reluctantly said goodbye to Petra and headed back home. It was mostly downhill, but the girls still had to be careful where they stepped. They were walking barefoot again, and for some reason, it seemed more treacherous to go down the slippery path than it did to climb up it. Maybe it was because the ground didn't seem so far away when you were walking uphill, but when you were walking downhill it sloped away from you and you could imagine yourself taking a big tumble if you slipped and fell. But the air was fresh and cool now, and an occasional *coquí* could be heard, getting a head start on the evening symphony of nightlife in the mountains. This time, they did not stop to rest, and when they reached their home, Pilar looked wiped out.

Pobrecita, thought Luisa. *Poor thing. Growing up is hard on a person; it takes the sap out of you, and Pilar is growing like a weed. She is almost as tall as me, already, and so thin. No wonder she has no energy.*

Luisa remembered what it was like to be that age. Thankfully, it was temporary, and Luisa was blessed with good health and a strong constitution. She hoped that Pilar would get past that awkward growing stage quickly and regain vitality.

A few days later, Ricardo announced that Moncho was needed on the farm; he was to begin working with his father, Sebastián and Juan José the next day.

"*Es tiempo*," said Ricardo. "It's time. I was younger than you when I started doing a man's work. Pilar will take care of the chickens, and Juanito can take over the caring of the goats and pigs all by himself, right Juanito?"

"*Sí, Papá.*"

The next morning, Moncho was up and out the door with his father, feeling like a man and eager to prove that he could work as hard as the others. Juanito looked forlorn all day long, missing the older brother that he had been shadowing for years. He declared that he didn't want to play with his younger sisters, as Chenta suggested he do after his chores were done. Instead, he pestered and teased the little girls, provoking them to tears on more than one occasion. At one point, Juanito and Vicenta were outside fighting over some battered old toy. Chenta marched out to the *batey*, snatched the disputed object out of their hands, and *fuá!* She threw it down the mountainside. That was the end of the children's argument! Juanito and Vicenta were left with their mouths hanging open in surprise.

"There you go! That will teach you!" barked Chenta. Then she added, as she marched back to the house. "Close your mouths, or you will catch flies."

Juanito whined to his father that night about having to stay home.

"Why can't I go, too, *Papá*? I want to learn to do the farm work, too."

"Not yet, *Mijo*," replied Ricardo. "You are still a bit too young. If you go along with us, you and Moncho will play more than work. I know how it is. I was a boy once, you know."

Juanito pondered over that for a moment. It was hard to imagine his father as a little boy. He continued petitioning his father for a little while to be allowed to go with Moncho and the men, but Ricardo said a firm no. Juanito was needed to care for the goats and the pigs, and to be the "man" of the house in the absence of the others. Somewhat pacified, Juanito accepted and stopped his pleading. He knew that if he continued, he would be considered disrespectful, and he might be disciplined for it. Ricardo's word was always final.

For his part, Moncho had come home exhausted from his first day working on the coffee farm, and shortly after supper he went to bed without even being told to do so.

In the months that followed, the family fell into their new routine. With Petra no longer living at home, Luisa was now the oldest child in the house and worked tirelessly alongside Chenta to care for the children, cook, clean, and do the laundry. And boy was there a lot of dirty laundry with nine people in the home, including two little ones still in diapers and two people coming home in very soiled work clothes! Thankfully, Pilar had stepped up to help Luisa with the laundry and the sweeping, and was even being taught to cook by Chenta. She was also very responsible about feeding the chickens and collecting the eggs. Luisa watched her carefully. She didn't want Pilar to overwork herself and get sick.

Moncho was learning a lot about farming. During the spring months, the men planted ñame and other root foods and harvested oranges, grapefruit, *guanábanas* (soursop), guava, and papayas, which Sebastián and Juan José took to town to sell every other Saturday. Ricardo and Moncho tended to the coffee plants which took four years to mature before they produced beans. They all took part in the picking, drying, roasting, and packaging of the coffee beans. It was their main source of income.

Spring gave way to summer, and avocados and mangoes were added to the crops that were harvested, even as the grapefruit, guavas, and *guanábanas* were done for the year.

With the farm producing so well and the men having successful sales of the produce at the farmer's market, there was money with which to buy fabric and sewing notions. Luisa and Petra were able to take another fun trip into town with Sebastián and Juan José. This time, instead of just daydreaming about the dresses they would make, the two girls fingered the bolts of cloth with intent to buy. Luisa purchased a dark blue material for a new dress for herself and a length of calico for Pilar in a pretty, brown and green print on a cream background. They purchased thread in coordinating colors.

"What about buttons?" asked *Doña* Juana.

"Oh, Chenta has a big jar full of buttons," replied Luisa. "I'm sure we can find the ones that we need in there."

With a nod, *Doña* Juana rang up the purchase. "Well, if you don't find what you need in that jar, I have a nice selection of buttons here."

During the warm summer evenings, after the little ones were safely tucked into bed, Luisa skillfully worked on turning the fabric into dresses. Pilar watched and learned as well. She already knew how to sew a nice hem and how to stitch around buttonholes, but Luisa now showed her how to cut the fabric to fit the body measurements, adding clearance for seams. Getting the necklines, shoulder seams, and sleeves accurately cut out was challenging without a pattern. Even using an old dress as a guide, it took some analyzing to cut out the sections of fabric correctly. It would not do to make a wrong cut and waste fabric. Chenta, too, was busy sewing little dresses for Vicenta and Bonifacia.

One afternoon in late summer, Luisa made a suggestion as she and Chenta were having their three o'clock coffee break.

"How about if we move Vicenta and *la nena* into my room? Pilar can come sleep with me, and the two little girls can sleep in the cot that Pilar has been using. That way, all the girls will be together in one room and the boys alone in the other. Eventually, we will have to move Toño into the room with his older brothers, but not for a few months yet, right?" Chenta's stomach was becoming decidedly rounder. Another baby would be joining the family that fall.

"I don't know how comfortable the little girls will be sleeping together on Pilar's cot," Chenta remarked. "I think we should put their twin bed in your room and put Pilar's cot in the room with the boys. It will be fine for Toño when he moves out of his crib."

"Oh, that's even better," said Luisa. "Our room will be just a little bit tighter, but not much. We will still be able to move around."

After the little ones got up from their nap, Luisa and Pilar got busy removing the mattress and taking apart the twin bed. Taking the cot out of their room was easily done, but putting the twin bed back together proved trickier. Luckily, the construction of the wooden bed frame was such that tools were not necessary. The side boards hooked into slots on the headboard and baseboard, and the mattress rested on slats that crossed from one sideboard to the other.

Vicenta and Bonifacia's few articles of clothing and personal belongings were moved into Luisa and Pilar's room. There was one small dresser with four drawers, one for each of the girls. Luisa claimed the top drawer, since she was the oldest, and Pilar took the second one, leaving the bottom two for Vicenta and Bonifacia. The little girls were jumping up and down about the change and kept running in and out of their new room. That night they giggled and talked so much at bedtime that Luisa had to tell them firmly that it was time to be quiet and go to sleep.

It was just a little inconvenient for Pilar and Luisa because they had to be very quiet when going to bed at night and getting up in the morning so as not to disturb their little sisters' sleep, but it was a small sacrifice, and they would get used to it. As the family grew and evolved, these changes were necessary, thought Luisa. All in all, though they were a little crowded in the house, they were a happy family, and Luisa gave thanks to God for their health and prayed that they would all stay that way.

Chapter 5

A New Sibling

That fall, as Chenta's body became heavier with the weight of the coming baby, Luisa found herself taking over more of the household duties. Chenta often complained of a backache or painfully swollen feet, so Luisa offered to do all of the cooking and the bathing of the little ones. She and Pilar continued doing the laundry together, and Chenta relegated herself to such tasks as mending clothes and shelling beans, which she could do while sitting comfortably.

Chenta was in her chair on the porch one morning in October, shelling *gandules*--the pigeon peas that were used in a traditional rice dish—when she felt the first contraction. It startled her, and she almost upset the bowl of *gandules*. She paused only momentarily, though, and continued with her task until the second contraction came several minutes later. Okay, now she was sure.

The youngest children were all playing in the *batey*, where Chenta could see them. Juanito was using a stick as a bat and a round guava as a ball. He lobbed the guava and Vicenta and Bonifacia ran squealing after it to see who could get it first. Even little Toño was trying to get into the game, and occasionally got the "ball" if Juanito hit it gently in his direction. Luisa and Pilar were down at the creek washing clothes.

"Juanito," Chenta called out. "Run down to the creek and get Luisa and Pilar. Tell them I need them to come right away."

Juanito was glad to comply. He normally liked to go to the creek when the clothes were being washed because it gave him the opportunity to splash and play in the water, but lately he had been told to stay with Chenta, in case she needed help with something.

His bare feet fairly flew down the path, and even before reaching the creek, as soon as he could see them he was calling out to them.

Luisa heard him and shouted back, *"¿Qué pasa?" What's wrong?*

"*Mami* needs you right now!"

The girls looked at each other and immediately began gathering up the soggy laundry. They hurried up the path to the house and arrived out of breath. Chenta was still in the chair, but her hands had stilled from their work of shelling. One hand clutched the bowl of *gandules*, and the other hand was splayed across her taught belly. Dropping the basket of wet laundry on the wooden porch floor, Luisa and Pilar rushed to Chenta's side. Pilar extracted the bowl of *gandules* from Chenta's grip.

"Should we send for *Papá* or for the *comadrona*?" asked Luisa.

"Eh! What can your father do? It's the *comadrona* who delivers babies."

"Okay," said Luisa, trying to think fast. "Juanito, do you remember how to take the shortcut to get to the Maldonado property—down to the ravine and up the trail on the other side?"

At his nod, she continued. "Go there and tell them that Chenta needs *Doña* Tiburcia. She lives in a cabin on their land, and they can send someone to get her and bring her here. Run, Juanito. Don't stop to play, and come right back so that we at least know that you delivered the message. Pilar, I need you to watch the three little ones. I have to stay with Chenta, just in case…" Her voice trailed off. She hoped that *Doña* Tiburcia would get there in time. Luisa didn't know anything about birthing babies. When Toño was born, Sebastiana was the one who had attended to Chenta until the *comadrona* had arrived, and Petra and Luisa had been relegated to caring for the younger children. But now the responsibility of staying with Chenta fell on her.

Juanito took off on a run, and Luisa assisted Chenta to her room. She found a clean nightgown, helped Chenta change into it, then settled her into the bed. Unsure of what to do next, she rubbed Chenta's hands and feet by turn until Chenta suggested she put a pot of water on to boil. Happy to have something constructive to do, Luisa went to do as Chenta bid. *I might as well get some rice cooking, too*, she thought, and she went to the sink to rinse her hands in the basin of water. *The others will need to have something for lunch.* She cut up some ham and used some of the prepared *sofrito* and *achiote* that Chenta kept in jars for seasoning and coloring, respectively, and added some of the freshly shelled gandules to the rice, water and salt. She included some minced *recao* leaves, too. The wide leafed coriander plant would provide the aroma and flavor that they were accustomed to experiencing in their Puerto Rican cuisine. She used a small hollowed out coconut shell to measure the rice and the water, but none of the other ingredients were measured. Luisa was a seasoned pro at cooking. She left the covered pot of rice simmering over a low flame and returned to check on Chenta.

Chenta was an old hand at giving birth, or so it seemed to Luisa. She was doing well for the present. But this was her fifth baby, and to Luisa's thinking, Chenta might pop that baby out at any moment. She admired her stepmother's bravery and no-nonsense approach to giving birth, but observed how Chenta closed her eyes during each contraction and expelled a deep breath when it subsided. The beads of perspiration on Chenta's upper lip did not go unnoticed by Luisa, either. She handed her a clean handkerchief that Chenta immediately used to dab at her face.

It seemed like an eternity before Juanito returned, all sweaty and dirty from his errand. "They are going to get *Doña* Tiburcia and bring her by wagon," he reported. He then plopped himself down on the porch steps to catch his breath. Pilar brought him a cup of water and Luisa thanked him and told him what a good job he had done.

Luisa was getting anxious because Chenta's contractions were getting closer together. Chenta only emitted low moans with each contraction and stayed calm, but Luisa was worried that the baby would decide to come before help arrived. She dipped a rag in cool water and placed it on Chenta's forehead, then stayed by her side. Luisa was relieved when she heard her father and Moncho come in for lunch. Pilar had seen them coming and had run to tell them the news that Chenta was in labor and that *Doña* Tiburcia had been sent for. Ricardo stepped into the bedroom to greet his wife and assess her condition.

"I'm sorry, *Papá*, but all I could do was make a pot of *arroz con gandules* for lunch. I didn't want to leave Chenta alone for very long," apologized Luisa.

"Don't worry, *Mija*. Rice is good food. You go get some lunch and feed the others, while I stay here with Chenta."

By the time Luisa and the children had finished eating their rice, a wagon pulled up and Leocadio Maldonado was helping *Doña* Tiburcia down. She hurried into the house, carrying her bag of provisions needed for the job of assisting in deliveries. Short and plump, with graying hair, the widowed midwife had delivered most of the babies in Juan González for almost three decades, including all of Ricardo's children. Ricardo greeted *Doña* Tiburcia, squeezed Chenta's hand, and left the room. He stepped outside, where Leocadio stood waiting.

"*Compai* Leocadio, thank you for bringing *Doña* Tiburcia. Come in and have a cup of coffee."

"*No, gracias, Compai.* I have to get back, but I was wondering if you would like me to take the children to my house for a few hours. My girls would be glad to entertain them and take care of the little ones. I can return them tonight so that they can sleep in their own beds."

"That would be great, *Compai*. Luisa, gather up the other children and go with *Compai* Leocadio."

"*Papá*, Pilar and the others can go, but I should stay here in case *Doña* Tiburcia needs me. At the very least, I can clean up the kitchen and serve her coffee or something, and make supper this afternoon."

Ricardo nodded. *"Está bien. Quédate."* All right. Stay.

The children clambered happily into Leocadio's wagon, and they took off for his property, Moncho riding next to Leocadio and the rest of them in the wagon bed. Juanito held little Toño on his lap and wrapped his arms around him protectively. Pilar did the same with Bonifacia, and Vicenta sat close by her side. Any time that they had the opportunity to go anywhere, it was a special treat, so they were excited.

Ricardo checked in with Chenta and *Doña* Tiburcia and then went to the kitchen, where Luisa was serving him rice in a hollowed out half of a coconut shell.

"*Buen provecho*," she said as she handed her father his lunch. *Bon appétit*.

She sat in the chair across from Ricardo, elbows on the table and chin resting on folded hands.

"So…another baby…good thing that we moved Toño to the boys' room last week and he has adapted well to sleeping on the cot," she said.

Ricardo merely nodded and continued eating in silence. When he finished, he went out to clean his machete. There would be no more farm work that day. He would occupy himself in the stable and check on the farm animals, instead. The children weren't around to do their chores, anyway, so he would keep himself busy doing them.

Luisa cleaned up the kitchen, intermittently checking in on Chenta and *Doña* Tiburcia to see how things were going and if she was needed for anything. *Doña* Tiburcia assured her that it wouldn't be much longer, and had Luisa provide her with some basins, water, clean towels and baby blankets.

Afterwards, Luisa decided to sit on the porch where she could still hear if her name was called and finish shelling the *gandules* that Chenta had been working on that morning. A sudden rain shower surprised her, but she was protected from getting wet by the roof's extension over the porch. Remembering the wet laundry that was balled up in the laundry basket, some of it still soaped up, Luisa thought, *Guess I'll just have to rewash it all tomorrow, if I can be somehow spared to go down to the creek. If I had finished the task the clothes wouldn't have dried on the bushes, anyway, with this rain shower.*

Her thoughts were interrupted by the thin wail of a newborn baby, and Luisa grinned and said aloud, *"Gracias, Señor."* *Thank you, Lord.*

She tiptoed inside and stood outside the curtained doorway to Chenta's room. "Is everything okay? Should I go get *Papá*?"

"Everything is fine. You have a baby sister. Go tell your father, but give me a few minutes to get Chenta and the baby presentable."

Much relieved, Luisa draped a towel over her head for protection from the lingering raindrops of the subsiding shower and hurried out to find her father.

That evening, as the family regrouped and everyone had a chance to see Chenta and the new baby, little Vicenta was the one who asked the question that they all wanted to know. *"¿Cómo se llama?"* *What is her name?*

Chenta smiled, and answered, "María Fermina."

"María Fermina," repeated Vicenta. "Can we just call her Fermina?"

"Claro," responded Chenta. *Of course.*

"Another little girl," observed Moncho. "We can't keep calling Bonifacia 'la nena' anymore because now there is another *nena*."

"It might be hard to break that habit, but we can try," said Pilar. "Bonifacia is such a big name for a little girl. We can at least shorten her name to Boni."

All agreed to that. In time, a nickname emerged for Fermina, as well, and she became simply Mina to all who knew her.

Mina was born on a Thursday. Ricardo and Moncho took the day off from farm work both the next day and Saturday, although Sebastián and Juan José worked as usual on Friday and took produce to town to sell on Saturday. On Friday morning, Luisa and Pilar prepared breakfast for the family, washed the dishes and did their morning chores, with Luisa checking in on Chenta and Mina every now and then. In the meantime, Ricardo hitched up the horses to the wagon and went to pick up *Doña* Tiburcia. The *comadrona* liked to visit new mothers and their babies at least once after the delivery. *Doña* Tiburcia was satisfied with Chenta's recovery so far and with Mina's breathing, nursing and overall appearance.

With both Ricardo and *Doña* Tiburcia there, Luisa and Pilar were free to go to the creek to rewash the laundry that they had begun the day before. *Doña* Tiburcia told the girls to take their time; she would cook a hearty chicken soup for the family's midday meal. That way she could serve Chenta some nourishing broth to help her regain her strength.

They took Moncho and Juanito with them and left Vicenta, Boni and Toño in their father's care. A neighbor boy, Carlos, came to play in the creek with Moncho and Juanito. Carlos was a couple of years older than Moncho, but as the only other boy in the vicinity, he occasionally spent time with Moncho. Ever since Moncho started working on the family farm, their time together was limited, so today they took advantage of the opportunity and had a great time wading in the creek and skipping rocks. Born with a defective foot that caused him to walk with a limp, Carlos was excused from working on his father's property, although Luisa noted that it did not impede the lad from hiking through their hills or wading in the creek.

When the clothes were finally washed and spread out to dry on the bushes in front of the house, the family enjoyed bowls of *Doña* Tiburcia's delicious soup. Their custom was to drop slices of avocado into the soup. The mixture of flavors and textures was amazing. After lunch and a final check on her patients, *Doña* Tiburcia was taken back to her cabin by Ricardo.

Luisa and Pilar sent Moncho and Juanito outside to play and put the younger children down for their afternoon nap. Chenta and baby Mina were also napping, so Luisa and Pilar tiptoed out to relax on the shady porch. Luisa knew that her rest would be short lived because Ricardo would return from taking Doña Tiburcia home and would expect his three o'clock coffee to be ready. After that, she would have to start peeling and cutting up *vianda* for their supper. But for the time being, she and Pilar would enjoy this moment of repose. Her favorite bird, the *ruiseñor*, was gifting her with his lovely melodic song, and a gentle breeze was caressing her face. In the *batey*, the chickens that were allowed free range during the daytime clucked and pecked. An immense feeling of gratitude and satisfaction filled Luisa's heart. God was good; life was good.

Chapter 6

Celebration

Baby Mina's baptism took place when she was two weeks old. Ricardo and Chenta took her to town, where she was baptized by *Padre* Irizarry at San Joaquín church. Ricardo's brother, Pedro, was the *padrino*—the godfather.

As they exited the church into the bright sunshine, Chenta covered Mina's face with a corner of her baby blanket and Ricardo shielded his eyes with his hand.

"*¿Vienes para la casa?*" *Are you coming to the house?* "We are going to celebrate."

Pedro slapped his brother on the back. "*Claro que sí. Pa' allá voy.*" *Of course. I'm going there.*

Luisa had been busily preparing food at the house while Pilar took care of the little ones as best she could. Moncho and Juanito rebelled a bit under Pilar's supervision, but they got their chores done and changed into clean clothes, at least. They were now in the *batey*, playing with a top, to the entertainment of Vicenta and Bonifacia. There was an art to winding the string just so, beginning with a loop around the crown of the top and then wrapping the string tightly from the tip upwards. Both boys could wind and throw the top well, but Moncho could also scoop the spinning top up onto the palm of his hand. Juanito was still practicing to perfect this trick.

Petra and Juan José were the first ones to show up, and Luisa gladly accepted Petra's help in the kitchen. Juan José was ready to take care of the horses of any guests that arrived on horseback. Ricardo and Chenta returned from town, and shortly afterwards, Rosa and Domingo arrived. They still had not seen the newborn baby.

Rosa cradled tiny Mina in her arms, cooing over the baby's sweet face and soft skin. She felt her throat tightening up. When would she be able to hold her own baby in her arms? She and Domingo had been married six years now, and she had miscarried two pregnancies already. The first one happened in the first trimester of pregnancy, and that was hard enough to bear, but the second one she carried almost full term. The baby girl was born too early and could not be saved. The *comadrona* had not even been able to get there in time to deliver the premature infant. It had been a traumatic event in the lives of the young couple. An unbidden tear slid down Rosa's face and fell onto Mina's tiny arm, and she quickly wiped it away, hoping that no one had noticed it. But Domingo had noticed, and he reached out to take the wee child from Rosa.

"Here, let me have a turn before everyone else gets here," he said. "I need to figure out my relationship to this little one. She is my wife's baby sister, so that makes her my *cuñada*, my sister-in-law. But she is also my sister's baby, so that makes her my *sobrina*, my niece. Ay, ay, ay, life can get complicated!"

"Maybe you can combine the two words and come up with a new term," suggested Juan José. "How about *cuñina*?" Everybody laughed, and Rosa was spared from any awkward attention.

As more people arrived, baby Mina was passed around from one willing set of arms to another, exclaimed over and blessed many times. It was customary to add, "*Dios la bendiga*—God bless her," after any compliment as superstition was common among them. If someone said, "*Ay, que linda*," referring to how cute the infant was, without adding, "*Dios la bendiga*," people thought that the baby might be getting what they called "*Mal de ojo*"—evil eye. They believed that it could cause some harm to the infant in the form of sickness or even death.

Before long, the *batey* was swarming with guests, many of them from Chenta's side of the family, including her parents, Eugenio and María Policarpia, and her sister, Antonia.

Antonia was married to Lucas Maldonado, a cousin of the Torres family's neighbor, Leocadio Maldonado, and they had five children ranging from eight years old down to two. Lucas had also invited his younger half-brothers, Eladio and Manuel de Jesús. Although Luisa had known them for years, she hadn't seen them in a long time. The first time she remembered meeting them was at Lucas and Antonia's wedding, some ten years earlier. In the years following, she had seen them several times at other gatherings, but they were still just pesky boys, and she was an uninterested little girl then. Things were different now.

When Lucas and Antonia arrived with their large group and joined Leocadio and Aquilina's family, as well as the other guests that were already there, there was a joyful melee of handshakes, hugs and kisses mixed in with laughter and booming voices. At first, Luisa didn't recognize Eladio and Manuel de Jesús. Then it dawned on her who they were. She stood on the porch and slyly watched the young brothers as they were busy greeting everybody. They were so tall and handsome now! Eladio had a neatly trimmed goatee that made him look very manly. Manuel de Jesús was clean shaven but wore his dark hair just a little bit long. Luisa liked the way it was shiny and wavy. Manuel de Jesús suddenly turned his head and looked straight at Luisa. Flustered and embarrassed at being caught studying him, she turned and ducked back into the house on the pretense of getting something from the kitchen.

Now what? She couldn't stay in the kitchen forever. She had to come out with something in her hands. Luisa sliced one of the loaves of bread that she had baked early that morning, put the slices in a basket, and carried it out to the table. The rest of the food was ready, so Rosa and Petra helped Luisa carry the various pots and bowls out. Ricardo called for attention and thanked everyone for coming, with special thanks given to his brother for accepting the responsibility of being Mina's godfather. Now, besides being brothers, he and Pedro would be *compadres*. No longer would he address his brother simply as Pedro; now he was *Compai* Pedro. He prayed a blessing over the food and invited all to partake of the meal.

Luisa was finally off her feet and was sitting with her cousin María de la Paz Torres and her friends, Felita and Dionicia Maldonado, their plates of food on their laps. The girls had not been all together for nine months, since Petra's wedding. Dionicia looked downcast. She was hoping that she would see Catalino again, but Luisa's *Tío* Canuto had not yet arrived with his family. Word had reached Ricardo that his first wife's mother,

Eusebia Nieves, was not well. She was now living with Canuto's family, and it was unclear if anyone from that household would be able to attend Mina's baptism celebration.

"Buen provecho."

Luisa looked up to see Eladio and Manuel de Jesús approaching the group.

"Gracias," Luisa answered. *"Igual."* Same to you.

"May we join you ladies?" asked Eladio, the older of the two.

The girls all assented, and the boys pulled up chairs. Their plates were loaded with rice and beans and stewed chicken, with a thick chunk of bread resting on the rice and slices of avocado garnishing the sides.

Luisa was glad that they were all seated in a group. She wouldn't have known what to say if she had been alone with the two young men. As it was, Eladio, Dionicia, and María de la Paz kept up a steady stream of conversation. Felita was more reserved and usually only spoke if someone asked her a direct question. The same was true for Manuel de Jesús.

After he was about halfway through eating his plate of food, Eladio commented on its flavor. "Help me solve this mystery: if Chenta was in town getting the baby baptized, and Petra is married and lives in her own cabin, who cooked all of this delicious food? Was it you, Luisa?"

Luisa looked up at him, and since she had food in her mouth, she only nodded. She couldn't help but notice how big and beautiful Eladio's eyes were. He had a bit of a husky physique overall, whereas Manuel de Jesús was slender yet muscular. *Farm boys grow up fast to become strong men*, she thought admiringly, as she swallowed what was in her mouth.

"This rice is excellent," continued Eladio.

"*Ya Luisa se puede casar,*" quipped María de la Paz. *Luisa can get married now.*

"*Pacita!!*" exclaimed Luisa, aghast.

"Well, you know the saying that we have...when a girl can make good rice, she is ready to get married," said María de la Paz, with a shrug of her shoulders. The others snickered, and even Manuel de Jesús smiled.

Luisa rolled her eyes but said nothing in response.

Suddenly, Dionicia's face lit up. Catalino was striding across the *batey* towards their little group. They all greeted him and invited him to get some food and join them.

"Did you come alone?" Luisa asked Catalino after he had sat down with his plate of food.

"Yes, Mama Sebia is not doing well, and *Mami* was going to stay with her and have *Papi* come with the kids, but in the end, he thought he should stick around the house, too. So, I came alone. I didn't want to miss this opportunity to see family and... friends." He looked directly at Dionicia when he made the last statement, and she blushed and lowered her eyes. She was sure that everyone could hear her heart beating!

Their circle got wider as Sebastián joined their group. Among the young men, their usual conversations revolved around agriculture and politics, but since they were socializing in a mixed group, the topics tended to be more generalized. They got caught up on local news, such as which young man was courting which young lady and what was going on in each person's family.

"Sebastián, when are you getting married?" asked Catalino. "You live all alone in that little cabin. Doesn't it get lonely?"

"No…well, sometimes…but most of the time I don't mind being by myself. If I want to be around a lot of people, I can just come here. I work from sunup to sundown, and after I fix myself something to eat at night, all I want to do is go to sleep."

"Really? You don't have your eye on someone? What about when you and Juan José go to town. Haven't you seen some pretty girls there?" persisted Catalino.

"Well, of course there are pretty girls," answered Sebastián, "but it's hard to get to know a person when you are working all the time. But you should know all about that. And hey, you are older than I am. Isn't it time for you to settle down?"

Now all eyes were on Catalino. He put all of his attention on his plate of food and mumbled, "Yes, yes. I'm working on that."

"And who might the lucky lady be?" pressed Sebastián, happy to get the conversation away from himself.

"I don't think he needs to answer that," said María de la Paz, with a little smirk. "It's pretty obvious."

Catalino said nothing but looked up from his plate and allowed his gaze to fall on the hapless Dionicia, who was blushing furiously, to everyone's amusement.

Altogether, it was a wonderful afternoon filled with laughter, food, conversation, and of course, the inevitable dancing to the *jíbaro* music that broke out once everyone had eaten their fill.

Chapter 7

Disaster

Five days after Mina's baptism, disaster struck the island of Puerto Rico.

That morning had started out just like any ordinary day. Luisa, up before the others, had ground and brewed the coffee and had served Ricardo and Moncho a breakfast of coffee, eggs and bread while Chenta remained in her bedroom nursing baby Mina. Father and son had gone off to work on the farm, and Luisa had continued on with her household work: cooking, washing dishes, sweeping, and taking care of younger siblings. When Luisa was busy, Pilar was a big help, watching Juanito, Vicenta, Bonifacia, and Toño. In addition, Pilar fed the chickens and collected and washed the eggs. Luisa and Pilar had washed clothes in the creek just three days earlier, so laundry was not on her mental list of chores that day. It was a good thing, too, since the sky was getting cloudy, and a strong wind was picking up. The clothes would have flown right off the bushes had she spread them out to dry.

Something was eerie about the weather. The air was extra muggy. Up in the mountains of Adjuntas, they were blessed with cooler temperatures and less humidity than in other parts of the island, but today the air was almost stifling, despite it being so windy.

Luisa had put dried beans to soak overnight, and now she set them on the stove to boil and soften. It took the rest of the morning for the beans to soften and for her to stew them with tomatoes, onions, garlic, sweet peppers, *recao*, spices, and chunks of ham and potatoes. Served with white rice and fried plantains, this made a hearty lunch. Typically, their big meal was in the middle of the day, and supper was lighter fare.

Ricardo and Moncho came home for the midday meal, and as he ate, Ricardo voiced his own concerns about the weather.

"Every *yagrumo* tree that I have seen today has its leaves upside down. Rain is coming, and I think it is going to be a big storm. The air is heavy."

"I feel it too, *Papá*, and it has me worried. If a big storm comes, will Petra and Juan José be safe in their little cabin? Will Sebastián be okay in his?"

Ricardo's answer was to simultaneously lift his eyebrows and shrug his shoulders. He continued eating in silence. His response only heightened Luisa's concern.

Chenta had her back turned and was spooning food into gourds for the children. "We have to have faith that God will protect us," she said. "And we must pray!"

Luisa went to stand in the open doorway and look out at the treetops swaying in the wind. A shiver ran up her spine.

Ricardo rose from his chair. "I think this afternoon, Moncho and I will dig up some yucca and other tubers. It will be helpful to have a supply of *vianda* in the house in case a storm keeps us housebound for a day or two. Luisa, you and Pilar and Juanito should make a couple of trips to get water, if you can, for the same reason."

"*Sí, Papá.*"

While the little ones napped that afternoon, and the others were getting the *vianda* and water as planned, Chenta made some chicken soup to serve for supper along with bread that she had baked. Luisa, Pilar and Juanito ended up making three treks up the mountainside for water, filling up their small water cistern and in addition having full jugs and cans in a corner of the kitchen. Ricardo and Moncho returned with two large sacks of sweet potatoes, yucca, and *malanga*.

The adults had their mid-afternoon coffee and discussed what further actions they could take to prepare for the storm.

"We need more firewood for the stove," observed Chenta. It was agreed that Luisa and Juanito would bring in more firewood, while Ricardo and Moncho went out to feed and care for the animals and see that they were all secure in the barn and chicken coop. Pilar was to watch the little ones as they got up from their naps, since Chenta would probably be busy nursing Mina.

The wind was really picking up and ominous dark clouds were gathering over the eastern hills. Luisa deposited the last load of firewood in the box near the stove and straightened to check on the soup that had been left simmering on the stovetop. As she stirred the soup, she again thought of her siblings. She wished she had some way of knowing that Sebastián, Juan José, Petra, Rosa, and Domingo were also preparing to hunker down for the approaching storm. Her sister and brother-in-law,

Sebastiana and Francisco, came to her mind as well, and she hoped that they were doing what they could to stay safe in their home in Ponce. But in the fall months there was always a danger of hurricanes; that was nothing new, and her older siblings had lived through more hurricane seasons than she had. Surely, they knew what to do.

Ricardo and Moncho came back into the house just as a loud bang sounded from the girls' bedroom. The wind had slammed one of the wooden window shutters closed. Luisa hurried to close and lock both shutters.

"Everybody get inside," said Ricardo. There was urgency in his voice. "Close all the windows and the kitchen door." The older children scattered to do as he bid. Ricardo shut and secured the front door.

Chenta was ladling soup for the children and sitting them down to eat. She looked around. "Where is Boni? Her food is served."

"Bonifacia, come and eat!" called Luisa. "Pilar, is she with you?"

"No, but she was here a little while ago," answered Pilar. "I'll check our room." She came right back out, shaking her head.

"Did you check under the bed?" asked Luisa. At Pilar's nod, she then asked the boys to check in their room to see if Boni was in there.

"No, she's not in our room," reported Moncho. "And yes, we looked under the beds."

Chenta looked in her room, but Boni was not there, either. "*¡Ay, mi madre!*" exclaimed Chenta, the worry evident in her voice. "Where can she be? Pilar!" she snapped. "You were supposed to be watching her!"

Ricardo unbolted and pushed the front door open against the howling wind, and he went out, calling Bonifacia's name. Luisa, Moncho and Pilar were right on his heels. They called out, "Bonifacia!" over and over again. Luisa checked the chicken coop and Ricardo went to the barn, but both outbuildings were still securely closed. Thinking that maybe the little girl was already inside when he had bolted the barn, Ricardo opened it back up and looked for her there, to no avail. He did the same in the chicken coop.

Could Boni have gone down to the creek? Luisa felt her throat constricting and her heart pounding in fear. "Bonifacia!" she screamed again, her voice now high pitched and desperate. She ran to the edge of the *batey* and peered through the foliage toward the creek. Her hair was coming loose from its braid and strands were whipping across her face, making it even harder to see.

The palm trees were bending over with the strength of the wind blowing from the east, their fronds stretching straight out like banners. Coconuts were known to detach themselves and fly like cannonballs through the air during hurricanes. Luisa shivered more from fear than from cold. As it was, leaves and small branches were being torn from trees and were scuttling across the *batey*. Not a single bird or *coquí* could be heard. Where were they all taking refuge? And where was Bonifacia?

Moncho was the one who found the little girl sitting in the dirt under the house, clutching the cat.

"*La gatita tiene miedo,*" she told Moncho. *The kitty is afraid.*

Moncho called out to the others, "I found her! Here she is!" He then coaxed Bonifacia out. She was still holding on to the cat. Ricardo rushed over, grabbed the little girl by the arms, and gave her a hard shake, causing her to lose her hold on the kitty. "You are supposed to answer when you are called!" he growled.

Bonifacia let out a wail and pointed to the cat that had scampered back under the house. Ricardo scooped her up and marched up the porch steps, with the others following.

Chenta took the crying child from him. Ricardo looked around, taking a silent inventory of his children before closing and bolting the front door again. With his hair all bushed out by the wind and his eyes still reflecting the anxiety of the last ten minutes, he looked like a wild man. Luisa was feeling a little weak-kneed, and she also looked around at all of her siblings, making sure that everyone was accounted for. Juanito and Vicenta were asking questions and Moncho was relating to them how he had found Bonifacia. Chenta was scolding the sobbing child even as she washed the tot's hands, and little Toño, unsure of what was going on, also began to cry. Amazingly, Mina was sleeping through all of this. Luisa caught a glimpse of Pilar's pale face as the girl slipped quietly into their bedroom, and she followed her there.

"Are you okay, Pilar?"

Pilar did not answer, but her slender shoulders were shaking with sobs.

"It's okay. Boni is fine. We are all together now." She sat down on the bed next to her sister and laid a comforting hand on her arm.

"But…I was supposed to be watching her. She could have gotten hurt, or…worse! Chenta is angry with me. I…" Pilar's voice choked up and she couldn't continue.

Luisa wrapped both arms around Pilar and laid her cheek against the girl's head. "I know, *Mamita*. Chenta was just scared. We all were. But these things happen, and you work so hard alongside of me. You do a lot around here, and watching the little ones is not easy. The bottom line is that taking care of her children is really Chenta's responsibility, and she knows it, whether she says so or not. Don't let her upset you. She loves you. Sh, sh." Luisa kept crooning comforting words to Pilar for several minutes until the younger girl's sobs subsided.

Eventually, a composed Pilar was able to rejoin the family, albeit with red-rimmed eyes. If Chenta noticed Pilar's puffy eyes, she didn't say anything. Luisa and Pilar walked past the rest of the family and on into the kitchen. By then, the others had already eaten, and the two older girls had the privilege of having their supper of soup and bread at the table by themselves. The table and the kitchen were not large enough to accommodate the whole family at mealtimes, so the adults and the small children usually ate there. The others normally sat in the living room or on the porch, balancing plates on their laps. Either that or they took turns sitting at the table. So, this felt like a treat.

Afterwards, Luisa put the dirty bowls and utensils in a bucket and poured water over them. They would have to wait until morning to be washed. The wind was fierce, and Luisa didn't even dare leave them outside in the sink that hung from the kitchen window. They would probably blow away in the storm.

The family huddled together in the cramped living room. It was already so dark that Chenta had to light two kerosene lamps. Rain was now beginning to pelt down on the tin roof, usually a pleasant sound that lulled them to sleep, but tonight was different. Ricardo tried to entertain his family with stories of his childhood in the mountains of Utuado, but his stories of bad storms that he had lived through only made his children more anxious. As the storm increased in intensity, the pounding of the rain on the roof became deafening, and listening to Ricardo became impossible, anyway. The wind was roaring and screaming by turns, and the wooden house shook with each gust. Would its short supporting pillars continue to hold the house up? Though this type of construction was common in rural Puerto Rico, especially in areas that were prone to flooding or mudslides, Luisa now wished that their house wasn't up on piers.

The little ones were allowed to stay up well past their bedtime. Luisa was not sure if it was to give them reassurance or to give the others someone to hold onto. One by one they fell asleep on laps and were reluctantly carried to their beds. If there was a way for them to comfortably stay together all night long, Luisa would have preferred that. She worried about part of the house collapsing on someone while they lie sleeping in bed.

Somehow, the roof was holding up, and there was only one leak in the kitchen. An empty cracker tin was placed under it to catch the drip. The ping of the drops hitting the can could not even be heard, so loud was the thundering rain on the roof and the wind whistling through the cracks in the walls. Occasionally, a mighty gust of wind seemed to lift up the edges of the zinc roof. The creaking and shaking of the whole house was fearsome.

Chenta gave up and went to bed, cradling tiny Mina close to her body. Ricardo finally tapped Moncho and Juanito on the shoulders and pointed to their bedroom. His voice could no longer be heard over the fury of the storm. Luisa saw that Pilar's eyes were drooping, so she got her up, and they also went to their bedroom. Miraculously, the little girls were still fast asleep on the small bed that they shared. She let Pilar cozy up to her in their bed and was relieved when the younger girl fell asleep quickly. Luisa wasn't sure that she would be able to sleep at all.

She lay still, listening to the relentless pounding of the rain and trying not to gasp each time the house shuddered with the blasts of wind. She remembered what Chenta had said earlier that day: "We must pray." Luisa closed her eyes and prayed silently. *Dear God, please spare my family and our house from destruction, and bring us safely through this hurricane. Please be with Sebastián, Petra and Juan José, and Rosa and Domingo. Protect Sebastiana and Francisco in Ponce, and all of my other relatives and friends and neighbors.* She repeated this prayer in her head several times until she felt an inexplicable peace invade her heart, in sharp contrast to the furious storm that raged outside. Luisa didn't even know that she had finally fallen asleep until the sound of her little sisters crying woke her up. Bonifacia had awoken first, and her crying woke up Vicenta, who also began whimpering in fear. Luisa brought both little girls into bed with her and Pilar, and they all promptly went back to sleep.

Hours later, Luisa felt rather than saw that it was daytime. With the house all closed up, everything was still dark inside. She got up carefully so as not to disturb the others and reached under the bed for the chamber pot. There would be no trips to the outhouse this morning, if the outhouse was even still standing!

A few minutes later, Luisa exited the bedroom, smoothing out her wrinkled skirt. No one had even bothered to change out of their regular clothes before going to bed. What a night! And the storm was still going strong.

Her father was in the living room, looking haggard and unkempt this morning. Luisa figured that she didn't look much better, even though she had slept for a few hours. Had he even gone to bed last night? The pounding of the rain on the tin roof and the roaring wind impeded any ability for conversation, so Luisa merely waved at her father as she passed through to the kitchen.

She poured water from a jug into a basin and washed her hands and face, then proceeded to grind coffee. The monotonous task of cranking the handle of the coffee grinder afforded her time to wake up and get the fuzziness out of her head, but at the same time, her thoughts were reawakening to new worries about the dangers that her relatives and friends might be experiencing in their homes. Luisa prayed that everyone would safely make it through the hurricane.

When the coffee was brewed and she had added milk and sugar, she poured two steaming cups and rejoined her father in the living room. It would be so different today with their normal routine disrupted. Ricardo and Moncho would not be going out to work. Everyone would be together in the little house at the same time. How would they ever keep the children entertained? What if the storm continued for two days or longer?

In the end, it didn't turn out to be so bad being trapped indoors. After a filling breakfast of oatmeal, Pilar made some paper dolls for Vicenta and Boni to play with, using the brown wrapping paper that came from the general store. When they tired of that, she dressed up Vicenta in one of Luisa's housedresses, and put one of her own on Boni. The little girls giggled and paraded around, pretending to be grown up ladies. Juanito put his father's straw hat on Toño, and everyone laughed at how funny he looked walking around with his head all but engulfed by the huge hat. Midmorning, Luisa put Moncho and Pilar to work peeling tubers to be boiled for their lunch, and Juanito played with the top, which entertained his little sisters and brother. Ricardo had the rare opportunity to enjoy his family and hold baby Mina.

Luisa had a difficult time washing dishes in the kitchen since she was unable open the window to use the sink outside. She poured water in two basins and placed them on the table. One basin held soapy water and the other one had clear water. She spread a towel on the table on which to set the clean dishes to dry. She had last night's dishes to wash as well as the sticky ones from that morning's breakfast. Luisa made a mental note not to cook oatmeal the next time they were in such a situation, but she sincerely hoped that they would not have to face another hurricane ever again!

Chapter 8

Aftermath

It was shortly after lunch when the storm finally showed signs of abating. Ricardo ventured out to check on the animals and returned to the house soaking wet.

"The animals are all fine," he reported, "just hungry, having missed their early morning feeding."

He had milked the desperate nanny goat and brought a pail of milk into the house with him, covered with a burlap sack that he had tied securely around the pail with twine. The wind was still strong and blowing twigs and leaves around, although it had subsided substantially.

By mid-afternoon, all was eerily calm again. Windows and doors were opened, and curious family members peeked out to the dismaying scene of broken branches and debris all but covering their *batey*. The youngest children were napping, but everyone else ventured out to assess the condition of their home and outbuildings.

"The outhouse is gone!" exclaimed Pilar.

Sure enough, the outhouse had blown away during the hurricane, but praise the Lord, the house, barn, chicken coop and bathhouse had apparently not suffered any serious damage.

Ricardo had just finished his three o'clock coffee and was lacing up his boots to hike up the hill to the Collado's cabin, when Juan José showed up with the welcome news that they were all fine—he and Petra and Sebastián. A section of the tin roof covering the bedroom of Sebastián's cabin had been ripped off, and he had taken refuge in his tiny kitchen with a damp blanket and pillow that he had managed to salvage from the bedroom before everything in there was soaked. When the storm abated, he had made the trek to the Collado's cabin.

"He is there now, napping in a hammock that we strung up in our living room, trying to make up for the little sleep he got last night," said Juan José.

"How was the path between your cabin and here?" asked Ricardo.

"There are several downed trees along the path, and everything is very muddy and slippery," answered Juan José with a shake of his head. "What a mess!"

Luisa brought a cup of coffee and some buttered bread to Juan José where he had remained on the porch, having declared that he was too muddy to go into the house. He and Ricardo discussed what their next course of action would be.

"Drink your coffee and rest up a bit," said Ricardo. "But you had better return home before it gets too dark. Come back early tomorrow morning with Sebastián so that we can put up new walls and a roof for the outhouse. I have some extra siding stored in the barn."

He hoped that the zinc panel that had been the outhouse roof could be located somewhere on the property. Fixing the roof on Sebastián's cabin would be a bigger project, and Ricardo didn't think they would be able to get the materials for the job right away.

"Sebastián is welcome to stay with us as long as necessary until his own place is livable again," assured Juan José. "No worries there."

The next morning, Ricardo set the children to clearing out the *batey*. It was treacherous to even pick one's way through the maze of branches, leaves, and pieces of the demolished outhouse. That area had to be cleared out first so that the men could have space to set up sawhorses, supplies and tools for the rebuilding of the outhouse. Luisa, Pilar and Moncho got busy with the project, and even Juanito and Vicenta were happy to help after being admonished about the dangers. Not wanting to ruin their shoes in the mud, they were all barefoot but watched where they were walking and stepped gingerly, afraid of stepping on a nail.

Sebastián and Juan José arrived early, as promised, and the men went to work reconstructing the outhouse, which was an absolute necessity. Even Moncho pitched in to help. The missing zinc panel had been located halfway down to the creek and dragged back up the hillside by Juan José and Moncho. By noon, they were done, and the men ate a hearty midday meal of *vianda* and stewed codfish. Then they left to evaluate the condition of the farm, or at least a section of it.

Ricardo came home very dejected. From what they could see, the coffee crop was ruined. With coffee plants taking four years to mature and produce beans, this was a huge setback to the family's financial situation. It would take years to get the farm back to its previous level of productivity.

During the next week, the men cleared the downed trees that were blocking paths and canvassed the entire farmland, salvaging what they could of the destroyed crops. They would not starve; there was still plenty of *vianda* to be had. Since the tubers grew underground, they were not harmed by the hurricane, although their identifying foliage above ground had for the most part been ripped off, making it difficult to know where the edible roots could be found. They had to rely on their knowledge and memory of which tubers had been planted where. Digging up the *vianda* was like finding hidden treasure.

Ricardo also brought home burlap sacks full of plantains, but most of them were not fully developed and were only fit to be fed to the pigs. However, many fallen oranges and papayas were still good to eat.

"I am thankful that the chicken coop was spared in the hurricane," declared Luisa. "Chicken and eggs make good side dishes to our abundance of *vianda*."

By word of mouth, Ricardo and Chenta had learned that all of their relatives and friends had survived the hurricane, and none of them had lost their homes or suffered substantial damage to them. Ricardo himself checked on their nearest neighbors, *Don* Eustaquio and *Doña* Sinforosa. Moncho's friend, Carlos, came to their house to tell them that his family was fine and so was their house. But there were many others in Adjuntas that did not fare as well.

It was ten days before Ricardo was able to make a trip into town. By then, building materials were unavailable, as suppliers in Adjuntas could not keep up with the demand. He would either have to wait until new supplies came in or take a trip to the larger town of Utuado on the chance that they would still have zinc panels available with which to fix Sebastián's cabin.

That night, a grim-faced Ricardo told Chenta and Luisa what he had learned while in town.

"The hurricane entered Puerto Rico from the east, between the towns of Fajardo and Humacao, and swept across Puerto Rico, affecting every part of the island. Over two hundred people died island-wide, and the agriculture of the entire island is in shambles."

"How many people from Adjuntas died?" asked Luisa, even as she feared what her father was going to answer.

"Our *barrio* of Juan González did not suffer any loss of life, and overall there was a minimal amount of damage to homes," was his reply.

Chenta and Luisa marveled at this news, and Ricardo went on to explain that this was due to the fact that their *barrio* was on the western slope of the mountain that was east of the town center. With the hurricane blowing in from the east, Juan González had been protected by the mountain itself. In the town center and in the *barrios* to the west of it, there were numerous houses that were now uninhabitable, displacing entire families. Generous neighbors had opened up their homes to provide shelter for those who were left homeless. Every municipality in Puerto Rico was clamoring for help from the Spanish government, but it seemed like Spain did not give much importance to rescuing its colony from the dire straits in which it had been left by the hurricane. People everywhere were growing very dissatisfied with the political, economic, and social condition of the island.

Luisa could not pretend to understand what all the issues were that were provoking the general unrest, but she did hope that help would soon come from the government. Her heart broke for the families having to double up in crowded houses with no hope of finding building materials to repair their damaged homes. Many did not even have crops to sell to provide the money with which to buy the needed supplies for rebuilding. Those who lived in towns depended on businesses like *Doña* Juana and *Don* Pepín's general store and the farmer's market to supply their food. What would they do when they ran out of food in their homes, especially if two families were sharing one dwelling? How many children would go to bed hungry night after night before a measure of normalcy returned to their lives?

That night, when she went to bed, she thanked God that her family was safe and petitioned Him on behalf of all the people in Puerto Rico who had lost loved ones, or their home, or their livelihood. Undoubtedly, there were people on the island who had suffered losses in all three areas. Tears slipped out from under Luisa's closed lids as she prayed herself to sleep.

Chapter 9

Mama Sebia

Everything seemed so much more difficult after the hurricane. Fetching water from the spring up the mountainside was quite a treacherous feat. The trail was all but obliterated by huge branches and small mudslides. Luisa feared that she or one of her siblings would slip and end up tumbling down the steep hillside to the ravine. So, they took their time, picking their way carefully in bare feet. There was no use ruining their shoes with the thick mud.

The water that they retrieved was not clear like it used to be, and it had to be boiled on the stove to kill any bacteria that might be in there and then cooled to room temperature before it was fit for drinking. The extra chore of boiling the water also used up more of their wood supply, and they were running low. Ricardo was hard pressed to find dry wood to cut on their drenched property.

Laundry could not be done for the first week after the hurricane. The creek water was all churned up and murky. Luisa thought that the clothes would come out of the water dirtier than when they went in. When the creek finally cleared up enough for her to venture down there to wash clothes, the pile of laundry for ten people was alarming. There was no way that she and Pilar could get all of it done in one day, so Luisa picked out one set of clothing for each member of the family for starters. Two days later, they went back down to wash more clothes. They hoped that by doing laundry every two or three days, they would catch up. It helped that Chenta was soaking the soiled diapers in a pail and washing them herself behind the house on a daily basis. She was also washing Mina's tiny garments when the baby spit up. Otherwise, she would have run out of clean clothing for the infant.

Thirteen days after the hurricane, on the evening of November 11th, Luisa was in the living room, sorting through the dirty laundry, pulling out the clothes that she intended to wash the next day, when Chenta said, "Listen! Someone is calling."

Everyone got quiet. Through the open door, among the singing of the *coquís*, another sound was heard coming from the hillside on the other side of the ravine. A person was hooting. Ricardo went out to the *batey*, cupped his hands around his mouth, and hooted back. He was letting the messenger know that he had heard their call.

He sat down on the porch and began putting on his boots. "Chenta, please prepare two flares for us. Moncho, get your shoes on. You are coming with me."

Chenta got two glass bottles and poured some kerosene into each one. She fashioned wicks out of strips of cotton cloth and lit them. Father and son took off into the night with their homemade lanterns.

They made their way down to the ravine, where they were met by Leocadio Maldonado with the news that Mama Sebia had passed away early that afternoon in the home of her son, Canuto. They were holding the wake at Canuto's house that night, and the burial would be the next afternoon at three o'clock. Canuto had ridden into town during the afternoon and had made the arrangements with the priest. As soon as he had returned to his house with the funeral details, his son, Catalino, had ridden over to the Maldonado farm, knowing that they could relay the message over to Ricardo.

Ricardo shook his head. "I am sorry to hear the news. May she rest in peace. There is no way that we can make it to the wake, but we will be at the funeral tomorrow. Or at least, some of us will go. Probably Chenta will have to stay home with the little ones."

Back at the house, Luisa was anxiously awaiting Ricardo and Moncho's return. She figured it was bad news of some sort; it always was, in these situations. The younger children were in their beds, and Chenta was in the living room, doing her mending by lanternlight, but Luisa and Pilar sat on the porch steps, talking quietly and waiting. The November nights up in the mountains were cool, and the girls were wrapped in their shawls. Luisa was enjoying the peaceful serenity which was in such contrast to the intense noise and fear that she had experienced during the hurricane. The *coquís* were not as numerous as they had been prior to the hurricane, but they seemed to be making a comeback. Their calling out of their own name, *"Coquí, coquí!"* was a comforting sound to Luisa's ears.

When father and son entered the *batey*, Luisa and Pilar got up and ceded their spots on the porch steps to them. Chenta came out with two glasses of water and took their lanterns from them.

"*¿Qué pasó?*" she asked her husband, her voice quiet and low with seriousness. *What happened?*

Ricardo lifted his eyes to his daughters who were standing in front of him, and spoke directly to them. "Your grandmother, Eusebia, has died. The burial will be tomorrow afternoon."

"Mama Sebia?" asked Pilar, sounding a little shocked.

Luisa merely nodded. "Well, Pilar, it was to be expected sooner or later. She was very old, and she has been sick for some time. Don't you remember we heard about it from Catalino at Mina's baptism? *Papá*, are we all going to the funeral tomorrow?"

"No, *Mija*. I will take you, Pilar and Moncho. We will leave Chenta at home with the younger children. Is that all right with you, Chenta?" At her nod, he continued. "In the morning, I will tell Petra and Sebastián. We can all ride into town together in the wagon."

Well, at least that is something to look forward to, thought Luisa.

That night, as Luisa lay in bed willing herself to fall asleep, she started thinking about Mama Sebia. She felt guilty about not feeling as sad as she thought she should be. She had known Mama Sebia all of her life and had seen her regularly, but she had never really felt a closeness with her grandmother. Try as she might, Luisa could not remember a single time that Mama Sebia had told Luisa that she loved her. To her recollection, she had never been hugged warmly by her grandmother or sat and had a heart-to-heart conversation with her. *Well, with so many children and grandchildren, it was a wonder that she even remembered my name*, thought Luisa wryly.

She tried to analyze her feelings for Mama Sebia, and after some moments realized that she had respected her grandmother and had maybe even been a little afraid of her. Certainly she was not grieving for her the way she had mourned the loss of her own mother.

What had it been like for Mama Sebia when Luisa's mother died? After all, that was her daughter! She had already lost several children by the time Ildefonsa died. How did a person survive that kind of sorrow? Perhaps Mama Sebia had not always had such a tough exterior; perhaps it was a protective shell that had hardened around her heart over time due to experiencing so much tragedy.

As Luisa finally started drifting off to sleep, a memory from long ago came to her mind, causing her to open her eyes again. It was the summer that she turned nine, and her brother Sebastián was fifteen. Mama Sebia had come to visit them, and upon observing how tall and strong Sebastián had become and learning how much he helped Ricardo on the farm, she had smiled and complimented the boy. Luisa had thought how nice it must be to get a compliment from Mama Sebia. *Sebastián is probably her favorite grandchild,* she had thought, a little jealously.

She, Petra and Sebastián had been sent out to fetch water. They were heading up to the spring, when there on the path was their father's mare. She was often let loose to graze, but they had been surprised to see her there nonetheless.

"Luisa, do you want to ride her?" Sebastián had asked on the spur of the moment.

"I've never ridden on a horse before," had been Luisa's dubious answer.

"I know! What kind of a country girl are you? And this is your own father's mare!"

So, convinced that it was high time that she tried it, Luisa had let Sebastián help her onto the mare's bare back. Without a saddle or reigns, Luisa hadn't known how she would hold on, but Sebastián had grinned and assured her that the old mare was incapable of going fast. He gave the animal a pat on the rump, and to their surprise, the mare had bolted forward, sending Luisa flying off. She landed on the ground right on her tailbone. Ouch! The mare trotted off, happy to be rid of her rider. Needless to say, that was the end of the horseback riding. Luisa had to be helped back to the house, as she was barely able to walk. With Sebastián and Petra supporting her on either side, Luisa took painful baby steps.

They had thought that they would get scolded for returning without the water, but that had not even been mentioned. Ildefonsa, of course, had been concerned about Luisa's injury, but Mama Sebia's anger had been explosive. She railed at Sebastián, calling him thoughtless, careless, and irresponsible.

"What were you thinking," she had demanded, "putting your little sister on a horse without a saddle, and her without riding experience? She could have been killed! Look at the child—she can hardly even walk!"

On and on went Mama Sebia, berating the grandson that she had praised not even an hour earlier. Luisa had smiled despite the pain in her tailbone. Mama Sebia did care about her, after all.

She was smiling again now, as she lay in her bed remembering that incident from long ago. Yes, Mama Sebia had loved her, although she was not prone to displays of affection or even loving words. *Thank you, God, for bringing this memory to my mind. I guess my grandmother cared for me after all, in her own way…and I guess I loved her, too.*

The morning dawned gray and rainy. The laundry chore would have to be put off for another day. That was probably for the best, as Luisa didn't think that she would have time, anyway. After helping Chenta prepare and serve breakfast for the whole family, washing the dishes, and sweeping the house, the morning was half gone.

Luisa began heating up water on the stove. She, Pilar, Moncho and their father would all need to take turns bathing in the bath house. She decided to go first, since her father was still not back from the Collado cabin, Pilar was washing the eggs that she had gathered that morning, and Moncho was taking care of the other farm animals. Luisa was going to wear, for the first time, the new dress that she had sewn months ago. It was a good thing that she had purchased the fabric and sewn the dresses for Pilar and herself when the farm was producing well and there was money for such things. If it were now, with the ruined crops, it would have been a different story. She was also thankful that she had chosen a dark blue colored fabric. Typically, people wore black clothes for funerals, but any dark color was acceptable. Pilar would be fine in her new dress, also. While not exactly dark, the green and brown print on a beige background was not too lively a pattern, and she was still so young that she would not be judged for not wearing suitable mourning clothes.

After Pilar was bathed and the two girls had changed into their new dresses, they fussed with their hair. Luisa decided to wear her hair down, and her long tresses reached almost to her waist. Pilar opted to have hers unbraided, also, and tied simply with a ribbon at the back of her neck.

Ricardo returned, and he and Moncho took turns in the bath house and changed into their best clothes. The four of them had the privilege of sitting together at the table and eating their midday meal before all of the others. Ricardo wanted to leave right after eating because they had to pick up Petra and Sebastián, and he wanted to get to town in plenty of time. Sebastián was still staying in the Collado's cabin, sleeping on a hammock, since they had not been able to acquire the necessary supplies to fix the roof of his cabin. So at least they only had to make one stop. Juan José was staying behind to work on the farm.

It was a good thing that they did leave the house early because the road was extra rutted, and Ricardo had to drive the team slowly. It had only been two weeks since the hurricane, and the roadways still had not been repaired. If the Spanish government was doing anything to help Puerto Rico recover, it was not apparent in the rural mountainous regions of the island. The local citizens had taken matters into their own hands to remove tree trunks and repair washed out roadways using picks, shovels, machetes and lots of hard labor. The road was passable, but caution had to be taken so as not to break a wagon wheel. It required Ricardo to put all of his attention and skills to use in driving the team of horses.

Padre Irizarry officiated the graveside burial service and many family members were in attendance. The news of Mama Sebia's passing had traveled fast via word of mouth. Eusebia Nieves Pérez was thought to be about one hundred years old at the time of her death, although no one knew for sure when she was born. She had outlived her husband, Juan de la Cruz Torres, by over twenty-six years, as well as all of her siblings. At her funeral, twenty-one of her grandchildren were present, along with their parents, and many of her nieces and nephews with their children and grandchildren. Rosa was there with her husband, Domingo, and they stood alongside Ricardo and his family for the service.

The next evening was the start of the Novena. It was to be held at Canuto's house and consisted of nine consecutive nights of praying the rosary for the eternal rest of the deceased. The *novenaria* was Canuto's wife, Anastacia Sáez. She led the participants in the prayers of the rosary and the accompanying litany.

Considering the distance that they had to travel to get to Canuto's house, Ricardo and his children were unable to make it to all of the nights of Eusebia's Novena, but they attended the first and last nights, as well as several in between. Those were late nights for them and a long time for children to sit still while the praying was going on. Luisa felt a little sorry for Moncho and Pilar, thinking that they might be bored with all the monotonous reciting of prayers. She was willing to endure it for the sake of propriety and because it afforded her the opportunity to be with her older siblings and other relatives and friends, even if it was for a somber occasion. In the last several months she had gotten into the habit of praying herself to sleep, and she felt a closer intimacy with God with that type of prayer. It was like having her own private conversation with the Lord. But at the same time, she had respect for the religion in which she had been raised, and repeated the Lord's Prayer and the Hail Marys along with the others.

When the Novena was over, life fell back into its usual pattern. The men worked hard to salvage some of the crops that hadn't been totally destroyed by the hurricane. Luisa and Chenta poured all of their energy into the domestic work necessary to make their home cozy and its inhabitants well cared for. Pilar and Moncho were growing and taking on more responsibilities, and the little ones were thriving. There was a lot for Luisa to be thankful for and she expressed her gratitude in her nightly chats with God.

Chapter 10

The Christmas Season

Christmas in Puerto Rico was not just one day; it was a whole season that began in early December and continued until after Three Kings' Day, January 6th. For the Torres family, the celebration was kicked off by the first *parranda* that they participated in. This Puerto Rican tradition was a social event featuring typical music, food, and drinks, and it was a highlight of the Christmas season.

Late one Friday night in December, the Torres family was awakened by the sound of someone playing a *cuatro,* several voices singing loudly, and someone playing a *pandero*—a tambourine—right on their *batey*! The house had been approached quietly so as to surprise the family while they were sleeping in their beds. That was the whole idea of an *asalto*; it was a sneak attack of sorts. Luisa's heart gave a happy leap, and she bounded out of bed. Pilar did the same, and both girls hurried to dress.

Vicenta sat up in her bed and rubbed her eyes. "Why are you getting up?" she asked.

"*Mamita*, we are getting an *asalto*!" Luisa replied, excitedly. "Pilar, help her get dressed, but if Boni wakes up, it's okay to let her stay in her nightgown. I have to go help Chenta get refreshments ready."

She left the bedroom and entered the living room just as Ricardo and Chenta were coming out of their bedroom, also fully dressed. The singing and the playing of the instruments continued outside with gusto until Ricardo lit a lantern. Then a cheer arose from the group in the *batey*, and cries of "We got them up!" could be heard.

Ricardo opened the door and invited the musicians in. Leocadio Maldonado was the one who had been playing the *cuatro*, and his daughter Felita had been playing the *pandero*. Besides Leocadio, his wife, Aquilina, and their four children, Luisa was surprised to see Leocadio's cousins, Eladio and Manuel de Jesús. She had not seen them for two months, since baby Mina's baptism celebration. The young men greeted Luisa as they entered, and she responded in like manner. Eladio's dreamy eyes still captivated Luisa's attention, but when Manuel de Jesús smiled at her and she noticed how one shiny lock of his dark hair threatened to fall on his forehead, her heart flip-flopped! What was going on with her? She was being silly. These two were guys that she had known for years. They were childhood friends, she reminded herself.

The living room was now packed with people singing, clapping their hands, and moving to the beat of the lively music. Ricardo brought out his maracas and contributed to the joyful noise. Luisa slipped out of the crowded room and into the kitchen to help Chenta prepare crackers, cheese, fruit, and drinks for the guests. They arranged everything on the table, and with a wave of one hand and the other hand pointing to the table, Chenta was able to communicate to the visitors without using words that they could come partake. From there, she went to her room to tend to baby Mina, who was crying in her crib. Luisa remained in the kitchen and Dionicia and her younger sister, Rosa María, joined her there.

"Did you hear us coming, or were you surprised?" asked Dionicia, as she helped herself to some cheese and crackers.

"I didn't hear a thing!" answered Luisa. "I don't know how you managed to sneak up so quietly in the dark."

"The full moon helped," said Dionicia. "Eladio and Manuel de Jesús planned this with my father. They wanted yours to be the first house. I hope you can come with us to the next ones."

"I don't know," replied Luisa. "We'll have to see what *Papá* says."

Eladio and Manuel de Jesús came into the kitchen and Luisa moved aside to give them access to the table.

"How have you been, Luisa?" asked Eladio, looking at her with those gorgeous eyes.

"Good, good," she replied. "And you?"

"Good, also. My brother and I are staying on Leocadio's farm now, in one of his cabins. We have been helping him to clean up and replant after the hurricane. There is a lot of work that still needs to be done."

"I know," answered Luisa. "Sebastián and Juan José work so hard with *Papá* and Moncho that I hardly ever see them."

Luisa felt eyes on her and turned her head slightly to see Manuel de Jesús looking at her. *He is the quiet one—silent and handsome*, she thought.

"*¿Quieres bailar?*" he blurted out, and he looked as surprised at his own question as Luisa felt.

"*Sí,*" was her simple answer, and she preceded him back into the living room. They danced to the *guaracha* music being played by Leocadio on the *cuatro* with Ricardo keeping the beat on the maracas. Leocadio had a nice singing voice, and the lyrics of the song were appropriately about celebrating the Christmas season with good food and music. The *guaracha* dance was performed by jauntily stepping side to side with the partners in the classic dance hold. Manuel de Jesús held Luisa's right hand in his left one, and his right hand was on her waist. Her left hand was on his shoulder. There was a good distance between them, but Luisa still felt a little giddy. *It is late at night. Normally, I would be sleeping right now,* she thought, as a way of explaining her emotions to herself.

Eladio was now dancing with Dionicia, and Pilar and Rosa María began awkwardly dancing together, each of them trying to lead, to everyone's laughter. Moncho, Juanito, Vicenta and Bonifacia were raiding the refreshments. Chenta, holding Mina, was sitting next to Aquilina, with Toño standing close to her, sucking his thumb.

About an hour after the *asalto* began, the group was ready to move on. They decided to give a surprise attack to the household of *Don* Eustaquio, the neighboring family on the way to the main road. An older couple, they had a married daughter that had moved to Utuado with her husband. It was decided that Ricardo, Luisa, Pilar, and Moncho would join the *parranda*, while Chenta stayed home with the five younger children.

This time Luisa got to have the fun of sneaking up as quietly as possible to the unsuspecting family and burst into singing along with the others. They were out there for almost ten minutes before they saw a light come on inside the house and they let up a victory cheer. That was so exhilarating—to make people get up and dressed, open up their house to an instant party and serve the guests refreshments. Eustaquio's wife, Sinforosa, served them *arroz con dulce*, which was a rice pudding especially popular during the Christmas season. Once again, Manuel de Jesús invited her to dance. She also danced with Eladio and even once with her father. It was nice not having to help out in the kitchen or play the part of hostess. There was more time for talking, eating, and dancing.

From *Don* Eustaquio's house they moved on to the home of *Don* Abelardo and *Doña* Elena, taking along *Don* Eustaquio and *Doña* Sinforosa. The group that descended upon *Don* Abelardo's family now consisted of thirteen people. *Don* Abelardo and *Doña* Elena had two girls, Camila, aged fifteen and Concepción, eleven, and their thirteen-year-old son, Carlos, who was Moncho's friend. What a party! They could all barely squeeze into the living space. After singing and dancing in that home for an hour and enjoying more food and drinks, Ricardo declared that it was enough partying for one night; they would head back home from there. It was now about two o'clock in the morning, and although they had all had a great time, it was really late. He didn't want Chenta to be worried.

When they arrived home, Pilar and Moncho were like zombies, not being accustomed to staying up so late. Luisa was sleepy, too, but oh, what a wonderful night it had been! Her prayer that night was very short. She fell asleep even before saying, "Amen." In her dreams, she was dancing and dancing and it felt wonderful to feel her partner's hand on her waist. But…who was she dancing with? His face was a blur.

That Saturday, Petra joined them in the making of *pasteles*, another tradition of the Christmas season. They were labor intensive to make, but so worth it, and it was fun to work together. Pilar wanted to be a part of the team, but she was needed to watch her younger siblings. On a recent visit, their sister Rosa had said that this year she would be making pasteles with her sister-in-law, Antonia. Anyway, Chenta's kitchen was way too small to have four women working in there at the same time.

Leocadio Maldonado had butchered one of his pigs, and he gave Ricardo a large section of pork. What a blessing! It took Chenta and Petra quite a while to cut up the meat into bite sized pieces. They then spent hours cooking the meat in a big *caldero* on the wood stove. They added Chenta's delicious *sofrito,* which she prepared with onions, garlic, sweet peppers, and *recao* leaves, and salt to taste. For coloring, they used *achiote*—lard that had been tinted orange with annatto seeds.

Meanwhile, Luisa had the task of peeling and grating the green bananas and the *yautía*—the taro root. To peel the very green bananas, she used a sharp knife to cut the ends off of each banana and score it all the way down its length. Then with a blunt knife, she separated and lifted the thick banana peel off the fruit, working her way all the way around until the entire peel came off. It took skill and practice to be able to do this without taking out chunks of the banana with the peel. The *yautía* was peeled like one would a potato, but underneath the rough skin the tuber was as slippery as soap and hard to hold onto. The vegetables were put in salted water as they were peeled until that task was completely done. This kept them from discoloring. Luisa alternated taking green bananas and *yautías* from the salt water to grate them, and every so often she mixed the gratings that were in the bowl to blend them well. Grating the green bananas and the *yautía* by hand was a strenuous task, and every now and then Luisa would be spelled by either Chenta or Petra. When the vegetables had been finely grated to a paste, salt was added to taste, and *achiote* was stirred and blended in to provide an appealing uniform color. This paste was called *la masa*.

For their part, Ricardo and Moncho cut down banana leaves and prepared them by passing them over the embers of a low fire to soften them. Then they cut off and discarded the center vein of each huge leaf. The leaves were then cut into lengths of about twelve inches and wiped with a clean damp cloth.

Now they were ready to begin assembling the *pasteles*. Their table was too small, and the kitchen was too cramped to work in for this part of the process, so Ricardo set up a long table on the porch by placing wooden boards on sawhorses. Chenta set up the ingredients in a production line: the banana leaves, *la masa*, the pot of cooked pork, a bowl of green olives, a small plate of capers, a bowl of garbanzo beans, a small plate of raisins, parchment paper, and lengths of string.

After enjoying their three o'clock coffee during a short break, the three women were revitalized and eager to continue with the making of the *pasteles*. It was now midafternoon, and Bonifacia, Toño, and Mina were taking their naps, so Pilar was free to help. Juanito and Vicenta were playing in the *batey*, within sight of the others as they worked. Pilar was all smiles as she took her place in between Luisa and Chenta in the production line. "I feel joy jumping around inside of me," she declared, giddily. "This is so much fun, and it means that Christmas is almost here!"

At the far left, Petra spooned six or seven tablespoons of *la masa* onto the center of one of the banana leaf sections and spread it out a bit, then slid it over to Luisa, who added three tablespoons of the meat mixture into the middle of the circle of *la masa.* On top of the meat, Luisa placed an olive and then passed it to Pilar, who was charged with adding capers, raisins, and garbanzo beans before passing the leaf to Chenta. Chenta had the artful task of carefully folding the banana leaf, wrapping it in the parchment paper, and tying it up with string like a little package. Granted, Chenta's part took the longest to do, but she was very adept at it and only once in a while had to ask the others to slow down.

The *pasteles* were boiled in salted water for about forty-five minutes and served with *arroz con gandules* as part of their Christmas feast. All across Puerto Rico, families were working together to cook traditional meals and gathering with friends and relatives to celebrate the joyous season.

On Christmas Day, the entire Torres family got dressed and rode into town in Ricardo's wagon to attend the *misa*—the mass in the Catholic church. Luisa thought that it was a minor miracle that no one had to stay home sick and that everyone was bathed, dressed and ready on time. Neighbors had spent time working on the dirt road, but it was still rutted and bumpy; Chenta held onto baby Mina tightly, and Luisa did the same with little Toño.

Everyone was wearing their best clothing. Luisa was wearing her dark blue dress, and Pilar was also wearing the same dress that she had worn for Mama Sebia's funeral. Chenta, Luisa and Pilar all had mantillas with them to drape over their heads as they entered the church. It was the custom for women to wear head coverings inside the church while men were to remove their hats before entering.

On the way into town, as they passed neighboring homes, people came out to their porches to wave and call out, *"¡Feliz Navidad!"*

The plaza of Adjuntas was festively decorated and a beautiful carved stone nativity scene was set up in the very center, with a wooden fence around it to keep the children out. It was set up the same way every year, and Luisa remembered when she was a little girl that she would have tried to pick up the figure of the baby Jesus had not the fence kept her from doing so. As it was, even though she was not a child anymore, she had a strong urge to reach out and at least touch one of the camels. The scene depicted a wooden shed with a straw thatched roof that protected the figures of Mary and Joseph gazing adoringly at baby Jesus in the manger. A large gold star was atop the roof of the shed. Outside of the shed, on one side were figures of the Three Wise Men bearing their gifts of gold, myrrh, and frankincense to honor the baby Jesus, with their camels standing behind them. On the other side of the shed were three shepherds with their lambs.

Luisa and her family were admiring the nativity scene when her sister, Rosa and brother-in-law, Domingo, approached them. Glad greetings, hugs, and kisses were exchanged all around. After hugging her sister, Luisa held her out at arm's length and pointedly looked at the white dress that Rosa was wearing, with a blue rope tied at the waist.

"¿Es una promesa?" asked Luisa. *Is it a promise?*

Rosa fingered the blue rope. "Yes, it is. I will be wearing this every day until the Lord answers my prayer and fulfills the desire of my heart."

"A baby?" whispered Luisa. At Rosa's nod, the two young women embraced again, and Luisa spoke softly in Rosa's ear. "I will pray for you, too, every night."

They all sat together in the church, and familiar faces were all around them. Leocadio Maldonado's family was seated across the aisle from them, along with Chenta's sister, Antonia, and her husband, Lucas Maldonado. Luisa leaned forward in her seat to discreetly wave at her friends, Felita and Dionicia, and was a little taken aback when both Eladio and Manuel de Jesús smiled and waved back at her. She quickly sat back in her seat and felt her face flush. Did they think that she had been waving at *them*? Those guys must think that she was a flirt! How embarrassing! Despite that, Luisa couldn't deny the little excited tingle she felt inside. It was nice to be noticed…and liked.

The Christmas mass was reverent, humbling and inspiring all at the same time. The heartfelt singing of the congregation, the delight of seeing friends and family all around her, the words that *Padre* Irizarry spoke, the fragrance of the incense, and the taking of communion, all combined to elevate feelings of peace and joy within Luisa.

Afterwards, instead of going back home, Ricardo directed the wagon to Leocadio's property. The family, along with other neighbors and relatives, had been invited there to celebrate Christmas. There was no exchange of gifts; it was just a time of gathering together and celebrating the birth of Christ with good food, conversation, laughter, music, and yes, the inevitable dancing. Perhaps one of the reasons why the Christmas season was so looked forward to was because it provided a respite from the usual hard work that was an integral part of their daily lives. These social gatherings were as important a component to everyone's health and wellbeing as were food, water, and air.

Chenta and other ladies helped Aquilina in the kitchen, so Luisa was free of hostess duties and was able to enjoy the company of her cousins and friends. The young people gathered together, and even though she was holding Mina, there were plenty of other arms willing to relieve her of her charge and give Luisa the opportunity to dance. And dance she did, with most of the young men that were there, including Eladio and her brother Sebastián.

At one point, Manuel de Jesús came to stand in front of her and asked, "Will you dance with me?"

"But there is no music playing right now," protested Luisa. "The musicians are taking a break."

"I know, but if I wait until the music starts back up, someone will beat me to the punch. It has been happening for the past hour. So can I have the next dance?"

Luisa laughed and nodded her head. When the musicians began to play again, Manuel de Jesús got his dance with Luisa, and several more after that.

And so continued the parties and *parrandas*, through New Year's Day—a day that brought everyone hope for the future of agricultural and financial recovery from the devastation of the hurricane. It also brought the sobering realization that the Christmas season would soon be over, and life would return to its unending cycle of the hard work and struggles that badgered the typical *jíbaro*. But the partying would not end until after Three Kings' Day. This day, above all, was looked forward to by the children, since they anticipated receiving gifts. Birthdays came and went, usually without any acknowledgement, much less gifts. Most of the people in Luisa's sphere didn't even know when their actual date of birth was, nor exactly how old they were. So, the receiving of a gift on Three Kings' Day was even more special to the children in these rural areas.

Chenta and Luisa decided to make a batch of *arroz con dulce* to have on hand for Three Kings' Day in case unexpected visitors dropped by or just for their family to enjoy. Everybody tweaked this traditional rice pudding to their own liking, but the basic ingredients were the same. Luisa had learned to make it the way Chenta did, since she was so young when Ildefonsa had passed, and Luisa couldn't recall her mother's version.

Chenta had put raw rice to soak for about three hours to soften it. It reduced the cooking time and gave the pudding a better texture. She now drained it and set it aside. She put four cups of water to boil and added some fresh ginger and a few cinnamon sticks to the water, along with a dash of salt. After simmering the spices for about ten minutes, she removed them and kept the water in the pot. Now she added the rice to the fragrant water and cooked it for about fifteen minutes over a medium flame until the water was absorbed. After the water was mostly absorbed, coconut milk and cream of coconut were stirred in. The rice mixture now had to be stirred every few minutes to avoid having it stick to the bottom of the pot. When the rice was soft, raisins and butter were added and stirred until well blended. At this point, the *arroz con dulce* was removed from the stove and spooned onto various plates to cool. Luisa liked to shape the dessert into round cakes and garnish them with ground cinnamon. After they cooled completely, the plates of pudding could be cut into wedges to serve to guests, or the entire plate could be given away to a family, often in exchange for a plate of *arroz con dulce* from that family.

Luisa's younger siblings were really excited to prepare their boxes of grass for the camels that night. After supper, they scampered around pulling up grass from the edges of the trail that led away from their *batey*. Pilar had declared that she was too old to fix a box for the camels, but Luisa had insisted she do it anyway.

The children placed their boxes of grass under their beds. This was intended as a treat for the Wise Men's camels. They hardly had to be prodded to go to bed that night. They definitely wanted to be obedient; the Three Kings would not bring gifts to naughty children.

The next morning, the grass in the boxes was half gone. What was left of it looked like it had been chewed, and broken pieces of grass trailed out of the bedrooms toward the front door, which had been supposedly left unbolted the night before. There were even a few clumps of mud on the floor, allegedly from the camels' hooves. But the children didn't notice the mess. They were focused on the surprises they found under their beds next to the boxes with their remnants of grass. Pilar had an assortment of new hair ribbons, Moncho and Juanito had new tops, Toño had a toy horse, and Vicenta and Bonifacia had newly sewn rag dolls.

Later, as Luisa swept the floor clean of all grass and mud, she couldn't hide the smile on her face at the expressions of delight from her younger siblings. All of the late nights that she and Chenta had spent working on the rag dolls had been worth it to see those little girls cradling their new dollies. Ricardo had given her the money to buy the other gifts on one of her trips to town with Petra weeks earlier, and Chenta had hidden the purchases in her room, where they would not be discovered. Knowing the financial plight that the family was in after the destruction of their crops, Luisa was grateful that they had managed to at least get those small gifts for the children.

Breakfast was a special treat of *arroz con dulce* and coffee. The last of their *pasteles* would be eaten for the midday meal. For the Torres family the Christmas season was officially over.

Chapter 11

Plans

Luisa plunged into the new year with fervor. She and Petra had talked about starting vegetable gardens to add variety to their households' usual diet. The climate in Puerto Rico afforded them the opportunity to begin a garden even in January. Petra had a perfect spot close to her cabin, and Juan José had begun to prepare the ground for their garden plot. Luisa, however, had no area close to the house that was suitable. There was one spot that she thought might work, although it was not as close to the house as she would have liked. It was down by the creek where she and Pilar washed the clothes. There was a wide, flat area on the bank of the creek, clear of trees and large bushes. Luisa talked to her father and pointed out the area. Ricardo looked it over and walked the perimeter of the proposed plot, declaring it good and promising to help Luisa clear out and prepare the soil or have Moncho help her with it.

Petra came for a visit, and the two sisters sat down with Chenta and planned their gardens over their midafternoon coffee. Chenta already had some herbs and spices growing right outside her kitchen window, such as mint, oregano and *recao*. Chenta reminded them that their garden might start with a few different kinds of plants, but others could be added during the year; their garden "crops" would vary according to the months when they grew best and could be harvested.

"That's great!" said Luisa, brightly. "We will not be eating the same things over and over. You know, after the hurricane, when so much of the agriculture was destroyed, it was a blessing to still have the root foods to eat. If we had had a garden, it would have probably been wiped out with the hurricane, but maybe we would have already had beans or squash harvested that could have supplemented the *vianda*."

They decided to start out with tomatoes, onions, lettuce, sweet peppers and *gandules*. Juan José would get the seeds the next time he was in town, and Petra and Luisa would get their tomato seeds started in planter boxes, hoping that they would germinate and be hardened by the time the garden plots were tilled and ready for planting.

Luisa wasn't sure how she would fit in time for tending to the garden in between all of her other household chores and duties as the oldest child, but she was willing to find a way. Thankfully, Pilar was a big help around the house.

"I can help you take care of the garden, Luisa," Pilar offered.

"Thank you, *Mamita*, I appreciate that. I think once the plants are established, even Juanito and Vicenta can be taught to pull weeds without harming the vegetables. It will be good for them to start helping out more. You already do quite a bit, Pilar."

"It's training for when you get married and I will have to do all of the work that you do now," said Pilar, with a wink.

"Ha! What if I am an old maid?"

"You are too pretty to be an old maid. Besides, I saw you dancing plenty during the Christmas parties. I think there are at least a couple of guys interested," insisted Pilar. "What do you think, Chenta?"

"I think that I am not in a hurry to marry off Luisa. She is too valuable to us here. *Pero el tiempo dirá.*" *But time will tell.*

"Anyway, if you are an old maid, that will be better for me. I won't have to do all of the work myself," remarked Pilar.

"That's right. We are partners, and you are a big help, but I want you to enjoy being young, too. I don't think I worked as hard as you do when I was your age. But then, I had three older sisters who did most of the work. Get some sun on your face. You are looking pretty pale."

Petra had a thought. "Why don't I come help you with your garden at least one day a week, and you two can come help me with mine once a week? That way, we can visit regularly, and the work will be more fun."

Luisa and Pilar both brightened at the idea, and the plan was approved by Chenta. They decided that once the gardens were established, Luisa and Pilar would go help Petra with her garden on Wednesdays, and Petra would come help them with theirs on Fridays.

Several days later, Juan José and Petra paid them a visit together. Juan José had purchased the seeds in town, as promised, and Petra had come so that she and Luisa could sit at the table and divide them up. Juan José sought out Ricardo, who was in the barn tending to the horses.

The sisters were happily entertained with their seeds and just chatting with Chenta and Pilar, when Petra lowered her voice and said, "You know, Juan José wanted to come with me so that he could talk to *Papá* about things that he heard in town."

"What kinds of things?" asked Chenta.

"Political stuff," replied Petra. "He hasn't said anything directly to me, but I overheard him and Sebastián talking about it."

At Chenta's and Luisa's questioning looks, Petra continued. "There is talk about people getting organized—to stand up to the Spanish government. There are a lot of people who are complaining about the way we are treated, about our lack of freedom, and about the economy of our island—things like that. Oh, and slavery. People want slavery to end, but the Spanish government isn't listening."

Luisa shuddered. Slavery was so disgusting, so horrible! The idea of people thinking that they could own other human beings and buy and sell them like they were livestock sickened her. She wished it would come to an end, or better yet, she wished it had never happened.

"Hmm," said Chenta, tapping on the table with her fingers. Luisa had seen Chenta do this many times when she was deep in thought or worried about something. "I thought that the government had set up a board of review or something like that to work with the demands of the people."

"Yes," said Petra, "but Juan José says that it isn't doing any good. All the petitions and requests that are made are voted down. There is talk about the people needing to organize and meet secretly, if necessary."

"What is going to happen?" whimpered Pilar, fearfully.

"Nothing is going to happen, *Mamita*," said Luisa, reassuringly. "Don't start worrying. Anything that might happen will be far away from us. You are safe here—we all are."

"That's true," added Chenta. "*Seguro es el pájaro en el nido.*" *The bird is secure in its nest.*

"Yes," agreed Petra. "We are safe in our own homes, up here in the mountains."

Pilar still looked worried, and she massaged her stomach absentmindedly with her hands. Luisa wasn't sure if Pilar's nerves were causing her distress or if she was getting another one of her stomach aches. She was getting them more and more often.

The next morning, Luisa arose and dressed quietly so as not to disturb the sleep of Vicenta and Bonifacia. She brushed and braided her hair, and then after taking a trip to the outhouse and washing her face and hands, she returned to the kitchen to begin her work there. Later, when her father and Moncho were eating their breakfast and drinking the freshly ground and brewed coffee, Chenta entered the kitchen, having already nursed and tended to Mina. Luisa excused herself and went back to the bedroom to wake up Pilar. Today was a laundry day, and they needed to get their other chores out of the way so that they could get started on washing the clothes down at the creek.

Pilar was awake but lay curled up on her side. Luisa could see that she was crying.

"*¿Qué pasa? ¿Qué tienes?*" *What is wrong? What ails you?* Luisa's voice showed genuine concern. Pilar had become a *señorita* a few months earlier, and she suffered from severe monthly cramps, sometimes even accompanied by a fever. She asked Pilar if that was what was going on now.

"No, it's not that," answered Pilar. "My stomach just hurts really bad."

"Okay, stay in bed. I'll go get Chenta."

Rushing back to the kitchen, Luisa told Chenta that Pilar was sick.

"What's wrong with her?" asked Ricardo, as Chenta dried her hands and left the kitchen.

"I don't know. She says her stomach hurts, and she was crying, poor thing."

"Well, Chenta will figure it out. We need to get going to work. "*Vámonos*, Moncho."

"*Adiós, Papá. Bendición.*"

"*Dios te bendiga, Mija.*" *God bless you, daughter.*

Juanito and Toño came into the kitchen, still sleepy-eyed and with rumpled hair. Luisa shooed them onto the porch to get washed up, admonishing Juanito to keep an eye on his little brother and help him wash his face and hands. Vicenta and Bonifacia had been awakened by Chenta talking to Pilar, and they came into the kitchen, too. She sent them out to get washed up, also, just as baby Mina started to cry. Luisa went to pick her up, thinking, *I will never get breakfast done with the baby in my arms, much less do the dishes, sweep the house and go wash clothes in the creek!* How do mothers juggle everything?

As the four children trooped in from the porch, Luisa told Juanito, "Sit here and hold Mina. Don't drop her now! I need to get breakfast ready for all of you."

"Where is *Mami*?" asked Juanito.

"Pilar is sick and Chenta needs to tend to her." Luisa turned to the stove and began preparing eggs for the children, but her mind was on Pilar.

Chenta bustled into the kitchen and immediately put water to boil on the stove. "I am going to make Pilar a tea from *guanábana* leaves," she informed Luisa. "That should help her stomachache."

"Do you have any on hand?" asked Luisa.

"No, and I would need some fresh ones, anyway. Juanito, give me Mina and go pick some leaves from the soursop tree. Run, *Mijo*."

By the time Juanito returned with the leaves and Chenta had brewed the tea, the children had been fed their breakfast and Mina had been passed around between Chenta, Luisa and Juanito several times.

This is crazy, thought Luisa. She was worried about Pilar because the girl seemed more pale and delicate than ever lately, and there were no doctors nearby, nor was there money with which to pay one, anyway. Up in the mountains, children—and even adults—sometimes died of stomach ailments. Gastroenteritis, Luisa had heard it called. Anemia was another condition that commonly afflicted and killed people, but Luisa didn't think that a stomachache was a symptom of anemia.

Chenta took the tea to Pilar, and Luisa followed, depositing Mina into Juanito's arms on the way. Pilar sat up in the bed and sipped at the tea until it was gone, then lay back down. Chenta massaged Pilar's stomach gently with chamomile oil, moving her hands in a circular motion as she prayed aloud, *"En el nombre del Señor todopoderoso."* In the name of the all-powerful Lord.

"Go to sleep, now, *Mamita*," whispered Luisa, as she brushed back Pilar's hair from her sweaty forehead.

Later, Luisa asked Chenta where she had learned what leaves or herbs were good for different ailments, and Chenta replied that she had learned from her mother, who had learned from *her* mother.

"Our people were using these natural remedies long before the Spaniards came," said Chenta, "and they have been passed down from generation to generation."

Apparently, they were good remedies because Pilar was feeling better in the space of two hours.

Chapter 12

Progress

"Luisa, the garden plot is ready for you now," announced Ricardo.

"Yes! *Gracias, Papá.* I will start planting this afternoon, then."

"What are you planning to plant?" he asked.

"Lettuce, sweet peppers, *gandules*…"

"Those are all above ground crops," he said. "*Es luna menguante.* This is the time to plant below ground crops."

"*Papá*, I've heard you talk about *la luna menguante*, but I am not sure what you mean by it."

"*La luna menguante* is the waning moon. This is the time after the full moon, when it is decreasing. All crops that grow below ground should be planted during this time so that the roots can get strengthened," explained Ricardo. "Were you planning to plant anything that grows underground?"

"Well…just the onions for now," replied Luisa.

"Then that's all that you should plant at this time."

"Oh," said Luisa, sounding a bit disappointed. "When can I plant the other things?"

"For plants that give their yield above ground, you should wait for the waxing moon, *la luna creciente*—the time when the moon is growing in illumination."

"So, I guess I will have to wait a couple of weeks before finishing my planting. Is that right?" Luisa asked.

"Yes, watch the moon and follow its phases," replied her father. "Sebastián and Juan José are planting *ñame* this week because of *la luna menguante*."

Ñame, or yams, was a crop that did well in the tropical climate of Puerto Rico, with its abundant rainfall. Ricardo had preserved some of the previous year's yams to use for the new planting season. The cut pieces of the tuber were treated with ash and allowed to dry before the men planted them in mounds and ridges.

"So, *Papá*, how did you learn all this about the moon's phases, and the proper time to plant different things?" asked Luisa.

"Well, I guess it is all written in a book called *Bristol's Farmer's Almanac*…if you know how to read. But our ancestors have been doing it this way since…well, I do not know since when, but this knowledge has been passed down from generation to generation.

"Interesting," murmured Luisa. Once again, she wished that she knew how to read. There was a world of information that could be obtained from books, apparently. But then, Chenta and Ricardo had a lot of practical knowledge that they had learned from their parents and grandparents, and Luisa had much to learn from them.

Pilar continued to do well, health wise. Luisa monitored her sister to make sure that she wasn't being overworked and was getting enough rest. At the first sign of a stomachache, Chenta or Luisa would prepare a tea for Pilar, whether it was made from *guanábana* leaves or from sweet spices—cinnamon, cloves, anise, and ginger. As the weeks went by, Pilar began to gain a little weight and lose her pallid complexion. She was blossoming into a lovely young woman.

All over Puerto Rico, farmers were still cleaning up their properties after the devastation of the hurricane and coaxing new life out of the land. Ricardo and Moncho were busy on the farm, replanting coffee plants. As they worked, they discovered that not all of their old coffee plants had been destroyed by the hurricane. A lot of them had survived. They had certainly taken a beating, but they were making a comeback. Still, there would not be much of a coffee crop for the next four years.

Luisa and Pilar were eventually able to plant the rest of their seeds. The first to reach maturity were the lettuce plants, and they were a welcome addition to their diet. The tomato seedlings had been transplanted into the garden plots and were flowering, as were the *gandules* and the sweet peppers. Once the gardens were established, the work was not difficult. Juanito and Vicenta had been trained and drafted into service to help pull weeds in Luisa's plot by the creek. They enjoyed the activity and were learning to identify the different vegetables by their leaves. After the midday meal was the best time to have Juanito and Vicenta work in the garden because they would be away from the house while their younger siblings took their afternoon naps. On more than one occasion, their bickering had disturbed the little ones' slumber, but the garden activity kept them entertained and at a safe distance. For added peace and security, Luisa separated the two and had them working on different vegetable rows.

It turned out that the time spent together gardening was good for Luisa and Pilar, also. The weekly trek to Petra's cabin and their older sister's visit to help with their garden plot was a welcome break in their routines. The joy of the three of them being together served as a tonic, with the fresh air, sunshine and healthy exercise contributing to their wellbeing.

Progress was also being made across the island in the reconstruction and repairing of homes and roads damaged by the hurricane. Shortly after the holiday season, Ricardo was finally able to acquire the lumber and zinc panels needed to fix the roof on Sebastián's cabin, and between the three men and Moncho, the job was finished in a day's time. During the hurricane, Sebastián had taken refuge in the Collado's cabin, sleeping on a hammock that they strung up in the living room. A couple of weeks later, after clearing out the soggy contents of his bedroom, he had moved back into the cabin, using the borrowed hammock in his own tiny living room space.

"Are you sure that you want to move back into your own cabin so soon?" Petra had asked him when he was preparing to leave. "You know that you are welcome to stay here as long as you need to."

"I appreciate your hospitality, but I think we will all be more comfortable if I move back to my own place," he had replied.

"But your bedroom roof is still not fixed. You know it rains almost every day. What are you going to do?" she had persisted.

"I have a tarp over the missing section of roof. For the most part, it keeps the water out. And I can hang the hammock in my living room just as well as here in yours. Anyway, you guys are still newlyweds. You need your privacy!" He said this with a wink. Petra had blushed and had offered no further arguments.

Now that his roof was repaired, Sebastián moved the hammock into the bedroom. He still needed to get a new bed, as his mattress had been soaked and ruined when the roof of his bedroom blew off. He would get one as soon as he had the money for it; in the meantime, at least he was back in his own bedroom and had a snug and secure roof over his head.

There was a third cabin on Ricardo's property—the one that had been vacated by a former employee and his family—but it too had suffered damage from the hurricane and was at present uninhabitable. Ricardo was focusing his attention on the farm since the crops were needed for their sustenance and to provide income for the family's other needs. That cabin's repair was not his highest priority at the present time, and he could not spare the time or money to fix it up yet.

A new litter of ten piglets had been born, as well as a batch of chicks, and darling twin goat kids. The farm was thriving, and along with the vegetable gardens, provided Ricardo and his family a sense of increasing prosperity and wellbeing. God was good!

On Easter morning, April 12, 1868, Luisa was up earlier than usual. She performed her morning personal hygiene routine, and then began her first chore of the day: grinding the coffee beans needed for the family's consumption. The droning sound produced by the coffee grinder served as a wakeup call for the others, aided by the rooster's crowing at first light. One by one, the Torres family members arose and were greeted cheerfully by Luisa as they entered the kitchen.

"It is *la Pascua Florida*, and we need to hustle to eat breakfast, do our chores and get dressed for church," she prompted each person.

Chenta was busy with Mina, now a plump six-month-old baby that she was still nursing. She also had to get Toño and Boni dressed and fed. Pilar supervised the making of the beds and then went out to feed the chickens and collect the eggs. Juanito fed the pigs and goats, while Moncho and Ricardo tended to the horses. They would hitch up the wagon later, when the family was ready to go.

Fixing breakfast for her large family was a project in itself, and when that was done, Luisa had a pile of dishes to wash. She hurriedly poured hot water into the two pans in the kitchen sink and added soap to one of them. She stood at the open window, leaning slightly out of it to wash the dishes on the sink that was suspended just below the window. Luisa smiled as she performed the task. She could hear her beloved *ruiseñor* singing cheerily, and it matched her mood exactly.

Everyone else was dressed and waiting on Luisa, so she had to hurry to change into her beige dress with large pink flowers. While not new, it was still in good condition, and it felt appropriate for the day and the season. Making sure that she and Pilar had their mantillas, Luisa joined the rest of the family in the wagon bed. As the young ladies of the house, Luisa and Pilar were awarded the privilege of sitting on the one bench in the wagon bed. The other children sat on the floorboards, atop burlap bags that had been placed there to keep their Sunday best from getting dirty. Chenta, of course, sat up front with Ricardo, and held Mina on her lap.

On the ride to church, Luisa breathed in the freshness of the morning and enjoyed the sounds of nature all around her. Her younger siblings were calm and content, for once not bickering or elbowing each other. They were happy to be going into town, also. There was little opportunity for conversation, and no one really felt the need to talk, anyway. It was a peaceful ride.

When they arrived to town, Ricardo found a shady spot for the horses and wagon, and the family walked around the plaza to where the church stood. Luisa was elated to see her sister, Rosa, on the church steps, standing next to her husband, Domingo. Luisa gave her a tight squeeze, then stood back and looked at her sister's smiling face. They didn't have to say anything. Rosa knew that Luisa *knew*. The white dress with its blue rope tie had been slackened at the waistline.

"When is your baby due?" Luisa asked, with tears in her eyes.

"In September," answered Rosa. "Pray for us that this time we get to keep this little one."

"You know that I will," asserted Luisa. "I have a good feeling about this one." Now the tears did spill out, but they were happy tears.

After Rosa and Domingo had greeted everyone else in the family, Chenta started herding them all into the church. Luisa draped her mantilla over her head and basked in the feeling of humility and modesty that came over her as she did so. She entered the church reverently, dipping her fingers into the holy water and making the sign of the cross. Her family did not attend church weekly, as people who lived in town were able to do, but the occasions when they did go were special to Luisa.

Rosa sat next to Luisa during the mass, and the congregation was dotted with familiar faces, many of them relatives. The choir sang beautifully and the sermon that *Padre* Irizarry preached on the resurrection of Jesus Christ was flawlessly delivered. Luisa left the church with a feeling of satisfaction in her soul.

Outside the church, they were able to greet friends and family members. Chenta's sister Antonia was there with her husband, Lucas Maldonado, and their children. Luisa got to see and hold their sweet new baby, Estevanía. Eladio and Manuel de Jesús were with them also, and they both approached Luisa.

"*¿Cómo has estado?*" Eladio asked her.

"I have been well, thank you. And you?" she responded politely. Eladio had those amazing eyes that Luisa had never seen on another person's face.

"You are looking well, Luisa." This was from Manuel de Jesús. *He is handsome, too, and has such a sweet, sincere smile*, thought Luisa.

She thanked him and returned the compliment. Luisa was embarrassed to realize that these two young men could make her blush just by greeting her. She turned away quickly to say hello to someone else.

They went straight home afterwards, but Rosa and Domingo followed them there. The Torres family enjoyed a lovely afternoon of cooking and eating together. They made a huge pot of *arroz con pollo* and had fried plantains and avocados to complement the meal.

Petra, Rosa, Luisa and Pilar indulged in sister talk that revolved around Rosa's pregnancy.

"I was pretty sick for the first three months, and could hardly keep anything in my stomach," said Rosa. "But that is over now, and I am sure glad I can savor this delicious chicken and rice… and my favorite thing—ripe, fried plantains! Mmmm. *Maduros*, with a little salt on them are so good! And this avocado is just perfect, not too green or too ripe. I could eat a whole avocado right now."

Her sisters laughed, and Petra said, "Watch out, or you will get fat, Rosa. I mean all over, not just a big belly. That's to be expected."

"How about you, Petra? You have been married over a year now. No baby coming yet?" asked Rosa.

"No, not yet. Not that I know of, anyway," shrugged Petra. "It's okay. I am not in a hurry. I am still enjoying the quiet, cozy cabin that Juan José and I have. And when I feel like holding a baby, I can just come over here." She had Mina on her lap and gave the baby a little jiggle with her knees for emphasis.

"Yes, and when she spits up on you or has a poopy diaper, you can just hand her back to Chenta and go on home. I've seen you do that!" remarked Pilar.

The sisters all laughed, and Petra said, "Sure. I'm no dummy!"

That night, in bed, Luisa's prayer was filled with gratitude for her family, their health, the progress made with the farm and the animals, and the opportunity to see extended family and friends on that joyous occasion: the celebration of Resurrection Day. She thanked the Lord for his many blessings, and prayed for her sister, Rosa, that she would be able to carry out her pregnancy for the full nine months and give birth to a healthy baby. Lulled by the serenading of the *coquís* outside her window, she fell into a peaceful sleep.

Two weeks after Easter, the family was surprised by a visit from Sebastiana and Francisco. With the road between Ponce and Adjuntas now repaired, they had been able to make the day-long trip to visit family members that they had not seen in over a year. They had arrived at Rosa and Domingo's home late Saturday afternoon and had attended church with them the next morning. Afterwards, the two couples had driven together up to Ricardo and Chenta's home in Juan González.

With excited greetings and hugs all around, the family settled down to a midday meal of *vianda* and *bacalao*. Petra, Juan José and Sebastián usually came to the Torres home on Sunday afternoons and had supper with them, but Moncho was dispatched to go inform them to come earlier because of Rosa and Sebastiana and their husbands being there.

With all of the family together, there was non-stop conversation to catch up on all of the events that had happened in the fifteen months since they had last seen one another. Sebastiana had a new baby sister to meet. She cuddled Mina and exclaimed over her mop of straight dark hair and her big brown eyes. They talked of the hurricane and the damage that it had caused around the island. Thankfully, because of the direction in which the hurricane had traveled, Ponce had not been hit as hard as the northeastern part of the island. Francisco only had to repair a section of the roof of their house. Then there was Mama Sebia's passing.

"I found out about it about a month later," said Sebastiana. "*Tío* Gregorio and cousin Mauricio were in Ponce and stopped by for a quick visit. I was very sad to hear the news. May she rest in peace."

"She lived to be very old," said Chenta, "and death is part of the cycle of life. What can anybody do about it? God gives and God takes away." She sighed, and then brightened. "I am sure that Rosa has already shared her happy news with you."

Rosa and Sebastiana's eyes met and the two sisters grinned widely. "Well, yes, she has," said Sebastiana, "and since we are on the subject, I have some news of my own to share. Well, *our* news, actually," she added, winking at her husband.

Shouts of congratulations, handshakes and hugs followed that announcement. Rosa clapped her hands and laughed at the family's response. Of course, she had known about it since the night before and thought that Sebastiana had picked the perfect moment to reveal her secret.

When they all calmed down again, Francisco explained that Sebastiana had her heart set on having their baby baptized by *Padre* Irizarry right there in Adjuntas. That was one reason why they had made the trip from Ponce; they wanted to see if it was possible to set a date that far in advance to baptize the baby.

"*Padre* Irizarry said that it was an unusual request," Francisco continued, "and that babies are usually baptized in the town in which they are born, but that he did not know of any church rule that prohibits him from baptizing our baby. He went ahead and wrote it on his calendar."

"We expect our baby to arrive in early October, very close to when Rosa and Domingo will be welcoming their little one," added Sebastiana. "So we set a date to baptize our baby on Sunday, December 27th. You know what that means, don't you? We will be here to celebrate Christmas with all of you!"

More cheers ensued and the family continued in their festive mood for the rest of the afternoon. Sebastiana wanted to see how Petra had fixed up her little cabin, so she, Petra, Rosa, Luisa and Pilar hiked up to it after assuring the others that they would take it slowly and rest frequently. The sisters' outing proved to be a lot of fun. On the way up they stopped at every flat area, sat on *yagrumo* leaves to catch their breath and talk, picked flowers, listened to the *ruiseñor's* lilting melody, and even caught a glimpse of a parrot high up in one of the palm trees.

Sebastiana and Rosa got the five minute tour of Juan José and Petra's little cabin and her garden, then sat around talking and drinking the coffee that Petra brewed for them in her tiny kitchen. Petra did not have enough chairs for everybody, so Pilar sat on an overturned bucket. She didn't mind; she was just glad that her older sisters had included her. Rosa and Sebastiana compared notes on their first trimester of their pregnancies, finding that they had had similar experiences with morning sickness. Both were now feeling fine.

"Enjoy this time now," said Petra with a shake of her head. "We have all seen how big Chenta gets and how difficult it is for her to move around when her time is close."

"That is part of the experience, for sure," said Rosa. "Remember, I have gone through that."

Her sisters nodded solemnly. "But this time will be different," said Luisa, softly. "I feel it in my heart, Rosa."

Not wanting to allow time for Rosa to become sad remembering the loss of her premature baby girl, Sebastiana quickly changed the subject. "When Francisco and I come to Adjuntas to baptize our baby, will we still be able to stay at your house, Rosa? You will have your baby by then, too."

"Oh, we will all fit somehow," responded Rosa, brightening visibly. "The baby will probably still be in our room, anyway, and your little family can stay in the second bedroom."

By prearrangement, Domingo came to pick up the five girls and bring them back to Ricardo and Chenta's house in the wagon. The men had enjoyed a few games of dominoes while the girls were at Petra and Juan José's cabin. Chenta prepared a delicious *asopao de gallina* for supper that had everyone smacking their lips. Her chicken stew was the best! Rosa, Domingo, Sebastiana and Francisco left shortly afterwards so as to get home before dark. It had been a wonderful visit, but it was hard to say goodbye. Francisco and Sebastiana would be leaving early the next morning to return to Ponce. They probably would not see them again until Christmas. By then, both Rosa and Sebastiana would hopefully be the mothers of healthy babies. It was definitely something to pray for every night until it came to pass.

Chapter 13

The Maldonados

Luisa was at the creek washing clothes with Pilar's help one morning in May. Juanito and Vicenta waded in the water near them, playing and getting clean at the same time.

"Look at the garden, Pilar," said Luisa. "There are tomatoes and green peppers ready to be picked. Won't those be tasty with our supper tonight?"

Pilar smacked her lips. "Oh, yes! We should come back in the afternoon to pick what is ripe. Juanito, stop it! Go farther away from me if you are going to splash water."

Juanito stopped his splashing, but stood where he was, knee deep in the creek. "Someone is coming!" he announced.

"Who?" Luisa turned her head to see who was coming down the trail from the house.

"Not from there," said Juanito. He pointed. "From the other hillside."

Luisa spun around and saw Manuel de Jesús beginning to cross over the makeshift bridge that spanned the creek a short distance behind where she was sitting.

"Buenos días," he called in greeting.

Luisa stood up off the rock that she had been sitting on and greeted him in return. She noticed his big grin at the same time that she heard Pilar's voice, low and urgent behind her. "Luisa! Your skirt!"

With a gasp, Luisa quickly untucked her hem from her waist and let it tumble down into the water, covering up her previously exposed legs. She could feel the blush creeping up her face from her neck to the top of her head.

Manuel de Jesús said nothing about it as he approached— just smiled, and Luisa could see the humor in his eyes.

He does have the cutest smile I have ever seen on a man, she thought, and blushed even more furiously.

Trying her utmost to regain some form of composure and dignity, Luisa primly asked, "To what do we owe the honor of your visit?"

"I have been sent here by Lucas and Antonia—Eladio and I are now living and working on their farm—to ask your family to their home on Sunday. Their new baby girl is being baptized and they want their friends and family to come join in the celebration. It will begin around noon."

"Oh!" breathed Luisa. "That's wonderful. Thank you. I will tell Papá and Chenta, unless you want to tell them yourself."

Manuel de Jesús looked up toward the house and replied, "I'm sure that is not necessary. Your father is working on the farm, and Chenta is probably busy. You were, too, so I will let you get back to your chore. I need to get back to work, myself."

Luisa merely nodded, and Manuel de Jesús smiled and nodded before turning and retracing his steps across the footbridge.

"*¡Adiós!*" called out Juanito, and Vicenta echoed him.

Manuel de Jesús waved at the children and disappeared on the path leading up the hillside.

Pilar and Luisa looked at each other but did not say a word as they sat back down to finish the laundry task. Luisa did not bother to tuck the hem of her skirt back into her waistline. What was the point? The bottom six inches of her skirt was already soaked.

When they returned to the house, Vicenta helped Luisa hang the clothes on the bushes, proud that she knew which ones to drape on the bushes near the house, where the shade would keep the colors from fading, and which ones to put in full sun to get bleached. Then she was hustled inside to get out of her wet dress and into clean, dry clothes.

At noon, Ricardo and Moncho came in for their midday meal, and Luisa took the opportunity to relay the message about the Maldonado baby's baptism celebration that they had been invited to. All eyes turned hopefully to Ricardo, waiting to get his confirmation that they would be attending. He concentrated on his plate of food, keeping them all in suspense before he answered.

"*Sí. Vamos.*" Yes, we are going. "Who came to bring the invitation?" he asked, as an afterthought.

Chenta answered for Luisa. "Manuel de Jesús came, but I didn't see him. Luisa and Pilar were washing clothes in the creek and he talked to them."

"He saw Luisa's legs," piped Juanito in a sing-song voice.

Ricardo stopped chewing his food, lifted his eyes slowly, and stared at Luisa. The look on his face was frightening.

"What, *Papá*? I was w-washing clothes, and I had my skirt hem t-tucked up so that it would not get w-wet. I let it down right away." Luisa was literally stammering.

"I don't want you talking to men unless they are here at our house with me or with Chenta, or when I am with you at a party or church," Ricardo said sternly.

"Put *Papá*, what was I supposed to do? He showed up when we were at the creek washing clothes. Anyway, he is not a *man*, he is Manuel de Jesús…you have known him all his life! His brother is married to Chenta's sister. He is practically family!"

"*No importa,"* was Ricardo's terse reply. *It does not matter.* "You cannot let any man take too much confidence. If you give a man an inch, he will take a mile. I know. Next time, make sure that he comes to the house to talk to Chenta or me."

"*Sí, Papá."* Luisa answered, respectfully. *"Con permiso."* She excused herself and went to her room, but not before glaring at Juanito, who looked sheepish. *Big mouth*, she thought.

The afternoon was busy as there was gardening to do, laundry to retrieve off the bushes, and clothes to sort, put away or iron, if needed. Luisa went through the children's clothing to make sure that they had something decent to wear to baby Estevanía's baptism party. She separated the selected items and admonished her younger siblings not to wear those outfits before Sunday. There wasn't much chance of that happening, anyway, since the children had "everyday" outfits and knew that the better items of clothing were reserved for outings to parties or church. As for herself, her dove gray dress was washed and ironed, and her shoes cleaned and shined well in advance of Sunday.

On Friday, Petra came for her weekly visit to help with Luisa's garden plot. She, Luisa, and Pilar chatted while pulling weeds. Juanito and Vicenta had the day off from gardening on the days when Petra came, and were playing in the *batey*. The sisters liked to have their private conversations without nosy little siblings around.

"Did you hear about the party at Lucas and Antonia's house this coming Sunday?" Luisa asked Petra.

"Yes, I did. *Papá* told Juan José when they were working together, and Juan José told me about it when he came home that evening. I cannot wait! I have not seen anyone since Easter, except for our immediate family."

"Did you hear what happened when Manuel de Jesús came to invite us?" asked Pilar.

"No, what?" answered Petra.

Luisa rolled her eyes.

"Pilar and I were down here, doing laundry at the creek," she began. "I had my skirt hem up between my legs and tucked into the front of my waistline, like always, so that I would not get my skirt wet. Well, when Manuel de Jesús surprised us with his visit, I stood up to greet him and he could see my legs."

"I told her, 'Luisa! Your skirt!' And she lowered it right away, but not fast enough," giggled Pilar.

Petra's mouth was hanging open, and Luisa gave her a woeful look. Petra closed her mouth but sputtered in an attempt to hide a snicker. In a matter of seconds, all three girls were giggling, and then laughing so hard that tears ran down their cheeks.

"I—was—so—embarrassed!" gasped Luisa, in between spurts of laughter.

"Yes," said Pilar, "and then at noon Juanito blurted out what had happened and *Papá* got angry."

Luisa and Petra both sobered. "He did?" asked Petra. "What did he say?"

"I told him that it was not intentional, but he said he does not want me talking to any man unless he or Chenta is around."

Petra just said, "Oh," but Pilar quipped, "Luisa, you will never get married if you can only talk to a man when *Papá* is sitting there next to you!"

The three burst out in squeals of laughter again.

On Saturday night, Luisa put salted codfish to soak in a bowl overnight. She was going to make *gazpacho de bacalao*— codfish salad—to take to the Maldonados' house. It was unfair to have their large family go to someone's home, even as invited guests to a party, and not contribute to the meal. Besides, it was just the custom in Puerto Rico. You never showed up at someone's house empty handed. You always had to take something. Ricardo had always been adamant about that.

The next morning, after the breakfast dishes were washed, dried, and put away, Luisa poured out the salty water from the pan of codfish, filled it with fresh water, and put it on the stove to boil. When it was tender and flaky, she drained it and let it cool before carefully removing all the fish bones. Using a fork, she broke up the filets into small flakes and poured a generous amount of olive oil and a small amount of vinegar on the fish. Next, she added sliced onion rings, cut in half, and chunks of fresh garden tomatoes and mixed the salad well. The last thing to be added would be avocado pieces, but she would wait until they were at the Maldonado home to do that; otherwise, the avocados would get brown, and the salad would become mushy.

Covering the pot with a snug lid, Luisa set it in a wooden box and laid three avocados in the box, as well. The food was ready. Now it was time to round up her siblings and help Chenta get them cleaned up and changed into the clothes that she had set apart for them.

Pilar and Moncho were self-reliant, of course, but from Juanito on down, they required hands-on attention. Luisa called them all out to the porch where she sat on a chair and had a pan of water and a couple of small towels. Instructing Juanito and Vicenta to wash their own faces and hands, she dipped one towel into the water and used it to clean the faces, arms, hands, and legs of Bonifacia and Toño, drying them off with the other towel. After inspecting Juanito and Vicenta for cleanliness, she sent them inside to change clothes. Chenta came out to take Toño in to get dressed, having already finished getting herself and Mina ready. Luisa took Bonifacia into the girls' room and Pilar got her into her clean clothes while Luisa got Boni ready. Then she slipped into her gray dress. Ricardo was already dressed for the party and was now hitching up the team to the wagon.

Luisa wished she had something new to wear, but the best that she could do was weave a new pink ribbon into her long braid and tie the end of it into a perky bow. Pilar, emulating her older sister, also wore her hair in a long braid down her back. Luisa was glad that she had sewn Pilar's dress with room to spare; the young girl was growing taller and filling out, but the dress that she had worn for Mama Sebia's funeral six months earlier still looked great on her.

When the Torres family arrived at the Maldonado home they were greeted by the aroma of a pig roasting on the spit. Lucas and Antonia liked to go all out for their parties. Lucas Maldonado was a successful farmer with more acreage than Ricardo. He had a larger home and more cabins on his land. What was amazing about Lucas is that he was a self-made man. His mother had died when he was only eight years old, and his father, José, had remarried. His stepmother, Moncerrate Sandoval, had given birth to three more boys—José Justo, Eladio, and Manuel de Jesús. Then tragically, José Maldonado had passed away, leaving Moncerrate with fifteen-year-old Lucas and three little boys under the age of six. Lucas had suddenly become the man of the house and had to work hard to support his stepmother and younger brothers. Thankfully, he came from a long line of successful Maldonados all with agriculture in their blood. His hard work had paid off; he and Antonia and their children lived comfortably. At the same time, Lucas still helped support his stepmother, Moncerrate, who now lived in town. José Justo had died at the age of fourteen, so as Eladio and Manuel de Jesús grew into young men, Lucas was determined to give them a leg up by recently employing them on his farm and providing them with lodging. Best of all, he was educating them about good farming practices and was a father figure to them, modeling how to be a good husband and father.

The younger Maldonado brothers were there to receive the Torres family when they arrived. Eladio held onto the horses' bridles as Ricardo alighted, and Manuel de Jesús helped the Torres children out of the wagon. Luisa was the last one to get out, handing down Boni to Pilar before placing her small hand into Manuel de Jesus's strong one. At the last minute, she stepped on the hem of her dress and almost toppled out of the wagon bed. In an instant, Manuel de Jesus had his hands on her tiny waist and lowered her easily to the ground. He kept his hands there for a second or two longer, just to make sure that she was steady on her feet, and then dropped his hands to his sides.

"*Gracias,*" whispered Luisa, braving a quick glance up to his handsome face. Manuel de Jesús wore a funny little lopsided smile, and Luisa wasn't sure what it could mean. Reaching back up into the wagon bed, she started to pull out the wooden box with the food she had brought, but Manuel de Jesús quickly said, "Here, let me!" They walked toward the house side by side, with Manuel de Jesús effortlessly carrying the box.

Ricardo, who had helped Chenta and Mina down from the wagon seat, was now starting to drive the team to the area behind the house, where he could unhitch his horses. As he turned the wagon to go around the side of the house, he looked over at Luisa walking with Manuel de Jesús. He wore a stern expression, but Luisa grinned at him and shrugged her shoulders as if to say, "It couldn't be helped." She thought she saw her father crack a small smile in return.

"Do you want me to put this on the food table?" Manuel de Jesús asked her.

"Could you please take it into the kitchen instead? I need to cut up the avocados and add them to the *gazpacho* before setting it out," Luisa replied.

"No problem," said Manuel de Jesús. "I cannot wait to taste it. *Gazpacho de bacalao* is one of my favorite things to eat."

"Really?" *I will have to remember that,* thought Luisa.

The baptism celebration for baby Estevanía was a huge success. Doña Moncerrate lovingly carried her newest grandchild around so that all in attendance could see the baby and offer the child a blessing. The food was amazing! The *lechón asado* was roasted to perfection and the *vianda, arroz con gandules,* and *gazpacho de bacalao* were delicious side dishes. Luisa received many compliments on her codfish salad and saw that Manuel de Jesús went back for seconds of it. As he returned to his seat in their circle of young adults, he winked at Luisa. She smiled and looked away, only to see Petra watching the whole exchange with a knowing look on her face.

"What?" Luisa asked her in a stage whisper. "He only winked because he was telling me that he likes my *gazpacho*."

"Oh, so now you two have a secret language?" responded Petra.

Luisa just shook her head and looked away, but she couldn't stop the little smile that played about her lips. She was sure that she had not heard the last of Petra's teasing, but she was not angry. It was all in fun, and for some reason, Luisa was actually enjoying it. She felt a tingling happiness inside of her that she could not explain.

Rosa and Domingo were at the party, also, since after all, Domingo, Chenta and Antonia were siblings. It was wonderful to see and visit with all the family and friends. Only sickness kept people from attending events such as baptisms or weddings. It was their main opportunity for socialization—a chance to break away from the never-ending cycle of hard work, and it buoyed everyone's spirits to celebrate life with food, music, and dancing.

Luisa danced so much that afternoon that she thought she would wear out her shoes. She danced with her brother, Sebastián, her brothers-in-law Domingo and Juan José, her cousins Mauricio, Catalino and Andrés, and with Eladio and Manuel de Jesús Maldonado. She only had one dance with Catalino, though. The rest of his time was spent with Dionicia Maldonado, Leocadio's daughter. Every time they were together for any social gathering it became more and more obvious that they were very interested in each other. It seemed likely that they would one day wed. Dionicia had just turned seventeen, so Luisa hoped that she would hold off getting married for another year or two.

After one particularly lively dance with Manuel de Jesús, Luisa sat down to rest, and Manuel de Jesús sat down next to her.

"You can't sit next to Luisa," announced Pilar, who was sitting on the other side of Manuel de Jesús.

Luisa pinched her lips together and shook her head at Pilar behind his back, but Manuel de Jesús was already asking, "Why not?"

Ignoring Luisa's silent messages, Pilar plunged on. "*Papá* said she can't talk to a man unless he is sitting with them, too."

"No," Luisa interrupted, "he did not say that. He does not want me talking to you…or any man…privately. At a party it is fine."

"And are you okay with me sitting next to you now, talking to you?" he queried.

"Yes, of course. You are fine. *I* am fine. *It* is fine." Luisa was stammering now, and Manuel de Jesús smiled at her discomfort. "Anyway," she added, "we have our little chaperone here, so all is well." She pursed her lips and pointed them in Pilar's direction.

"Ha!" exclaimed Pilar. "Not unless I leave!" With that, she stood up and flounced off.

To be truthful, Luisa was not entirely sure that her father would not be upset at her if he saw her sitting next to Manuel de Jesús, engaged in conversation with him, without others joining in. She hoped she would not hear about it later, but she was willing to take the chance.

As it was, the guests began leaving soon after that, and Chenta began rounding up her brood while Ricardo went to hitch up the horses to the wagon. The lovely party was over. Luisa retrieved their empty pot from the food table and the wooden box, which had been left in the kitchen. Setting the pot in the box and picking them up, she whirled around and almost ran into Manuel de Jesús. He just grinned down at her and took the box from her.

"Such a gentleman!" remarked Luisa.

"That's just the way I was raised to be," answered Manuel de Jesús, as they headed out of the house. "I don't think your father should have any objections to you talking to me. I am a decent man."

"Of course you are," said Luisa, but she couldn't stop the blasted blush from creeping up her face. "He has nothing against you."

"Good, because I hope that we have the opportunity to see each other again. Are there any more babies that need baptizing that you know of? Weddings being planned? Funerals?"

Luisa laughed. "I don't know of any events happening in the near future, but I am sure that something or other will need to be celebrated before long."

They had arrived at the wagon, and Manuel de Jesús set the box inside the wagon bed and helped Luisa up.

"Until the next time, then," he said. "Take care of yourself!"

That night, as she drifted off to sleep, a tired but incredibly happy Luisa breathed a prayer of thanksgiving for the wonderful day and the blessing of being with family and friends.

Chapter 14

Rebellion

Two weeks later, Ricardo did bring up the subject of Luisa socializing with Manuel de Jesús. Petra had come over for her usual Friday visit and gardening time with Luisa, but they were up at the house having lunch first. Ricardo had come in for his noon meal, and Petra took advantage of his presence to ask his permission about something.

"*Papá*, can Luisa go to town with me tomorrow? It has been a while since we have tagged along with Sebastián and Juan José. I have some shopping to do, and Luisa and I want to get fabric for new dresses."

"*Sí, hombre*," interjected Chenta. "We have not sewn any new clothes in a year, and the little girls are in sore need of new dresses. I could use a new one, too. Luisa can pick out the material and notions. She has good taste and knows what we need."

"Can I go, too?" pleaded Pilar.

"Not this time, *Mamita*," said Luisa, gently. "Chenta will need you to stay and help her with the little ones."

"I never get to go anywhere!" whined Pilar. "It's not fair!"

"No, you are the one not being fair," chided Petra. "You were at a party just a couple of weeks ago, remember?"

"Yes," said Ricardo. "The party where Luisa was deep in conversation with Manuel de Jesús every time I looked her way. You know, he and Eladio go to town on Saturdays also, to help Lucas sell the produce from his farm. Are you hoping to secretly meet him there?"

"Honestly, *Papá*, I had not even given it any thought," responded Luisa, a little tartly. "I did not know that he went to town on Saturdays. But now that I know, I will have to look for him while I am there and bat my eyelashes at him."

"Luisa!" exclaimed both Chenta and Petra. Pilar's mouth dropped open in surprise.

"No need to be impertinent," Ricardo reprimanded.

"*Lo siento*. But I don't like you suspecting me of behaving badly."

"There is nothing going on between the two of you?" queried Ricardo.

"No…not yet, anyway."

"So, he has not declared any interest in you?" persisted her father.

"No, he has not, and if you prohibit me from even talking to him, he never will declare himself, nor will anyone else. I will be an old maid, like Pilar says!"

"*Papá*," said Petra slowly. "Luisa is almost twenty. I was already promised to Juan José and we were planning our wedding when I was her age. I also remember Mamá telling me that she married you when she was twenty years old."

"Yes, she did," said Chenta. "Also, plenty of girls run off with men because their fathers will not even let them talk to a man. They rebel."

Luisa just stood there with her arms folded across her chest and arched an eyebrow at her father, who had looked up at her from his seat at the table. He half smiled, but it looked more like a grimace.

"*Está bien, Mija*. Go to town with Petra and the guys."

"And if I happen to see Manuel de Jesús, can I talk to him without you hearing about it and getting upset with me?" asked Luisa.

"Sí, *Mija*. I trust your judgment."

Luisa smiled and bent over to kiss her father on the cheek. Behind her she could hear Pilar mutter. "I knew she was his favorite child!"

Petra and Luisa had a grand time the next day, browsing through the general store and picking out all the fabric and notions needed for the five dresses that Chenta, Luisa and Pilar would be sewing for their household. Petra would also be sewing a new dress for herself, and she selected material with a beige background and flowering vines in hues of peach, brown and green. For Vicenta and Bonifacia, Luisa picked out a pattern of pretty blue flowers on a white background that Chenta would fashion into matching dresses. The material for Pilar's dress had sweet sprigs of salmon-colored flowers and green leaves, also on a white background. For Chenta, Luisa chose a brown and tan print. The hardest choice was picking out fabric for her own dress. She narrowed it down to two and enlisted Petra's help in making the final decision. In the end, they decided on a profuse pattern of red and blue-violet flowers with olive green stems and leaves.

Doña Juana chatted as she rang up the purchases and wrapped them in brown paper, tied with string. *Don* Pepín was busy helping another customer, so *Doña* Juana took advantage of the opportunity to ask about the rest of the Torres family.

"How is your stepmother? Is she expecting another baby? That woman can sure pop them out, can't she? How do you all fit in that house? How are your older sisters? One of them moved to Ponce with her husband, didn't she? Do you see her often? The other one, Rosa, comes in here every now and then, and I can see that she is expecting a little one. I hope that she can keep this one. It is such a shame that she has lost two already. What about you, Petra? Any baby on the way, yet? And you, Luisa, when are you going to find a husband?"

Luisa and Petra could hardly keep up with *Doña* Juana's questions, but they answered them as quickly and briefly as they could, and as soon as it was possible, they said their goodbyes and escaped from the store. Hugging their parcels to their chests, they hurried a short distance from the store before dissolving into giggles.

"*Doña* Juana knows everyone and everything, or at least she tries to!" remarked Petra.

"I know! I felt like helping her tie up the packages so that we could get out of there sooner!" was Luisa's reply.

They returned to where Juan José and Sebastián had set up their produce stand, and lo and behold, Lucas and Eladio were there with them. The two men greeted the girls cordially and then went back to their conversation, which was political in nature. Luisa thought that their expressions were grim, and her heart gave a little fearful leap. For some time now there had been rumors of unrest, and it seemed like something was brewing, but Luisa did not know exactly what. The girls settled themselves in the wagon to put their purchases away and to bring out the food that they had packed for their midday meal.

"*Nos vemos*," Eladio called out to them as he and Lucas went back to their own stand, which Manuel de Jesús had been left tending.

Later, after finishing their simple lunch, Petra and Luisa sat on one of the plaza benches in the shade of a huge ceiba tree, just chatting and watching people as they strolled by. They were within sight of the produce stand and saw when Manuel de Jesús approached it and began speaking with Sebastián and Juan José. They couldn't hear all that was being said, but did hear Sebastián say, "…over there…" and point in their direction. Luisa's heart gave a little leap as she saw Manuel de Jesús look her way and then begin walking toward them.

"*Buenas tardes*," he said in greeting. "I heard that you were here, and I wanted to come say hello."

"Good afternoon to you, too," Petra responded for them both. "Yes, I had shopping to do, and asked Luisa to accompany me. It is more fun that way."

"I am pleased to see you both," he said, but he was looking only at Luisa. "Would you care to go for a stroll around the plaza?"

Luisa looked at Petra, then back at Manuel de Jesús. "We would both have to go," she replied.

"Yes, of course. Both of you," Manuel said, politely.

"The girls stood up and began walking away with Manuel de Jesús. Luisa was in the middle and Manuel de Jesús on the side nearest the street; a gentleman always tried to protect the ladies from the dirt or mud kicked up by passing horses. Petra turned and called out to her husband. "We will be back in a little while."

Manuel de Jesús took advantage of the moment to tell Luisa, "You look very nice."

Luisa was just wearing her beige dress with the large pink flowers. She couldn't wait to sew her new dress and have something different to wear. But she thanked Manuel de Jesús and wracked her brain for something to talk about as they strolled.

"I have to say that I was pleasantly surprised that you came to town today," said Manuel de Jesús. "So, you just came to keep your sister company?"

"Oh, I had some shopping to do as well—fabric with which to make dresses," explained Luisa.

"I see. Will you be doing the sewing, or Chenta?"

"Both of us will do the sewing, and Pilar is learning now, so she will also help. I will make my own and supervise Pilar in sewing hers. Chenta will make her own dress and the ones for the little girls."

Manuel de Jesús looked impressed. "My mother does not sew, but then, with only boys, there was probably not much need. I am just wondering if there is anything that you cannot do."

Luisa laughed self-consciously. "There are plenty of things that I do not know how to do, and some things that I do are not really enjoyable. Sewing is one of those things; I take satisfaction in seeing the finished product but do not enjoy the process. I would rather be in the kitchen, cooking, or even outside, working in the garden."

Petra had been accompanying them in silence, knowing that she was not the focus of Manuel de Jesús's attention, but now she spoke up.

"Do you know what is going on? Why is there so much political talk among the men?"

Manuel de Jesús shook his head. "There are murmurings about taking action against the Spanish government, which many consider oppressive and unfair. I am not much involved in it, but we have been invited to attend some meetings."

"What meetings? Where?" pressed Petra.

"Secret meetings here in Adjuntas, in Peñuelas, Mayagüez, Lares, and San Sebastián…and probably other towns, too."

Petra didn't question him any further, but both she and Luisa looked worried, so Manuel de Jesús was quick to add, "I don't think it is anything for you to be concerned about. Juan José is not involved in any political meetings, nor is Sebastián, to my knowledge."

"And you?" Luisa could not keep from asking.

"Me, neither." Manuel de Jesús smiled down at Luisa.

Satisfied, Petra and Luisa continued their walk, enjoying the sights and sounds of the busy plaza, from the farmers selling their produce, to the children running and playing, to the elderly gentlemen seated on the benches recollecting their youth. It was a welcome break in scenery for Luisa, and she enjoyed the extra time spent with Petra, but she was a country girl through and through.

As if reading her thoughts, Manuel de Jesús now asked Luisa, "Would you ever want to live in town, do you think?"

"Not me," declared Luisa, with a decisive shake of her head. "I love the mountains, the streams, the *ruiseñor* serenading me, the rooster waking me up and the *coquís* singing me to sleep."

"So do I," responded Manuel de Jesús.

Luisa felt Petra surreptitiously nudge her with her elbow, as if to say, "Aha!" and Luisa nudged her back as if to say, "Shh!"

The summer months passed with Luisa and Petra literally enjoying the fruits of their labor, as they harvested beans, sweet peppers, onions, and tomatoes. The squash plants were spreading and flowering, and Luisa could see the beginnings of squash developing on some of them. The extra hours of daylight were welcome to the women for getting some sewing done by natural light instead of by flickering lantern light. By summer's end, the females of the Torres household had new dresses, and everyone was anxiously awaiting news of Rosa's delivery of a healthy baby.

Chenta, Petra and Luisa had discussed the upcoming event, and how they could give Rosa the support that she needed. In the end, Petra volunteered to go stay with Rosa when her time was near so as to be with her when Domingo went to get the midwife, and to lend a hand after she delivered. Since Petra had no children to take care of and Luisa was needed to help Chenta with the large Torres brood, she felt that she was the logical candidate.

Petra was at Domingo and Rosa's house only two days before the blessed event occurred. Word came to Ricardo and Chenta on Sunday, September 27th that their first grandchild had been born the day before. They learned that Rosa's delivery had been difficult, and while the infant girl was fine, Rosa would be needing bed rest and attention.

Luisa was excitedly looking forward to seeing the baby and to visiting with her sisters, but she had to wait until the following Sunday, since Ricardo could not take a day off from the farm until then. Sebastián was going, too, and he was already at the main house. Chenta was concerned about taking all the children to Rosa's house because with their constant runny noses and playing in the dirt, she didn't know what they might transmit to the newborn baby. So, since she wanted to go, too, Pilar was told that she would have to stay home with all of her younger siblings. Pilar was extremely upset about this.

"How am I supposed to watch all of them by myself?" She gestured toward the other children. "Moncho won't listen to me, Juanito and Vicenta are always fighting, Boni is always hiding somewhere and I have to go look for her—remember what happened during the hurricane? —and Toño is always running away and getting into mischief. Mina cries all the time and only wants to be held. I can't handle all of them! What am I? A slave? Lord help me, I hope slavery is abolished soon so that I can have a life!" she finished, sounding on the verge of tears.

Chenta stood as tall as her five-foot, one inch frame would allow her and placed her hands on her hips. "Are you done with your rebellious rant?" she demanded. "You are not a child anymore, you are a *señorita*. Any day now Luisa could be getting married and I will need to depend solely on you. It is time to start practicing now. Moncho, look at me! You are to help Pilar with the children. Pull equal weight, do you hear me? Juanito, if you do not behave and listen to Pilar and Moncho, you are going to get it when we come home. That goes for you, too, Vicenta.

No fighting, or you will both get a spanking that you will not forget! Now listen," she said, talking to Pilar and Moncho, "we are not leaving here until after lunch, and we are not staying long at Rosa's house. We will be back in time to cook dinner, so no need to worry about that. Put the three youngest down for a nap when they start getting fussy, and when they wake up, give them some milk and bread or some fruit to hold them over until suppertime."

Not another word of complaint was heard from Pilar. Ricardo, Chenta, Sebastián, and Luisa left in the wagon shortly after lunch, waving goodbye to the seven children standing forlornly on the porch. Well, six were standing. Pilar was carrying Mina on her hip. As they drove off, they could hear Toño begin wailing for his mother. Luisa whispered a prayer that all would go well with Pilar and the others in their absence.

It was an intimate gathering at Domingo and Rosa's house, with only the eight family members there, counting the baby. Chenta crooned over the wee child, who was both her niece and her step-granddaughter, and Ricardo looked proud and pleased to be holding his little grandbaby. Sebastián grinned widely and declared that baby Micaela was perfect. They presented Rosa with a few gifts for the newborn. Chenta had sewn and embroidered several darling little tunics, and Luisa had crocheted a border around a soft flannel blanket. Baby Micaela would stay warm in the chilly mountain evenings during the approaching winter months.

Petra served coffee and slices of a cake that she had baked, and they all had a lovely visit. Ricardo, Chenta, Sebastián and Domingo lingered over their second cups of coffee and another helping of cake, but Rosa felt the need to get back into bed. She was still a little wobbly on her feet. With tiny Micaela tucked at her side and Petra and Luisa sitting at the foot of her bed, Rosa began talking about her birthing experience. Petra interjected with comments from her perspective as the midwife's assistant.

"This was my first time being present at a birth," said Petra, directing her comment to Luisa. "You know, when Chenta gave birth to Toño, Sebastiana and I stayed with her until the *comadrona* arrived, and then we left the room, just like you did when Chenta had Mina. But this time, I was present for the entire delivery."

"Oh," breathed Luisa, in awe. "What was that like?"

"What was it *like*?" Rosa gave a snort of laughter. "A lot of pain. I mean, *a lot*! But *Doña* Tiburcia was wonderful—so kind and compassionate. She kept me calm and reminded me that the pains were necessary and that they were actually good. Pains meant that a baby was coming. Pains meant that my body was doing what it had to do to deliver the baby. It was all natural."

"That's right," added Petra. "She said that if there were no pains then it would be a bad delivery, a bad sign that things were not right."

"And I know what that is all about," said Rosa, sadly. "When I lost the little baby girl that I carried for eight months, there was no progression of pains, just one big pain and a very quick delivery."

"That was so horribly tragic. I remember that as if it were yesterday," said Luisa. "But look at you now! You are the mother of the prettiest baby I have ever seen."

"She does have a sweet face, doesn't she?" agreed Rosa. Petra and Luisa murmured their assent.

"So, going back to your delivery, how long were you in pain? Petra, were you scared? How did you get *Doña* Tiburcia here?"

"I delivered in the evening," said Rosa, "but I started with my labor pains early in the morning, which I am thankful for, because Domingo was still in the house…not that I was letting him go anywhere far; I knew my time was close. He woke up Petra and then hitched up the team and went to go get *Doña* Tiburcia."

"He was gone about three hours," said Petra, continuing with the narrative. "I have to say that I wasn't scared, though. I knew babies usually take a long time to make their appearance, unless they are coming early, and that wasn't the case this time. I also felt that since Rosa had worn her promise dress and God had blessed her with a pregnancy, He would complete the job that He had started and give her the baby that she yearned for."

"I felt the same way, too!" exclaimed Rosa.

"When *Doña* Tiburcia arrived, she of course knew Rosa's history and reassured her that everything would be okay. After checking to see that the labor was progressing normally, she made Rosa a comforting tea of marjoram."

"I am not sure what the purpose of that was—what it is supposed to do—but it tasted good," laughed Rosa.

"So then…the delivery?"

"That was the most exciting and beautiful thing I had ever seen," admitted Petra. "I mean, we have all seen kittens, puppies, piglets and goat kids being born, but this—this was my niece coming into the world. And I was helping, doing whatever *Doña* Tiburcia asked me to do and fetching whatever she needed. I think it is the most important thing I have ever done in my life. And then to see God's amazing creation—a new life, complete with ten fingers and ten toes, a scrunched up red face, and a mop of dark hair on top of her head…" Petra could not continue, and the three sisters wiped tears from their eyes at the emotion they were all feeling.

Baby Micaela stirred and whimpered, and Rosa gathered up the little bundle to her breast.

"We will leave you alone so that you can get your rest and nurse Micaela in privacy," said Luisa. "How long do you need to stay in bed, anyway?"

"Well, you know they call the period of rest and isolation following a child's birth *la cuarentena*, meaning forty days, right? Well, *Doña* Tiburcia says that is outdated. Most women do not get to lounge around nearly that long, despite the name. It depends on the mother's health, so it can be as little as a day or two or as long as is necessary. I happened to lose a lot of blood during the delivery because there was a bit of a problem getting the placenta out, so *Doña* Tiburcia is still coming around to check on me, but I am getting stronger day by day."

"She really is a sweet woman," added Petra. "She doesn't just deliver the baby and leave. She takes care of the whole family. She told me I should give Rosa lots of chicken broth the first few days, so I did."

"And she refused to take any money! She said it is her calling to help women deliver babies and that her reward comes from God." Rosa shook her head in wonder and began unbuttoning her blouse to nurse Micaela. Luisa and Petra slipped out of the room.

True to her word, Chenta made sure that they kept their visit brief so that they could be back home to release Pilar and Moncho from their babysitting duties and get supper prepared for the family. Luisa was relieved to find all of her younger siblings safe and sound. Pilar was composed and admitted that she felt that she had everything under control. She said that Moncho was a big help, especially with Juanito and Vicenta.

That night, after the younger children were sent to bed, Ricardo and Sebastián sat on the porch talking about the news that Sebastián and Juan José had heard in town the day before, when they went there to set up their usual produce stand. Sebastián had told Ricardo, Chenta and Domingo about it that afternoon, but Luisa had been in the bedroom with Petra and Rosa and had missed out on the conversation. She and Pilar now joined Ricardo, Chenta, and Sebastián on the porch as the latter filled them in on the details of the happenings, as best he knew.

On September 23rd, an uprising had occurred in the town of Lares. It had been planned for some time, the result of the political and social unrest that had been brewing on the island for years. The repression widely felt under the Spanish government, the issue of slavery, and the critical economic crisis due to increasing tariffs and taxes were contributing factors. This was enhanced by the devastation caused by the hurricane of the previous year and the subsequent lack of recovery aid from the Spanish government.

"There were about 500 rebels that gathered on a hacienda just outside Lares," related Sebastián. "They marched into the town of Lares on foot, looted stores and businesses owned by Spaniards, and then took over the city hall. They even took some Spanish merchants as prisoners."

"Yes," added Ricardo. "Sebastián also heard that the rebels entered the church and placed a flag that they had made up on the altar in symbolism of the revolution."

Luisa felt her heart beating in her throat and a knot forming in her stomach. "What happened after that?" she asked, alarmed. "Did the Spanish army come and open fire?"

"Not then," said Sebastián. "The insurgents proclaimed the Republic of Puerto Rico there in the church, and they named Francisco Ramírez Medina as the president."

"Who is he?" asked Pilar.

"Well…I am not sure," admitted Sebastián. "He is Puerto Rican, that much I know—not a Spaniard—and he was part of this whole movement. Somehow I guess he was chosen as the best one to be president. They also declared that any slaves who joined the movement would be set free. Anyway, the rebels moved on to San Sebastián del Pepino the next day, but they were met with strong resistance from the Spanish militia, so they went back to Lares, where they were surrounded by the militia and the rebellion was stopped."

"Did anyone die in the process?" asked Luisa.

"I do not know," responded Sebastián.

"So, Puerto Rico is still under Spanish rule?"

"Yes."

"Were people arrested?"

"That is what I heard."

"And we still have slavery?"

"For now, yes."

"Did anything good come out of all of this?"

"Time will tell."

"Enough questions for now," said Ricardo. "Pilar looks scared to death."

Indeed, the young girl did look very frightened. Luisa put her hand on Pilar's arm. "Don't worry, *Mamita*. We are safe up here on our mountain. I have told you this before. Look, all of that happened three days before Micaela was born, and we are just now learning of it."

"Yes, *Mija*, put your trust in the Lord above. He will take care of us." This was from Chenta.

"Hey," said Luisa. "How about if I make us some hot cocoa and we sit out here and look at the stars. The *coquís* will serenade us. Does anyone else want any?"

"No, thank you. I am going to head to my own cabin," said Sebastián. "Tomorrow is a workday. That is the life of the poor—work, work, work!" He winked at his sisters, said, "*Bendición*" to his father and Chenta, and strode off into the night.

Luisa prepared the hot cocoa and she and Pilar sat together on the porch steps, breathing in the freshness of the evening air and absorbing the sounds of the night critters.

"I know that scary things are happening all around us, and we don't know what the future holds," said Luisa, soothingly, but you know the saying that we have— '*no hay mal que por bien no venga.*' Basically, it means that something good always comes out of bad things."

Pilar nodded, but said nothing.

"Anyway," continued Luisa. "Just think about your brand-new little niece. She is a doll! You will see her soon, and in the meantime, you did a good thing today, taking care of the younger ones so that the rest of us could go see the baby. Tonight, despite things that we heard about that have happened out there in other towns, we are safe and happy here and have a sweet little niece. God is good."

Luisa draped an arm over her younger sister's shoulder and continued speaking softly. "Do you know that when I go to bed every night, I usually pray myself to sleep? Not regular prayers, like when we are in church or at a Novena. It is more like talking to God and telling Him how I feel or what I am worried about. You should try it, too, Pilar, and see what peace it brings to your heart. Come on. Let's get to bed. I can't wait to pray and give thanks to the Lord!"

Chapter 15

Growing

Rosa and Domingo had *Padre* Irizarry baptize baby Micaela on November 8th, when she was forty-two days old. After all her explanation to Luisa about the *cuarentena* not necessarily being forty days anymore, Rosa ended up taking that exact amount of time to feel normal and strong again. Petra had stayed with Rosa and Domingo for two weeks and then returned to her home. Juan José had paid his wife a visit over at Rosa's house, something he had done every two or three days during the time she was there. When he was about to leave, Petra had said, "Wait. I need to get my bag and kiss Micaela goodbye."

"What? You are coming home? Tonight?" Juan José was clearly overjoyed.

"Calm down," said Domingo, with a laugh. "Yes, you are getting your bride back. The honeymoon will continue."

"Don't talk nonsense," said Petra, with two red spots burning on her cheeks. "We have been married for almost two years now. Hold on, I will be right back. Wait for me."

"Of course I will wait for you!" exclaimed Juan José with a big grin on his face.

Petra did not see Micaela again until they were standing outside the church on her baptism day, a month later, and for Luisa it had been five weeks since she had seen her niece. They both declared that Micaela was half grown already.

"Look at those cheeks! I don't think that I have ever seen such chubby cheeks on a baby before!" cried Luisa, as she accepted the sweet bundle that Rosa was handing her. Micaela was wrapped in the light baby blanket that Luisa had given her.

"Well, it is no wonder. Micaela wants to nurse all the time. I can barely find the time to cook or do laundry. Babies are a blessing, but they do take up a lot of time being cared for!" Rosa smiled and looked tenderly at her daughter as she said this. Anyone could tell that she did not resent for one minute the work that being a new mother required.

After the solemn rite in which Justo and Eugenia Torres, cousins of Domingo's, were named the baby's godparents, everyone went to Rosa's house for the celebration.

Domingo and Rosa had fixed up their little house over the years since they had been married and it was looking cute, thought Luisa, as Domingo helped her down from the wagon. Luisa liked the flowers that were growing in front of the house and the welcoming chairs on the wide porch. Someday, she would like to have a house like this, but she would be satisfied with a tiny cabin like the one that Juan José and Petra were in.

The kitchen in Rosa's house was larger than the one that Chenta and Luisa had at home, and Luisa admired how tidily things were put away on the two shelves that were near the window. Rosa even had a buffet cabinet with two glass doors,

a surface that pulled out for cutting vegetables, and two drawers on the lower part. The piece of furniture was painted green,
and the white ceramic knobs had pink flowers on them. Luisa
thought that it was just beautiful.

Petra and Luisa had shooed everyone but Rosa out of the
kitchen, declaring that the three of them could handle all the
food preparation. Chenta and Policarpia had both tried to insist
that they also help.

"Go out on the porch and enjoy your grandchild, *Doña*
Carpia," said Luisa, using the older woman's nickname. "And
you keep her company, Chenta. You deserve some time off."

"So do you, *Mija*," Chenta answered. "You work as much as
I do, or more. You are young and need to have some fun."

"Oh, I will have fun, working here in the kitchen with Rosa
and Petra, no need to worry about that!" laughed Luisa.

Petra was already busy adding chicken, rice, potatoes, onions, garlic, capers, and seasonings to a huge pot of water to
make an *asopao*, a thick, hearty soup. Rosa was cutting up cheese
and slicing bread to serve as appetizers, and Luisa began cutting up mangos and papayas to also serve ahead of the meal.
The sisters chatted as they worked. Luisa had brought a pot of
gazpacho de bacalao from home and she was adding the avocados
to it now.

"Luisa," began Rosa, "I couldn't help but notice that Chenta
is expecting another baby. I guess when I saw her five weeks ago
it either was not so obvious, or I was just unaware of anything
but Micaela at that time. When is she due?"

"I don't know for sure," replied Luisa. "You know that she
never talks about these things. She has a round figure anyway,

which is probably why you did not notice it before, but now it is at the stage where there is no denying it."

"I would think that she only has two or three months left," observed Petra. "What are they going to do? You are already bursting at the seams at that house."

"I have been wondering that myself," Luisa admitted. "The babies always stay with Papá and Chenta until another baby comes, but there is no other place to put Mina at this time. I suppose that they can leave Mina in their room while the new baby still fits in the cradle. After that, I do not know. We already have four girls in one room and three boys in another. It does not seem right to put Mina in with the boys, even if she is only a year old."

Petra turned from the stove and wiped her hands on her apron. With a huge smile on her face and a wink she said, "Well, now that we are talking about babies…guess what?"

"What?" exclaimed both Rosa and Luisa at the same time.

"No!" gasped Luisa.

"Yes," affirmed Petra.

With squeals, the sisters threw their arms around each other in a three-way hug.

"When?" asked Rosa, after they had disentangled themselves. "You are not showing yet, but I should have known. You were with me for two weeks. I don't remember you feeling sick."

"I figure that the baby is coming in May. And no, I have not felt very sick, just once in a while a little bit nauseated, but so far nothing major."

"What did Juan José say when you told him?" asked Luisa.

"I just told him last night. I wanted to be sure first. He became crazy with joy. You should have heard him shouting. I think Sebastián may have heard the commotion all the way at his cabin," she said, laughing.

"When it is your time, I will come and stay with you, at least during the daytime and go home at night," said Luisa. "But I do not think that I want to be the midwife's helper, like you were, Petra. It might scare me so much that I will not want to get married and have children of my own."

"That is true," replied Petra. "Having seen what Rosa went through…but then, *Doña* Tiburcia was so sweet and comforting and made everything seem so natural, that I am not afraid to give birth. Rosa was a great example, too. If she can be brave and strong, so can I."

"Yes, well, I am still an impressionable *señorita*. I think I will let *Doña* Tiburcia handle the delivery all by herself. She is capable and experienced."

"That is still a long way off, but maybe you should get off your feet now, Petra," said Rosa.

"Oh, no, I am fine!" answered Petra. "Luisa, look out the window! See who just got here."

Luisa turned to look and saw that it was Eladio and Manuel de Jesús, who had arrived with Lucas, Antonia and their children.

"Who is it? Someone special?" asked Rosa. "You have been keeping very quiet about this, Luisa. Which one is it? Eladio or Manuel de Jesús?"

"It is no one. There is nothing happening yet," she answered, a little stiffly.

"Oh, come on, Luisa," chided Petra. "He sought you out in town to take a walk around the plaza. I was there. I saw how he looked at you, and you like him, too! It is Manuel de Jesús," she added to Rosa.

"Hmmm. I still see the two of you as little children, playing together at Chenta and *Papá's* wedding. But you are both grown up now. He turned out quite handsome!" said Rosa.

"Shh! Voices carry, you know." Luisa wiped her hands on her apron. Then, thinking better of it, she removed her apron and picked up the plate of cheese and bread in one hand and the bowl of fruit in the other. "I will just take these out."

Her sisters grinned at her. "Go," said Rosa.

"And don't hurry back," added Petra. "In fact, stay there. Your work here is done."

Luisa winked at them both as she slipped out the door. She was glad that she was wearing the new dress that she had sewn during the summer. She had no way of knowing that the bits of green color on the stems and leaves of the fabric's pattern exactly matched the green flecks in her brown eyes.

It almost seemed like Manuel de Jesús had been watching for her, because no sooner was she setting the appetizers out on the table, than he was right there by her side.

"*Hola,*" he greeted her.

"*Hola,*" she responded. "*¿Cómo estás?*"

"I'm well, thank you. Better now than I was a minute ago." He smiled at her, and she turned her head away to hide the maddening blush. Was she going to do that every time he talked to her?

"Help yourself to a little something to take the edge off your hunger until the food is ready. Petra is making *asopao*. I also made *gazpacho* that I am going to go back in to get."

She darted back into the house, and Petra and Rosa both looked at her, not even trying to hide their curiosity.

"Well?" asked Petra. "What happened?"

"Nothing," said Luisa. "I just came back in for the *gazpacho*."

"Oh, that's right. He loves your *gazpacho*. Smart girl!"

"Did you make your *gazpacho* to use as bait for a *man,* you brazen girl?" Rosa asked, feigning shock.

"Lower your voices! He is right outside!" Luisa fairly bolted for the door in her eagerness to get away from her teasing sisters.

Back outside she went with the *gazpacho,* and Manuel de Jesus's eyes lit up. "I was hoping you would bring more of your *gazpacho*. No one else makes it as delicious as you do."

He served himself some *gazpacho* and bread, and asked, "Can you sit with me, or do you have to go back inside?"

"I can sit with you. Let me fix myself a plate and I will join you. But aren't you going to have any cheese or fruit?"

"I can eat cheese and fruit anytime," answered Manuel de Jesús, "but your *gazpacho* is something that I do not get to eat very often. The last time I had some was at the party for my niece's baptism, and that was several months ago."

Luisa couldn't help feeling pleased at the compliment that he was paying her. They joined the circle of friends and relatives that included Eladio, Sebastián, Catalino, Dionicia, María de la Paz and Pilar. Later on, the circle widened to include Domingo and Juan José, and eventually, Rosa and Petra, after the *asopao* was done. Baby Micaela, understandably the center of attention at her own baptism party, was passed around from one person to another to be admired and often given a blessing: *"Dios la bendiga."*

When it was Luisa's turn to hold the infant, she stared lovingly into the child's face, trying to decipher who she now looked like. "As she grows, she changes. At first she looked like Rosa, but now I see a lot of Domingo in her," she observed.

Manuel de Jesús leaned in to get a better view of the baby. Eladio, sitting across the circle, watched him and Luisa as they gazed at the tiny child.

"I just got a vision of the future," he declared slowly and distinctly. Everyone turned to look at Manuel de Jesús and Luisa, who innocently looked up to find themselves the focus of the group's scrutiny.

"What? Oh!" exclaimed Luisa. Manuel de Jesús shuffled his feet in the dirt of the *batey* in an expression of embarrassment. The baby was quickly handed off to the person on Luisa's right, amidst giggles and snickers from the others in the group.

The older generation had their own circle and within theirs, Toño, now two-and-a-half, still preferred to stay shyly by Chenta's side. Mina, on the other hand, at thirteen months was standing and taking short walks before plopping down on her bottom. Thrilled by her new ability, she toddled from one person to another, holding on to their knees for support as she made her way sociably around the circle. Looking over at them, Luisa noticed how Chenta had absentmindedly rested her hand holding the coffee cup on her bulging belly. *Our family is growing*, she thought. *Sebastiana must have had her baby by now. Soon I will have another sibling, and eventually more nieces and nephews.*

Turning her attention back to the circle of familiar faces of which she formed a part, Luisa wished that time would not go by so quickly. She enjoyed her life as it was, surrounded by family, all in good health, good friends, with the land and the island's economy slowly beginning to recover from the hurricane. She wished that things would stay this way always, but she knew that growth and change were inevitable. The future was both exciting and frightening in its unpredictability.

Her prayer that night in bed was a little different. *God, I don't know what the future holds for me or for anyone in my family. It could be wonderful, but I know that bad things could also happen, because that is just the way life is. Babies are born, and people die. The land produces, and then hurricanes come. But whatever happens, God, please be by my side. Give me strength to handle whatever comes my way. And thank you for today, for the good time that we all had, for Your blessings, for baby Micaela, and for Petra's good news. I pray that Sebastiana has delivered a healthy baby and that we can see that family soon. Amen.*

Chapter 16

Another Wonderful Christmas Season

"*Papá*," began Luisa one evening in early December, as Ricardo was relaxing on the porch. "Where is Mina going to sleep when the new baby takes over her crib?"

"The baby can be in the cradle for the first few months," said Ricardo.

"But after that? When the baby outgrows the cradle, will you just get another crib for your room?"

Ricardo shook his head slowly. "No. There isn't enough room in there for two cribs."

"I was thinking," Luisa continued, choosing her words carefully. "I'm the oldest. Maybe I should move out to make room for Mina to come into the girls' room."

"Move out? What do you mean by that? Where are you thinking of going?"

"Well, there are different possibilities. I could move in with Sebastián," ventured Luisa.

"That's not possible. Sebastián's cabin only has one small bedroom. Where would you sleep?"

"I don't know," Luisa answered, doubtfully. "On a cot in the living room?"

"That's ridiculous," grumped Ricardo. "That's no place for a *señorita* to sleep. Sebastián would not be comfortable with that, either."

"Then maybe I should take a job as a maid or a cook for some well-to-do family—maybe in Arecibo or in Ponce. They would provide a room and meals for me, plus a salary."

"No!" Ricardo's voice was firm. "No daughter of mine is going to leave this house until she is married."

"Then…?"

"I will just have to add on another bedroom to this house. I have been giving it some thought lately. I did not think it would be needed just yet, but considering the situation more carefully, I think we will get started on it right after the Christmas season is over. You and Pilar can move into the new room and Vicenta and Boni can share the old room with Mina when the new baby arrives."

"Yes! I like that plan, *Papá*!" exclaimed Luisa. "But where exactly will you add the room? Will it cost a lot of money?"

"No, it will not cost much. You see how our front porch runs the length of the house? The pillars are already in place and so are the floor and the roof. I just need to enclose the end of the porch with three walls. You will have to go through the girls' room to get to yours, and you will have one window. It will not be a big room, but it will fit a bed and maybe have some extra room for your belongings."

"Oh, so we will have a smaller porch…I hope the rest of the family doesn't mind," said Luisa.

"They have nothing to say about it, and they will get used to it soon enough," replied Ricardo.

Luisa stood up and walked to the end of the porch. "How far out will the room go?" she asked.

Ricardo stood up also, and indicated where the wall would go that would divide the room from the rest of the porch. "It will be as long as the girls' room is, but narrower. The width will be a little less than what you see on the porch floor, after the walls are in."

Luisa's eyes were shining as she visualized her future room. "I am going to find Pilar and tell her. Gracias, *Papá*." She gave her father a quick kiss on the cheek.

Pilar was just as excited about the prospect of having a bedroom solely for her and Luisa. They predicted that this year they would not feel the customary let down after the joyous Christmas season was over since they had something wonderful to look forward to in January.

The next morning, after the breakfast dishes were washed, dried, and put away, Luisa began making *empanadillas (*meat turnovers). It was Saturday, and the Torres family had been invited to a party at the home of Lucas and Antonia. Knowing that Manuel de Jesús was going to be there, Luisa had considered making her *gazpacho de bacalao*, but the tomato plants in her garden had stopped producing. Also, she did not want it to be obvious that she was trying to impress Manuel de Jesús. If she had to be honest with herself, though, she was hoping he would like her *empanadillas*, too.

Luisa was only ten years old when her mother died, but making beef *empanadillas* was something that she had watched her mother do many times, and that was the one recipe of her mother's that she used. Everything else she had learned from Chenta.

She began by mincing beef. This was a time-consuming task, but Luisa was able to sit at the table to do it. Through the open window she could hear her beloved *ruiseñor* serenading her, and through the open kitchen door she could catch glimpses of her younger siblings playing in the *batey*. Normally, Ricardo and Moncho left the house early to work on the farm on Saturdays, but because they were going to the Maldonado's for a social gathering that was to begin in the early afternoon, they had stayed home that morning. Instead, they were working in the barn, cleaning it out and reorganizing the tools and feed. For once, Juanito was playing nicely with Vicenta and Bonifacia. He had a length of rope that he was wriggling on the ground to resemble a snake's movement. The girls and little Toño were having a fun time jumping over it. Chenta sat on the front porch watching the children play and entertaining Mina, who wanted desperately to join her older siblings out on the batey. Now round and heavy with child, and suffering once again from swollen ankles, Chenta was limited in her ability to work around the house. Pilar was taking advantage of the empty house to sweep it clean.

With the meat finally minced, Luisa cooked it in a pot with onions, garlic, green peppers, capers, *recao* and achiote, adding salt to taste. Then, leaving the meat to cool, she made the dough.

Using flour, water, lard, and salt, Luisa kneaded the dough until it was well blended and of a pliable consistency. She rolled out a ball of the dough on a floured board on the kitchen table and cut out circles by pressing down and twisting half of a small coconut shell. She spooned a little mound of meat onto the center of a circle, added a couple of raisins to it, dipped her fingers in a bowl of water and wet the circumference of the dough. She folded the circle in half, and dipping a fork into flour, used it to pinch the edges of the meat turnover together, making a pattern of tiny lines all around the edge. Pilar, finished with her chores, came in and helped Luisa with this part of the process, and when they were done, she counted over two dozen beautiful turnovers.

Now came the job of frying them. Standing over a hot stove frying two or three *empanadillas* at a time was a tiring job, even if the December mornings in the mountains of Adjuntas were cool. The tiny kitchen was stifling, as the only ventilation was the occasional breeze that blew in through the window or the kitchen door that opened out to the porch.

Chenta sent Pilar down to the creek with Juanito, Vicenta and Bonifacia to supervise them while they splashed and got clean in the shallow water. She kept Toño and Mina with her and used soap, a pan of water and a wash rag on them.

The *empanadillas* were all fried, with crisp golden-brown edges, bumpy dough on the outside and savory meat on the inside. They had taken most of the morning to prepare. Luisa put them in a deep pan which she covered with a clean kitchen towel, hoping that no one would sneak any while she was getting ready. She was so hot and sweaty that she was tempted to bathe using just cold water, but she remembered that a neighbor woman—*Don* Abelardo's wife, Elena—had suffered a facial palsy when she bathed in cold water after being overheated from cooking. She did not want to go through life with her mouth twisted to one side like *Doña* Elena. So Luisa cleaned up the grease splatters on the stove and set water to heat up for the adults to use in the bathhouse.

An hour and a half later, the family was all bathed and dressed for the fiesta, and they loaded up their wagon and took off for their first party of the Christmas season.

Luisa's heart skipped a beat when she saw Manuel de Jesús approaching their wagon as Ricardo pulled up to their home. He helped the children out and then held out his hand to assist Luisa. This time she was careful not to step on the hem of her dress. She did not want a repeat of what happened the last time he was helping her alight! Manuel de Jesús seemed to remember that incident, also, as his eyes were twinkling with merriment. He lifted her pan of *empanadillas* out of the wagon and sniffed appreciatively.

"Mmmm. Something smells good! *¿Empanadillas?*"

"Yes," Luisa answered simply.

"I can't wait to taste them," he declared.

Later, as they were seated with the other young people, all balancing plates of food on their laps, Eladio held up one of Luisa's *empanadillas* and asked, "Did you make these, Luisa?"

At her nod, he announced to the group, "Another delicious treat out of Luisa's kitchen."

"Chenta's kitchen, really, although I spend more time in it than she does, nowadays," replied Luisa, drily.

"You grew up in that house and yet you don't feel free to call that your kitchen?" he asked.

"Well, no. Chenta is the woman of the house. She has everything where she wants it and likes everything returned to its place, which I do not blame her for wanting...but I think it would be wonderful to have my own place and organize my kitchen to my liking," responded Luisa.

Eladio looked across the circle at his brother, who was sitting next to Luisa. "Did you take note of that, Manuel?"

Amid giggles and guffaws from the others, Luisa turned to stare open-mouthed at Manuel de Jesús. He was looking back fixedly at his brother, nodding his head as if to say, "You are going to get it, now!" But there was a little smile playing around his lips. He was amused, not angry.

Deciding to ignore all that teasing, Luisa changed the subject.

"I heard Eladio call you Manuel just now. You have always been Manuel de Jesús to me. Does your family ever call you Manolo or some other nickname?" she asked.

"No," he answered. "Eladio is the only one who calls me Manuel sometimes. Everyone else says Manuel de Jesús. No one has ever called me Manolo."

"I see."

"What would you like to call me?" he asked, looking into her eyes.

"Oh!" There was that dratted blush again. She had been doing so well this time until now. "I'm used to calling you Manuel de Jesús...but once in a while I may just say Manuel."

He nodded. "That's fine with me."

The musicians began playing and soon everyone was dancing in the Maldonados' *batey*. This first party of the Christmas season was followed by *parrandas* and other parties. The typical foods of the season were enjoyed by all: *pasteles*, *arroz con gandules, lechón asado, arroz con dulce, empanadillas*, and *tembleque,* a firm Puerto Rican coconut pudding.

On Christmas morning, friends and family gathered outside San Joaquín church. The Torres family was overjoyed at finding that Sebastiana and Francisco had arrived safely from Ponce and they had a healthy baby girl, whom they had named Pilar.

"You named your baby after me?" asked Pilar, incredulously.

"I did, little sister," answered Sebastiana, as she placed her baby in Pilar's arms. "I was twelve years old when you were born and I remember clearly how you looked as a newborn. When I saw my own baby for the first time, I thought, 'She looks just like Pilar did when she was born,' so we named her the same as you."

Blinking back tears, a radiant Pilar cuddled her newest niece to her chest. "My namesake," she whispered. "I love you already!"

Rosa and Domingo were there with baby Micaela, now a chubby three-month-old. Petra was not showing much yet, but her dress had been let out at the waistline.

The family all gathered together, the festively decorated plaza, the reverent mass, and the sounds of Christmas music all contributed to the joy of the season.

Sunday, December 27th was baby Pilar's baptism day, and the Torres family hosted a celebration at their home in the afternoon. The invitations had been hastily made outside of the church after the Christmas Day mass, since Ricardo and Chenta wanted to make sure that Sebastiana and Francisco were going to be able to make the trip from Ponce, first, and confirm with *Padre* Irizarry that the baptism was going to take place as planned. Even so, the party was well attended by uncles and aunts, cousins and neighbors. Luisa helped Chenta prepare the food in the kitchen, but when it came time to set the food out on the makeshift table in the batey, there were plenty of hands willing to help carry out bowls and pots. Rosa, Petra, and Aquilina had brought plates and cutlery from their own homes to supplement what Chenta had in her kitchen, and most of the attending families brought food to share. With all of her sisters there to help, Luisa was not confined to hostess duties. She was able to sit in the circle of young people and dance to the music provided by Leocadio, *Tío* Canuto and *Tío* Gregorio. At one point, while dancing a *guaracha* with Manuel de Jesús, Luisa saw Sebastiana sitting at the edge of the *batey* in between Rosa and Petra. The three sisters were sharing some juicy tidbit of news and looking over at her. Sebastiana grinned widely and waggled her eyebrows at Luisa. Luisa shook her head reprovingly at her sisters, but could not hide her smile. She sincerely hoped that Manuel de Jesús had not seen any of that.

On New Year's Eve, the Torres household received a *parranda*. Luisa and Pilar set out cheese, crackers, and fruit, as well as slices of a cake that they had baked that day. After an hour of merrymaking in their house, Ricardo and the oldest three Torres children joined the parranda. They only went to one other house, though, because Ricardo did not want to leave Chenta home alone for long with just the younger children, being that she was getting close to her time of delivery.

For Three Kings Day, the children were overjoyed with their gifts. Once again, Luisa had purchased items on a recent trip to town with Petra, Juan José and Sebastián, and Chenta had hidden them in her room. Moncho had received a jackknife and he was one proud twelve-year-old. Juanito had received a new top, as his old one had taken an accidental spin off of the *batey* and down the mountainside, and he had not been able to retrieve it. Vicenta was pleased with her miniature tea set, and Bonifacia was enthralled with her tiny set of tin dishes and cups. The two little girls were able to combine their toys to play house in the dirt under the mango tree. Toño got a little boat that he could float in a pan of water. He loved it; that boy was happiest when he was playing with water. Little Mina received a hand-stitched stuffed dog made from a soft flannel fabric. It was sweet to see her carry that doggie around all day long. She did not want to be separated from it for a minute. Pilar had not set out grass for the camels this year, but there was a present for her anyway: a new brush and comb set. It was inexpensive, but Pilar thought it was beautiful.

The Christmas season was over, and it was time to begin working on the addition of the new bedroom. On the morning of Friday, January 8th, Ricardo sat at the kitchen table eating his breakfast of eggs, ham, and bread. He took a gulp of his hot coffee and addressed Luisa, who was at the stove.

"*Mija*, I am going to town today to buy the wood I need for your room. Do you want to go with me to pick out fabric for the door curtain?"

Luisa whirled around to face her father. "Oh, yes, *Papá*, I would love to go! When are you leaving?"

"Right after breakfast, as soon as you can get ready."

"Can Pilar come, too? She would love that, and it will be her room, too," pleaded Luisa.

Ricardo pondered the request for a moment or two. "*Está bien*. Moncho will be here to go for help if Chenta needs it." He sounded a bit hesitant.

"Well, it is Friday, and Petra always comes on Fridays. I'm sure she will be willing to just stay in the house with Chenta instead of going down to work in the garden."

"That is true. It is settled then. You had better go get Pilar up. I want to make this a quick trip to town and back. I am hoping to get started on the room this afternoon," said Ricardo. He rose from the table. "I will go hitch up the horses to the wagon."

Luisa pushed the pan of eggs to the back of the stove, wiped her hands on her apron, and hurried out of the kitchen. When she woke Pilar up and told her they were going to town, the girl fairly flew out of the bed. She was dressed, washed, and eating her breakfast in record time.

"I have to gather the eggs before we leave," said Pilar.

"No, we are leaving now," said Ricardo. "Chenta, tell Juanito to do the chicken coop chores today and have Moncho tend to the other animals."

"Yes, and please explain the change in plans to Petra when she gets here. Tell her I will see her when we get back," added Luisa.

The girls climbed up on the wagon seat with Pilar in the middle. What a treat! Neither of them could remember ever going to town with their father like this. Ricardo drove the team in silence, deep in his own thoughts, but the girls chatted between themselves, pointing out things they saw along the way and talking about their new room.

Luisa dared to interrupt her father's reverie by asking, "*Papá*, are we going to be moving our bed into the new room? If we are, where will Vicenta and Boni sleep? They are getting too big for that little bed."

"I am going to buy enough wood to make a new bed for you two girls, and get a mattress for it. Vicenta and Bonifacia can have your old bed and Mina can sleep in the twin bed."

"Oh, that's perfect!" exclaimed Luisa. Pilar just grabbed Luisa's hand in both of hers and squeezed it. She was so happy.

Ricardo began the construction that afternoon. With Moncho's help, he measured and cut the studs and nailed them in place to frame the space that would be Luisa and Pilar's bedroom. Petra got to see that much of the process, having stayed until after their three o'clock coffee. After that, she went home to begin cooking supper for her husband. Sebastián came by late in the afternoon and helped Ricardo frame the window opening. Now it was easy to picture the space as a bedroom. The new mattress was leaning against the house, and Luisa could see that when the bed was assembled, it would take up most of the space in the small room.

Luisa wanted to help, but there was really only room for the men and Moncho to move around, and she knew that she would just be in the way. So instead, she cooked her father's favorite meal for dinner: white rice, stewed pink beans, and fried chicken. She garnished his plate with slices of avocado when she served him. The normally serious Ricardo smiled at his daughter, acknowledging her appreciation.

The next day was Sunday, and it was usually Ricardo's only day of rest, but he was back at work on the room right after breakfast. He measured and cut the boards for the siding, and the sounds of the saw and hammer continued for most of the day. Sebastián came and worked on making the window shutters. He had a gift for carpentry and enjoyed the change of pace from farm work. Late in the afternoon, before the last wall was up enclosing the room, Sebastián sawed out an opening for the door leading from the girl's room to the new bedroom.

"During the week, probably tomorrow or the day after, I will come and frame the doorway, and also install a bar over the top so that you can hang your curtain," Sebastián promised. "I will also help *Papá* make the new bed. By the middle of the week, you girls will be sleeping in your new bedroom."

And so it was. By Wednesday, all of the work was done. Luisa and Pilar had each hemmed one end of the curtain, one end having a wide hem open at the sides to slide over the rod. Sebastián had also attached clothing pegs on the wall nearest the foot of the bed. There was no room for a dresser. Their undergarments and nightgowns would remain in the small four-drawer dresser that was in their old room, with one drawer for each girl. When Mina moved in, they would have to put her things in the same drawer as Bonifacia's.

Because of the narrow width of the room, the bed had been pushed against the wall. The sheets and light blanket were on the bed and their pillows in place. There had been a short discussion on who was to sleep against the wall.

"Do you know what I noticed?" Pilar asked Luisa, coyly.

"No, what?"

"I used to sleep on the cot against that other wall, and you slept closest to me, and Petra closest to the outside wall. Then after Petra got married and moved out, you moved over and I got to sleep in the big bed with you, and Vicenta and Boni got their twin bed put in where my cot used to be. Now we are moving into this other room, and you should keep sleeping on that side of the bed, against the outside wall, because it means that you will be the next one to marry and move out."

Luisa shook her head. "I see your logic, and it was a nice try, but it is not going to happen. In the other room, Petra and I had space to get out of bed without disturbing the other person. Now, in this smaller room with our bed against the wall, it's a different story. You need to sleep against the wall unless you want to be the first one up, grind and brew the coffee for the family, and cook breakfast."

At Pilar's baleful look, Luisa continued. "So, since I am always up first, I need to be on the side of the bed closest to the doorway. That way I can get up without disturbing your slumber, little sister." With a wink and a swish of her skirt to punctuate her statement, Luisa turned and left the room. That was the end of the discussion!

That night, snug in their new bed in their clean new room that smelled slightly of sawdust, Luisa prayed an extra blessing on her father and brothers for the construction of the new bedroom.

In the midst of her prayer, her mind started wandering. *How long will I be enjoying this new room before I get married and move out? What if Pilar is right and the person who sleeps closest to the outside wall will be the next to get married? That would not be good. Pilar will not be old enough to marry for at least five more years. I will be an old maid by then!*

Unbidden, an image of Manuel de Jesús entered her mind, and she drifted off to sleep with her lips curved into a smile.

Chapter 17

Juana Ramona

"When are you going to move Mina out of the crib and into the girls' room?" Luisa asked Chenta one afternoon in early February as they were enjoying their mid afternoon coffee. She could see that Chenta's time to deliver was imminent.

"Not until after the new baby is born," replied Chenta.

"What if Mina throws a fit about another baby being in her crib? She might feel jealous or unwanted."

"I plan to keep the baby in the cradle for the first two months or so," said Chenta. "Mina will still have her crib until the baby outgrows the cradle.

"But won't the baby's crying in the middle of the night wake Mina up?" questioned Luisa.

"Maybe, but if that happens, I will deal with it then. I don't want to move Mina out of the crib until the new baby is here and we know that it is healthy and strong."

Luisa set her coffee cup down slowly and looked at Chenta in surprise, processing what her stepmother was saying.

"Are you afraid that moving Mina out of your room before you deliver could somehow jinx the wellbeing of the new baby?" she asked.

Chenta shrugged her shoulders, and murmured, "Well, you never know. Things like that happen sometimes."

Luisa was hard put to find the words to respond to that, but she finally said, "You know, for a woman of faith, you have a lot of superstitions."

Chenta gave a sheepish half smile. "I know," she admitted. "Sometimes the ideas that were passed down from my mother and grandmother are hard to shake. I do trust God and respect His will, but…I will still wait until after the baby is born to move Mina to the other room."

A few days later, Chenta went into labor. It happened in the wee hours of February 9th. Ricardo woke Luisa up and told her that he was going to hitch up the wagon and go for *Doña* Tiburcia. Would she mind staying with Chenta until he returned with the midwife?

"Of course, *Papá*. Don't worry, and be careful. I will take care of Chenta," Luisa assured Ricardo.

Deciding not to attempt dressing in the dark bedroom and not wanting to disturb her sisters, Luisa tiptoed out of her room and through the little girls' room barefoot and in her nightgown. She went straight into Chenta's room to check on her.

Whispering so as not to awaken Mina, Luisa asked, "How are you doing, Chenta?"

"I'm doing fine," Chenta responded. "I'm still in the beginning stages. But your father did not want to delay going for the *comadrona*. After all, this is my sixth baby."

"I know. Don't start pushing until after *Doña* Tiburcia gets here!" teased Luisa.

Chenta smiled and patted the bed next to her. "Come lay down. I will wake you up if it gets rough."

Luisa accepted the invitation, although it felt very strange. She had a fuzzy memory of napping next to her mother when she was a small child, but she had never lain down next to Chenta.

She must have dozed off because the sound of Mina's crying woke her up. Luisa sat up in the bed, startled. The first rays of daylight were coming in through the cracks and the rooster was crowing lustily.

"Are you doing okay, Chenta? Is the baby coming?"

"Not yet, but the pains are getting closer and stronger. Just tend to Mina, please. Hopefully your father will be back soon."

Luisa opened the shutters of the bedroom window to let in the light and then lifted Mina out of her crib. "*Ay,* you have a wet bottom, little girl," she crooned to the tot. "You definitely need a clean diaper. Let me grab one from here and I will change you in another room. I have to get dressed and washed up, so I think I had better wake up Pilar to give me a hand. Coffee needs to be ground and brewed, little ones fed their breakfast…*¡Ay, ay, ay!*" She continued talking to Mina as she carried her into her bedroom to rouse Pilar.

When Ricardo arrived with *Doña* Tiburcia forty-five minutes later, Luisa was dressed and sitting in a chair next to Chenta. She had gulped down some freshly brewed coffee and was now helping Chenta drink sips of tea. Pilar had scrambled eggs for the younger children, and Moncho had buttered bread for them. Juanito had Mina on his lap and was sharing his eggs with her. Vicenta, Bonifacia and Toño were almost done with their breakfast. Water was already boiling on the stove for *Doña* Tiburcia's needs. Luisa was so relieved to see the midwife! She hurriedly gathered the items that *Doña* Tiburcia requested and gratefully left the room. Preparing a cup of coffee for the older woman, she took it in to her.

"*Ay, Mija*, how did you know I needed some coffee?" the midwife exclaimed. "Your father was in such a hurry that I didn't have time to brew any for myself. I am surprised that he let me change out of my nightgown before loading me in his wagon." She winked at Luisa as she took the steaming cup of coffee from her.

Pilar and Moncho had things under control in the kitchen, but Ricardo downed a cup of coffee and then hustled all of the children except Luisa out to the barn. It was best if they were not in the house during the birth of the baby. Picking up Mina, he said to the others, "*¡Vámonos!*"

A minute after they had trooped out, Luisa could hear Chenta moaning. *They got out of here just in time*, she thought. As she washed the breakfast dishes, Luisa silently prayed, *Lord, please help Chenta deliver a healthy baby, and let it happen quickly.*

No sooner were the dishes washed dried and put away, then Luisa heard *Doña* Tiburcia encouraging Chenta to push. Moments later, a crying baby announced its arrival. Luisa rushed to stand outside the curtained doorway.

"*¡Así se hace!*" *Doña* Tiburcia was saying, joyfully. *That's how it is done!* "*Tienes otra niña hermosa.*" *You have another beautiful girl.*

Luisa clapped her hands and exclaimed, "*¡Gracias a Dios!*" *Thank God!*

"Is everything okay?" asked Luisa through the curtain. "Can I go tell the others?"

"Yes, Mija," responded *Doña* Tiburcia. "Go tell them that you have a healthy baby sister, but keep them out for a while. Let me get these two cleaned up and presentable."

Luisa wasted no time in sharing the good news with the rest of the family.

Her father beamed, but Moncho slapped his forehead. "Another girl! Juanito, we are really outnumbered now!"

"Doña Tiburcia said you can't come in the house yet, so if you are finished taking care of the animals, go play in the *batey*. No fighting, though!" admonished Luisa.

"I still have not gathered the eggs," said Pilar.

"Go ahead and do that and you can come into the kitchen to wash them, but the rest of you stay out. Moncho, don't let Mina or Toño out of your sight. Juanito, you help with the little ones, too. You are getting big now." With that, Luisa turned and headed back to the house with Ricardo.

Doña Tiburcia remained with them most of the day and had lunch with them. She liked to stay with the mother and new-born baby for at least a few hours to make sure that they were both healthy and stable. Luisa cooked a hearty chicken stew for lunch, giving Chenta only chicken broth for her first meal, per *Doña* Tiburcia's instructions. The children were allowed to come in and see their new baby sister briefly, and then were shooed out so that mother and baby could rest.

After they had their three o'clock coffee, *Doña* Tiburcia declared that Ricardo could take her home now.

"What are you naming the new baby?" she asked, as she was gathering up her things.

"Juana Ramona," responded Ricardo.

"Will we call her Juanita?" asked Moncho.

"No, that's too close to my name," protested Juanito.

"How about Ramonita or Monín?" suggested Luisa.

"Monín!" was the unanimous cry.

Luisa was anxious to tell Petra about Monín's arrival, but didn't feel that she should leave the house. Ricardo and Moncho were taking a second day off from farm work, so the next day Luisa sent Moncho and Pilar to the Collado's cabin after their morning chores were done.

"You might as well have lunch there with Petra and Juan José," she said. "Maybe you two can pull weeds in her garden, too, since we won't be going there tomorrow."

Pilar and Moncho were happy to be the messengers and set off on their adventure. They returned close to suppertime, announcing that they had indeed helped pull weeds and that Petra would come see the baby as soon as Juan José could bring her in the wagon. She was now six months pregnant, and Juan José did not want her traipsing up and down the mountain in her condition. Sebastián had joined them for lunch at Petra's house as was his custom since he worked with Juan José on the farm. Moncho was thrilled to have had a break from farm work for two days in a row and to be able to spend time with his older brother. Although they all worked on the farm, Ricardo and Moncho were usually in a different area than Sebastián and Juan José. Even if they were in the same part of the farm, they worked hard and there was no opportunity for talking and laughing.

Little Mina was intrigued with her new baby sister and had to be supervised carefully because she wanted to rock the cradle every time she saw the newborn in it. She did exhibit some jealousy and cried when she saw her mother holding and nursing Monín. Luisa and Pilar gave Mina extra attention and took her outside as often as they could to be entertained by the kittens or to play on the porch with Toño.

Monín was baptized on Sunday, March 14th. *Tío* Canuto Torres and his wife, Anastacia Sáez, were the godparents, and the family celebrated the event in the customary way. Family members and friends had been invited to partake of food, music and dancing in their *batey*. Luisa was so busy that day that she felt like a spinning top. She wouldn't allow either Chenta or Petra to help her, so Rosa handed chubby Micaela to Petra and worked with Luisa to prepare and serve the food for the visitors. Pilar was enlisted again to help with the little ones. There were so many small children running around!

When Luisa finally sat down with a plate of food, the others had already eaten and were dancing in the *batey*.

Manuel de Jesús took the vacant seat next to her and greeted her with "There you are! *Buen provecho.*"

"*Gracias,*" she responded. "Did you get enough to eat?"

"More than enough, and it was delicious as always," he complimented her. "You must be exhausted."

"I am worn out," she admitted. "I don't think that I will even have the strength to dance, much as I enjoy it. But you should go find someone to dance with and have a good time."

Manuel de Jesús just shook his head slowly and gave her one of his little smiles. "If I want to really enjoy myself, I don't need to move from this chair. I would rather sit and talk to you than dance with someone else."

Luisa lowered her gaze, but could not stop the fluttering in her stomach. She strove for composure and changed the subject. "So what is new since the last time that I saw you?"

"Not too much. Lucas is keeping Eladio and me busy working on the farm. It is harvest time for oranges and grapefruit, among other fruit."

"I know. Same here on my father's farm. We are thankful for those crops since the coffee crop is not as good as it was before the hurricane."

"I see that you are going to have another niece or nephew sometime soon," Manuel de Jesús said, with a nod in Petra's direction.

"Yes," sighed Luisa. "I am so happy for her and Juan José. They are really excited. I am getting a lot of experience with babies. We have two in diapers here, Rosa has Micaela, and Petra is now expecting…I love babies, but sometimes I feel like I need to escape somewhere."

Manuel de Jesús looked a little startled. "Well don't go running off with the first person who asks."

Luisa laughed. "I'm not going to go running off with anyone. I was just saying that because I am wiped out right now. I love our mountain and I love my family. No one is going to pry me away from them."

Manuel de Jesús didn't know if he liked that answer or not.

Chapter 18

New Arrivals

Easter Sunday was two weeks later, on March 28th. The Torres clan attended the church service in town, with the exception of Chenta, who stayed home with Mina and Monín. The Collados also chose to stay home, since Petra felt that the long wagon ride to town on jutted roads would make her feel even more uncomfortable than she was. Baby Collado had an annoying way of jabbing pointy elbows into her ribs. She was not sure how she was going to endure another six weeks until the baby arrived. She and Juan José did feel that the short wagon ride to her father's house that afternoon would be doable, however.

Luisa was looking forward to the Easter mass and to seeing everyone that she knew at church. She and Pilar rode up front with Ricardo this time, and the girls were wearing their newest dresses, the ones that they had sewn the previous summer. *It's time to sew new dresses,* thought Luisa. *The little girls can barely fit into their clothes.* For now, though, she was fine in her pretty dress with the profusion of tiny red and blue-violet flowers. The pattern on Pilar's dress was similar, but the flowers were salmon-colored. Pilar had long lost her pallid, sickly complexion and now looked every bit an unassumingly attractive young lady. In the bed of the wagon, Moncho, Juanito, Vicenta, Boni, and Toño rode comfortably, also attired in their best clothing.

Rosa, Domingo and baby Micaela were waiting for them in front of the church, and sat with them during the mass. Toward the end of the service, Micaela began to fuss a bit, so Rosa had to take her outside. Afterwards, as the congregation spilled out into the warm sunshine, Luisa looked around to greet her friends and cousins. She was trying not to be obvious about looking for Manuel de Jesús, but when someone tapped her on the shoulder she whirled around, hoping it was him. Alas, it was *Doña* Sinforosa, their closest neighbor, who was standing next to her husband, *Don* Eustaquio. A tall, handsome young man was with them.

"Luisa, I would like to introduce you to my nephew, Victor Avilés. He is the son of my brother, Simón, who lives in Arecibo," began *Doña* Sinforosa.

"*Mucho gusto,*" said Victor and Luisa, almost simultaneously. *Pleased to meet you.* They shook hands cordially.

"Luisa is the daughter of Ricardo Torres, our closest neighbor up the mountain," *Doña* Sinforosa explained to Victor. To Luisa, she added, "He just got here, and he doesn't know anybody yet."

"Will you be visiting long?" Luisa asked Victor politely.

"I am staying with my aunt and uncle for a while, and if I find work here, I hope to remain in Adjuntas," he replied.

"Well, I wish you luck," said Luisa, and with a nod and a smile to all three of them, she turned to seek out her family.

Since they had recently had a big party at their house, Ricardo and Chenta opted to just stay home for Easter supper with the family, including their adult children that lived in Adjuntas. That's why it was such a surprise when Victor Avilés showed up at their house that afternoon.

"*Buenas tardes*," he said in greeting. *Good afternoon.* "I am Sinforosa's nephew. I did not have the pleasure of meeting you at church today," he said to Ricardo, who was sitting on the porch with some of the family. "But I did meet your daughter, Luisa."

He and Ricardo shook hands. "*Mucho gusto*," said Ricardo. "This is my son, Sebastián, my sons-in-law, Domingo and Juan José, and my daughter, Petra."

Victor shook hands with all of the young men and nodded to Petra. "*Señora*," he said, acknowledging the introduction.

Juanito, who had been playing in the *batey* with his top, ran over to the open kitchen door and called out loudly, "Luisa, there is a man here that you met."

Luisa came to the kitchen door, wiping her hands on her apron, and the surprise showed clearly on her face when she saw Victor. He smiled at her and lifted a hand in greeting.

"Oh," was all that Luisa could say at first, then, "I am in the middle of cooking and cannot leave the stove. Umm. Nice to see you again." She ducked back inside to tend to the *tostones* that she was frying. She had peeled green plantains, cut them into thick slices and had fried them once. Then she had flattened them and was frying them again. When fried twice to a golden brown and salted, they made a tasty side dish.

"Who is it?" asked Rosa.

"It is *Doña* Sinforosa's nephew, who is visiting from Arecibo. She introduced him to me today after church. But what is he doing here?" Luisa wondered aloud.

"Why don't you go out on the porch and find out?" her sister answered. "I can tend to the *tostones.* Obviously you made an impression on him, and he is wasting no time calling on you."

"Oh, stop your teasing!" rebuked Luisa. "I do not find that funny. I barely said two words to him outside the church. Anyway, how do we know that he doesn't want to speak to *Papá* about something?"

"Fine, then. I will go out. I will take him a glass of water. I am sure that he is thirsty after walking here from his aunt's house, and it is a warm day. I will be right back."

Rosa stepped out on the porch with a glass of water for their guest, and introduced herself. "Hello, I am Rosa, another one of Ricardo's daughters." She handed the water to Victor and pointed to Domingo. "I am his wife, and that is our little girl that he is holding."

Chenta also came out on the porch, carrying baby Monín and was introduced to Victor. Vicenta, Boni, and Toño had joined Juanito in the *batey* and Moncho had plopped himself down on the porch steps. Pilar came out of the house carrying Mina, who had just woken up from her nap.

"What a nice big family you have," said Victor. "It's very quiet at my aunt's house, with no children there, and my uncle was taking an afternoon siesta when I left. I told my aunt that I was going to wander on up here to visit. I hope you all don't mind."

"Not at all," said Chenta. "Moncho, go get another chair from inside for our guest. Victor, we are going to be eating soon. I hope you can stay."

"That would be very much appreciated. I would like to get to know your family," was his polite reply.

Later, as they were finishing the delicious dinner of white rice, stewed pink beans, and tender chicken in *salsa criolla* (Creole sauce), with crisp *tostones* on the side, Victor complimented the cooks.

"Oh, Luisa gets most of the credit," said Rosa. "I just helped her. She is very capable of doing it all on her own. You should see all the dishes that she prepares. She is a wonderful cook!"

Luisa felt like a cow being offered up for sale. If she had been close enough to kick Rosa, she might have done that, but since she was too far away, she just glared at her.

Victor did not notice Luisa's discomfort. He was intent on asking her father a question. "So, *Don* Ricardo, I am searching for work. Are you looking for more workers for your farm? You probably know that my uncle has his small farm leased and lives off of those proceeds. There is no opportunity for me to work there."

Ricardo shook his head. "I am sorry. There are four of us already working here on my farm—Sebastián, Juan José, Moncho and myself. I cannot afford to hire anybody from outside the family. Were you raised on a farm in Arecibo?"

Victor smiled wryly. "No, actually, I do not know much about farm work, but I was willing to give it a try. My parents live in town in Arecibo, and my father owns a store."

"I am surprised that you are not working for your father in his store," commented Sebastián, looking fixedly at Victor. "That would seem the likely choice."

"Well, yes, it is…it was…I mean, I did work in my father's store for several years. It is just that…well, I just wanted a change of environment," Victor responded lamely.

"What kind of store does your father have?" asked Juan José.

"General merchandise. He sells just about anything that you need for your home, except furniture."

"Maybe you could see if *Doña* Juana and *Don* Pepín will hire you to work in their store here in Adjuntas," suggested Petra. "It is right on the plaza, and they are always busy, plus they are getting older now."

"But maybe you are tired of that kind of employment and want a change," observed Domingo.

"Oh, no, I am not tired of it. I actually like working in stores, and I know how to do it all, ordering supplies, working the cash register, balancing accounts, taking inventory…"

"So why did you stop working in your father's store then?" queried Moncho.

"Moncho!" admonished Ricardo. "Do not enter in the conversation of adults!"

"Oh, that is all right," said Victor affably. "If your son is man enough to work on the farm alongside of you, then I do not take offense to his question. But I am afraid that I must be taking my leave now. I should get back to my aunt's house."

With profuse thanks and compliments on the meal, Victor said his goodbyes and departed down the path.

"Well, what do you think about that?" asked Sebastián when Victor was out of earshot.

"He didn't answer my question," said Moncho.

The following Sunday, Victor came calling again, but this time he came during the mid afternoon.

"I have good news," he said as he shook Ricardo's hand. "I found work in *Don* Pepín's store. Please thank your daughter for the suggestion."

"Oh, good," said Ricardo. "When do you start?"

"He hired me on the spot, and I have been working there for three days already," replied Victor.

"Come have a seat," offered Ricardo.

Victor took a seat on the porch and commented on the quietness. "Where is the rest of your family?"

"The little ones are napping, the boys are playing in the creek, and I believe that Luisa and Pilar are preparing the afternoon coffee. Vicenta is around here somewhere. She doesn't take naps anymore."

"I see," said Victor. "I did not have a chance to talk to Luisa last week. I was hoping that I could visit with her today or maybe go for a walk with her."

Ricardo pursed his lips and said, "Hmm! She will be out here shortly, serving us coffee. You can sit and talk to her here while you have a cup of coffee."

Victor nodded slowly and gave a half smile. He understood.

Pilar was the one who brought out the two cups of coffee for the men. The girls had heard the voices on the porch, and Luisa had prepared a cup for their visitor, but she had sent Pilar out with the coffee.

"*Gracias, Mija*," her father said. "Go ask Luisa to bring her coffee out here and join us on the porch."

Pilar delivered the message and sat down at the table with a grin to sip her coffee with Chenta. Luisa rolled her eyes, picked up her coffee cup and went out on the porch.

Half an hour later, after a rather stilted conversation with Luisa and Ricardo, Victor left. He would have stayed longer if he had been given the opportunity to go for a walk with Luisa or at least talk to her alone, without her father there as a chaperone.

Luisa did not know what to make of it when the following Sunday, Victor again came calling in the early evening. He had not wanted to impose by showing up at suppertime, plus he was hoping that Luisa would be free to go for a stroll with him.

Once again, nearly the whole family was there, with the exception of Rosa, Domingo and Micaela. Most of them were out on the porch, enjoying the coolness of the evening. The doves were beginning to coo and the first *coquís* of the night could be heard. Luisa normally enjoyed sitting outside after sundown, listening to the beginnings of the nighttime symphony of critters on their tropical mountain and relaxing at day's end. But, she was finding it hard to relax with Victor there. She understood that as a newcomer to the area he was lonely, and her large family offered much more entertainment than could be found in Eustaquio and Sinforosa's cabin. Still, she was just a little bit annoyed that her peace and tranquility were interrupted, as well as the intimacy of the family gathering. She sighed inaudibly and turned her attention back to the conversation.

"There is talk about reconstructing the church since it has deteriorated so much in recent years. I guess the hurricane caused a lot of damage to the building," Victor was saying.

"Oh, really? You overheard that while working at *Don Pepín's* store?" Sebastián asked.

"Yes…well, no…I heard it at the bar after work on Friday."

At Sebastián's raised eyebrow, Victor hurried to add, "It is actually a good place to catch up on what is happening in town. I guess when men drink a little rum they loosen up their tongues more." He grinned at Sebastián, but his smiled dimmed when it was not returned.

"Luisa, would you like to go for a little walk with me?" Victor abruptly asked.

A little startled by the unexpected request, Luisa glanced at her father and then back at Victor. "Oh…yes…I suppose, if it is all right with you, Papá."

Ricardo shrugged his acquiescence. "Do not go far. You have a posse here waiting to go after you if you take too long."

Victor was not sure if he was joking or not, but he assured Ricardo that they would not be gone long.

They walked slowly down the path in the direction of his aunt's house. "I hope your family does not mind me coming by like this on a regular basis. I would like to get to know you all better, but…especially you."

Luisa did not lift her eyes from the path. She was unsure of how to answer him. In fact, she did not know how she felt about the interest that this young man was showing in her. He was handsome. He was a relative of their long-time neighbors. He had a job. Were those the things that mattered the most? Did she even really want him coming over to see her? She remembered what Manuel de Jesús had said to her a few weeks earlier: "Don't go running off with the first person who asks." She had to smile. At the time, there had been no one else showing any interest in her, but now there was.

Victor had been waiting patiently for Luisa to say something. "So?" he prodded. "Is it all right with you?"

"Is what all right with me?"

"Is it all right if I come calling."

"Oh! I…I don't think so…I mean, my sister is going to be needing my help soon. And Chenta always needs me. I am the oldest in the house now, and I have so many responsibilities. I really don't have time…"

"For a short walk once a week?"

"Well," Luisa hedged. "I suppose if you put it that way, I can spare time for a short walk once a week. But I do not want this to be considered…I do not want you to think…"

"All right, then!" exclaimed Victor. "I will come on Sunday evenings and we can take walks and get to know each other better." He almost sounded like he was gloating. Luisa hoped that he understood that they were not entering into a formal relationship of any kind.

For the next few Sundays, Victor and Luisa went on their evening strolls, and they talked. Victor seemed pleased during their time together, but Luisa continued to feel uneasy. Something was not right, but she could not put her finger on it. There was something missing. Perhaps her family was the problem. She just did not see them warming up to Victor and accepting him the way that they had with Domingo, Francisco and Juan José when her sisters were being courted. The men in her family did not say much to her about him, but she sensed that they did not trust Victor completely. Even her sisters did not tease her the way that they had about Manuel de Jesús.

As May rolled around, Luisa began taking daily trips to Petra's cabin. She rose early, ground and brewed the coffee, and hurriedly did her morning chores. On laundry days, she and Pilar worked quickly to get the job done so that she could go to Petra's cabin as soon as possible, but on all of the other days she was there by midmorning and stayed until after their three o'clock coffee. Chenta took over her kitchen again and Pilar was left to carry the burden of helping Chenta with the little ones. They were all sacrificing for a short time because Petra was nearing her time to deliver and she should not be left alone in her cabin all day. Juan José was making sacrifices, also, shortening his work day so that he could stay with Petra a little longer in the mornings and coming home a little earlier in the evenings. She was still alone part of the time, but not for very long.

One morning, only an hour or so after Ricardo and Moncho had left for their work on the farm, Moncho came running down the path with the news that Petra had already given birth to a baby boy!

"What? Already?" Chenta and Luisa exclaimed at the same time.

"What happened? When? Who told you? Have you seen the baby? Is the midwife still there?" Luisa was firing questions at Moncho so fast that he could not even get in a reply.

"Let him talk," said Chenta.

Pilar had come in from the chicken coop with a basket of eggs, which she set on the table. She was excitedly waiting to hear the details, also.

Moncho's chest was still heaving from having run most of the way back home, and he was laughing, too, so it was hard for him to answer.

"Sebastián told us. He is the one that had to go get *Doña* Tiburcia last night after dinner, and she is still there. The baby was born this morning, so Juan José is not working today. Papá told me to come tell you all, so that Luisa can go if she wants to."

"Of course I want to go!" Luisa had been removing her apron as Moncho was talking and was already heading out the door.

Chenta was pushing Moncho down into a chair.   "Sit and rest and drink a glass of water before you go back to work."

Luisa ducked back inside. "Chenta, can Pilar come with me this time? Can you manage without her this once?"

At Chenta's nod, Pilar hugged Chenta and dashed out the door with Luisa.

Chapter 19

Choices

Luisa continued going up to Petra's cabin daily to help her sister out until the new mother got her strength back. Tiny Francisco Collado was just precious! Luisa referred to her nephew as "*el granito de café*"—the little coffee bean—because he was small and his skin color was the beautiful warm brown of roasted coffee beans. She adored baby Francisco and was so glad that she got to see him grow day by day, at least for the first few weeks of his life. Luisa knew that her daily visits had to come to an end and she would not see her little coffee bean as often, but they had formed a bond that she hoped would never be broken. Already the infant was as comfortable in Luisa's arms as he was in his mother's. Luisa knew how to calm him when he was crying and understood what his different types of fussing meant—when he was hungry, when he was tired, or when he just wanted to be held. Rocking the little one while her sister rested was a special time for Luisa. She would gaze at the perfect little face with its adorable button nose, trusting eyes, and sweet mouth and dream of one day rocking a baby of her own in her own cabin.

Francisco Collado was baptized on Sunday, June 6th, and the celebration was held at Ricardo and Chenta's house because it was a much larger space. Manuel de Jesús had been chosen as the godfather and his mother, Moncerrate Sandoval, had been asked to be the godmother. Luisa was looking forward to seeing Manuel de Jesús again. She had not seen him since Monín's baptism, which was in mid March.

The day of the baptism, Luisa dressed carefully in her best dress, the one that she had worn on Easter Sunday. There still had not been any opportunity to go into town to purchase fabric for new dresses, much less time to sew them. But she had washed and pressed her dress and cleaned and shined her shoes. Pilar was going, too, and they helped each other with their hair. Luisa plaited a ribbon in Pilar's braid, but chose to have her own braid coiled at the nape of her neck and secured with hairpins. Some short wavy tendrils of hair were left loose to frame her lovely face.

"Okay, come on, let's go," said Luisa. "We don't want to keep *Papá* waiting, or he might leave without us."

The rest of the family stayed home. Chenta was enlisting Moncho and Juanito to help with the younger children while she began cooking. Luisa had made sure that everyone's best clothing was ready for them to change into before the guests arrived.

As they passed *Don* Eustaquio's cabin in the wagon, Victor waved at them from the porch. *"Te veo después."* he called out. *I will see you later.*

Luisa waved back, but did not respond. Pilar looked at her intently, trying to read any emotion on her sister's face, but Luisa's expression was impassive.

"Did you invite him to the party?" Pilar asked.

Luisa shrugged. "Not directly, but his aunt and uncle are coming. Why wouldn't he come also?"

"But are you happy that he is coming?"

"I am happy that all of our neighbors are planning to come. It is a special day," replied Luisa, noncommittally.

"But are you happy that *he* is coming?" insisted Pilar.

"What are you getting at?" asked Luisa, a little annoyed.

"What Pilar wants to know," interjected Ricardo, "is if you have feelings for Victor."

"Well, why didn't she come out and say that?" said Luisa crossly. "No, I do not have feelings for Victor."

Pilar still was not satisfied. "But he comes over almost every Sunday, and you go for walks."

"So?"

"So, he likes you."

Luisa did not respond right away. "I guess he does," she finally said. "But I do not like him…that way. To me, he is just our neighbor's nephew…a…a friend. Not even that. I would call him an acquaintance. Nothing more."

Ricardo cleared his throat. "Be very careful, *Mija*, not to encourage Victor if you do not have feelings for him. It would not be right to lead him on."

"So, what should I do, then?" asked Luisa, with a tinge of exasperation in her voice. "He just shows up and expects me to go for a walk with him."

"I think you can figure that out for yourself," was all that her father said.

They were silent the rest of the way into town, and Luisa tried to shake off her irritation and bring her focus back to the joy of the occasion. Once at the church, all of her attention was on baby Francisco. She reached out eager arms to take the baby from Petra and cooed into the sweet face right up until it was time to relinquish the babe to be baptized.

She greeted Manuel de Jesús with a smile and gave his mother a kiss on the cheek. Manuel de Jesús smiled back, but said nothing. He and his mother took their places by Petra and Juan José as they waited for *Padre* Irizarry to perform the rite. Manuel de Jesús did not so much as look Luisa's way after that.

He is taking his duties as the godfather seriously, thought Luisa, as a way of justifying his aloof behavior. She was happy that he had been asked to be the baby's godfather but wondered why she wasn't chosen to be the godmother instead of Moncerrate Sandoval. *I could not love that baby more,* she said to herself. *I would have been a wonderful godmother. Oh, well. As long as God gives me breath, I will be there for my little coffee bean. I may not be his godmother, but I am his aunt, and no one can take that honor away from me.*

That afternoon the Torres' *batey* was swarming with guests. In addition to Manuel de Jesús and Moncerrate, most of the friends and family that had attended Petra and Juan José's wedding almost two and a half years before were now celebrating the birth and baptism of the Collado's first child. Among those missing on this occasion were Sebastiana and her husband, Francisco, although Luisa looked around for them just in case her older sister wanted to surprise them all like she had done for Petra's wedding. Sadly, they were not there, and neither was Mama Sebia anymore. Luisa felt a pang as she remembered her family's most recent loss.

As had happened during Petra's wedding celebration, Petra's mother-in-law, Felipa, helped Chenta in the kitchen, and so did Rosa, so Luisa had the freedom to greet guests and mingle. Luisa had prepared her signature *gazpacho de bacalao* and only had to add the avocados at the last minute before placing the bowl among the array of dishes already on the food "table." She was surreptitiously watching to see if Manuel de Jesús served himself some, but she didn't even know where he was. She finally saw him standing with Eladio, Sebastián, Domingo, and Juan José beneath the mango tree. Her cousin Catalino was absent from the group of young men. He had declared his feelings to Dionicia Maldonado and Leocadio had given Catalino permission to court his daughter. They would be getting married early the next year and would occupy one of the cabins on the Maldonado farm.

Leocadio and Aquilina arrived with their family, and as expected, Catalino was with them. He spent so much time with the Maldonado family that Leocadio joked about now having one more mouth to feed, but that once the young couple was married, he would be down two.

Tío Gregorio and *Tía* Paula arrived with their brood. Luisa was happy to see her cousin, María de la Paz.

"Pacita!" exclaimed Luisa, giving her a hug. "I am so glad that you are here. Are you hungry? Do you want to serve yourself some food?"

"In a little while," answered María de la Paz. "Let's just sit together and talk first."

"I like that idea." The girls claimed a couple of chairs in the shade of a *flamboyán* tree, its abundant clusters of reddish orange flowers forming a protective canopy.

"What is new with you?" asked María de la Paz.

"Not much. Well, that's not true. I have been busy dividing my time between my house and Petra's cabin, helping her out until she got on her feet again. With eight younger siblings in our house, there is always a lot of work to do here, although Chenta is doing most of the cooking again, and Pilar helps out a lot."

"I do not envy you all the work that you have to do, Luisa. But I bet you like spending time in Petra's cabin with her and her baby."

"Oh, he is so adorable! I have the hardest time greeting Petra when I first walk into her cabin because all I want to do is push past her to see the baby and pick him up," admitted Luisa. "And it is nice and quiet there with only one child in the house," she added.

"Did you hear that Catalino and Dionicia are officially *novios*?" asked María de la Paz.

"Yes, I did. That was no surprise. Do you remember Petra's wedding day, when they were first eyeing each other and they danced together? I had a hunch even back then that they would fall in love."

Luisa looked around her and sighed. "Things are already so different after only a couple of years. People pairing off and getting married, babies being born right and left…it is all good, but I don't know…somehow I miss the good old days. We are not even sitting together as a group anymore. Catalino and Dionicia are over there by themselves, Rosa and Petra have their husbands and babies…we are here by ourselves. What are we—the old maids?" She said the last part a little too loudly because the musicians had begun to play, and she wanted her voice to be heard over the music.

María de la Paz laughed and said, "Hardly. Here comes someone for you right now."

Luisa turned her head to see who it was and had to suppress the dismay she felt at seeing Victor, not Manuel de Jesús approaching.

"*Hola*, Victor. Have you met my cousin María de la Paz?" she asked, as soon as he was within earshot. "Pacita, this is Victor, *Doña* Sinforosa's nephew. He is visiting here from Arecibo."

"*Mucho gusto*," said Victor. "But I am not just visiting anymore. I have a job in town and am looking for a place to rent there to be close to my work."

"Wonderful," said María de la Paz, smiling up at him. "It is a pleasure to meet you."

Do I detect interest there? You can have him, Pacita! Luisa had to smother a giggle at her own thoughts.

But Victor was holding out his hand to Luisa and asking her to dance. Reluctantly she put her hand in his and let him lead her to the center of the *batey*. A few others were already dancing, but Luisa still felt awkwardly conspicuous. With Victor's hand on her waist and her right hand in his left one, she peered past his shoulder to the group of young men hanging out under the mango tree. Manuel de Jesús was looking at her, his eyes serious and his face unsmiling.

Well, what are you doing standing way over there instead of coming to talk to me? I could have been dancing with you, instead!

Luisa's thoughts silently voiced her disappointment over her current situation.

"This is our first time dancing together. I have been waiting for this moment for a long time," Victor commented, smiling down at Luisa. "I wanted an excuse to put my arm around you and hold you close." He tried to draw her nearer to him as he said this, but Luisa resisted.

"Come on, loosen up," he murmured intimately.

"No," said Luisa tersely. "I cannot."

"Oh, I understand. Is your father watching? We can sneak away for a little while and no one will notice. I want to hold you in my arms, and you will be more comfortable if we are alone."

Luisa stiffened even more. "What are you saying? Do you think that I act one way in front of my father and another way when I am out of his sight? Have I given you reason to believe that I want to be alone with you and act in a way that my father would disapprove of?" Luisa was beginning to tremble.

"*Mi amor*, don't get upset," began Victor in a soothing voice.

"*¿Mi amor?* Victor, I am not *your love*. I thought I made that clear on our first walk together," Luisa said between gritted teeth.

"But that was weeks ago. I have invested a lot of time getting to know you. You should know how I feel about you. I can take you away from here, and we can have a life together…" He again attempted to draw her closer.

"No!" exclaimed Luisa, giving Victor's chest a push with her left hand as she tried to disengage her right hand from his. Instead of letting go of her hand, Victor tightened his hold on it and grabbed her other wrist.

"May I cut in?"

Luisa had not noticed Manuel de Jesús approaching and felt immense relief when she saw him.

"*¡Sí, por favor!*" she said, gratefully.

"Luisa, I would like to finish our discussion. Let's go take a walk." Victor increased the pressure on her wrist almost imperceptibly, but Luisa felt it and glared at him. Her lips were pressed together and her feet firmly planted where she stood.

"It doesn't look like she wants to continue your…discussion," Manuel de Jesús said, his voice even and controlled.

Victor dropped his hands.

"Fine," he spat out, looking from her to Manuel de Jesús, "if that's the way you want it. You have made your choice!" He strode away angrily.

Luisa turned to Manuel de Jesús, humiliated by what he had witnessed and by the tears that were forming in the corners of her eyes.

He sighed and said, "Come on. You need to sit down."

He led Luisa to a couple of chairs on the edge of the *batey*. Luisa struggled to compose herself. She did not trust herself to speak; she knew her voice would be all wobbly.

"I had to interrupt your dance," began Manuel de Jesús. "You looked uncomfortable and angry, and I wanted to make sure that you were all right. Are you upset that Victor walked off just now?"

"Upset? No. I am glad he is gone."

"But isn't he…aren't you two…seeing each other? Isn't he courting you?"

"What? Where did you get that idea?" Luisa looked at Manuel de Jesús incredulously.

"Well…from him. He has been telling everyone that you are his girl. That's why I have been giving you space."

"Oh, no, no, no. That is not true at all, and it never will be," said Luisa firmly. "I hope he gets a place in town like he says he plans to and moves away from his aunt's house. I wish him a happy life, but I do not want to be a part of it. I think I made it clear this time. He insulted me by suggesting that I…that he and I… " She shuddered. "Ay! How am I ever going to shop in *Doña* Juana's store if he is working there?"

Manuel de Jesús smiled. "Don't worry. He is the one who will have to hide his face when you see him at the general store. You stood up to him. You stood your ground, and he should know better than to say anything bad about you. Do you know the saying, *A mojo con ají no se le paran las moscas encima*? It means that your brave and upstanding character will serve as a shield against insults or abuse."

Luisa let those words sink in. She felt validated and respected by Manuel de Jesús. The tears threatened to appear again, but she fought them back. Instead, she raised her chin, looked into his caring eyes, and whispered a heartfelt "*Gracias*."

Chapter 20

Moving On

"I am going down to the garden plot to see what I can pick to go with our dinner tonight," Luisa informed her father as she stepped lightly down the steps onto the *batey*. He and Sebastián were lazing on the shady front porch, enjoying their day of rest.

"Okay, *Mija*," said Ricardo. "I didn't know that you were still tending to your garden. I thought you had let it go wild."

"No, I haven't been able to take care of it as much as it needs, and it is a sorry mess, but I think I can still glean something out of it. Now that I will not be going to Petra's cabin every day, I can dedicate more time to pulling weeds. See you in a bit."

Luisa felt lighthearted as she swung her basket and picked her way down the path to the creek. She was barefoot, and somehow that made her feel more carefree, like a child going out to play. As she drew closer to the stream she could hear the water gurgling over the rocks and a *ruiseñor* singing lustily in a tree overhead.

You poor garden, she thought, *I am sorry that I have had to neglect you so, but I will try to fix you up. In the meantime, let's see what you have for me.*

She was bending over the rows of string beans, happily discovering that there were still quite a few ready for picking, albeit the last of the crop, when she heard someone approaching. Straightening up, she searched the path along the bank to see who could be coming, and her breath caught in her throat when she saw that it was Victor. Rooted to the spot where she was standing in the middle of her garden, she waited for him to say something when he got close enough. She herself was rendered speechless.

"*Hola*, Luisa," he greeted her warmly, as if they had not had a heated argument just one week before. She said nothing and regarded him warily.

"I guess you are surprised to see me," he continued speaking amiably. "I just thought I would stop by and let you know that I found someplace to rent in town. I am leaving my aunt's house this afternoon to go get settled into my new abode."

Luisa finally found her tongue. "That's nice. That will make it convenient for you, since you work in town. Goodbye and good luck." When he didn't make a move to leave, she added, "You had better go now. My father does not allow me to talk to men when I am alone."

"He let us go on walks together every Sunday for several weeks," Victor pointed out.

"Yes. He gave us permission to do that. That was different. He does not know that you are here. So please leave."

Victor nodded, and his lips twisted into a smirk. He tilted his head to regard her candidly, letting his eyes sweep down her worn housedress to her bare feet and back up to her now blushing face. "You know," he said ignoring her dismissal, "you can have a different life than this if you choose to. My invitation is still open. I would love to have you come to town with me. You can leave all of this hard work and primitive lifestyle behind you."

He stepped closer and reached out to put his hand on her arm, but Luisa jerked back.

"Don't touch me!" she warned. Inwardly, she was wondering if her voice would be heard up at the house if she screamed.

"Why? What will you do? Call for your father to come save you?" he asked, as if reading her mind. "You are such an innocent. Your father would probably be happy to have one less mouth to feed. You are on your way to becoming a spinster, tucked away up here on this mountain. You are lucky that there is someone like me interested in you."

Luisa straightened up to her full five foot two inch stature. "Well, I am not interested in *you*…a man who does not respect me *or* my father. You misjudge us both. Now leave before I do scream, and believe me, he is sitting on our front porch, and I *will* scream loud enough for him to hear!"

Victor snorted. "You are nothing but a cold fish and a prude. Good luck getting a man to marry you." With a sneer and a haughty final raking look up and down Luisa's slim form, he turned and strode away.

Luisa stood there watching until he disappeared around the bend in the trail. Their brief encounter had left her rattled. She peered into her basket to see how many green beans she had collected. Not enough, she decided, and bent to quickly pick more, casting frequent nervous looks upwards toward the path. But he was gone, and Luisa hoped that she had seen the last of Victor. She made her way back up to the house.

Her demeanor must have given her away because Sebastián asked, *"¿Qué pasa?"*

Her father saw it, too, and echoed, "What is wrong?"

Luisa set her basket down on the wooden porch floor and lowered herself into a chair. "Victor just came up to talk to me while I was down by the creek."

"You know that I have said that I don't want…"

"I know. *Papá*," Luisa interrupted, her voice sounding weary. "I told him that, and I sent him away. He is not coming back."

"What did he have to say?" asked Sebastián, his voice low and level.

Luisa glanced up at Sebastián, and then looked away. She could not tell them *everything* that Victor had said or implied. It would only cause more trouble. "He found a place in town and is moving there this afternoon. He came to say goodbye."

Ricardo regarded his daughter silently, but Sebastián muttered, "Good riddance."

Now Luisa and Ricardo both turned their heads to look at Sebastián. "Listen," he said, "the guys were talking last week at the party we had here. Nobody really likes or trusts Victor. He is getting a reputation in town. I have seen him myself when we go to the plaza to sell our produce. He likes to flirt with the girls that walk past the general store. Plus he spends his Friday nights in the bar." He grimaced, and added. "It is not exactly criminal behavior, but all the same he is not someone that we consider good enough for you. And no one knows much about his background or why he really moved here from Arecibo."

"Why didn't you say something sooner?" queried Ricardo.

"I would have said something if I had seen Luisa genuinely interested in the guy. But I have been watching you, sister, and you did not act like a woman in love around him."

"*Uy, no*," responded Luisa with a shudder.

Ricardo chuckled. "She did tell Pilar and me that she did not have feelings for him. I hope you let him off easily, Luisa."

"Well, if telling him, 'Don't touch me or I will scream,' is letting him off easily, then I guess I did," said Luisa, with an impish smile.

Ricardo and Sebastián looked at her in shocked surprise, and then burst out laughing.

"Well done," said Sebastián, approvingly. His sister could take care of herself.

A couple of weeks later, Luisa and Pilar rode into town with Sebastián and Juan José to shop while they sold produce at the plaza. Pilar was elated at the opportunity to accompany Luisa. Petra was staying home with her baby, but had asked her sisters to pick out some fabric for a new dress for her as well as some cotton material for Francisco. Petra was grateful that Chenta had passed along used baby clothes, but she wanted to sew and embroider a few new tunics for her fast-growing boy.

Luisa was a bit nervous about encountering Victor in the general store, but she recalled what Manuel de Jesús had said about Victor being the one who would have to hide his face. Those were encouraging words, even if she had a hard time imagining Victor doing that. He was too arrogant. Yet Luisa knew that she had nothing to be ashamed of; she had acted in a proper and respectable manner, and she need make no apologies for her conduct.

The tinkling bell announced their entrance into the store. Pilar breezed in eagerly; Luisa a little less so, but with head held high. *Doña* Juana greeted them from behind the counter, and Luisa returned the greeting, noting that Victor was standing next to his employer. *Don* Pepín stuck his head out from behind the curtain that separated the store from the back room, waved at the girls, and disappeared again. With a few softly spoken words to *Doña* Juana, Victor picked up the broom and headed outside, presumably to sweep the wooden sidewalk clean. Luisa breathed an audible sigh of relief and headed to the fabric section with Pilar.

Doña Juana could not contain her eagerness to chat and hurried over to the girls.

"Look at this new material that came in," she said, indicating some colorful bolts of fabric. "Are you needing new dresses for a special occasion? Is someone in your family getting married?"

At Luisa's shake of her head, the older woman continued, "Oh, I guess not. You would be next in line. Your older sisters are already married. Unless it is Sebastián…but no, I have not heard of him having a *novia*. Now when Victor first started working here, he said he was courting you, Luisa, but a couple of weeks ago he said he decided to break it off." She cast a searching glance at Luisa as she said this, trying to read her reaction.

"Oh, *he* decided to break it off?" Luisa shook her head. "Never mind. We were not courting, anyway. I was just being neighborly to a newcomer."

"I see." *Doña* Juana seemed disappointed that there was not a juicier story there. She would have liked to relate to other store patrons just how brokenhearted Luisa was to have been rejected by Victor.

Suddenly brightening, *Doña* Juana continued, "Well, Victor is such a charming and handsome young man. Intelligent and hardworking, too—he is a great help here at the store. He would make a fine husband for some lucky girl. In fact," she snuck another sly look at Luisa here, "he is already seeing another young lady—a neighbor of his aunt Sinforosa."

"A neighbor? What neighbor?" Both Luisa and Pilar halted their browsing and stared at *Doña* Juana.

"I thought that would interest you," she said with a knowing smile. "Do you know Camila?"

"Camila?!" both girls exclaimed in unison, and Luisa asked, *"¿La hija de Don Abelardo y Doña Elena?"* Don Abelardo and Doña Elena's daughter?

"La misma," affirmed *Doña* Juana, with a nod of her head. *The same one.*

"But she is only a girl, several years younger than me," declared Luisa. She and Pilar looked at each other, and Pilar added, "I think she is in between your age and mine."

Doña Juana shrugged. "Apparently Victor does not think that she is too young, and neither do her parents."

The tinkling bell and the arrival of another shopper pulled *Doña* Juana away, much to Luisa's relief.

"Let's hurry up and make our selections and get out of here before Victor wears out the wooden planks of the sidewalk with all of his sweeping," Luisa said.

June slipped into July, and the Torres women were busy during the evenings sewing their new dresses. Luisa was thankful for the long summer days that provided them with natural light long after the dinner dishes were washed, dried and put away. *Maybe that is why we tend to sew new dresses in the summertime,* thought Luisa. *The winter days are too short, and it is dark by the time we are done cleaning up the kitchen. Sewing by lamplight is too hard on the eyes.*

Her life had returned to a normal routine that included time for gardening, sewing, and visiting her little coffee bean. Sunday evenings with the family gathered on the front porch were delightful, and Luisa was thrilled not to have to go on walks with Victor anymore.

Chenta had devised a baby carrier for Petra to use when trekking down from her cabin for a visit. "My mother used to have one like this," she reminisced, as she adjusted the cloth around baby Francisco. "I remember her carrying my baby sister, Magdalena, on her back when we walked to my grandmother's house. I had five younger siblings, each of us only a year apart. *Mami* needed her hands free to hold on to the other little ones. Of course, my older sister, Moncerrate, helped her a lot, and I tried to, too, but I was only about six or seven at the time. Domingo is a couple of years younger than me, and he was a little rascal. If someone didn't hold on to him, he would run off!"

"Didn't your father have a wagon?" asked Pilar.

"He did have a wagon, but there was a path between our house and my grandparents' house that the wagon could not go on. It was just for walking, like the one that you take to hike up to Petra's cabin. *Mami* would get mad at *Papi* about something, and she would gather up all of us kids and take us to her parents' house. We would even take the goat with us!" Chenta chuckled at the memory.

"Really?" asked Luisa, incredulously. "How long would you stay at your grandparents' home?"

"Oh, not very long," Chenta answered, with a shake of her head. "There really wasn't room for all of us at Mama Juana and Papa Manuel's place. They probably encouraged her to take us back to our house, but *Mami* would hold out stubbornly until *Papi* came to convince her to go back with him."

"That's funny," Petra said. "I can't imagine *Doña* Carpia being so feisty. She does not seem that way now."

"Well, she was young," murmured Chenta. "People sometimes change as they get older and their circumstances change. It is not easy when you have so many children. Mothers can get overwhelmed and short-tempered."

"You have a lot of children to care for, Chenta," Luisa pointed out, and then added, with a twinkle in her eye, "Thank you for not getting angry with *Papá* and dragging all of us over to your mother's house."

Chenta and Petra laughed, and Petra said, "Yes, thank you for setting a good example for us, Chenta."

One Sunday afternoon in early September, Moncho's friend, Carlos, came to visit him. Usually, they headed for the creek with Juanito in tow and spent their time splashing, throwing rocks or looking for Taíno petroglyphs on the boulders that edged the other side of the creek. Today, he appeared content to stay on the porch with his friend's family, sipping on the glass of water that Luisa brought him, although he seemed to have something on his mind.

"Are you all right?" Chenta asked him. "You look sad. Are you hungry? Would you like something to eat?"

Carlos shook his head, and smiled wanly. Did all mothers think that food was the answer to everything? "I *am* sad…and worried."

"Why, *Mijo*?" Chenta prodded gently. "Is everyone okay at your house? Is your mother sick?"

Carlos looked furtively over at Luisa and then back at Chenta. He sucked in a big breath of air and blew it forcefully out of his mouth, making his vibrating lips produce a sound.

"It's Camila," he finally said. "She ran off with Victor. He took her away with him to his place in town."

"Oh, no!" moaned Luisa, and she squeezed her eyes shut.

"*¡Ay, bendito!*" exclaimed Chenta. "Your poor mother!"

"I know," said Carlos, mournfully. "She won't stop crying. And *Papi* is so angry. I couldn't take it anymore, so I left the house and ended up here."

"When did this happen?" asked Luisa.

"My younger sister discovered that she was gone yesterday morning. Well, at first she didn't realize that she was gone," Carlos explained. "She thought that Camila had just gotten up before her, but when she wasn't anywhere in the house, and no one knew where she was, *Papi* and *Mami* started to suspect the worst. They looked around and saw signs. Her clothes were gone, and the window of her bedroom was unlatched."

"No one heard her leaving?" wondered Chenta.

"I didn't hear anything. Concepción says she might have heard something but thought she was dreaming. She feels really bad that she didn't wake up and stop Camila from sneaking out."

"And…do you all know for sure that she went away with Victor?" Luisa asked.

Carlos sighed heavily. "Yes, *Papi* went into town yesterday and found out where Victor lives. Well, that really wasn't difficult. *Doña* Juana told Papi that Victor was renting a couple of rooms over the bar, and that he was probably there now since he had asked for the day off from the store. *Papi* went there and confronted them. Camila said that she had run away of her own free will and did not want to go back home with *Papi*. She wanted to stay with Victor. There was nothing that *Papi* could do. He said he felt like punching Victor in the face, but he refrained from doing that."

Ricardo grunted. "Yes, that would only have made things worse."

"I feel terrible," said Luisa, and everyone turned to look at her. "Oh, not because of…I did not have any feelings for Victor. I was glad when he stopped coming to see me and surprised when he started courting Camila right away. But I feel bad because I should have gone to warn her to be careful. I guess I thought that it would look suspicious if I did because she would think I was jealous or resentful that he was seeing her now. After all, I have never visited her before, and to all of a sudden pay her a visit would have seemed strange." She groaned. "Camila is so young! She let herself be swept away by the first man that showed her any attention."

"But why would you even think of warning Camila?" Chenta queried. "How could you know that he was even capable of doing such a thing?"

"Any man is capable," remarked Ricardo. "It has to do with whether or not he has respect for a young woman and her family." He looked into Luisa's eyes with new insight. "*Mija*… did he….?"

Luisa's expression became sorrowful. "He suggested…no, outright invited me to go with him…to his place in town. I did not want to stir up trouble by mentioning it to you or Sebastián. I rejected him and he left right away, and I thought that was the end of that, but now I feel guilty that Camila fell for his smooth talking."

"Hey," said Carlos, "my father feels guilty because he allowed Victor to come calling on Camila. My mother feels guilty because she thinks she should have known that her daughter was scheming to run away. Concepción feels guilty because she didn't wake up and stop Camila. Luisa feels guilty because she didn't warn Camila, and I feel guilty because I didn't realize that Victor did not respect my sister. In the end, Camila is responsible for her own actions and none of us should feel guilty." Carlos's discourse showed great maturity for a fifteen-year-old, and the others nodded in agreement and murmured words of assent.

"I should probably get back home," he said now, and he stood up to leave.

"Be kind to your mama," Chenta said softly. "Her mother's heart is broken."

"I know. I will. Thank you all for listening."

He was several steps away already when Luisa called out after him. "I will be praying for Camila and for your whole family."

Carlos acknowledged her words with a nod and a wave.

Luisa did pray. That night and for many nights to come she included Carlos and his family in her bedtime prayers, asking for the angels to protect Camila and for God to comfort *Don* Abelardo, *Doña* Elena, Carlos and Concepción. She did not mention Victor in her prayers. She did not know what to say about him. It was difficult to pray for someone for whom she held resentment.

Chapter 21

The Declaration

Leocadio and Aquilina welcomed a new baby boy that fall and named him Rosendo. They had thought that they were done having children because Aquilina was over forty years old, and she had not conceived in five years. She had actually thought that she was going through "the change" and was several months along before she realized that she was carrying another child. Thankfully, the surprise pregnancy had proceeded without difficulties, and Rosendo was born healthy and robust, the largest of their seven babies. With *Doña* Tiburcia living in a cabin on their property, Aquilina had expert care during the birthing of the baby and in the weeks that followed.

The celebration of Rosendo's baptism was a joyous affair. It had been months since relatives and neighbors had gathered for an afternoon of food and fellowship, ever since Francisco's baptism party in early June. Chenta prepared a huge pot of *fricasé de pollo* (chicken fricassee), made more delicious by homegrown onions, bell peppers, cilantro, carrots and potatoes from Luisa's garden. In addition, Luisa had baked *flan de coco* (coconut custard). Their contributions to the community potluck were carefully placed in boxes, and Luisa held the box with the *flan* on her lap on the wagon ride to Leocadio's house. Whenever the wagon lurched over a bump in the dirt road, Luisa held the box up off of her lap to mitigate the impact of the jostling. She was relieved when they finally arrived and the *flan* was still intact, without a single crack in its smooth surface. She was also glad that none of the caramelized sugar had leaked out of the box onto her new dress! This was her first time wearing the dress that she had spent weeks working on during the summer evenings. Luisa loved the moss green background, the pattern of delicate ferns and sprinkling of rose-colored flowers. The dress even still had that new-fabric smell to it.

There were plenty of young men already there to offload children and help ladies alight from the wagons, as well as to care for the horses. Moncho jumped out of the wagon almost before it came to a complete stop, eager to work with Leocadio's son, José, who was close to him in age. Both boys already were experienced at caring for horses. Catalino and his younger brother, Andrés, helped offload Ricardo's wagon of the children and food. As usual, Luisa was the last one to alight. She handed the flan over to Andrés, but as she prepared to climb out of the wagon bed, it was Manuel de Jesús who was there to meet her with a smile and a strong outstretched hand.

Her feet were on the ground now, but Manuel de Jesús still held her hand in his. Looking up into his eyes, Luisa felt like she had a little *coquí* jumping around inside her stomach. It was the strangest feeling. Her fingertips were tingling, too.

Manuel de Jesús gave her hand a gentle squeeze before he released it, but didn't take his eyes off of her.

"Me alegro que estés aquí," he said, softly. *I am glad that you are here.* "You look so pretty in that dress!"

Luisa was surprised that she was even able to speak. *"Gracias.* I am happy that you are here, too." That sounded so bold to her own ears, and she felt the dreaded blush beginning to happen.

"Hey, you two," Catalino called out, startling them out of the moment. "Better get out of the way or you will be run over by the next wagon that arrives."

With a sheepish grin, Manuel de Jesús put his hand under Luisa's elbow and guided her out of the way.

"You don't have to play the part of hostess today, do you?" he asked.

"No, not this time. There are plenty of women to help out in the kitchen. But I do want to say hello to Aquilina and see who else is here. Do you know if my sisters have arrived?"

"They have. Go greet everyone. I should stick around out front here to assist with the families that are arriving, but I hope you can spare some time to visit with me a little later," he said.

"Oh, yes, of course!"

Manuel de Jesús gave her a funny lopsided smile and lightly touched her arm before turning away. There went that imaginary *coquí* in her stomach again!

Luisa found Aquilina and had a chance to hold Rosendo, exclaiming over his ruddy complexion and the reddish-brown fuzz on his head. *It is true that we Puerto Ricans come in all colors,* thought Luisa, even within one family unit. Dionicia had a beautiful bronze complexion while her brother, José, was nick-named *"el Cano"* due to his blond hair and freckled skin. Luisa imagined that little Rosendo would soon be referred to as *"el Colorao"* because of his coloring, if indeed people weren't already calling him that.

Next, she greeted her sisters and their babies. Rosa's Micaela was an adorable, curly-haired one-year-old, already toddling around on chubby legs. She was wearing the cutest little pink dress that Rosa had sewn for her, and she showed off her dimples when she smiled at everyone. Petra's Francisco was almost six months old, growing bigger every day and now sporting two bottom teeth, but he was still Luisa's "little coffee bean." Since she saw him frequently and was nearly as familiar to him as his own mother, Francisco waved his arms and gurgled at Luisa. She took that as her cue and picked him up, holding him close and nuzzling his sweet-smelling neck. Francisco chortled with delight. He loved his *Tía* Luisa!

Leocadio called for all the guests to gather around. He thanked everyone for joining in the celebration of their newest—and last, he hoped—child. After the chuckling died down, he offered up a prayer of thanks for the feast that they were about to indulge in, asking God to also bless the many hands that had prepared the food.

Luisa continued holding Francisco while Petra served herself a plate of food, then offered to watch Micaela also while Rosa got hers.

"When are you going to eat, Luisa?" asked Rosa.

"I'll eat later," she replied. "I'm not worried about the food running out. There is an overabundance of it." She sat in Rosa's chair, holding both Francisco and Micaela on her lap, and chatted with Petra until Rosa returned with her food. Then ceding the chair to Rosa, she handed Francisco back to Petra and took

Micaela with her to find María de la Paz and Dionicia so that Rosa could be free to enjoy her meal.

"There you are!" she greeted Dionicia, who was sitting in the shade holding Rosendo. "How convenient is it to have a baby brother to practice on with changing diapers and burping! Maybe this time next year you will be expecting one of your own," she teased.

Dionicia flushed with pleasure at the thought. "I know. Can you believe it? In a few months, I will be a *señora*. That sounds so old!"

"Yes, and you are younger than I am. You beat me! I don't even have a *novio*."

"No, but you have a *pretendiente*," declared Dionicia.

"No, not even that," said Luisa. "I don't know where you got the idea that I have a suitor."

"Luisa," said the younger girl, a little impatiently. "Anyone can see that Manuel de Jesús is crazy about you, and you like him, too. Admit it!"

Luisa looked around to make sure that they were not being overheard by anyone. She lowered her voice. "I do like him. But nothing has been declared. We have not even had an opportunity to talk."

"So go give your niece back to her mother and go find him," urged Dionicia.

Luisa laughed. "I am not that brazen. If it happens, it happens, but I am not going to hunt him down. I *will* return my niece, though, and go get myself a plate of food."

So saying, Luisa took Micaela back to Rosa and made her way to the food table. She was eyeing the array of dishes when Manuel de Jesús came up behind her and touched her elbow to get her attention. She looked up at him, at his quirky smile and kind eyes, and her breath caught in her throat.

"Are you hungry? If you can wait a little bit, I would like to speak with you now because I am afraid that time will get away from us, and you might go home before we have a chance to visit."

"I can eat later," she replied, and waited to see what he suggested.

"All the chairs seem to be taken," he observed, "but we can head out behind the house, toward the barn. Will you get in trouble if you go for a short walk with me?" he added, with a teasing grin.

Luisa shot him a coy look. "I am willing to risk it," she said, and marveled at her own brashness.

They strolled around the side of the house toward the barn, but seeing that there were several men and boys in there tending to the horses, he veered to the right. "How about if we sit on the back steps, instead?" he suggested. "There are people within sight, but out of earshot."

Manuel de Jesús took out his clean, white handkerchief and spread it out on one of the wide steps for Luisa to sit on. As he lowered himself next to her, she looked toward the barn. It was some distance from the house, and the men inside were in the shadows, but she thought she saw her father among them.

"Are you all right?" asked Manuel de Jesús. "Do you feel uncomfortable here? If you feel that this is not proper…"

"No, it's fine," Luisa assured him. "Thank you for being so considerate, though. There are some men who do not care about propriety."

"Yes, I know who you are referring to, and that is one reason why I needed to talk to you, Luisa. You gave me a scare, you know. I thought he…I thought you…I thought I had waited too long."

Luisa stole a sideways glance at Manuel de Jesús and saw him nervously clasping his hands together, but she didn't say anything. She waited.

"We have known each other for so many years. We have both lived in Juan González all our lives and have watched each other grow up. We played together as children…but when I saw you that day a couple of years ago…it was at Mina's baptism...I knew…"

Luisa sucked in her breath. She remembered the moment that he was alluding to, when she saw him turn his head to look at her and caught her staring at him. Flustered, she had ducked into the kitchen. It had been a turning point for her, too.

Manuel de Jesús continued his monologue. "After that moment, every time I saw you at another party, or at church, or well, anywhere, I just wanted to be with you…to talk to you… and dance with you. There was no one else that I wanted to spend time with. Others saw it and they teased us—Eladio and your sisters—but I actually took that as confirmation that we belonged together."

Now Luisa's heart was thumping so hard that she could hardly breathe. *Could this really be finally happening?*

"I felt that we were still young, and I wanted to be able to provide you with a house and furnishings and things…so I was taking things slowly…but then Victor moved in with his aunt and wasted no time calling on you."

"Oh, but I didn't..."

"I know. I was so jealous when I saw you dancing with him. But then I noticed your countenance and realized that you were not enjoying being with him. I couldn't stop myself from butting in."

"I am glad that you did," said Luisa, now daring to look at Manuel de Jesús.

"Luisa," he said her name tenderly, and did not need to say anything more. His eyes said it all. Luisa felt the tingling in her fingertips again. Such a strange sensation! *This is what was missing with Victor. I never felt anything like this when I was with him,* she thought, marveling at the revelation.

He reached out and took one of her hands in his. "I would like to talk to your father…about coming to call on you. Would you be okay with that?"

Luisa nodded. Without taking her gaze from his, she said, "I think he is in the barn. He may even have seen us sitting here together. You can go talk to him now, if you like."

"I do want to talk to him right away, but…at the same time I don't want to get up from this step yet. I don't want this moment to end." He laughed self-consciously.

"Me neither," she admitted.

They were both laughing as he helped her stand up, and he did not let go of her hand.

"Manuel," Luisa whispered, "I am so happy!"

"So am I." He gave her hand a squeeze before releasing it, and bent to retrieve his handkerchief. Giving her his signature lopsided smile, he said, "Here I go!" With that he turned and strode off toward the barn. She watched him walk away, saw him folding up his handkerchief and stuffing it in his back pocket. She breathed a silent prayer that her father would be open to the courting request, but she felt optimistic about it. It felt right, and her father must have seen it coming. He would not be surprised by what Manuel de Jesús was going to ask. Luisa all but floated around the side of the house in search of Dionicia or her sisters. She had to tell someone!

Chapter 22

Courtship

Ricardo gave his blessing, and Manuel de Jesús began courting Luisa each Sunday afternoon, without missing a beat. Luisa put extra love into cooking the Sunday dinner because Manuel de Jesús had a standing invitation to share it with them. He was always appreciative of her efforts.

Those were blissful evenings with Manuel de Jesús joining in the family time on the porch as if he had always belonged there. He could talk agriculture with Ricardo, Sebastián and Juan José, and they could all relate to one another. He was often the fourth person around the domino table. He usually brought greetings and tidbits of news to Chenta from his sister-in-law, Antonia. Just one year younger than Chenta, the two sisters were very close and loved this added opportunity to keep informed of one another. Chenta was thrilled at the budding romance between Manuel de Jesús and Luisa. If they got married, it would be another link between Ricardo's family and hers.

Luisa's siblings were all welcoming of her suitor, but little Toño, normally painfully shy, attached himself to Manuel de Jesús like to no one else. It was not unusual for Manuel de Jesús to be playing dominos with Toño perched on his knee the whole time, and when it was the boy's bedtime, it had to Manuel de Jesús who tucked him in. After the younger children were sent to bed, the rest of the family visited a while and then one by one went inside, or—in the case of Sebastián and the Collados—to their own cabins, giving Luisa and Manuel de Jesús some time alone. He never stayed very late; as a farm worker, his days started early, same as with the men in the Torres family, and he still had to ride his horse back to Lucas and Antonia's farm in the dark. But those few moments of sitting on the porch by themselves, talking quietly and holding hands were special. When he stood to take his leave, he would draw her close in a tender embrace and give her a kiss on the forehead or on the cheek. He was very respectful.

Luisa went through her daily chores with a light spring in her step and a song on her lips. Although she was a caring and considerate person by nature, she became even more loving in her treatment to all those in her circle. On Sundays, she was especially jubilant with the anticipation of a visit from her *pretendiente*. Sebastián noticed it first and remarked to her one day, "There's the look I was expecting to see!"

"What do you mean?" asked Luisa.

"The look of a woman in love," her brother explained.

Luisa blushed and ducked her head demurely, but she could not hold back a smile.

"I am happy for you, sister," he said. "It's about time, too. I could see that the poor guy was smitten a long time ago, and I never thought he would get up the nerve to tell you how he felt about you. I guess it took Victor trying to get close to you to spur him into action."

"Ugh. Victor," said Luisa. "I wonder how Camila is doing. Have you seen her in town?"

"I saw her once. She walked past our produce stand on the way to the general store. She didn't say anything to us or even look our way, and then I saw her going back the other way shortly afterwards. My guess is that Victor did not want her there at the store when he was working and sent her back to their place above the bar. He still likes to stand outside the store and flirt with the girls that walk by."

"Poor Camila," murmured Luisa. "She must feel like a prisoner there."

Sebastián shrugged. "You know, we have the expression here in Puerto Rico that a man has 'taken a girl' if he convinces her to leave her family and go with him without getting married first. But really, unless he ties her up, gags her mouth and throws her over his shoulder, he is not actually taking her. It was Camila's decision to go with him."

"Yes, but I wonder if she really knew what he was like. After all, Victor can be very nice and polite as long as he thinks he is getting his way. But he will turn mean if anyone opposes his wishes, like I did. Since Camila agreed to his scheme of running away together, maybe she had not seen the mean side of him yet."

"I think by now she has," said Sebastián. "She did not look happy when I saw her."

"Poor Camila," Luisa said again.

The Christmas season was approaching, and Luisa needed to make a trip into town to buy gifts for the children's Three Kings' Day as well as some items that she and Chenta needed in the kitchen. The thought of entering the general store and seeing Victor did not bother her that much this time. Surely by now he had heard that Luisa was being courted by Manuel de Jesús.

Luisa rode into town early one Saturday morning with Sebastián and Juan José. Neither Petra nor Pilar were able to accompany her. Petra felt that it was too much trouble to get Francisco up, changed, fed, and dressed for a wagon ride into town at that early hour. Pilar would have liked to go, but Chenta needed her help around the house since Luisa was going to be gone until mid afternoon. Besides, Luisa could hardly pick out a present for Pilar if she was there at the store with her. Pilar was fourteen now, way too old to expect anything for Three Kings' Day, but Luisa wanted to indulge her younger sister, anyway.

Sebastián and Juan José insisted that Luisa ride up front with them. They were all slender and the bench seat could hold all three of them, even if they were a little crowded. Luisa felt special and protected, riding between the two men.

"You know, you will probably see Manuel de Jesús today. He is usually at the plaza the same days that we go," said Juan José as they made their descent down the mountain in the wagon.

"Really?" responded Luisa, lightly.

"Oh, don't try to pretend that you hadn't already thought of that," said Sebastián, and Luisa laughed out loud, admitting her guilt.

The three of them continued their lighthearted conversation all the way into town. They parked in their customary spot and began offloading the wagon. Luisa wanted to help, but she was not allowed to. Sebastián pointed out that the crates were too heavy for her to lift, and anyway, she worked hard at home every day. She should relax and enjoy her morning off. He helped her out of the wagon and she settled herself on a nearby bench some ten feet away from them.

After they were done setting up, Sebastián came over to where she was sitting and asked, "Hey, do you want to take a walk with me?"

She was up in an instant. "Where are we going?"

"Oh, just around the corner of the plaza, to the side that faces the church. There are some friends that I want to go say hello to." Luisa looked up at Sebastián and he winked at her. A smile overtook her face.

Manuel de Jesús's face lit up when he saw them approaching. "Luisa! I didn't know that you were coming to town today. Hola, Sebastián," he said, shaking hands with him but barely taking his eyes off of Luisa.

"I have some shopping to do. I am here by myself this time. I mean, without one of my sisters, just with Sebastián and Juan José," she replied.

"If Eladio doesn't mind handling the stand by himself for a while, you can accompany Luisa to the store, if you like," offered Sebastián.

"I would be honored. Is it all right with you, Luisa?"

She nodded her assent, and Eladio agreed with a dismissing wave of his hand. The young couple strolled off in the direction of the general store, and Sebastián returned to his own produce stand.

"You look beautiful," Manuel de Jesús told her as they walked side by side, but not touching. He was unsure if Luisa would be comfortable with a public display of affection such as hand holding, but he knew that he wasn't comfortable with it. Not yet.

"I look the same as always," responded Luisa. "Nothing is different. You have seen this dress on me plenty of times."

"No, not the same," he insisted. "Your face looks more beautiful every time I see you."

Remembering what Sebastián had said about the look of love on her face, Luisa said nothing in reply, but she did smile at him. As their eyes met, Luisa marveled at how they managed to continue walking forward without bumping into someone or tripping on a tree root. Somehow they made it to the store without mishap and entered to the sound of the tinkling bell on the door.

Victor paled when he saw them but quickly recovered his composure and welcomed them to the store. He remained behind the counter and *Doña* Juana was helping another customer, so Manuel de Jesús and Luisa were free to browse and select the items that she wanted to buy. It was fun having Manuel de Jesús weigh in on the appropriate gifts for the children; he was very much involved and was as anxious as Luisa was to get presents that would bring joy to the youngsters. Conveniently, when it was time to have the items rung up and wrapped, Victor was busy restocking shelves and *Doña* Juana was available to help them at the counter. She chattered non-stop about how she had heard that they were courting and was thrilled to offer them her congratulations.

"Victor has his Camila, you know," she said, lowering her voice to a whisper, "although I hardly ever see the poor girl. I told him it wasn't proper for them to be living together without being married. He should make an honest woman out of her." She shook her head and pursed her lips disapprovingly. "Well, it is none of my business, and he is not my son, but he is my employee, so I can't help but let him know what I think of it."

Murmuring their thanks, Luisa and Manuel de Jesús left the store, breathing a sigh of relief once they were outside. They walked leisurely around the plaza, in no big hurry to get back to the produce stands. When they reached the Maldonado's stand, Eladio assured them that he was doing fine by himself, so they continued on to her brother's stand. Manuel de Jesús climbed nimbly onto the wagon to store Luisa's purchases under the seat, then hopping down, declared that he felt compelled to go back and spell his brother, despite Eladio saying that it wasn't necessary. Luisa approved of his sense of responsibility and urged him to go back to his stand, thanking him for helping her with her shopping and carrying her packages for her.

He reached for her hand, oblivious to anyone who might be watching them, and his voice had a husky edge to it as he said, "I enjoy every minute that I get to spend with you, so this was a treat for me. If we don't see each before the farmer's market ends this afternoon, I will see you tomorrow night." He gave her hand a gentle squeeze before releasing it. Luisa watched him walk away and turned to find both Sebastián and Juan José grinning at her.

"What?" she demanded, putting a hand on her hip saucily. "Oh, stop it! I am going to get our lunch out, if one of you will help me up into the wagon."

It was some time after they had all eaten and Luisa was relaxing on the bench near their produce stand, enjoying the sights and sounds of the bustling plaza, when she was startled to see a girl approaching her.

"Camila?" Luisa barely recognized her. She looked thinner than Luisa had remembered her, and her hair was hanging loosely around her face. She looked unkempt and had shadows under her eyes. Upon closer observation, Luisa could see a glaring red bruise on Camila's cheek that her flowing tresses failed to cover up.

Camila sat down on the bench next to Luisa, casting fearful looks toward the general store as she did so.

"I have been watching for you every time your brother comes to the plaza to sell," she said, hurriedly. "Victor does not like me leaving our place or walking around the plaza. He would get angry if he knew I was here talking to you. I saw you from our window above the bar. You were walking with Manuel de Jesús, so I could not pass up the opportunity to come talk to you."

"What's wrong? Are you unwell?" asked Luisa, with genuine concern in her voice.

Camila's eyes filled with tears. "No, I am not well. I want to go home. Please! Can I ride home with you and your brother? Will you take me to my parents house, if they will take me back?" her voice trailed off as a sob escaped her.

"I...I am sure that they will, Camila. Your mother will be much relieved to have you back, of that I am sure." Luisa patted the girl's arm, and added, "Let me talk to my brother."

Camila clutched Luisa's arm. "I can't let Victor see me. Sometimes he stands outside the store, and if he sees me here, he will be furious. Please help me!" Tears were now streaming down Camila's face.

Luisa looked over to the produce stand and saw Sebastián staring at them with a questioning look on his face. She summoned him urgently with her hand. When he strode over to them, Luisa quickly apprised him of the situation. Sebastián clenched his jaw and his eyes took on a steely look.

"Go stand behind the wagon with Camila, so that you are both out of view from the general store," he said, brusquely. "We will pack up and leave immediately."

The girls hastened to do as he said, and after a few quick words to Juan José, the two men wasted no time loading the unsold crates of produce into the wagon. When they were ready to leave, with the reins already in Sebastián's hands, Juan José helped Luisa and Camila up and they settled themselves on the bench in the wagon bed, directly behind the driver's seat. As they drove off, Camila kept her face averted, hoping that even if Victor stepped outside of the store he wouldn't see her.

Camila cried most of the way home. She had nothing with her other than the clothes that she was wearing, so Juan José produced a clean handkerchief for her to use to mop up her tears. Every now and then Camila made short comments like, "He was not who I thought he was," "I am sorry I agreed to run away with him," and "I hope my father lets me come home." Luisa held her hand and offered soothing words to comfort the girl.

The sound of the approaching wagon and team brought Camila's family out onto their porch. At first, they only saw Sebastián driving the team with Juan José next to him, and didn't realize that Camila was sitting behind them. When *Doña* Elena saw Juan José helping the girls down, she let out a cry.

"*¡Ay, Mija!*"

"*¡Mami!*" A sobbing Camila ran straight to her mother's arms. Carlos and Concepción pressed in close to them, trying also to hug their sister. Their father, Abelardo, stood just a few feet away, head down and thumbs in his pants pockets, but he withdrew a hand to wipe a tear from his eye. Luisa and Juan José remained near the horses, and Sebastián was still on the wagon seat, holding the reins. After a few moments, they looked at each other questioningly, wondering if they should just leave the family alone to their reunion. But Camila broke away from the group embrace and faced her father hesitantly. He looked at her with red-rimmed eyes, and reached out to her. He gathered her in his embrace, with one hand on the back of her head, and let the girl sob into his chest.

Doña Elena blew her nose on her handkerchief and indicated with her hand that the others were to come in, so Sebastián got down from the wagon and tied the horses' reins to the porch railing. Luisa and Juan José went up the porch steps and greeted the family.

"*Entren, entren,*" said *Doña* Elena. *Come in, come in.* "I am so grateful to you for bringing our Camila home."

Concepción hurried to bring out a pitcher of water and glasses for everyone. She didn't want to miss out on the conversation when it started. It took a few minutes for Camila to get enough control of her emotions to speak, but once she did, she poured out the story of how Victor had changed from the nice, loving guy that she thought he was into a jealous, controlling man who spent hours in the bar every evening. She was not allowed to leave their rented rooms to even go for a walk around the plaza. He accused her of horrible things when he was the one who was always flirting with other women. Last night she had waited up for him. He was later than usual and was drunk when he finally came in, then was angry with her because his food was cold. She had dared talk back to him saying that it was his fault that the food got cold while he was in the bar, and he had smacked her across the cheek.

"I never once saw you raise a hand to *Mami*," she said tearfully to her father. "I cannot live with a man who mistreats me so."

"Of course not!" grumped her father. "If I see him…"

Doña Elena and Camila both immediately protested, begging him not to do anything or even go near Victor. "He has caused our family enough pain," said *Doña* Elena.

Sebastián cleared his throat and spoke. "We should get going."

Don Abelardo stood up to shake hands with Sebastián and Juan José and to thank them again for bringing his daughter home. He looked back at Camila and asked, "And how did that come about?"

"I saw Luisa and Manuel de Jesús from the window, and I thought that it was my chance to get away…while Victor was working," explained Camila. "I waited until after Victor had his lunch and went back to the store, and then I went down and looked for Luisa. I was afraid that they would pack up and leave early, and I would miss my opportunity to get a ride home."

"Manuel de Jesús probably wondered what happened to us, if he noticed that we left early and in such a hurry," said Luisa. "I will explain it to him tomorrow night when he comes…if it is all right with you…I know it is personal…"

"No, no, that's fine," said *Don* Abelardo, with a wave of his hand. "*No se puede tapar el cielo con la mano.*" *You can't cover up the sky with your hand.*

"We know that the truth of what has happened to our family has to come out in the open," said *Doña* Elena with a sigh. "But we also know that you are good, caring people, and you are not judgmental."

"Of course not," said Luisa, sincerely. She gave *Doña* Elena a hug and one to Camila, and then went out the door with Sebastián and Juan José. All of Camila's family followed to see them out.

Even with the stop at Camila's house for that hour, they were still going to be arriving home earlier than expected. Luisa knew that they would be relating the afternoon's events to her family, albeit with care and consideration for their neighbors' situation.

Later that night, as Luisa lay in bed next to Pilar, she prayed that her younger sisters would not ever get entangled in the snare of such a man as Victor. She thanked God that she had had the wisdom to discern that Victor was not the type of man for her, and that she had broken off all personal contact with him. Unfortunately for Camila, he had then sought that young girl out and had succeeded in convincing her to leave her family for him.

Bless Sebastián and Juan José for having the valor to do what was right and help Camila get away from Victor. Thank you also, God, that Camila's family welcomed her back home and that they still love her. That is the kind of love that You have for us, isn't it? We disappoint You and yet You welcome us back into Your loving arms. Camila's sad story has been a lesson for me. It is far easier and more enjoyable to live in such a way that pleases You, Father, instead of suffering the consequences of our behavior and having to ask for Your forgiveness. I know that You are a loving and forgiving Father, but I do not want to displease You. Help me to always do Your will. Amen.

Chapter 23

Doubts

In the weeks that followed, as neighbors gathered for Christmas parties and church services, the word spread that Victor was no longer working at the general store in town. In fact, he had vacated the rented rooms and moved away from Adjuntas. Everyone assumed that he had moved back to Arecibo.

Camila was content to stay at home and help her mother with the domestic duties. Luisa saw her when she went on a *parranda* to the girl's house close to midnight one Saturday night. *Don* Abelardo and *Doña* Elena graciously opened their door and set out refreshments for the group, but when the party moved on to another house, Camila's family did not join them. Their wounds needed time to heal. Luisa continued to remember them in her prayers every night.

Things were understandably awkward between *Doña* Sinforosa and *Doña* Elena, especially since they did not live far from one another and had been neighbors for over ten years. *Doña* Elena felt hurt by how Victor had disrespected her family and ruined her daughter's reputation, not to mention how he had physically and emotionally mistreated her. *Doña* Sinforosa was embarrassed about her nephew's behavior but still felt a measure of familial loyalty. After all, he was her brother's son. It wasn't until after *Don* Eustaquio and *Doña* Sinforosa made a trip to see her brother in Arecibo, that things got patched up between the two neighbor women. Carlos was the one who came over to tell the Torres family the whole story.

He showed up on a Sunday after dinner, when the whole family was gathered at Ricardo and Chenta's home. Manuel de Jesús was there, as well, playing dominoes on the porch with Sebastián, Juan José and Moncho. Ricardo was sitting that game out, sipping on a refreshing beverage that was made from the bark of the *maví* tree, and enjoying the interaction between ten-month-old Monín and her seven-month-old nephew, Francisco. The babies, held on the laps of their mothers, seemed to have their own form of communication with one another. It was delightful to see how they were already best friends. Pilar and Juanito were on the porch with the older family members, but the rest of the children were playing either in the house or on the *batey*.

"*Buenas tardes*," Carlos greeted them.

"*Hola, Carlos. ¿Cómo estás? Súbete*," Chenta responded. *Hello, Carlos. How are you? Come on up.* Pilar went into the kitchen to pour a glass of water for their visitor.

"What's happening?" said Moncho.

"Well, I have news to share with all of you about Victor," said Carlos.

The domino players set their tiles face down on the small table and leaned back in their chairs, curious as to what they were about to hear. The others on the porch were also definitely interested, but Ricardo hurried to say, "Wait a minute. Is this gossip?"

"No, I wouldn't call it that. I mean, my mother actually asked me to come here and tell you all about it," the boy replied.

"And what about Victor's aunt and uncle?" Ricardo insisted.

"They are the ones that told my parents about Victor. Everything is all right between them and my parents again."

"Oh, good," sighed Chenta. "So, go on then."

"*Don* Eustaquio and *Doña* Sinforosa took a trip to Arecibo the other day. They left very early in the morning and came back home at night. They went to visit Victor's father, Simón. They thought they would see Victor there, but *Don* Simón said that he hadn't seen Victor since before Easter, when he moved from Arecibo to Adjuntas."

Carlos gratefully accepted the glass of water that Pilar brought him, took a few sips, and continued with his narrative. He told them that *Don* Simón had asked Victor to leave home the previous spring and find work elsewhere. Victor had become inappropriately involved with a young lady in Arecibo, and the girl's father had threatened Victor with legal action. In addition, the girl had older brothers who were not above inflicting physical punishment on Victor. And finally, Simón was losing business at his store because Victor worked there and many disapproving townspeople sided with the girl and her family. People who had been loyal clientele were starting to shop at other stores in that large town. So Victor had come to Adjuntas, and his loving aunt and uncle, unaware of what the young man was running from, had taken him in.

"I wonder where he went now," mused Luisa, aloud.

"*¿Dónde irá el buey que no are?*" said Sebastián. *Where will the ox go and not plow?* "Wherever he went to, the young ladies better watch out, because he is not going to change his ways."

"How sad," said Chenta. "He had so much potential. He had a good job in town, but with regards to relationships, he was going about it all wrong."

"*Está más perdido que un juey bizco,*" remarked Manuel de Jesús drily. *He's more lost than a cross-eyed crab.* Juan José snorted and Moncho snickered. Several of the others chuckled and made random comments, until Ricardo put a stop to it.

"That's enough. We need to focus on what is important here. I hope my sons will learn how not to act and my daughters will be alert to warning signs and not fall victim to men that lack good intentions."

Luisa and Manuel de Jesús's eyes met across the expanse of the porch, and he smiled at her. She gave him a small smile in return and then spoke to Carlos.

"So you said that your mother and *Doña* Sinforosa are friends again?"

"Yes," he replied. "*Doña* Sinforosa was so sorry about everything that had happened and she assured *Mami* that she had not known about Victor's history. If she had known, she would have warned my parents."

"That's good. I am glad," said Chenta and the others murmured their agreement.

"Well, we best fold up this domino game," said Sebastián. "It's starting to get dark."

"Yes, and I had better get back home," said Carlos. Ricardo and Chenta thanked him for his visit and sent their greetings to his family, and the boy departed.

Sebastián and the Collados also took their leave, and the rest of the family went inside. Only Luisa and Manuel de Jesús remained on the porch. They sat on the top step, their favorite spot. They could gaze up at the stars from there.

"You are being really quiet," Manuel de Jesús observed after they had sat in silence for a little while. "What are you thinking about?"

Luisa shrugged. "Oh, just about Camila and her family—how they suffered when she left with Victor, and how even though Victor is gone, the consequences of what happened remain. And yet, I do not think badly of Camila. She was young and innocent, and she was deceived by a man that she thought she knew."

Manuel de Jesús nodded. "What your father said—about hoping his daughters would not fall for men that did not have good intentions—I am glad that you did not fall for Victor. But," he added, taking her hand in both of his, "I hope you have fallen for me. You should not doubt that I have good intentions."

Luisa glanced up at him, but didn't answer. Instead, she rested her head against his shoulder.

The Christmas season proceeded with the usual activities and traditional foods. Luisa, Chenta, Pilar and Petra had spent a day making pasteles, and when they were surprised with a *parranda* that night, Pilar joked that the musicians had followed their noses to the Torres home. They had indeed eaten *pasteles* and *arroz con gandules* that night for dinner, and the tantalizing aroma lingered in the air. However, there weren't enough *pasteles* left over to serve the group of nine that came to their house that night—Leocadio and four of his children, Catalino and his brother, Andrés, and Eladio and Manuel de Jesús. So, instead, Luisa and Chenta served fruit, cheese and bread. It happened to be New Year's Eve, and it was a Friday, so Manuel de Jesús and Luisa were thrilled to have an extra night together that week, plus to be able to bring in the New Year together. It boded of good things to come for them. They danced in the cramped living room, shoulder to shoulder with Catalino and Dionicia, Eladio and Felita, Andrés and Pilar, and Moncho and Rosa María. Even Ricardo and Chenta joined in for a couple of dances.

Ricardo, Luisa, Pilar, Moncho and Juanito joined the *parranda* and they all went to *Don* Eustaquio and *Doña* Sinforosa's house next. As the midnight hour approached, *Don* Eustaquio brought out a bottle of *pitorro* and poured out several small glasses of the Puerto Rican moonshine to serve to the adults.

"Who wants some *lágrima de montaña?"* he offered, using another common term for the rum drink—tears of the mountain. Manuel de Jesús accepted one.

"You are not really going to drink that, are you?" a surprised Luisa asked.

"Why not?" answered Manuel de Jesús. "We are celebrating the new year. Do you want to taste some?"

"No, I do not! And I did not know that you drank."

"Well, I do not *drink*…as in regularly. I do not hang out in bars or get drunk. It is just one small glass, here with friends—to celebrate the end of this year and the start of the new one."

As if on cue, *Don* Eustaquio lifted his glass and toasted to the new year, wishing all present much health, happiness, and prosperity.

"And love!" added Catalino, wrapping his arm around Dionicia's waist.

"And love!" echoed the others, and they all downed their drinks.

Luisa pressed her lips together and said nothing.

"*A bailar*!" shouted Leocadio, and the musicians started up with a lively Christmas tune.

"Come on, let's dance," proposed Manuel de Jesús, getting up from his chair.

"No." Luisa stayed seated.

Manuel de Jesús looked down at her frowning face and said, "Okay, then, let's step out on the porch and talk." He held out his hand to Luisa, but she ignored it. She stood up and brushed her way past the dancing couples to the front door.

Out on the porch, she sat on one of the rocking chairs. Manuel took the other one and asked, pointedly, "What is wrong? Why are you angry with me?"

Luisa did not answer right away. She rocked the chair agitatedly and took a moment to formulate her thoughts while Manuel de Jesús waited patiently. Finally, she spoke.

"I thought that I knew you well. All this time I had no idea that you liked rum. When I think of Camila, and how Victor got drunk and…"

"Oh, so that's what it is? You are comparing me with Victor? Luisa, I am not Victor, and I don't like you comparing me to him." He was not shouting, but he had to speak loud enough to be heard over the music, conversation and laughter that spilled out of the open doorway and windows of the house. "No, I take that back. *Do* compare me to him! You said you thought that you knew me well. You *do* know me well! I am not some stranger that rode into town a few months ago. You have known me since we were children. When have you heard people say that I go to the bar or get drunk? When have I ever been disrespectful to you? Have I ever proposed that we do something improper, like run away together – as Victor did?"

Luisa glanced up at him briefly, and shook her head. The difference in behavior between the two men was like night and day, and she realized how unfair she had been to even consider them at all similar.

He continued, "That is probably the only drink I have had all year. I am not opposed to having a drink once in a while. Has your father never touched rum? Speaking of your father, he gave me his blessing to court you. Do you not trust his judgment? Chenta, Sebastián, Juan José…they all seem to approve of me. Do you think they are all wrong?"

Luisa was not prone to crying, but she was really fighting back the tears now. Unable to speak, she looked up at him with brimming eyes. Manuel de Jesús groaned, and standing, pulled Luisa to her feet. "I am sorry that I upset you," he said, placing his hands on her arms and drawing her gently to himself. She allowed the embrace and laid her cheek on his chest. "Do you forgive me?" he said against her hair. "Yes," she said softly, and added, "Do you forgive *me*?"

His arms were wrapped around her now, and he rested his chin on the top of her head. "There is nothing to forgive. You do not need to apologize for the things that worry you. Just always talk to me, Luisa, especially if you have doubts about me…about us. Tell me how you are feeling. I promise to listen and to try to ease your worries."

She tilted her head back to look at him, and he cupped her face with his hands and used his thumbs to tenderly wipe away two tears that had escaped her eyes. He kissed one wet cheek and then the other, and Luisa sighed contentedly.

"This time last year I could only imagine and dream about holding you close like this," he said, huskily. "Now I can't wait to see what will happen in the next twelve months. Happy New Year, Luisa."

"Happy New Year, Manuel."

Chapter 24

De Una Boda Sale Otra

Dionicia and Catalino's wedding day had finally arrived – February 26, 1870. The Maldonado household had been abuzz with activity for weeks, and the families all around them in Juan González had been eagerly anticipating the long-awaited event. The Maldonado property was set up to accommodate the large group of friends and family that were expected to attend the celebration.

It was a minor miracle that Aquilina had been able to sew Dionicia's beautiful cream-colored wedding dress, considering that she still had six children in the house, including an infant, and the sewing had been done during the shorter winter days. But her oldest daughter, Felita had helped immensely with the project, and Dionicia had also helped with the hemming and with sewing on the lace edging. The dress, though fancier than any that Dionicia had ever owned before, would still be practical enough to be used on future special occasions. In their mountain community it was unheard of to splurge on a gown that would be only worn once.

In the Torres home, Luisa had arisen early to grind and brew the coffee and to give Chenta a hand with preparing the breakfast. They needed to be at the church early; Ricardo was going to be standing alongside Catalino and Dionicia as one of their witnesses. This time the entire family was going to attend the wedding ceremony, and from there, they would go directly to Leocadio and Aquilina's house. The morning chores were hurriedly completed, and then the family dispersed into their bedrooms to put on their best clothes, which had been washed and ironed the day before. Luisa and Pilar helped five-year-old Boni and two-year-old Mina, into their pretty dresses, but Vicenta, almost eight years old, only needed help with her hair. Moncho got himself ready and then dressed Toño. He had learned that if he did it the other way around, the little boy would get his clothes dirty before they even left the house. Or more accurately, he would get himself all wet. That child was a human water dousing rod! He could find water in a flash and soak himself in it before anyone noticed what he was up to. Chenta got baby Monín dressed, and the one-year-old looked sweet in her new tunic. Mina and Monín, only a year apart, had the same straight, dark brown hair and large dark eyes. Their features were so similar that Luisa imagined they would look like twins as they grew older. Boni's mop of lighter colored curls was distinctive, but oh so hard to get untangled! Pilar was gentle and patient with her, so Boni would not let anyone else get the tangles out of her hair.

Finally, they were all ready and loaded into the wagon. Sebastián, Petra, Juan José and baby Francisco were riding in the wagon and team of horses that the Collados had purchased in recent weeks. Across the ravine, on the other hillside, a beaming Leocadio was loading his family into their wagon, with the bride occupying the seat of honor on the front bench between her parents. In the neighboring barrio of Vegas Abajo, a nervous Catalino was urging his parents and his siblings to hurry. He didn't want to be late for his own wedding! Canuto and Anastacia smiled indulgently at their son; they remembered how nervous and excited they were at their own wedding some twenty-seven years earlier.

Manuel de Jesús Maldonado was in a happy mood as he drove his brother's wagon and team of horses to the front of their house. Today he was going to see Luisa, and it was only Saturday! He would get to see her two days in a row. At the church he would sit with her, and at the celebration he would talk to her, eat with her, laugh with her, and dance with her. He was looking forward to all of it, but the thought of holding her in his arms while they danced had his heart racing. Whistling a cheery tune, he jumped down from the driver's seat and helped load his nieces and nephews into the wagon. Antonia and little Estevanía would be riding up front with Lucas. Manuel de Jesús and Eladio were riding their own horses to the wedding, though, as their brother's wagon was too crowded with his large family.

When he entered the church, Manuel de Jesús had to let his eyes adjust to the dim interior before he located the Torres family already seated in pews near the front. He greeted the family with a wave of his hand as he took the open spot next to Luisa.

"Te ves bella," he told her quietly. Luisa just smiled up at him. He told her that she looked beautiful almost every time that he saw her. True, she did take extra pains with her appearance when she knew that they were going to be together and

more so for a wedding, but nevertheless it pleased her to hear the warmth in his voice when he complimented her.

The wedding ceremony was simple but reverent. Luisa was proud that her father had been chosen as a witness; he was respected and well-liked in Juan González, and looked handsome in his brown suit. Seeing Dionicia standing next to Catalino, bringing to fruition their plans and pledges to one another, Luisa felt her eyes misting. Dionicia was young, two months shy of her twentieth birthday, but she was marrying the love of her life. They looked so good together—both slender and dark skinned, like a matching set of bronze figurines. Luisa glanced over at the bride's parents, Leocadio and Aquilina, and saw their faces glowing with love and pride for their beautiful daughter. Canuto and Anastacia looked equally happy to see their son at the altar, having his union with Dionicia blessed and anointed by *Padre* Irizarry.

That afternoon the party at Leocadio's was the best one that Luisa had ever remembered attending. The aroma of roasting pig tantalized everyone's nostrils as they arrived, and the planks on sawhorses that served as a food table were laden with all kinds of tasty dishes. The Torres family was contributing three round cornbread cakes that Luisa had baked the night before. She wanted to take something that would transport easily and that would not spoil while they were at the church.

Manuel de Jesús was already there when the Torres family arrived in Ricardo's wagon. The trip from the church to Leocadio's house in Juan González was much faster on a single horse than in a loaded wagon.

"I was going to ask you to ride with me on my horse, but I didn't quite dare suggest it," said Manuel de Jesús, when they were finally seated together, holding their plates of food. "I could see that you were wearing a new dress, and I didn't think you would want to get on a horse in it."

"I don't want to get on a horse, period," Luisa responded. "I fell off of one when I was a little girl, and I haven't been on one since."

"How is it that I did not know about that?" mused Manuel de Jesús. "We have a lot to learn about each other."

"It was so long ago. My mother was still alive."

"Are you afraid of horses?" he asked.

"Let's just say that I respect them," she said with a laugh. "Okay, yes, I guess I am a little afraid of them."

"I could help you get over that. My horse is gentle, and I would hold onto his bridle, if you want to try it," he offered.

"I don't know," she answered, shaking her head. "Sebastián was the one that got me on my father's old mare that time, and he has made several attempts to get me back on a horse over the years, but I think he has given up on that. I'm just not interested. I still remember the pain in my tailbone very vividly!"

"Speaking of Sebastián, here he comes," noted Manuel de Jesús.

Sebastián was indeed approaching them and they were also soon joined by Eladio, Felita, María de la Paz, Andrés, Pilar, and Rosa María, all carrying plates of food. They formed a circle with their chairs. Eladio set his food down on his chair and approached Luisa. Taking her plate from her, he handed it to Manuel de Jesús and then pulled Luisa up from her seat.

"I haven't had a chance to tell you how happy I am that you and Manuel are courting," he said. Grinning widely, he gave her a bear hug and a kiss on the cheek. Surprised and flustered, all Luisa could do was laugh.

"You are truly a prize. My brother is a lucky man," Eladio continued. "Manuel has a good heart, and we have all known for a long time that he is crazy about you, so I am glad that he finally took the next step. You two belong together."

The others in the group agreed with hoots and hollers, and a blushing Luisa took her seat again, and reclaimed her plate of food.

When the music started up, Catalino escorted his bride out to the middle of the *batey* and led her in their first dance together as husband and wife. Dionicia looked absolutely radiant, and she and Catalino could not take their eyes off of each other or wipe the smiles off of their faces. They were a joy to behold, and Luisa sincerely hoped that their marriage would be long and happy.

Soon the *batey* was full of couples moving to the rhythms of Caribbean music. Manuel de Jesús and Luisa were in the middle of it all, dancing to the lively beat of the bongo drums, *güiros* and *maracas*, and the melodic picking of the *cuatro*. Leocadio was an excellent *cuatro* player with a pleasant singing voice. He had gathered together the best musicians in Juan González to play at his daughter's wedding. One of them was Luisa's *Tío* Gregorio, who was skilled at playing the *bordonua*, and Luisa's *Tío* Canuto (the father of the groom) was a master *tiple* player. Luisa remembered that the three of them had played at Petra's wedding three years earlier. The music and dancing continued throughout the afternoon and into the evening, culminating with the *seis chorreao*, the fastest of the *jíbaro* dances.

"*Amigos*," announced Leocadio, in his booming voice, "this will be the musicians' last song of the night. Join us in ending the celebration of Dionicia and Catalino's wedding with a *seis chorreao. ¡A bailar, todos!*" Everybody dance!

Manuel de Jesús began dancing with his hands clasped behind his back, while Luisa had her left hand on her hip. With her right hand she swished the skirt of her dress back and forth. Their feet moved in little steps to the rapid rhythm, and their bodies swayed from side to side. Later, as the batey filled with dancing couples, they shifted their poses. Luisa now used both hands to hold and shake her skirt and fell into line with the others as they snaked around the *batey*. It was a musical finale to the hours-long celebration and when the last note was played, the dancers were exhausted but jubilant. Cheers and clapping arose to congratulate the bride and groom once again and to thank the musicians.

The wedding was over. Families gathered up their children and their empty pots and serving dishes and began taking their leave. Luisa found Dionicia and gave her a long hug.

"I am so happy for you," she spoke into Dionicia's ear. "May God bless you and my cousin with love, joy and good health for many years to come!"

Manuel de Jesús and Luisa managed a quick hug as the rest of her family was climbing into their wagon. He kissed her on the forehead and spoke softly. "I will see you tomorrow night."

By the time Ricardo pulled the wagon up to their own home, the little ones were all asleep and had to be carried inside and readied for bed. Pilar and Juanito were a big help with this task. Moncho went with Ricardo to unhitch and care for the horses.

As exhausted as she was from the day's activities, Luisa had a hard time falling asleep that night. She lay in bed listening to Pilar's even breathing and reflecting on the perfection of that day. The ceremony at the church had been well attended, and the celebration at Leocadio and Aquilina's house was truly the best ever. Leocadio always did like to celebrate in a big way, and by *jíbaro* standards, he had thrown a lavish party for his daughter and her groom. Because Leocadio was well-loved on their mountain, every family that Luisa personally knew had been there, plus some that she didn't know.

Realizing that she was too keyed up to sleep, Luisa closed her eyes and began her nightly chat with God. Starting with Dionicia and Catalino, Luisa prayed for everyone who she could think of that she had seen that day, until she finally drifted off.

The next afternoon, Luisa was cooking dinner when Manuel de Jesús arrived. She heard him ride up and heard him greeting her father and Sebastián, but she was at a critical point in the process of making the chicken and rice and could not leave the stove. The *sofrito*, salt and *achiote* were in the water, the chicken and capers had been added, and she was just waiting for the liquid to boil before adding the rice. Sebastián had told Manuel de Jesús that Luisa was in the kitchen, so he entered it quietly and came to stand behind her.

"Mmmm! That smells good!" he said. He put one hand on her waist as he leaned over her shoulder to get a look at what she was making. "*¿Arroz con pollo?* One of my favorites!" Just that slight touch on her waist and his close proximity was enough to make Luisa tingle.

"Everything is 'one of your favorites'," she answered, laughing. Adding the rice, she stirred the pot and waited for it to begin boiling again, then stirred it once more, covered it and lowered the flame. Dinner would be ready in half an hour. Anyone knew better than to lift the lid of a pot when rice was being cooked, though. That would ruin the rice and earn the culprit a stiff scolding. With no food to spare, the family would have to eat the rice even if it turned out undercooked or soggy, or they would have to go to bed hungry.

No worries with Luisa's rice, though—it was cooked to perfection, and slices of avocado and bread rounded out the meal. Sebastián and Manuel de Jesús were the only "extra" dinner guests, if they could even be called that. Juan José and Petra were usually there on Sundays, also, but having been at Leocadio's house all afternoon for the wedding just the day before, they had opted to have a quiet evening relaxing in their own cabin. After dinner, Manuel de Jesús asked if Luisa would accompany him on a walk. Luisa accepted, but couldn't help but think of the walks that she had had to endure with Victor for several weeks in a row. This was so different! She went happily with Manuel de Jesús, and once they were out of sight of the others on the porch, he reached for her hand. They ended up down at the creek, near the site of her garden plot and the area where she and Pilar washed clothes. Manuel de Jesús found some huge yagrumo leaves and arranged them on the bank for them to sit on.

"Luisa," he said, once again taking her hand in his. "I had such a good time at the wedding yesterday. It was so special to be with you for so many hours straight. I honestly did not want the day to end."

"I know. Me neither. It was the best party ever—the food, all the families together, the music, the dancing—"

"—and the prettiest girl by my side," he finished. "Dancing with you was, for me, the best part, and I didn't have to share you with anyone."

"Although I did dance with Sebastián and Eladio," said Luisa impishly.

"Our brothers don't count," declared Manuel de Jesús. "But Luisa, when I walked into the kitchen this afternoon and you were standing at the stove, cooking…the sight of you there…I don't know. I guess for a minute I imagined that we were married, and you were cooking dinner in our own cabin," he said, and chuckled a little self-consciously.

Luisa said nothing, but her heart skipped a beat. She dared lift her gaze to his.

His voice was serious now. "Luisa…will you will have me? As your husband?"

She nodded, too full of emotion to speak. He lifted her hand to his lips and kissed her fingers, never taking his eyes from hers. He found the courage to continue speaking.

"Maybe it was being at the wedding yesterday, too," he said. He looked at her lovely brown eyes with the flecks of green and at her sweet fresh mouth, and he plunged on. "You know that old saying, *'De una boda sale otra'*—although this usually refers to a couple who meet at a wedding and end up getting married—It got me thinking…I wish that we could start planning our wedding.

Luisa sucked in her breath. She saw the sincerity in his eyes and the hopefulness that was reflected in their depths, and she found her voice.

"What is holding us back from beginning to plan?"

Manuel de Jesús let out the breath that he had been holding and smiled wanly. "I don't have a house for you. We need to know where we would live."

"My father has an empty cabin on the property," Luisa said. "It is in between Sebastián's cabin and Petra's. It is actually bigger than either one of them, but it was damaged during the hurricane and still has not been repaired."

"I could work on it—repair it—if your father is agreeable. I have been saving up my money for a while now, but it would take me years to get enough money for a cabin and furnishings. I don't want to wait that long, Luisa."

"Me, neither," she whispered.

Manuel de Jesús caressed the side of her face and tilted her chin up gently. His lips met hers in a tender first kiss. Luisa's heart was pounding so hard that it all but drowned out the lilting melody of the *ruiseñor* singing in the treetops.

Chapter 25

The Cabin

Manuel de Jesús and Luisa spoke to Ricardo that very night. They waited until Chenta and Pilar went in to get the little ones ready for bed. Moncho and Juanito had gone inside, too, and Manuel de Jesús took that opportunity to speak up, saying that he and Luisa had something they wanted to discuss with him. Sebastián made a motion to get up, but Luisa said, "Stay. We want your opinion, also."

With lots of reassuring glances between him and Luisa, and her hand held firmly in his, Manuel de Jesús told them that he and Luisa wanted to begin preparing for their wedding day. Ricardo's mustache twitched, and his eyes took on a twinkle. Sebastián sat back in his chair and winked at Luisa. His look of approval warmed her heart.

"Well, *Mijo*, that is good news. I want my daughter to be happy, and I know that you love her and will be good to her. The bad news is that we will miss her when she gets married. I hope you plan to make a home here in Adjuntas."

"Actually, *Papá*," said Luisa, "I was wondering if we could fix up the vacant cabin on the farm and live in that one after we are married."

"I have been saving up money for a while now," said Manuel de Jesús, "and it is not enough to buy land or a house, but I could use it to cover the cost of repairing the cabin. Well, hopefully, that is…I am not sure how extensive the damages are."

"Well, let's plan on checking it out," said Ricardo. "Why don't you come earlier in the day next Sunday? The four of us can inspect the structure and see what it will take to fix it up."

Handshakes and hugs all around sealed the deal. Sebastián left to go to his cabin, and Ricardo headed inside. A jubilant Manuel de Jesús and Luisa took their favorite spot on the porch steps.

"I can't believe this is all falling into place," said Manuel de Jesús, with wonder in his voice.

"That is because it was meant to be," answered Luisa. "It all feels so right, doesn't it?"

"Yes. Like my brother said, we belong together. Now I cannot wait until next Sunday to see what condition the cabin is in. I hope it is fixable."

"Me, too. It would be so perfect to live close to Petra and Juan José, and Sebastián would be on the other side. It is what I always hoped for, to have a home of my own but to stay close to my family."

After a few more minutes of quiet conversation and star gazing, Manuel de Jesús stood to take his leave. Luisa walked with him to the edge of the batey, where he had tethered his horse. Untying the reins, he turned around and Luisa walked right into his arms. With a surprised chuckle, he wrapped his arms around her and held her close for several moments. It felt so good! Luisa tilted her head back, and Manuel de Jesús lowered his head for a sweet kiss—her second ever kiss on the lips. With a sigh, he released her and mounted his horse.

"Until next week, Luisa. Take care of yourself."

"You, too, Manuel. *Adiós*."

The week dragged by slowly for Luisa in her eagerness for the following Sunday to arrive. On Monday, she and Pilar had laundry to do, so that ate up a large chunk of the day. They took their time with the task and let Juanito, Vicenta, Bonifacia and Toño play in the creek while they worked. They stayed where the water was shallow, and the older ones watched the younger ones carefully. Toño was overjoyed at being allowed to go to the creek with the others, now that he was four years old. He loved the water and still had the little toy boat that he had gotten for Three Kings' Day when he was two.

"I remember when I used to get to play in the creek instead of sitting on a rock scrubbing dirty clothes," said Pilar, with a sigh.

"So do I," answered Luisa. "But that is part of growing up. You have to take on adult responsibilities and leave playing to the children." Seeing Pilar's grimace, she added, "Oh, it is not all bad. There are good things that come with growing up."

"Yes, like having a *novio*," teased Pilar.

"Yes, there is that." Luisa could not hide the happy smile. "What do you think about having Manuel de Jesús as a brother-in-law?"

"You know the answer to that," said Pilar. "Everybody likes him. He was already almost like family. Plus, he makes you happy. It will just be hard for me to get used to having you live somewhere else." With that last thought Pilar now looked a little downcast, so Luisa was quick to comment.

"Oh, but we may be moving into the vacant cabin near Petra's after we are married. That's not far at all, is it? We still see Petra at least twice a week even though she doesn't live in our house anymore. I will be close by if you need me, sister." Pilar looked up and flashed Luisa a dimpled smile.

Luisa continued speaking. "We are going to go inspect the cabin this coming Sunday to see if it is fixable. It has not been lived in for several years, and there was some damage done to it from the hurricane. So we will see." Her voice trailed off as her thoughts wandered with different possible scenarios of what they would discover during their inspection on Sunday.

"Luisa, do you remember the time that Manuel de Jesús came by to invite us to Estevanía's baptism party and he saw you with your dress all tucked up into your waistband?"

"*¡Ay, Dios mío!* That was so embarrassing!" Luisa rolled her eyes. The two girls shared a good laugh over the memory and continued on with other funny incidents that had happened in their family. It made the time sitting on the hard rocks washing clothes pass more pleasantly.

On Wednesday afternoon, Luisa and Pilar hiked up to Petra's cabin after their youngest siblings were put down for their afternoon naps. Petra and Luisa had replanted their gardens and had recently resumed their weekly gardening visits. When they arrived, little Francisco was napping, so Petra came out onto her front step with a finger to her lips. Luisa and Pilar sat on the steps to catch their breath and drink the water that Petra brought out to them. After they felt restored, they all moved to the garden plot to pull weeds and chat. They were close enough to the house to hear if Francisco woke up, but far enough away that they could talk without disturbing his nap. Their conversation revolved around Dionicia's wedding at first.

"What a great party that was!" exclaimed Petra. "There were so many people, and everyone was enjoying themselves. I have never seen Leocadio so happy."

"And why wouldn't he be happy?" said Luisa. "He loves to throw a big party, he was playing his *cuatro* along with the other musicians, and his daughter just got married."

"Dionicia and Catalino are going to live in a cabin on his property, right? So he will still have his daughter close by. Catalino is going to work on the farm, too. That all worked out perfectly."

"Tell her about you and Manuel de Jesús, Luisa," urged Pilar.

Petra was curious. "What about you and your handsome *novio*?"

"Only that we are ready to start making our own wedding plans," Luisa said with a happy laugh.

"And about the cabin," prodded Pilar.

"Yes, you know the vacant cabin up here near yours? Manuel says he wants to see if he can fix it up so that we can live in it."

"What, really?" Petra was ecstatic. "We will be close to each other? But did *Papá* approve this plan?"

"Yes, we are going to inspect it this Sunday to see what needs to be done to repair it—*Papá*, Sebastián, Manuel and I—we are all coming up here together to look at it."

"Well, Juan José and I will have to go, too, and give our opinion. Ha ha! Oh, but why wait until Sunday? Why don't we go now, after Francisco wakes up from his nap? It is just down the trail a short distance, practically just around the bend."

"I like that idea!" Pilar said. "I was not invited to come on Sunday, so I would love to look at it today."

And so it was that after the baby woke up from his nap and was fed, the three girls set out, with Francisco carried on Petra's back in the carrier that Chenta had made. Just as Petra said, the cabin was only a short walk away, out of sight from Petra's cabin, but reachable within minutes. They stood in the *batey* and studied the cabin in silence.

"It does need work, I can see that, but I have faith that it can be restored to a habitable condition," said Luisa, slowly. "It will take some time, though."

"Can we go inside?" asked Pilar.

"I think we had better not," said Petra. "It might not be safe. The floor could be rotted out."

Luisa sighed. "Well, we will see what the men say on Sunday. I guess we should not get our hopes up yet."

"It doesn't hurt to dream," said Petra.

"No, it doesn't hurt to dream." Luisa smiled, and stroked Francisco's head. "What do you think, my little coffee bean? Would you like your *Tía* Luisa to be your neighbor? You could come over to visit me every day. Wouldn't that be wonderful?"

Francisco gurgled in reply. "I think he likes that idea," said Petra.

The three girls turned back to Petra's cabin, and after enjoying a cup of *café con leche,* Luisa and Pilar left to hike back down to their home.

It was finally Sunday! Luisa was happy to hear the rooster crowing, and she eagerly left her bed and put on her old beige dress with the large pink flowers. It did not make sense to wear one of her better dresses for the outing that was planned for that day. But at the same time, she did not want to wear one of her everyday outfits that she wore for working around the house.

As often happened, especially on Sundays, Luisa was the first one up. After a quick trip to the outhouse, she washed her face and hands on the porch using a basin of water and a towel, then went back into her room to brush and braid her hair. She went about quietly so as to not disturb her sisters' slumber. There was no need to get them up, as the family was not going to be attending church that day.

The sound of the coffee grinder going round and round did serve as a wake-up call to Chenta and Ricardo, though, and it was not long before they emerged from their bedroom. Soon enough, the rest of the family got up, one by one, and Luisa and Chenta were busy serving breakfast. Chenta made a big pot of oatmeal. Later, as she stood washing the sticky bowls in the sink that hung just below the outside of the open kitchen window, Luisa recalled the time when they had eaten oatmeal the morning of the hurricane. Without being able to open the kitchen window and use the sink during the storm, she had had an even harder time washing those dishes. She remembered that she had used basins and towels on the kitchen table, and that it had been quite an ordeal.

Looking out the kitchen window at the lush vegetation that surrounded their home, she could appreciate how much growth there had been in the two-and-a-half years since the hurricane. Thoughts of the hurricane brought her mind back to the cabin that they were going to check out later on. Luisa hoped that the damages it had sustained were not too severe.

With the dishes done and the tiny kitchen tidied up, Luisa joined her father and Moncho on the porch. The morning was still fresh and cool and the doves were cooing, the sound oddly comforting.

"When do you think that Manuel de Jesús will get here?" Ricardo asked.

"He did not say exactly…just that he would come earlier, as you suggested. Are we walking up the trail to the cabin or riding in the wagon along the road?"

"We are riding in the wagon," her father answered. "Moncho will help me hitch up the horses after Manuel de Jesús gets here, right son?" Moncho nodded.

Pilar came from the chicken coop with a basket of eggs that she had collected. The hens, let loose by Pilar, came cackling and scuttling into the *batey* ahead of her, and Vicenta came trailing behind.

"I am training Vicenta to do chicken coop duty," said Pilar, with a grin. "When Luisa gets married and moves out, I will be too busy doing all of the things that she usually does around here."

Luisa laughed. "That is not going to be for some time yet, but it is good that you are thinking of the future."

"Listen!" exclaimed Moncho. "Someone is coming."

The sound of an approaching horse could indeed be heard, and soon Manuel de Jesús was alighting and tying the reins of his horse to a shrub at the edge of the *batey*. Luisa met him halfway and they had a quick hug before turning and walking back to the house with their arms around each other. Manuel de

Jesús shook hands with Ricardo and Moncho and greeted Luisa's sisters. Vicenta giggled shyly and ducked into the house, nearly colliding with Toño who was tearing out of the house to see his idol. Manuel de Jesús scooped the boy up in a big hug and spoke a few words quietly to him before setting him back down.

Pilar was waiting demurely and when she had the opportunity, asked, "*¿Te traigo café o agua?*" *Shall I bring you coffee or water?*

"Well, if you have coffee on hand, I will accept a cup. Thank you."

After a half hour of repose and cups of coffee for all of the adults, Ricardo and Moncho hitched up the horses to the wagon and drove to the front of the house. They rode off with Luisa seated up front between her father and her future husband. Moncho stayed on the porch, comforting little Toño, who was sad to see Manuel de Jesús leaving so soon.

All along the bumpy wagon ride, Manuel de Jesús held Luisa's hand in his, using his thumb to give her hand soft caresses, and every now and then one of them would give a little hand squeeze. Then they would look into each other's eyes and smile. It was all part of the language of love. Luisa's heart was full.

They stopped at Sebastián's place, and he climbed into the back of the wagon for the remainder of the ride to the vacant cabin. Upon arrival, Manuel de Jesús helped Luisa down and then pulled her into his arms. "This could be our future home!" he said, joyfully. He gave her a little squeeze before releasing her.

Sebastián had jumped down from the wagon bed and was already beginning to circle around the perimeter of the house, checking for any obvious damage to the pillars that held the house off of the ground. The others followed behind him. Luisa did not know much about carpentry or home construction, but as they walked along the right side of the house, she noted a flat area that might make a suitable garden plot. Looking up at the house, she saw a sink hanging askew beneath a window. *That must be the kitchen window,* she thought. *Perfect! I can look out over the garden as I am doing the dishes and check for vegetables that need picking.*

The foursome circled the house and Sebastián commented, "I do not see any damage to the pillars, but I would have to crawl under the house to check the ones that I cannot see from here."

He went up the porch steps, stopping on each one to bounce and stomp on it. Declaring them safe, he went on to inspect the porch. "Good so far," he said. Luisa was elated. She loved, loved, loved front porches. She could already picture herself seated there enjoying the evening coolness with Manuel de Jesús. Her stomach gave a happy lurch.

"The front door needs to be repaired," observed Ricardo.

"That's easy," responded Sebastián. They were all inside the house now, and Sebastián was looking up as he walked across the living room. "The roof is going to be a big project. The whole thing needs to be re---*ay!!*" His foot had gone right through a rotten floorboard, but Manuel de Jesús caught him before he fell over. Extracting his leg, Sebastián brushed off his pants and flexed his foot. "I am fine. But be careful. Luisa, maybe you should wait outside."

"No, please! I will be careful. I really want to see the whole house," she answered quickly, then added impishly, "I promise to look where I am walking instead of looking up towards the roof."

Sebastián grinned and gave her braid a little tug. "All right, little sister. We will all be cautious."

In the end, inspection of the two-bedroom house revealed that besides needing a new roof, some new floor joists, new floorboards in the living room, and repaired or replaced doors and window shutters, the walls also needed shoring up. Sebastián said that some angle braces would help with that problem. The outhouse also had to be rebuilt and a separate bathhouse constructed, since the hurricane had destroyed the old ones.

"We might be better off just tearing it all down and building a whole new cabin," remarked Ricardo.

Manuel de Jesús looked crestfallen. "How long would that take? I do not have that much money saved, either—not enough to build a cabin, unless it is a one room shack."

"What is your opinion, *Mija*?" All eyes turned to Luisa, and she responded, "I already love this place and can imagine us living here. If Sebastián thinks it can be fixed, and if there is enough money to do it, I would be happy to go with that plan."

"I was talking to Lucas about this place and how we were going to see if it could be made livable, and he offered the wood from a cabin that he is taking down on his land. Most of it is good, usable lumber," said Manuel de Jesús.

"That would be an advantage," said Ricardo, nodding. "That would stretch out your money. So are we going ahead with repairing instead of rebuilding, then?"

"Yes, but there is one thing that is on my mind," Luisa said. "I was thinking that Petra and Juan José might want to take this place for themselves since they already have a baby, and who knows if they will have more children. Their cabin only has one bedroom."

"I know the answer to that," said Sebastián. "Petra says she wants to stay in her cabin because she has already made it their home. She says she has *Papá's* permission to add on a bedroom and a front porch."

"That is true," affirmed Ricardo.

"Really?" asked Luisa. "I would like to have her see the house inside, first, though and make sure that she really does not want this one for herself. She said that she and Juan José would come over today and inspect it with us, but she probably did not know that we would be here this early. I think I will walk over and tell her that we are here."

"You do that while we start planning what to do first," said Sebastián. "I want to help with the repairs. I actually enjoy carpentry, and this will be my wedding present to you two."

"Thank you!" exclaimed both Manuel de Jesús and Luisa. The two young men shook hands and Luisa left to go see Petra.

That night, as they were seated alone on the porch steps of the Torres home, they talked excitedly about their future. Petra and Juan José, having been warned about the hole in the living room floor, toured the inside of the vacant dwelling and reiterated that they preferred to enlarge the cabin that they were in and stay there.

"After we are married and moved into our house, I can help Juan José make the improvements to his cabin," said Manuel de Jesús. "I will be experienced by then. I expect to learn a lot from Sebastián."

"When do you think you will start working on our place?" asked Luisa.

"Sebastián says that we need to start on the roof first, to make the house water tight, although I think we should start with the outhouse. We will need that for when we are working there all day long."

"That's true," said Luisa with a little laugh.

"During the week, after my work on the farm is done, I can start taking apart the cabin that Lucas offered. I am sure that Eladio will help me with that, too. Next Saturday we are not selling produce in town, but Sebastián and I will go in to get building supplies. If we get back early enough, we will start working that same afternoon."

"That's exciting. And then on Sunday you can tell me everything that you got done on Saturday."

"You know that it is going to take months to get the house repaired, don't you? I only have every other Saturday to work on it. God forgive me, but I think I am going to have to work on Sundays, too. I will still come to see you in the evenings."

Luisa was pensive. "Well, don't kill yourself working," she finally said. "I want you alive and well on our wedding day!"

Manuel de Jesús had been holding her hand, and now he raised it to his lips. "It will be hard to wait for that day, but at least we know that it is coming. The problem of where to live has been solved. That is progress. For now, though, I had better head home. It is a long ride and my workday on the farm begins right after sunrise."

Luisa walked with him to get his horse. In the seclusion of the evening shadows they shared a few lingering kisses and a long hug. Releasing her from their embrace, Manuel de Jesús tilted her head up for one more light kiss before mounting his horse.

In her bed that night, Luisa gave thanks to God for the events of the day, the generosity of her father in providing a future home for her and Manuel de Jesús, and for Sebastián's offer to help with the home repairs. She drifted off to sleep with happy thoughts of everything that she hoped the future would bring.

Chapter 26

Sebastián

During the month of March, much progress was made on the cabin. Manuel de Jesús and Eladio did take down the small cabin on Lucas's property in an area that Lucas wanted to use for farming. Lucas lent Manuel de Jesús his wagon and team to transport the used lumber to Ricardo's property on Friday afternoon. On Saturday, March 12th, Sebastián and Manuel de Jesús went into town to purchase materials, and that afternoon they began constructing the outhouse walls over the existing septic hole and wooden floor. On Sunday, they added the door and the zinc roof. One project was done!

Manuel de Jesús had brought a set of clothes to change into after using Sebastián's bathhouse. He did not want to go courting in filthy work clothes. He trotted his horse over to the Torres home along the wagon trail, but Sebastián took the shortcut on the footpath. The two young men arrived at Ricardo's house in time for Sunday dinner. Their hard work had produced a hearty appetite, and they savored every bit of the delicious dinner of *arroz con gandules* and *empanadillas.* Afterwards, too tired to play dominos, they sat on the front porch visiting with the rest of the family.

"We have had a good start," Sebastián reported. "But next weekend we will not be able to get much done, since we will be in town selling produce on Saturday. I want to wait to begin on the roof until we have two full days to work, so maybe we can repair window shutters in the meantime."

"When you do start on the roof," Juan José spoke up, "I would like to help."

"*Gracias,*" said Manuel de Jesús. "I appreciate your offer to help. When the time comes for you to begin working on expanding your cabin, you know that I will help you in return."

Later, as Luisa and Manuel de Jesús shared their short time alone on the porch steps, they tried to map out a tentative plan for their wedding.

"If all goes well, Sebastián thinks that we will be done with the roof by the end of this month," said Manuel de Jesús. "I think it will take all of April to finish the rest of the repairs. We will see how it goes."

"There is no furniture in the house," said Luisa. "When Petra and Juan José got married, their cabin already had most of what they needed. But the furniture in our cabin belonged to the family that used to live there, and they took it with them when they moved to Utuado."

Manuel de Jesús nodded. "Well, one thing at a time. I guess it is too soon to know when everything will be finished and ready for us, but I am hoping that by June we can get married."

They looked at each other then, the excitement of the thought causing their eyes to gleam. Manuel de Jesús stood, pulling Luisa up with him.

"Come on. I have to leave now, but walk with me to my horse."

There in the shadows, Manuel de Jesús pulled Luisa close. She marveled at how well she fit into his arms, with his chin resting on the top of her head. They stayed that way for several moments, then Manuel de Jesús pulled back and kissed her forehead, then her nose, then one cheek, and then teasingly, the other cheek. Finally his lips rested on hers. Pulling back again, he cupped her face in his hands and gazed into her luminous brown eyes.

"In a few more months," he said, his voice low and husky, "I won't have to stop kissing you. I won't have to say goodbye." He sighed, and gave her one last quick kiss before releasing her and mounting his horse. Luisa watched him until he was out of sight, and then walked slowly back to the house, her mind and heart filled with dreams of the future.

The following Saturday, was a farmer's market day for Eladio and Manuel de Jesús as well as for Sebastián and Juan José. Since the wagons and teams had to be taken back to their owners' properties, and with the long distance between the two farms, there would not be enough daylight hours left for Manuel de Jesús to ride back over and get any work done on the cabin. They decided that on the weekends when they went to town to sell produce, they would only work on the cabin on Sundays.

Sebastián was in his element the next day, showing Manuel de Jesús how to make and hang window shutters. Out of the four windows in the house, only one had to be completely remade; the shutters for the other three only needed repair or re-adjustment. Each of the two bedrooms had a window and there was one window in the living room, opening up to the porch. These window shutters were narrower, hinged on the sides and pulled together in the middle. They were closed and locked at night with a little piece of wood that swiveled onto a u-shaped bracket. The kitchen window was the one that had to be remade, and it was different from the other three.   It was all one piece, with hinges on only one side, like a door. Sebastián first cut four pieces of plank and nailed them together to form a frame that was smaller than the kitchen window opening. He then cut four lengths of board the height of the window opening and nailed them to the outside of the frame he had made. The four boards fitted closely together, with no gaps in between. Then he attached the metal hinges and he and Manuel de Jesús hung the shutter. From the inside of the kitchen, the window shutter swung out to the left. The lopsided sink was straightened out and reinforced so that it hung securely below the window. The adjustments and repairs to the other windows were easily made that afternoon. Another project was done, and Manuel de Jesús had learned new skills, thanks to Sebastián.

"Have you seen your brother when he is building some-thing?" Manuel de Jesús asked Luisa that night, as they sat on the porch steps. "He gets real enjoyment out of it."

"I noticed that when he was working on the bedroom that he and *Papá* added on for Pilar and me," Luisa responded. "He does such a good job, too."

The following weekend, the last one in the month of March, Sebastián, Manuel de Jesús and Juan José worked on the roof of the cabin both Saturday and Sunday. With two full days, they accomplished a lot, but were not totally done. They removed all of the old zinc panels, repaired and replaced roof rafters as needed, and began putting on the new zinc panels that Manuel de Jesús had purchased. Realizing that he had not bought enough new ones to cover the entire roof, they planned to reuse the better panels from the old roof on the back side of the house, where they would not be noticeable. It was not the rainy season yet, but they covered the unfinished portion of the roof with a tarp, nevertheless, in case it rained before they could finish the project.

The first Saturday of April was a farmer's market day, but on Sunday they made more progress on the roof. April 9th and 10th were good working days; the roof was finished, and the walls were shored up with angle braces. April 16th was another farmer's market day, and the next day was Easter Sunday, so no work was done on the cabin that weekend.

Luisa thought that a weekend off would be good for the men. They had been working so hard for over a month! She was also looking forward to attending church with the family and Manuel de Jesús. Familiar faces were all around them that morning in church—Rosa, Domingo and Micaela were seated in the pew in front of theirs, as were Juan José, Petra, baby Francisco and Sebastián. Dionicia and Catalino were right behind Luisa, sitting in the same pew as Leocadio, Aquilina and their large brood of children. On the other side of the aisle to their left were Lucas, Antonia and family. In the pew behind them sat Eladio, his mother, Moncerrate Sandoval, *Tío* Canuto, *Tía* Anastacia, Andrés and Margarita. A few rows behind them were *Tío* Gregorio, *Tía* Paula, the four children that were still living at home (including María de la Paz), three adult children and their spouses, and three grandchildren. Attending church on a holiday such as Easter was almost like going to a family reunion. Luisa felt like she was related to half of the people seated in the church that day. Indeed, if a person had the Torres surname and was living in Adjuntas, they probably were related to her!

As usual, *Padre* Irizarry delivered an excellent sermon centered on the sacrifice that Jesus had made by dying on the cross. Luisa's heart was touched to the core at the realization that God loved her so much that he gave up His only son as atonement for her sins. The deep sorrow felt about the horrific pain and death that Jesus endured served to heighten the overwhelming joy of His amazing resurrection from the dead. Easter Sunday, more than any other day of the year, filled Luisa with peace, hope and a sense of spiritual renewal.

Milling outside the church after the mass, meeting and greeting family and friends, Luisa couldn't help but remember that it was exactly one year since *Doña* Sinforosa had tapped her on the shoulder and introduced her to Victor Avilés. So much had happened in one year! Luisa spotted Camila outside the church with her parents, *Don* Abelardo and *Doña* Elena and her siblings, Carlos and Concepción. Camila saw her looking at her and waved. Luisa waved back, glad to see that Camila appeared happier and healthier than the last time that she had seen her.

Eventually, Ricardo and Chenta ushered their family to their wagon and made their way back to their home. While Sebastián always was with them on Sunday afternoons, and Petra, Juan José, and Francisco were usually also there, Rosa, Domingo and Micaela were seen less frequently. It was nice having almost all the family together. Only Sebastiana and her little family were missing, since they lived in Ponce.

Chenta had prepared *pollo guisado* (stewed chicken), white rice, and stewed pink beans. Luisa had harvested some early green beans, which she boiled, and had also made *domplines* (fried dumplings). It was a feast!

They were seated on the porch and around the *batey*, eating, talking and laughing. Sebastián, seated near Luisa and Manuel de Jesús in the shade of the mango tree, bit into a golden brown dumpling that had been fried to perfection. The outside was flaky and the inside was white and fluffy, and still steaming.

"Mmmm. We haven't had *domplines* in a long time. I am going to miss these when I am gone," he said casually.

"What do you mean by that?" asked Luisa. "Gone where?"

"I have decided to move to Ponce. I enjoy carpentry and want to try my hand at it in the city, where there are more job opportunities, and the pay is better."

"But what about the farm? You help *Papá*!"

"*Papá* has Juan José and Moncho...and eventually, hopefully Manuel de Jesús," he replied, glancing over at his future brother-in-law and smiling.

"Does *Papá* know about this?" Luisa asked faintly.

"Yes, of course. We have discussed it. I have been thinking about it for some time—since I helped build your bedroom, actually. Lately, working on the cabin repairs, I realized how much more I enjoy that type of work than farming. *Papá* agrees that I should go try it."

"When do you plan to move?" Manuel de Jesús asked.

"Not until I am done with your cabin repairs," Sebastián assured them. "Or at least, not until I reach a point where I think that you can finish the work without me."

Luisa had lost her appetite. Sebastián noted the sad look in her eyes and spoke kindly to her. "Look, you have this great guy right here who is going to be by your side. You will be making a new life together. I am a lot older than you. I want to see more than just Adjuntas. Maybe in Ponce, besides finding work in something that interests me, I will also meet my future partner in life."

Luisa smiled wanly. "I know. I think it will be a good move for you. But…are you going to be here for my wedding?"

"I will definitely come back to Adjuntas to be present when you two stand before the priest," he promised.

Luisa's eyes filled with tears, but she blinked them away. She didn't want Sebastián to feel bad about leaving. He had every right to seek out a better life for himself. The life of a farm laborer was harsh and often unprofitable. Sebastián was still young and strong. He could carve out a better existence in Ponce. "I will hold you to that promise," she now said to her brother. "I want to dance with you at my wedding!"

"Ha! If I can pry you away from Manuel de Jesús, you mean!" teased Sebastián.

Manuel de Jesús waggled his eyebrows while giving Luisa a sidelong look, and she laughed despite herself.

That night, during her evening prayer time with God, Luisa thanked Him for the wonderful day that she had enjoyed, first being spiritually renewed and uplifted in church, and then surrounded at her family home by the people that she most loved. She prayed a special prayer for Sebastián that God would bless and protect him in the adventures that awaited him in Ponce.

She hoped that besides finding work as a carpenter, he would also meet someone special and fall in love. Of course, that brought her thoughts back to Manuel de Jesús. He had stayed to help clean up after her adult siblings had gone home. When they finally sat down on the porch steps for their private time together, the *coquís* were lustily calling out their names, "*Coquí, coquí.*" The doves were cooing gently, the melodic sounds blending together in an audible expression of peace. Those last moments shared together on Sunday nights were so sweet and special to Luisa and Manuel de Jesús. Luisa snuggled under the light blanket and drifted off to sleep savoring the memory of their good night kiss.

Chapter 27

Tragedy

The following Saturday, Manuel de Jesús stopped by Ricardo's house before going up to the cabin to work with Sebastián. Luisa was surprised to see him, and a little embarrassed. She had not been expecting him and was dressed in one of her everyday housework dresses. If Manuel de Jesús noticed, he did not say anything. Ricardo and Moncho had already left to work on the farm, but the remaining family members came out to the porch to greet him, with Pilar holding fourteen-month-old Monín on her hip. Manuel de Jesús got straight to the point of his impromptu visit.

"My cousin Leocadio is sick in bed. It is some kind of stomach ailment, and Aquilina is worried because she has never seen him so sick. If he is not better by Monday, she plans to send Catalino to town for the doctor."

"*¡Ay, Dios mío!*" exclaimed Chenta. "Is there anything that we can do? Do you think that I should go help Aquilina?"

"*Doña* Tiburcia is there, and she has already been preparing him teas. Aquilina does not leave his side, so Felita and Dionicia are taking care of the younger children and cooking the meals." Manuel de Jesús shook his head sadly. "I went to see him last night. It is so strange to see the big guy lying helpless in a bed."

Chenta's eyes clouded over with worry. "I think I will bake some bread for the family and have Ricardo take me over there this afternoon, anyway. I will take some of my herbs, too, in case Aquilina and *Doña* Tiburcia are low on their supplies."

Manuel de Jesús's eyes sought out Luisa's. "See you tomorrow night?" She nodded, and managed a small smile. She was worried about Leocadio, too.

After Manuel de Jesús left, Chenta began the process of baking the promised bread. She had kneaded the dough the night before and had set it to rise, intending to bake for her own family this morning. They would have to do without bread today, but that was all right. Meanwhile, Luisa, Pilar and Juanito went up the mountain trail to fetch water. Eight-year-old Vicenta was charged with watching her four younger siblings while her mother was busy in the kitchen for the short while that it took her to get the oven hot and the bread dough ready.

Despite the freshness and coolness of the morning, the climb uphill to get water wore the girls out, although it did not seem to faze Juanito. The boy was gifted with boundless energy. He gallantly offered to fill all the water containers while the girls rested on *yagrumo* leaves, and they gratefully accepted. Luisa watched Juanito as he carefully filled each jug and pail with clear, cold spring water, ensuring that not a single twig or leaf entered one of the containers. *He's not a little boy anymore,* she thought.

He is getting big. It won't be long before Papá recruits him to work on the farm.

"Do you think that Juanito is going to have to start working with *Papá* and Moncho on the farm soon?" asked Pilar.

"I was just thinking about that!" exclaimed Luisa, looking at Pilar in surprise. "That is funny that we were both thinking the same thing at the same time!" The girls shared a laugh. "He might," Luisa said, "but I hope he doesn't. Juanito is our little man of the house right now, and he is useful for a lot of things. Remember how he ran to Leocadio's house to tell them that Chenta needed *Doña* Tiburcia that time—when she was going to give birth to Mina? Neither you nor I could have run that fast, plus I had to stay with Chenta, and you had to take care of the younger children."

The girls fell silent again, each lost in her own thoughts, until Pilar spoke softly. "I hope that Leocadio gets better soon."

Luisa nodded. "That is just what I was thinking, too."

Once back at the house, Luisa took over the kitchen, enjoying the fragrance of the baking bread while she set pink beans to boil in a pot. She had left the dry beans soaking overnight to shorten the time needed to cook them. While the beans boiled, she chopped fresh onions from her garden, cut up some tomatoes and new potatoes, minced a few cloves of garlic and several *recao* leaves, and diced a large piece of ham. She wished that she had some squash to add to the beans, too, but those plants were just beginning to flower. Luisa stewed all of these ingredients with the softened beans and added Chenta's savory *sofrito* and prepared *achiote.* The result was a flavorful and nutritious accompaniment to the white rice that Luisa was going to make. The time working alone in the kitchen gave Luisa the opportunity to lose herself in her thoughts and to pray for Leocadio.

Chenta came in and checked on her bread. Declaring it ready, she pulled the loaves from the oven. The aroma was mouth watering! Luisa knew that Aquilina and the children would enjoy the bread. Pilar had been entertaining Mina and Monín in the living room and had a hard time keeping them out of the kitchen. They began clamoring for *pan* and when Pilar told them that they couldn't have any because it was for the Maldonado family, they began to wail.

"They do not understand why they cannot have any bread," Luisa told Pilar. "Here, let them each have a cracker to hold them over until the food is ready. You know the old saying, *'A falta de pan se come galletas.'" When you don't have bread you eat crackers.*

With the beans stewing in one *caldero,* Luisa started the white rice in another one, and then began slicing ripe plantains. Sweet fried plantains, sprinkled with a little salt, would make a tasty side dish to the rice and beans. The plantain harvest was in full swing, and the family had been eating either green or ripe plantains every day for the past two weeks. Sometimes they made *tostones* out of the green plantains or cooked slices of them in their soup or stew, but Luisa's favorite way to prepare them was by frying slices of ripe plantains.

Ricardo and Moncho came home for the midday meal, and when Ricardo heard the news about Leocadio, he told Moncho that they would not be working on the farm that afternoon. Instead, he hitched up the team of horses after lunch and drove to Leocadio's house with Chenta. She had prepared a basket with the still-warm loaves of bread wrapped in a towel and an assortment of herbs and spices that were commonly used to alleviate stomach ailments. Using squares of the heavy brown paper saved from general store purchases, Chenta had made packets containing anise, ginger, cloves, and cinnamon. She had a clever way of folding the paper so that the little packets held the seeds inside, and nothing spilled out.

Luisa settled Toño, Mina and Monín down for their afternoon nap, and sent Juanito, Vicenta and Bonifacia out to play in the creek under Pilar's supervision. Time dragged as she anxiously awaited to hear more about Leocadio's condition. Washing the dishes and cleaning up the kitchen took up some of the time, but Luisa eventually found herself able to relax on the shady front porch. For several minutes, she watched the chickens strutting around the *batey,* pecking and clucking contentedly. The cat came out from under the house, stretched, and then ambled up the porch steps to rub against Luisa's leg. She reached down a hand to pet the kitty, remembering the time that Boni had been under the house with the cat while the family searched frantically for the little girl. That was the day that the hurricane had hit. Had it really been almost three years since the hurricane? *So much has happened since then,* she thought. *Both good things and bad things…and what will tomorrow or the next day bring? Anything can happen at any time – something wonderful, or a tragedy.*

Luisa did not like the way her thoughts were going, so she went in to get the mending basket. If she kept her hands busy, maybe her mind would be less so.

It was close to suppertime when Chenta and Ricardo returned from their visit to the Maldonado family's home. Luisa was almost finished preparing the evening meal; she had concocted soup out of the leftover rice and beans from their midday meal by adding them to a pot of broth. She had fresh green beans that had just been picked the day before, when she and Petra had worked in Luisa's garden, and she put those in the soup, as well. Peeled green plantains were sliced and sitting in a bowl of salted water, waiting to be drained and patted dry before being fried twice to make *tostones*.

Leaving the soup simmering over a low flame, Luisa went out the kitchen door to the porch as soon as she heard the wagon returning. Moncho helped Chenta down and Ricardo drove around to the back to unhitch the horses.

"*Vete ayuda a tu papá,*" said Chenta, and Moncho reluctantly followed the wagon to help his father, as he had been instructed to do. He really wanted to know how the visit to the Maldonados had gone, but he obeyed. He might find out about Leocadio from his father, but if Ricardo was in one of his silent moods, Moncho would have to wait till later to find out.

Chenta went wearily into her room to change into her housedress, and the others had to wait until she emerged and joined them on the porch. Luisa was the one who asked the question.

"How is Leocadio?"

"Very sick," responded Chenta, as she lowered herself into a chair. When we got there, we found out that they had decided to send Catalino to town to get the doctor instead of waiting until Monday. But before we left to come home, Catalino was back with the news that the doctor was unavailable. I guess he was out making house calls and was not expected back in his office all day."

"Oh," said Luisa, somberly. "Did you go into Leocadio's room to see him?"

"Yes, I did. He was not able to talk to me, though. He has had a fever for several days and has not been able to eat or drink anything except to take a few sips of tea. I don't think I have ever seen *Compai* Leocadio quiet—him with that loud voice and big laugh, always so happy."

"Is Aquilina all right? She is not sick, too, is she?" asked Luisa.

"No, no one else is sick, but they are very worried."

"Of course," murmured Luisa. She looked around at her siblings, all sitting quietly. Their subdued behavior told her that they were also concerned. She forced a wobbly smile. "Supper is almost ready. Let me serve some soup for the little ones so that it can cool a bit before they eat, and then I will get started making the *tostones*."

On Sunday, Sebastián and Manuel de Jesús arrived during the afternoon, somewhat earlier than usual. They reported that they had accomplished a lot during their two days of work and had reached a stopping point.

"The floor joists are done, and I showed Manuel de Jesús how to replace the rotted floorboards. There are several in the living room that still need to be replaced and a few in one of the bedrooms," said Sebastián. "I am really satisfied with the progress we have made."

"Of course, when the repairs to the cabin are finished, we will still need a bath house and furniture," added Manuel de Jesús.

"But it is coming along," said Ricardo, nodding his head. "That is good work."

Luisa prepared a simple supper of pieces of fried pork served with boiled green plantains and green beans. No one complained. The food was tasty and filling.

Afterwards, Pilar washed the dishes and Chenta cleaned the stove and table, so that Luisa could have more time to visit with Manuel de Jesús. The men debated on whether or not to play a game of dominoes. They decided that none of them were really in the mood for a game. Instead, they sat around talking, and Ricardo told how shocked he had been to see Leocadio looking so weak on Saturday afternoon. Manuel de Jesús said that he had stopped by Leocadio's house Saturday night on his way home and that there had been no change in Leocadio's condition.

"At least he isn't worse, then," said Sebastián.

The sun had gone down and the night critters had begun producing their sounds. It started with one lone *coquí* at dusk that was soon joined by others as the darkness around them grew. The doves liked to roost in a tree near the house; their cooing seemed almost like a lullaby to Luisa.

Chenta was inside, readying the little ones for bed with Pilar's help, and the others were out on the porch. During a lull in the conversation, a distinctly lower-sounding coo came from the doves.

"*¡Escucha!*" said Ricardo. *Listen!* "Did you hear that?"

"Hear what?" asked Moncho.

"Those doves…listen, there they go again!" Ricardo's brow furrowed as he spoke. "My mother used to say that when doves changed their call to a low, sad one, it was not a good omen. Something bad is going to happen."

They all looked at each other, but no one said anything. No one dared voice their thoughts aloud. Luisa did not know what to think or believe. Was it superstition? Or was it really an omen? How could a bird know that something bad was going to happen?

Eventually, they shook off the gloom and began talking about other things. The men discussed the work on the farm for the next week. It was time to plant *ñame* and to harvest oranges, grapefruit, soursop, guava, and papayas. The coming Saturday would be a farmer's market day, and they all hoped to have good sales from their produce.

Luisa did not find this conversation in the least bit boring. She was happy that their farm was producing abundant crops again, as it meant that Sebastián would come home with more household items that he could purchase with the money from the sale of their produce. They were running low on salt, sugar, rice, beans, and other staples. Maybe she could go to town with them on Saturday to buy fabric for new dresses. She would discuss this with Chenta and see if Pilar could be spared to go into town with her. Or perhaps Chenta would like to go into town with Pilar, and Luisa could stay home cooking and caring for the children. Chenta did not get to go to town to shop very often, and maybe she would enjoy picking out the fabric this time and getting whatever else was needed for the family.

From the other mountainside, the sudden sound of someone hooting and calling echoed across the ravine. All conversation halted. Ricardo and Sebastián jumped up from their seats. Sebastián strode out to the edge of the *batey* and answered the call. Turning back to the house with a grim expression on his face, he announced that he was going to go down to the meeting place in the ravine.

"I will go with you," said Manuel de Jesús. Luisa went inside to tell Chenta. Flares would be needed to light the way, and Chenta knew how to make them better than anyone else.

Waiting to hear and know what had happened was excruciating. With the younger children already in their beds, the rest of the family sat on the porch, talking quietly about anything and everything except about what news Sebastián and Manuel de Jesús might learn at their rendezvous in the ravine. When the young men returned, it was Manuel de Jesús who choked out, "My cousin…Leocadio…is dead." Luisa went straight into his arms, sobbing.

"How can that be?" asked Luisa, her head buried in Manuel de Jesús's chest and her voice muffled. It was incomprehensible that their big, jovial neighbor, who was like an uncle to the Torres children, was gone. Luisa could hear his booming voice and see his laughing face. She could picture him playing his *cuatro* and singing.

He was loved by so many people in Juan González and throughout other parts of Adjuntas. He and Ricardo had been *compadres*, since Ricardo was the godfather of Leocadio's oldest daughter, Felita. The Torres family and the Maldonado family had been very close, but Leocadio had been Manuel de Jesús's blood relative. The pain that he was experiencing at the loss of Leocadio was at least as great as Luisa's, if not greater. She wrapped her arms around Manuel de Jesús's waist and hugged him tight. Behind her she could hear Chenta and Pilar crying and the others sniffling and whimpering.

In the tree at the edge of the *batey*, the doves, having delivered their ominous warning, went back to their normal sounding coos.

Chapter 28

Broken Hearts

The next week was an emotional blur. Sunday night, after receiving the news that Leocadio had passed away, Ricardo hitched up the wagon and he, Chenta and Sebastián rode to the Maldonado farm. Manuel de Jesús rode there on his own horse. Luisa would have liked to go with them, but she did not feel that it was fair to leave Pilar in charge of seven younger siblings for so many hours at night, even though the children would hopefully be sleeping the entire time. Ricardo said that they would probably come home from the wake some time after midnight, but there was a chance that they would stay there until daylight. If that was the case, Pilar would feel overwhelmed trying to cook breakfast for everyone and tend to Mina and Monín, who were still so young and dependent.

As it turned out, Ricardo, Chenta and Sebastián did not return until after daybreak. Ricardo and Chenta were so exhausted that they went straight to their room to sleep for a few hours. Moncho took care of unhitching the horses from the wagon.

Sebastián was going to hike up to his own cabin to sleep, but Luisa convinced him to lay down on her bed since both she and Pilar were already up. Manuel de Jesús had stayed at the wake until after midnight and then had ridden on to the cabin that he shared with Eladio. The road between the two Maldonado farms was in pretty good condition, and his horse knew the way even in the dark.

The burial was that afternoon, and the entire Torres family attended. It was a lot of work to get everyone fed, bathed, and dressed on time, but it was worth it so that no one had to stay home with the little ones and miss the funeral. There was a huge turnout for Leocadio's funeral; the man was so well loved and respected in their town. *Padre* Irizarry officiated. The family was grateful to the parish priest because although Catalino had not been successful in getting the doctor to see Leocadio, he had stopped by the church on the way home to notify *Padre* Irizarry of Leocadio's grave illness. The kind priest had gone to see Leocadio on Sunday immediately after the mass and had conducted the holy sacrament of final rites to the ailing man. This gave the grieving family some measure of comfort.

When Luisa approached Dionicia to offer her condolences on her father's passing, the younger girl dissolved into tears. Luisa held her for a long time, her own tears falling freely. As the casket was lowered into the ground, Dionicia's brother José could be seen a short distance away, crouching down and sobbing quietly. Moncho was bent at his side, head bowed and with one hand on José's shoulder.

After the burial, people made their way up the mountain to attend the first night of the Novena at the Maldonado home, many of them bringing food to contribute to the communal meal. Just as she had done for Mama Sebia's Novena, Canuto's wife, Anastacia Sáez, led the participants in the praying of the rosary. She was an experienced *novenaria* and knew the litany by heart.

By the time Ricardo pulled the wagon into their own yard late Monday night, the little ones had fallen asleep and had to be carried into the house. Luisa helped Chenta get them undressed and into bed, going through all of the motions mechanically. When she finally was in her own nightgown and had slipped into bed beside Pilar, Luisa was too emotionally exhausted to either pray or sleep. She lay there on her back with her tears trickling down the sides of her face, wetting her hair. Her heart broke for Leocadio's family. He and Aquilina had been married over twenty-five years and had seven children. Little Rosendo was just a six-month-old baby! It was at his baptism party that Manuel de Jesús had declared his feelings to Luisa. She remembered how jovial Leocadio had been that day, joking that he hoped that Rosendo was their last baby. Well, he certainly was! Hot tears now streamed out of Luisa's eyes and rolled into her ears. She swiped at them angrily with her hands. She rolled onto her side and closed her eyes to try to stop the flow. Then she thought of Dionicia, a bride of only two months who should be glowing with newlywed happiness but instead was an emotional mess, grieving the death of her loving father. Now Luisa's pillow was wet, and she had to blow her nose. Creeping out of the bed into the adjoining room she searched in her dresser drawer until she found a handkerchief and tiptoed back with it to her room. She blew her nose as quietly as she could. Pilar was sleeping through all of this, but the poor dear had cried plenty throughout this sad event. She needed her rest.

Back in bed, Luisa tried to pray, but she just couldn't. She didn't have any words to say to God except to ask Him why. *Why did this have to happen to Aquilina and the children? Why Leocadio? He was a decent man, a devoted husband, and a wonderful father. He loved everyone, and everyone loved him. What is to become of Aquilina and her family without Leocadio's support? Who will run the farm? Baby Rosendo will never know his father!* The tears streamed out again, and Luisa realized that she had stopped praying and had been letting her thoughts rant.

Eventually, she fell into a restless sleep. In the morning, her eyes were swollen, and her body felt heavy. She went outside to use the outhouse, washed her face and hands listlessly, and plodded barefoot into the kitchen, still in her nightgown. She was standing there, trying to think of what she was supposed to do when Chenta walked in. She took one look at Luisa and stopped in her tracks.

"What's wrong?" Chenta asked. "You look lost. Are you awake, or are you walking in your sleep?"

"I am awake," mumbled Luisa. But she didn't smile and she was still standing there without moving.

Chenta looked at her askance. "Luisa, go get dressed. And brush your hair, please."

Luisa complied, walking past Chenta without so much as looking at her. Chenta watched her go with a perplexed look on her face. *Luisa is definitely not herself today,* she thought. *She is behaving strangely.*

Throughout the week, others in the family noticed the change in Luisa, but if they commented among themselves, Luisa did not hear. She attended every single night of the Novena with her father. Some nights the whole family went, other times

Chenta or Pilar stayed home with the five youngest children. Manuel de Jesús attended every night of the Novena as well. He sat next to Luisa, but they both refrained from any public display of affection, not even hand-holding. It didn't seem appropriate under the circumstances. The nine nights of rosaries extended through the weekend following Leocadio's death, so Manuel de Jesús did not visit Luisa at her house on Sunday night as he normally did.

The weekdays following the last night of the Novena passed with Luisa performing her household duties woodenly. She was not rude or mean to anyone, but she seemed to have lost her usual smiling, pleasant personality.

Lucas and Anastacia, Ricardo and Chenta, and others in the community visited Aquilina every few days to see how they could be of help. With the support of family and friends, the grieving Maldonado family was figuring out how to go on living without Leocadio. Thankfully, Catalino had been there long enough to know how Leocadio liked to run his farm, and he took over the supervision of the workers, with thirteen-year-old José as his apprentice. Felita was twenty-four and unmarried; she could run the household as well as her mother. When grief overtook Aquilina, and she had days that she was unable to get out of bed, Felita took over. Dionicia lived with Catalino in a small cabin on the property, so she also came to the main house every day and helped care for her youngest three siblings. The family was hobbling along. They were going to make it; it just was going to take time.

Luisa wasn't so sure about herself. She couldn't seem to snap out of her sullen mood. She went through the motions of cooking, gardening and doing laundry that week, but her heart wasn't in any of it. She didn't know what was wrong; she felt like crying all the time, although she wouldn't allow herself to give in to that emotion. She also had a difficult time concentrating on even the smallest things. On Wednesday, Pilar had asked Luisa if they were going to go to Petra's house to work in her garden as usual.

"Oh, is today Wednesday?" Luisa responded, sounding confused. "I guess that I lost track of the days. No, I don't think we will go today."

Pilar did not press the issue, but when Petra came on Friday, she commented on it.

"What happened on Wednesday? I was waiting all afternoon for you to come up to my cabin. Was one of you sick?"

"No…not sick, exactly," said Pilar, cautiously. Petra was looking at her, so Pilar let her eyes slide over to Luisa, who appeared lost in her own world. Petra and Pilar made eye contact again, and Petra nodded knowingly.

"Well," she said brightly. "Let's go down to your garden and see if I can manage to help you out a little bit with Francisco on my back. He is getting heavier every day."

"We can take turns holding him while the other two pull weeds," suggested Pilar.

"What do you say, Luisa?" Petra asked. "Do you want to hold your little coffee bean first, while Pilar and I work on one of the garden rows?"

Luisa's eyes seemed to come alive for a split second, and indeed, when they reached the garden, she extracted Francisco from Petra's infant carrier. Holding the baby close, she buried her face in his sweet smelling neck. Francisco squealed in delight at first, but after a little bit he protested. He arched backwards and reached up his little hands to pat her face. Then, leaning forward, he tried to give her a slobbery open mouthed kiss, which is all that he knew how to do yet. Luisa laughed, but it came out sounding like a sob. Petra and Pilar looked at her in surprise, and then at each other. Without saying a word, they knelt down to begin pulling weeds. The three girls each took a turn holding Francisco, but their time in the garden was much shorter than usual, and noticeably awkward, lacking the usual chatter and laughter.

On Sunday, two weeks after Leocadio's death, Manuel came courting in the late afternoon. Luisa did not come out to meet him while he tied his horse's reigns, and she was quiet and serious all through supper. She insisted on doing the dishes, leaving Manuel de Jesús on the porch with the others. When she was finally done in the kitchen and had no further excuse, she joined him on the porch. The family sat around talking and being entertained by Juanito and his top. He had learned several new tricks with it and took pleasure in showing off his talent. Moncho leaned against the porch railing, offering Juanito encouragement and advice. Toño was perched on Manuel de Jesús's knee, sucking his thumb.

"Take your thumb out of your mouth," Chenta reprimanded the boy. "*Ya tú estás grande.*" *You are already big.* Toño complied reluctantly, and Manuel de Jesús gave him an approving one-armed hug.

Ricardo had Mina on his lap and was jiggling his leg absentmindedly as he talked with Sebastián and Juan José about the farm work that they needed to do the next day. Chenta was holding Monín. Both tots were getting sleepy. Pilar sat on the steps with Bonifacia, patiently combing out the tangles from Boni's curly hair in preparation for the girl's bedtime; Boni still wouldn't let anyone else perform that task. Pilar's gentle combing of Boni's hair was making the little girl drowsy. Vicenta sat next to Petra, making funny faces at baby Francisco to make him laugh.

Luisa saw and heard all of the activity and conversation around her, but she did not contribute to it. It all felt almost like too much. She felt like getting up and walking away, maybe going for a walk, but couldn't figure out how to do that without calling attention to herself or being rude. So she sat there in silence.

When Sebastián spoke, though, he caught Luisa's attention. "I have decided to leave next weekend. I am moving to Ponce."

"So soon?" asked Manuel de Jesús.

"Yes," Sebastián replied. "I know that we are not finished with the repairs to the cabin, yet, but I am confident that you can take it from here."

Manuel de Jesús nodded, and Juan José spoke up. "I will help you finish."

Sebastián continued. "After Leocadio died, I just got to thinking. Life is short. I should not put off what I want to do any longer. Tomorrow is not promised to anyone, and you know the saying—*'Para nadar hay que tirarse al agua.'*—to swim you have to jump in the water. If I want to earn a living doing carpentry, I need to go to the city."

"How are you going to get there?" asked Moncho.

"Juan José has offered to take me in his wagon," answered Sebastián. "We will leave early on Saturday and get to Sebastiana and Francisco's house by evening. Juan José will spend the night and leave early on Sunday to come back home."

"Are you going, too, Petra?" asked Pilar from her seat on the porch steps.

"No," she answered. "I considered going, but it is a long day of travelling there and then back the next day with the baby, with only one night to rest in between. Juan José says that he will take us for a longer visit another time."

"I hope that they can come visit us soon," Pilar said, wistfully. "We have not seen them since the Christmas before last. Sebastiana's little daughter, Pilar, is the same age as Rosa's Micaela. She must be so big, walking and maybe even saying a few words, like Micaela."

"Yes, it would be nice to see the whole family," said Chenta, sighing as she stood up with Monín. "I need to get these little ones off to bed. Pilar, if you are done with Boni's hair, can you bring Mina in and help me with her?"

When the two toddlers were settled into their beds, Pilar came back out for Toño, but the boy insisted that Manuel de Jesús be the one to tuck him in.

"This is our cue to leave," Juan José said to Petra. He stood up and reached down to take Francisco from her.

"Same with me," said Sebastián, standing up and stretching. He grinned at a sudden thought. "This will be my last week of farm work!"

After they had left and one by one the others headed inside, Manuel de Jesús and Luisa took their customary seats on the porch steps.

"It feels like forever since we have had a chance to sit here enjoying the stars and each other's company," remarked Manuel de Jesús. "And yet, it has only been two weeks since Leocadio died. Of course, we didn't get a chance to sit here like this that night."

When Luisa did not comment, he took one of her hands in both of his. "You have been awfully quiet tonight," he said softly. "What is going on with you? Are you feeling all right?"

Luisa only lifted her shoulders and gave her head a small shake, as if to say, "I don't know."

Manuel de Jesús glanced at her, released his left hand from its hold on hers and put his arm around her, instead. He caressed her arm soothingly. "It has been a difficult two weeks for everybody. I know that losing Leocadio was a shock. And now that Sebastián is leaving, it is another change for all of us. Working with him on the cabin every weekend like we have been doing, he has become like a brother to me. It is a head start, because in a few months we will be *cuñados*. It is hard to believe that little Toño is going to be my brother-in-law, also." He chuckled. "But he will not stay little forever." Manuel de Jesús looked at Luisa again and with his arm still around her gave her a little squeeze. "Hey, are you ever going to talk to me tonight?"

Luisa sighed and finally spoke. "I'm sorry. I am just not myself these days. I...you are right...losing Leocadio was a big shock, even though we knew he was sick. I feel so helpless seeing how much Aquilina, Dionicia and the others in that family are suffering, and I can do nothing to ease their pain."

"You can pray," offered Manuel de Jesús, gently.

Luisa made a grimace. "I am not having an easy time doing that, either, lately. I do not understand why God had to take a good man like Leocadio so soon. He wasn't even old."

"We do not have to understand everything that God does," said Manuel de Jesús, "but we have to accept it. No, Leocadio was not an old man, maybe fifty years old, but he had lived a good and full life. He had a loving wife and seven healthy children, a farm, a house, and many friends. He was very sick for several days, but now he is no longer suffering…he is in Glory."

"No, *he* is not suffering," Luisa replied, a little sharply, "but his *family* is now suffering. I don't know how they can take it. If it hurts me this much, how much more brokenhearted are they? How can they even survive the pain? It is not just going to be for a few days, and then they will feel better. They will miss him for the rest of their lives!"

Manuel de Jesús removed his arm from around Luisa and sat in silence for a few minutes, once again holding her hand in both of his. Eventually, he spoke. "I am not sure how to answer all of that. I think you need time to sort this out. I had better get home, anyway." He stood up and pulled Luisa to her feet.

She held his hand as they walked to where his horse was tethered, and he drew her into his arms. Luisa lay her head against his chest and listened to his heartbeat and his breathing. It was comforting, and his arms around her felt so good and so natural. But how long would she have him around to hold her like this? What if she never saw him again? *What a terrible thought!* She silently reprimanded herself. But what *if* she never saw him again for some reason? That would be devastating, but how much more tragic would it be if something happened to him after they were married and had children? Luisa shuddered, and Manuel de Jesús tightened his arms around her in response. Slowly releasing her, he brought his hands up to cup her face and give her a good night kiss.

"I will see you next Sunday. Get some rest, Luisa," he whispered. With a trickling caress down the length of one of her arms, Manuel de Jesús turned and mounted his horse. As his horse picked his way around the bend in the road, Luisa felt two tears roll slowly down her cheeks.

On Wednesday, Luisa and Pilar hiked up to the Collados' cabin to work with Petra in her garden. Luisa was still uncharacteristically quiet and serious, and Petra shared her concerns about her sister to Juan José that night.

"I am worried about Luisa," Petra confessed. "She has lost her sparkle since hearing the news about Leocadio."

"I know. I noticed that last Sunday," her husband replied.

"But here it is Wednesday, and she still is not getting back to normal," insisted Petra.

"Maybe a change of scenery would do her good. What do you think of inviting her to go to Ponce with Sebastián and me next Saturday? Even just that quick trip to see Sebastiana and the baby might shake her out of her moodiness."

"Yes," agreed Petra. "What a wonderful idea!" Then having another thought, she added, "or maybe she could stay there with them for a couple of weeks. Could you go back to get her?"

"I could, or maybe the Laboys might want to bring her home and let the rest of the family here see their baby. They have not visited Adjuntas in well over a year."

"I think it is a good idea. How can we make this happen?" wondered Petra.

"Let me talk to your father tomorrow when we are working on the farm. He can take the idea home to Chenta, and we will see where it goes."

The next day, Ricardo listened carefully to Juan José's suggestion. He, too, had been concerned about Luisa's behavior and promised to speak to Chenta that night.

On Friday, when Petra came down the trail with little Francisco on her back, she sought out Chenta first and the two communicated silently, locking eyes. Chenta gave Petra an almost imperceptible nod.

"Let's have coffee first, before going to work in the garden," Petra suggested. "Chenta, do you need help preparing it?"

"No, it is almost ready. I will serve it, and you three girls can take your coffee out onto the porch. I will join you there in a minute."

Luisa offered no objection and did not seem to notice anything unusual going on. She went out on the porch, carrying little Francisco. Petra brought out both her coffee cup and Luisa's, with Pilar following, carrying her own cup of *café con leche*.

Once they were all seated, Chenta brought up the subject of Sebastián's approaching move to Ponce. Choosing her words carefully, she expressed that she and Ricardo thought it would be good for Luisa to go along and stay with Sebastiana and her husband for a couple of weeks.

"It will help you clear your head after all that has happened around here lately," she explained. "I hope that the Laboys can bring you back and stay for a few days. We all want to see them and their baby girl. But if they can't, then Juan José will go back for you."

Luisa's eyes had opened wide and she listened in surprised silence until Chenta was done talking. She looked over at Petra, and got a smile and a nod from her. "It will be good for you, Luisa," Petra said softly.

"Chenta, you need me here," was all that Luisa said.

"Nah!" said Chenta, with a dismissive wave. "We will miss you, yes, but Pilar is a huge help."

"Yes," affirmed Pilar. "I can do almost everything that you do now, and remember, when you get married I will have to take over all of your chores, anyway."

"Oh!" exclaimed Petra. "How are we going to let Manuel de Jesús know that you are leaving? If you decide that you want to go, that is."

"You should go," Pilar piped up. "You are lucky. I never get to go anywhere."

Luisa smiled at Pilar's standing complaint, and indeed it was the first smile that anyone had seen on Luisa's face in two weeks. It was a fleeting smile, gone as fast as it had appeared. "Maybe you should go instead of me. But yes, I will go. Don't worry about getting word to Manuel de Jesús. It is better if he doesn't know that I am leaving…until I am gone."

The other three exchanged looks but did not respond to that comment, even though they were not sure how it could be better that way.

Instead of working in the garden, Petra and Pilar helped Luisa pack for her trip. Early the next morning, Luisa was off on her adventure with Sebastián and Juan José. It was her first time leaving Adjuntas or even spending a night away from her family home. She was glad to be able to spend that extra time with Sebastián and was looking forward to seeing Sebastiana and her little family. She tried not to think of Manuel de Jesús, but he entered her thoughts, anyway. He would be going to the farmer's market with Eladio that morning. He knew that Juan José and Sebastián would not be there at their usual spot. Would he still go to work on the cabin on Sunday all by himself? Luisa did not know, but he had said that he would see her Sunday afternoon. She forced herself not to think about what he would say when he arrived at her house and found her gone.

Luisa did not learn until sometime later just how shocked Manuel de Jesús had been when he arrived at the Torres home on Sunday afternoon. He had been looking forward to sharing about the progress he had made that day on their cabin and had found Luisa gone. She had not even said goodbye nor sent word to him that she was going to go to Ponce. Had he known of the plan, he would have gone to her house Friday afternoon to hold her in his arms one more time. Had he ever even told her that he loved her? Surely she knew that he did, but now he lamented that he had probably never actually told her so. Was she having second thoughts about marrying him? Her behavior had been so altered lately. He had attributed it to grief, but maybe it was something more. What if after staying there for two weeks she decided that she liked Ponce and didn't want to come home? Tortured with these alarming thoughts, a brokenhearted Manuel de Jesús did not stay for supper even at Chenta's urging. Refusing someone's hospitality was sometimes considered an insult, so he mumbled an apology, said a polite goodbye, and left.

He was glad that his horse knew the way home. As lost as he was in his confused thoughts, Manuel de Jesús was barely aware of his surroundings until he saw that he was approaching his brother's property. He was relieved to see that Eladio was still at the main house, and that he had their cabin all to himself for a while. He did not want to talk to anyone. After caring for his horse, Manuel de Jesús readied himself for bed and feigned sleep when Eladio entered their cabin later that night. He would eventually have to explain this turn of events to Eladio…but first he would have to make sense of it himself.

Chapter 29

New Surroundings

After traveling all day, Luisa, Sebastián and Juan José had arrived at the Laboy home in the early evening. Neither Juan José nor Sebastián had been there before and were going by the directions that Francisco Laboy had given them when they had been in Adjuntas for baby Pilar's baptism. They made it to the general vicinity and stopped to ask a man if he knew which property belonged to Francisco Laboy and Sebastiana Torres. Luckily, the man was able to direct them to the correct house. It was on a small plot of land with a horse stable behind it. The Laboys were surprised to see them, but welcomed the unexpected company enthusiastically. Sebastiana was giddy with joy at seeing Luisa and excited to know that she would be staying for two weeks. After they unloaded the two burlap sacks containing *vianda* and fruit that Ricardo had sent, Francisco accompanied Juan José to the Laboys' horse stable and helped him unhitch the team from the wagon. He had his own team of horses and wagon which he used in his work as a teamster, hauling lumber, produce, furniture, and making general deliveries of all kinds.

Once back in the house, Francisco assured Juan José that he needn't return for Luisa; they would gladly take her home at the end of her stay. He and Sebastiana had been thinking of making a trip to Adjuntas soon, anyway, and this just firmed their plans. When Sebastián informed them that he was moving to Ponce to pursue a career as a carpenter, both Francisco and Sebastiana insisted that he stay with them as long as he wanted.

"Because of my line of work, I know a lot of people in Ponce. I think I may know someone who is looking to hire another carpenter," said Francisco. "I will introduce you to him and put in a good word for you."

Sebastián thanked them both and accepted their generous offers of lodging and help finding employment. He shared that eventually—once he was established in steady work—he wanted to find a place of his own.

"While you are here, Luisa, you can sleep in the bed that is in Pilar's room, if you do not mind sharing that space with her. After you go back home, we will move the baby's crib into our room, and Sebastián can have that room all to himself. For tonight, you two guys will have to bed down on the living room floor."

"No problem there," said Juan José. "I will be getting up early to head back home."

"I am always up early. I will help you hitch up your horses," Francisco offered.

Although her visitors told her that Chenta had packed food for them to eat along the road, Sebastiana set out bread, cheese and fruit for her guests.

"Who knows when you had your supper," said Sebastiana. "It was probably hours ago. I do not want any guests of mine to go to bed hungry."

So they all partook of the repast and while they ate they caught the Laboys up on the happenings back home in Adjuntas. Sebastiana was saddened to hear about Leocadio's passing.

"He was sincerely one of my favorite people in Juan González," she remarked mournfully. "He was as close to us as our uncles, and so very kind and generous. He will be missed, for sure."

Noticing Luisa so quiet and withdrawn, Sebastiana urged her to go to bed. "Pilar is in her crib, but she is a pretty sound sleeper. You will not disturb her at all."

"I will set out a couple of straw ticks and pillows for you two guys," said Francisco. "It is warm enough that you will not need any blankets."

"It is a lot warmer down here than it is up in the mountains," remarked Juan José. "And I think something bit me."

"Oh, yes, there are mosquitoes here. That is something that I had to get used to when we first moved to Ponce," said Sebastiana. "So, thank you for reminding me. I need to get out a *mosquitero* for Luisa's bed."

So saying, she went to retrieve a mosquito net from the linen closet and entered baby Pilar's bedroom. Luisa trailed behind her, carrying the burlap sack into which she had packed her belongings. She peeked at her little niece through the netting that covered the crib. Pilar had grown so much! Luisa looked forward to getting acquainted with the tot. Sebastiana unfolded the *mosquitero* and hung it from the four posters of the bed with loops that had been sewn into the corners of the net for that purpose.

"Have you ever used one of these?" asked Sebastiana, speaking softly so as not to awaken Pilar. Luisa shook her head, and Sebastiana said, "I didn't think so. You are at such a high altitude in Juan González that there are no mosquitoes, but down here in Ponce it is a different matter. You will have to get used to sleeping with the *mosquitero*. Just don't forget that the net is there if you get up in the middle of the night to use the chamber pot, or you might get tangled up in it." Sebastiana smothered a giggle. "Come on," she added. "I will show you where the outhouse is and the water pitcher and basin so that you can get ready for bed."

On their way to the back door, Luisa noted that the straw ticks were already on the living room floor for Sebastián and Juan José and that Francisco was tidying up the kitchen. She marveled at that. She had never seen her father do any kind of housework whatsoever.

Half an hour later, Luisa was in bed. She had not been sleeping well during the past two weeks but after the day-long journey in a jolting wagon, her body gave in to exhaustion, and she slept soundly. In the morning, she awoke feeling very disoriented. Where was she? It took her a minute to fully wake up and realize that she was not in her own bed at home but rather in a strange new place with a mosquito net obscuring the view of the little girl sitting up in her crib calling for her mama.

Luisa emerged from under the *mosquitero* at the same time that Sebastiana came into the room. "Oh, you are awake," said Sebastiana. "Why am I not surprised with this little one making such a ruckus?"

Baby Pilar looked from her mother to Luisa and then back again. She stuck two fingers into her mouth. "Look, Luisa, I don't know if you were too little to remember, but our sister Pilar used to suck on those same two fingers. Isn't that funny?" She picked up Pilar. "Look, *Mamita*, this is your *Tía* Luisa. She is going to stay with us for two weeks. Your mama is so happy about that!" She exited the room with the tot and left Luisa alone to get dressed.

A little later, as Sebastiana was serving some bread, eggs and coffee to Luisa, she related that she had been up since before dawn that morning.

"I didn't want Juan José to leave without having breakfast first," she said. "And of course, I had to make some for Francisco and Sebastián, too. Juan José left right after breakfast, hoping to get back home to Petra before dark. Francisco and Sebastián went to the stable to feed the horses and they still haven't come back. They must be having a good talk." She smiled at Luisa. "It is so good to have company from Adjuntas. I get homesick for the family."

Luisa was sitting at the table with little Pilar on her lap, feeding the baby bits of egg. "Everyone is going to be so happy to see you when you take me home," said Luisa. "It has been too long. Why haven't you come to visit in over a year?"

"It has been one thing after another. Either the baby was sick, or I was sick, or Francisco had too much work and could not take several days off in a row. He was working for a store, making deliveries, but the owner was working him to death for a pittance and only giving him Sundays off. Francisco finally decided to quit that job and go into business for himself. He figured that if he was using his own team of horses and wagon and having to pay for the upkeep of the animals and the equipment, he might as well be independent and be able to charge more."

"That is smart," Luisa said, nodding her head. "And it is going well?"

"Yes, he has established himself as a reliable teamster and has quite a few customers that solicit his services on a regular basis. So, now that he can make his own schedule, we have been talking about taking a few days off to finally go to Adjuntas." Sebastiana dimpled and continued. "Now that I am over my morning sickness, I can handle the trip and tell the family the good news."

"You are having another baby? That's wonderful!" Luisa reached out a hand to squeeze one of Sebastiana's.

Sebastiana laughed with delight. "I thought for sure you would guess before I told you. I am already starting to show a little, see?" She stood up to show Luisa her tiny bulge.

"If you say so," said Luisa, with a laugh. Luisa was starting to feel like her old self again. Her family was right. She had needed to get away for a bit.

The men came back in from the stable and the foursome made plans for the day.

"On Sundays, we like to go to the noon mass, then come home, have lunch and settle Pilar down for her afternoon nap," Sebastiana explained. "If you are up to doing that today, we could use the remainder of the morning to give you a little tour of Ponce. It is a pretty town and much larger than Adjuntas."

Sebastián was raring to go get the lay of the land of his new surroundings, but Luisa said that she needed to iron a dress since everything that she had packed into the burlap sack had come out wrinkled. Sebastiana fired up the stove again and set the iron on it to heat up. Eventually, they were all dressed in their Sunday attire. The horses were hitched to the wagon, and they were off on their sightseeing adventure.

"As you can see," began Francisco as they drove to the main road, "we live on the outskirts of town. The road that you came on from Adjuntas is called "*la Carretera del Café*"—the Coffee Road—because it connects the coffee growing towns of Utuado and Adjuntas to the port of Ponce. We will take that road all the way into town."

They passed many humble homes along the way, some of which were little more than shacks, but once they entered the main part of town, Luisa saw houses and buildings vastly different from the mountain cabins that she was used to. Even the houses near the plaza of Adjuntas did not look as impressive as these in Ponce.

Francisco stopped his team of horses in front of an imposing two story structure adorned with six tall columns along the front. "This is *Teatro la Perla*, a theater that was built five or six years ago. They hold musical concerts here," he explained.

Luisa was not sure what a musical concert was. Maybe she would ask Sebastiana later on, privately. She did not want to appear ignorant in front of Francisco. They drove up and down the streets of Ponce so that Sebastián and Luisa could get acquainted with the town and the style of the buildings. Many of the homes were very pretty, colorfully painted wooden structures with balconies and tall front doors. Luisa had never seen houses built so close to one another. She thought it might be nice to be able to stand on the balcony of one's house and wave at or even have a conversation with a neighbor next door.

Their tour ended at the plaza in the center of the town, where Francisco found a shady place to leave his team and wagon. At one side of the plaza stood the beautiful cathedral of *Nuestra Señora de la Guadalupe.* Luisa and Sebastián both stood and gawked at its elaborate architecture. They had never seen a building like it. The front façade of the cathedral was flanked by octagonal towers that were three stories high, with glass windows on each of the eight sides on all three stories. Two tall pillars were on either side of the massive wooden front doors. The cathedral was so much larger than their church back home in Adjuntas! Sebastián and Luisa were in awed reverence as they entered and dipped their fingers in the holy water to make the sign of the cross. Once they were seated and the mass began, Luisa found that it was very similar to their masses in San Joaquín Church. *Padre* José Balbino David spoke with a heavy Castilian accent, and his voice echoed in the cavernous building, but Luisa listened attentively to his message. One thing that he said stuck with her. It was a scripture from the Bible that said, "Trust in the Lord with all your heart, and do not lean on your own understanding." The priest explained it to mean that we do not always understand why God allows some things to happen, but we can trust Him in the good times and the bad because He loves us and will help us through those times of sorrow and difficulties.

When they were back at the house, Luisa asked Sebastiana if they attended church every Sunday. Sebastiana answered, "We go on most Sundays. Of course, there are times when one of us is sick or it is raining too hard…or some such reason. But, we only have one child and we live close enough to town—it's not like getting a houseful of children ready and traveling all the way down the mountain from Juan González to get to church. We really like that we are able to go regularly."

The next morning, Sebastián was up early and left with Francisco, who took him to meet Diego Ramírez, a man who owned a construction company. *Don* Diego was always busy, often overseeing the construction of more than one building project at a time. Francisco knew him because *Don* Diego sometimes hired him to haul materials. Francisco's suspicions were correct: *Don* Diego was in need of another carpenter, and he hired Sebastián as an apprentice on the spot solely on Francisco's recommendation. Thankfully, Sebastiana had had the foresight to pack a lunch for Sebastián as well as the one she had prepared for her husband. Francisco left to do his delivery runs, promising to swing by at the end of the work day to pick up Sebastián. Needless to say, Sebastián was elated at finding employment as a carpenter so soon.

During the next few days, Sebastián and Luisa fell into the routine of life in Ponce. They both felt at home in their sister's house, although Luisa felt bad about Sebastián having to sleep on the floor. After all, he was working hard at his new job while she was living quite the life of leisure.

Sebastián assured her that he was fine sleeping on the floor. "See? I put one straw tick on top of the other, and it is quite comfortable."

Luisa did help Sebastiana out with the housework, but it really was not much compared to all that she was used to doing at home in Juan González. Much of her time was spent entertaining little Pilar, and that was not work at all. It gave her pleasure, but it also made her miss her baby sisters and Petra's baby boy—Luisa's little coffee bean.

During the evenings, after the baby went to sleep, the four adults indulged in conversation, and it was a special time for the three siblings. Sebastián was six years older than Luisa, while Sebastiana was five years older. When they were both still living at home, Luisa was just a young kid in their eyes, much the way Luisa regarded her sister Pilar. Francisco and Sebastiana had been married for four years and had so far spent all of them in Ponce. Since moving away, they had only visited the family in Adjuntas three times. Sebastián and Luisa were used to seeing each other every Sunday afternoon and sometimes on a Saturday, but they were usually with all the rest of the family. The three of them had never before had this much quality time together as adults, and it turned out to be a wonderful time of bonding and reminiscing.

Sebastián laughed as he shared a memory during one of their evening conversations. "Sebastiana, do you remember the time that we couldn't find Luisa? She must have only been about three at the time. You and Rosa and I all fanned out, looking for her everywhere, even down at the creek, and our mother was frantic. Mario was just a baby, not even walking yet."

"I do remember that!" exclaimed Sebastiana.

"Really? You couldn't find me? That's funny. The same thing happened to us with Boni the day of the hurricane. She sure gave us a scare! So, where was I, and who found me?"

"Well, after we looked under the house and in the barn and everywhere, Sebastián went up the trail towards the spring where we fetch water."

"And there you were, about halfway up to the spring," finished Sebastián, "just lying on the ground face up, peaceful and content, unaware of the commotion you had caused. You were gazing at the clouds and listening to the birds."

Luisa smiled. "I still like doing that, but I hardly ever get the chance to anymore."

Sebastián regarded Luisa candidly. "It's nice to see you relaxed, little sister. You work really hard at home, and lately you haven't been yourself."

Francisco and Sebastiana were both looking at her, too, and Luisa felt embarrassed. She didn't know how to answer her brother, so she just lifted one shoulder in a half shrug and remained silent. Sebastián sensed her reticence and changed the subject, launching into a discussion about all the construction that was currently going on in Ponce and about how he really liked his new work as an apprentice carpenter. He was grateful that he had the opportunity to learn a real trade and expand his knowledge of construction.

"I have already made a few new friends. Two of them are brothers—Pedro and Pablo Millán—and they told me that they don't live too far from here. They have offered to take me to work in their wagon if I walk over to their place in the mornings. I think I want to try doing that, Francisco. If it works out, it will free you to go about your deliveries without first having to take me to the construction site every morning."

"Oh, I don't mind doing that at all," responded Francisco. "But if you want to try riding with the Millán brothers, it will probably be a good thing in the long run. Remember that I will be taking some days off to go to Adjuntas pretty soon, so it would be good for you to set up another way to get to work."

With the attention diverted from her, Luisa was able to lose herself in thought. What was going to happen when she returned to Adjuntas? Was Manuel de Jesús angry at her for taking off without saying anything to him, not even a goodbye? Would they be able to pick up where they left off and continue with their wedding plans? Did he even want to get married now? Did she? Wouldn't it be better to sever the relationship now before they reached the point where they could not live without one another? If that was the best thing to do, then why did it hurt so much to even contemplate it?

Luisa rose abruptly from her chair and excused herself. "I am going to bed. Good night, all." She walked briskly away, leaving the others to murmur their responses to her retreating back. Luisa did not see how the other three exchanged looks, nor did she hear their quietly voiced concerns about her after she had ducked into the bedroom.

Laying on her back in the bed, Luisa tried to pray, but the words would not form themselves. Where was that closeness that she had become accustomed to feeling with God in her nightly chats with Him? *God, are You there? What should I do? What will happen when I return to Adjuntas? I feel confused, God. I feel like I am being swept along in life, heading towards marriage and a family of my own. It is what I always wanted, but now I am afraid. I am afraid of this strong current that is moving me along to who knows what kind of grief and sorrow in the future. God, please help me understand Your plan for my life.*

It was nothing like the nightly prayers that Luisa had gotten used to saying during the past few years, but at least she was talking to God again.

Chapter 30

Trusting in God

On Saturday, Francisco loaded everyone into his wagon and took them to the beach. It was the first time that Sebastián and Luisa had seen the Caribbean Sea, and they were mesmerized by the turquoise waters and the white sand. The sounds of the seagulls and the surf were soothing to Luisa's soul. She stood barefoot at the water's edge, watching hypnotically as the frothy waves swept up over her feet and then retreated. As her feet sunk into the saturated sand, she stepped over to another clean, firm area of sand, awaiting the next wave, ready to experience the sensation again and again. Meanwhile, Francisco strung up a hammock between two palm trees and wasted no time stretching out in it for a nap, while Sebastián went for a long walk along the beach. Sebastiana set out a blanket and a picnic lunch in a shady spot near a stand of sea grapes. Baby Pilar played contentedly in the sand under her mother's watchful eye, and after she had eaten her lunch, fell asleep on the blanket with the sea breeze caressing her rosy cheeks. Eventually, Luisa joined Sebastiana and the baby on the blanket, but she could not take her eyes off of the majestic and seemingly endless sea. That day at the beach was an unforgettable experience for both Luisa and Sebastián.

Luisa had been in Ponce for a week and was adapting to the change in environment. There were things that made life decidedly easier in Ponce. There was a general store that was not too far from the house. The Laboys kept a few chickens but did not grow any crops on their small plot of land, so most of their food was either purchased at the general store or from the vendors that came around in horse-drawn carts selling fruits and vegetables.

Living on the outskirts of town also made it convenient to go to church. Luisa was glad that they had fair weather on Sunday morning and were able to attend mass again. This time *Padre* David spoke on the subject of grief. He said that there was a season for everything—a time to cry and a time to laugh, a time to grieve and a time to dance. There was nothing wrong with grieving. Jesus wept when he learned that his good friend, Lazarus, had died. He understands our grief. *Padre* David quoted a scripture from the Bible, "The Lord heals the brokenhearted and bandages their wounds." He went on to say that after a period of mourning, it is time to wipe your tears and move on. Expanding on what he had preached the week before about trusting God in the good times and the bad, *Padre* David said that God would help us get through the times of sorrow and give us the strength to move forward. Luisa listened in amazement. It almost felt like the parish priest was speaking directly to her, telling her exactly what she needed to hear. When they exited the dark cathedral into the bright sunshine, Luisa felt lighter in spirit than she had in weeks.

Another thing that was convenient about life in the Laboy home was that water was readily available from a pump that was near their horse stable. Francisco could pump water for his horses' trough and either he or Sebastiana pumped water for the household needs and carried it to the house in pails. Sebastiana's kitchen sink was *inside* the kitchen window, not hanging below it on the outside, so she could wash dishes even if it was raining outside. She still used two pans in her sink when washing dishes, and the waste water was poured down the drain and out into a bucket. Sebastiana used that gray water for watering the herb garden that was outside her kitchen window, just like Chenta did back home in Juan González.

The Laboys did not have a separate bathhouse like the Torres family did in Adjuntas. Instead, a section of their back porch was walled in, and the bathing took place there, although in similar fashion to how the Torres family bathed—using pans of water and a tin cup as a scoop.

The outhouse was in the back yard, halfway between the house and the horse stable, but off to one side. What Luisa disliked about that is that the neighbors' houses were so close that anyone and everyone could be watching when she had to visit the outhouse. For some odd reason, she was embarrassed to think that others might take notice of her trips to "do her business." She missed the privacy of her mountain home.

Mondays were laundry days in the Laboy household, and Sebastiana used a scrub board and soap in a tub of water on a table on the back porch to perform this chore. She had a second tub that contained clear water for rinsing the clothes. Luisa thought that this was definitely an improvement over lugging laundry down the path to the creek, having to sit on a rock to scrub the clothes on another rock, and then toting the heavy, wet laundry back up the trail. Sebastiana wrung out her wash by hand and hung it to dry on a clothesline that stretched between two tree trunks in her back yard instead of draping it over bushes as Luisa did in Adjuntas.

Standing to wash her clothes at the table on Sebastiana's back porch, Luisa had no need to have the back hem of her skirt tucked up into the front of her waistband to keep her skirt from getting wet, like she did at the creek back home. The memory of the time that Manuel de Jesús had come to invite the family to Estevanía's baptism party popped into Luisa's head. She couldn't hold back a smile remembering how embarrassed she was to have him see her bare legs and how Juanito's blurting out about it had sparked a reaction with her father.

Remembering that incident and the grin on Manuel de Jesús's face brought a pang to Luisa's heart. She missed him. She longed to see his kind eyes again, hear his voice, feel his arms around her, and savor his sweet kisses. And as convenient as life was in Ponce, Luisa missed the melodic singing of her ruiseñor, the calming sound of the water rushing over the rocks in the creek after a heavy rain, sleeping in her own bed without a *mosquitero*, and hiking up the mountain to fetch water or visit Petra and her little coffee bean, baby Francisco. Luisa was homesick.

At least she had Sebastiana's baby to play with and get to know. Little Pilar was a sweetheart of a child and had already taken to her *Tía* Luisa. On Tuesday, ten days after her arrival, Luisa was sitting at the table with Pilar on her lap. The baby was gnawing on a piece of Luisa's banana. Luisa's portion disappeared quickly, but Pilar massacred her piece until she had some banana on her tunic and some squished in her little fists.

Sebastiana used a wet cloth to wipe Pilar's hands and clothes. Rinsing out the cloth, she returned to clean Pilar's face with it. The little girl squawked in protest and turned her head from side to side, trying to avoid the face washing.   She wriggled off of Luisa's lap to pick up her rag doll that she had left on the living room floor. Plopping down on her bottom, she proceeded to remove the doll's clothing.

"That will keep her busy for a while," remarked Sebastiana. "She will get the doll undressed and then get frustrated trying to put the clothes back on her. Just wait and see." Sebastiana sat back down across the table from Luisa and decided it was time to have a heart to heart talk with her sister.

"Sebastián mentioned that you have been really down since Leocadio died. The family was really worried about you and hoped that this trip would do you good," she began.

"It has been a nice change," murmured Luisa. "It is my first time away from home, so it was an adjustment at first. But your home is very comfortable." Luisa purposely avoided commenting on her family's concern about her.

Sebastiana tried a different approach. "Tell me about what is going on with you and Manuel de Jesús. When I was in Adjuntas for Pilar's baptism, Rosa and Petra said that there was some interest—on both sides, I hope. Did anything more develop between you two?"

Luisa let out a little laugh and looked down demurely. "Yes, well, the interest was definitely there for both of us, but it wasn't until *Doña* Sinforosa's nephew tried to woo me that anything happened. Manuel de Jesús finally declared himself to me at the baptism party for Leocadio and Aquilina's last baby. That was last fall, and he has been courting me every Sunday night since then, except for during the Novena for Leocadio..." Luisa's voice trailed off as she recalled the sorrow experienced during that time. Then she perked up again. "He and Sebastián have been working on the empty cabin on the farm—the one that is very close to Petra's—and we are going to live there after we are married. Well, we are supposed to—I mean, if we get married..." Luisa's voice trailed off again and her countenance changed.

"What do you mean, if? What is going to stop that from happening?" Sebastiana asked. At that moment, Pilar let out an annoyed shriek. Luisa looked over in time to see Pilar fling her rag doll's uncooperative garment across the wooden floor. Sebastiana quickly gathered a pan, some tin cups and a spoon and placed them on the floor in front of Pilar. The tot immediately began stirring imaginary food in the pot, "cooking" for her naked baby doll.

Sebastiana sat back down, her brow furrowed, and gave Luisa her renewed attention. Luisa was glad to have had a moment to think about what she was going to say, but she still had a hard time expressing her scattered emotions coherently. "I do care for Manuel de Jesús...a lot. And that is what scares me. If we continue courting and get married, those feelings are only going to grow, I would think. What if something happened to him after we were married and had children? How would I be able to survive that?"

"Luisa!" exclaimed Sebastiana. "Why are you thinking of what could happen? You should be enjoying this time of your life. Courtship is such a sweet time. You shouldn't be thinking of what could happen."

Luisa shook her head sadly. "It *was* a really sweet time... until...look what happened to Aquilina. She lost the love of her life and is left with seven fatherless children! There are days when she cannot get out of bed because she is grieving so much. My heart breaks for her because I do not know how she can go on." Luisa's eyes filled with tears, and she looked down to try to hide them, but they spilled out and splashed on the table.

Sebastiana hesitated only a moment and then spoke gently to her sister. "Luisa, what would you have thought if after Leocadio died Aquilina had gone on *como si nada*—as if nothing had happened? Wouldn't you have suspected that she never even loved him? Wasn't Leocadio a blessed man, having a loving wife? Aren't you glad that they had a happy marriage? Aquilina is hurting now, yes, and misses her husband terribly, I am sure, but I am willing to bet that she is not sorry that she married him and had him by her side for all those years. If she had never married him, she would not be a grieving widow now, but she would also have lost out on all the blessings that came her way as a wife and mother. Look, Luisa, bad things happen. That's life. It is going to hurt a lot sometimes. But, you know what? If you are not hurting, you are not really living. Dead people do not feel pain."

Sebastiana reached over and laid a hand on Luisa's arm. "Have you ever slept wrong and woken up with your arm 'asleep'—with it feeling really heavy and having no sensation?" At Luisa's nod, she continued. "You could poke a needle in your arm and not feel a thing, but that would not be good, would it? You want your arm to wake up and have feeling again, so you rub it and slap it until the numbness goes away. For us to be truly alive, we have to be able to feel pain. Another example is when you are sick with a fever and an upset stomach or body aches. You feel awful and weak. Then when you get better, you are so happy and grateful because you remember how you felt when you were sick, and now you can enjoy eating again and doing what you like to do. Do you see what I mean?"

Luisa's tears had stopped, and she was nodding her head, but she still did not say anything. Sebastiana continued. "Do you remember when you asked me why we had not gone to Adjuntas in over a year, since Pilar's baptism? I said that I had been sick part of the time. Well the truth is that I was pregnant a year ago at this time. I was waiting for the morning sickness to go away so that we could take a trip to Adjuntas, and then...I lost the baby."

Luisa gasped in surprise and then said, "Oh, no, Sebastiana. I am so sorry!"

"We were, too. I cried. Francisco even cried. It was a very sad time for us. Our babies would have been close in age, like Mina and Monín, and it would have been so much fun." She shook her head. "It is very painful to lose a baby like that, but even so much worse to carry a baby for eight months like Rosa did and then give birth to a stillborn child. And yet look how happy Domingo and Rosa now are with little Micaela. The pain that they experienced did not stop them from trying again. And Francisco and I have moved on from that grief and are thrilled to be expecting again. Will I carry this one full term and give birth to a healthy baby? I do not know. But Luisa, we just have to trust the unknown future to God. He loves us and wants the best for us. He will give us the strength to go on when tragedy comes into our lives."

Pilar, tired of her play, came up to her mother with her third and fourth fingers in her mouth. Sebastiana picked her up and cuddled her to her chest. "She is getting sleepy. It is her nap time." She placed a kiss on Pilar's head and rocked her little one in her arms.

All of a sudden, Luisa felt an intense yearning in her being. She wanted what her sisters had. She wanted a loving husband and babies to cuddle. She thought of Aquilina and she did not pity her anymore. Aquilina had been happy with Leocadio and had seven children that would forever be a reminder of the love that they had shared. The intensity of her grief was a reflection of the immense love and joy that she had experienced in her marriage to Leocadio.

"What are you thinking, Luisa?" asked Sebastiana softly.

Luisa cleared her throat. "I am thinking that I want to go home. I want to see Manuel de Jesús. I miss him, and I miss Adjuntas. Ponce is nice, but I have a cabin waiting for us to finish getting ready, and I have a wedding to plan. Except...I left without saying goodbye to Manuel de Jesús. He didn't even know that I was leaving. He may be angry with me."

Sebastiana pursed her lips and shook her head even as she continued to rock her child. "He probably was not happy that you left so suddenly that way, but he is a good man, Luisa, and if he truly loves you, that is not going to be enough for him to break off your engagement."

Luisa smiled warmly at Sebastiana. "Thank you. I needed to hear everything that you said." She bit her bottom lip and then grinned widely. "And now I need to go home! When can we leave?"

That evening, they made their plans as they sat around the supper table. Francisco said that he needed to work the next two days to do scheduled deliveries, but that he could take Friday off and let his customers know that he would be unavailable Monday and Tuesday as well. They would leave Friday morning and take Luisa home, then go stay with Rosa and Dolores until Tuesday morning.

Luisa was not sure how she was going to make it through two whole days and three nights before leaving for Adjuntas. She was sure that she was not going to get any sleep, but that night after a heartfelt chat with God, she fell into a peaceful sleep.

Sebastián was relieved to see Luisa be her cheerful old self during those last two days in Ponce. They were enjoying the evening air on the front porch during her last night, talking enthusiastically about their plans for the future—his in Ponce in his new career and hers back in the mountains of Adjuntas.

"You only have one more night of sleeping on the floor," Luisa told him with a wink. "I bet you will be happy to take over the bed when I am gone."

"I didn't mind sleeping on the floor. It's been worth it to have you here these two weeks, sister," he replied. "The trip did you good, as we hoped it would. Manuel de Jesús may be a little sour in the mouth because you left in such a hurry without telling him, but give him a big kiss and see how he sweetens up in a hurry."

"Stop it!" she laughed, slapping his arm playfully.

It does sound like a good idea, though, she admitted to herself.

Chapter 31

Reunited

Luisa was up before dawn the next morning, eager to be on her way. She had the coffee ground and brewed by the time Sebastiana entered the kitchen.

"My, someone is in a rush to get home!" Sebastiana teased. "As much as I have enjoyed having you here, I am glad for your sake that you are going back home. And I can't wait to see the family again after so long since our last visit. I am as excited as you are! Let's get breakfast going quickly."

Within an hour, they were ready to leave. Sebastián gave Luisa a big hug and murmured encouraging words in her ear. He told her that Manuel de Jesús already felt like a brother to him and that he was a perfect fit in their family. He reminded her of his promise to return to Adjuntas for her wedding. Luisa pulled back from their embrace and looked up at her brother. She told him how glad that she was that they had had those two weeks together. It had made his move from Adjuntas to Ponce easier for her to bear, seeing how much he was enjoying the transition. Also, just having that extra sibling time together had been so special.

The drive to Adjuntas seemed never ending to Luisa. They stopped for a rest and refreshments at a roadside business on the north end of Barrio Guaraguao. After a filling lunch of white rice, stewed beans, *lechón asado*, and fried ripe plantains, they continued on their journey, arriving in Juan González close to suppertime. Since they were getting there earlier than antici-pated, Luisa had a thought.

"Francisco, do you think that you can take the left fork and drive up to Petra's cabin first? I want to see if Juan José will take me with him into town tomorrow when he goes to the farmer's market."

"No problem," Francisco responded. "You want to go to the farmer's market because…?"

"Silly!" cut in Sebastiana. "She wants to go see Manuel de Jesús!" She laughed gleefully. "You can't wait to see him, can you?"

A little embarrassed, Luisa offered an explanation. "Well, I have no other way of letting him know that I am back. He lives pretty far from us, you know."

Sebastiana gave her sister a sidelong knowing look, her lips twisted in a teasing smile.

"All right, fine!" admitted Luisa. "I can't wait to see him. I need to talk to him and make sure that he is not angry with me, and to know if we are moving forward with our wedding plans."

"I wish I could be there to witness that encounter," admit-ted Sebastiana. "Maybe I can convince Francisco or Domingo to take me into town tomorrow morning to do some shopping at the farmer's market."

"Or not!" retorted Luisa good naturedly. "Give us some privacy, please!"

"The plaza is a public place. You will have plenty of eyes watching you. What difference would a couple more pairs of eyes make?"

The two sisters continued with their teasing banter the remainder of the way, with Francisco quietly listening and enjoying their conversation. As Luisa had requested, he pulled in front of Petra and Juan José's cabin. After their joyful exchange of hugs, showing off the babies and making use of the outhouse, arrangements were made for Juan José to pick up Luisa in the morning. They didn't stay long, as they had to drop off Luisa and make it to Domingo and Rosa's house before they retired for the night.

Pulling his wife away from her parents' home was harder for Francisco. Chenta insisted they eat supper first. Luisa was virtually attacked by all of her younger siblings, so happy were they to see her back home. Chenta and Ricardo quickly realized that Luisa was emotionally back to normal as well, to their great relief.

The Laboys left to go to Domingo and Rosa's place and the little ones were settled into their beds. Pilar helped Chenta clean up the kitchen; they wouldn't let Luisa do anything, insisting that she must be tired from the journey. So Luisa joined Ricardo on the front porch and hesitantly informed him of her plan to go to town with Juan José in the morning. Even though she was no longer a child, her father was still the head of the household and she needed his approval of her plan.

"I need to talk to Manuel de Jesús," Luisa explained, candidly. "He must have been surprised and upset when he realized that I had gone to Ponce without letting him know first."

Ricardo nodded. "He was," he said simply. "He didn't come work on the cabin last weekend, either. I know because I went by there to check and maybe have a word with him to explain that we were the ones that suggested you go to Ponce. There really wasn't time to inform him about it before you left because it was a last minute decision. We did try to talk to him when he came courting the day after you left, but I don't think he heard anything that we said. He was too shocked that you had left, and he wouldn't stay for supper."

Luisa turned worried eyes to her father. "I hope he will hear me out tomorrow."

"He will, *Mija*. In light of everything that happens in life, this situation is nothing. *Son pajitas que le caen a la leche*— crumbs that fall into the milk."

"I hope that you are right," breathed Luisa.

Later, lying in her own bed next to Pilar, Luisa offered up a fervent prayer. *God, I am so thankful that I am home again. Bless my family for looking out for me and suggesting the trip to Ponce. It turned out to be a good thing in many ways. Sebastián is going to be happy there. Thank You for providing him with a job so quickly, and for Francisco and Sebastiana's support while he establishes himself there. Bless Sebastiana for talking me through my fear of the future. I trust You, Lord. I know that You want the best for me and that even though bad things happen, You are there to give us comfort and the strength to continue. Be with me tomorrow, Lord, as I go speak with Manuel de Jesús, and give me the right words to say. Amen.*

Eladio Maldonado drove the team of horses skillfully along the road toward the town of Adjuntas. He glanced over at his brother, sitting sullenly and deep in thought next to him. It had been a long two weeks since Manuel de Jesús had discovered that Luisa had taken off for Ponce. His brother had been despondent ever since. Manuel de Jesús had finally told him about Luisa leaving. Even though Eladio had offered encouraging words numerous times, they had not had much of a positive effect.

"I hope you perk up before we get to the plaza," Eladio now said to Manuel de Jesús. "Otherwise, you will scare away our customers with that face."

Manuel de Jesús offered a half-hearted apologetic smile. "Sorry," was all that he said.

"Hey, Juan José should be there today. He probably will have an idea of when Luisa will return since he was the one that took her to Ponce."

"Maybe."

"Are you going to go work on the cabin tomorrow?"

"No."

"Why not?"

"What for? What if she doesn't want to come back?"

Eladio grunted. *"Las aguas siempre vuelven a su cauce."* The *water always returns to its channel.* "Once you two are over this hump, things will get back to normal. You belong together." He glanced over at Manuel de Jesús again. "You have told her that you love her, haven't you?"

"Not in so many words, but she should know it. We were planning to get married."

"So you haven't actually said those three words?" At Manuel de Jesús's silence, Eladio groaned. "Man, first chance that you get, you need to tell her."

"I know. If I get the chance to, I will."

Luisa took extra pains with her appearance. She put on her best dress, even if it was only for a trip to town and not a special occasion. Who was she kidding? It wasn't just a trip to town; it *was* a special occasion…she was going to see Manuel de Jesús. At least, she hoped that he would be there. There was no guarantee, although the Maldonado brothers normally were at the farmer's market on the same days as Juan José.

Pilar had risen early, too, and she now sat on the bed, watching Luisa's nervous preparations. Luisa was brushing out her long hair, preparing to braid a blue ribbon in it.

"Here, let me do that for you," offered Pilar, standing. "I don't think your fingers are very nimble this morning," she added with a wink.

"Thank you, Pilar. You are right. My braid would probably come out crooked."

"Why are you so nervous?" Pilar asked, as she was finishing off the braid with the blue ribbon tied in a perky bow. "It's going to be all right, you know. Manuel de Jesús adores you."

Luisa turned around and gave Pilar a tight hug. No words in reply were necessary.

Luisa could hear Chenta in the kitchen, serving some coffee and bread to Moncho. He had been recruited to go to town with Juan José on their farmer's market days, now that Sebastián had moved away. If she had known that ahead of time, they could have eliminated the stop at the Collados' cabin last night since Juan José had already planned to stop by the house to pick up Moncho. But no matter, Sebastiana and Petra had been happy to see each other.

Entering the kitchen, Luisa greeted Chenta and Moncho cheerfully and poured herself a cup of coffee. *Starting tomorrow, I need to get back into the kitchen early to grind the coffee and help Chenta with breakfast,* she thought.

Juan José pulled up and they were on their way to town before the rest of the family was up. They kept up a lively chatter along the way, with Moncho and Juan José asking questions and Luisa relating about her experiences in Ponce. Luisa was glad for the distraction of the conversation. It made her less anxious about seeing Manuel de Jesús.

As they entered the town and drove around the plaza to their customary spot, Luisa was scanning the area where the Maldonados usually set up their produce stand. They were there! Her heart began pounding even before Moncho helped her down. Juan José gave her a wink and a smile. Luisa smiled back nervously, squared her shoulders and set off in the direction of the Maldonados' stand.

Manuel de Jesús set the last crate of oranges out and straightened up. He had been busy offloading the wagon and had not noticed Juan José pulling into his regular spot around the corner of the plaza. Early shoppers were starting to mill around, and they partially blocked his view, but…that young woman walking towards him looked like…it *was* Luisa! He stood transfixed, not taking his eyes off of her. She looked prettier than ever. His heart was thumping in his chest. Here was his opportunity to tell her how he felt about her.

Luisa approached him slowly, oblivious of the pedestrians who stopped short of bumping into her and abruptly changed their course to walk around her. Her eyes were on Manuel de Jesús. He was so tall and handsome, but he looked so serious! She stopped a short distance from him and smiled tentatively at him, trying to coax him into one of his cute smiles.

"Manuel," she said softly, but bravely. "I'm back." She almost laughed at the absurdity of her statement. "I mean, I am back to my old self. I have a lot to explain…about how I was affected by Leocadio's passing…about my fears…about the trip to Ponce…"

"Luisa," Manuel de Jesús took a step closer to her. "I need to talk to you, too. I have been so slow and awkward about expressing my feelings for you. I thought you knew how I felt, but then you left, and I was afraid that I was too late."

"No, you were not too late. I knew how you felt. We have been planning our wedding! But I left without saying goodbye. Do you still…are we still…?" She stepped closer.

"Luisa," he breathed, "I love you. I have loved you for the longest time. That day when I saw you standing on your front porch, the day of Mina's baptism—I took one look at you and thought, 'There is my future wife.'"

"I love you, too, Manuel." In an instant, she was in his arms, and it felt so good.

Manuel de Jesús wrapped his arms around her. It was amazing how well she fit into his embrace, as if God had fashioned her precisely for him. He never wanted to let her go.

Luisa never wanted to move from his embrace. For as long as God gave them life, this is where she wanted to be.

They remained that way for a long time. People passed by them, some smiling at young love, others frowning at the audacity of the younger generation. Finally, remembering Sebastián's joking suggestion from her last night in Ponce, Luisa stood on tiptoe and planted a kiss on Manuel de Jesús's lips. She was rewarded with one of his lopsided grins and a follow up kiss of his own. They had a lot to talk about, but it could wait.

From off to one side, Eladio had been slyly watching the encounter between his brother and Luisa. Now he looked down the street at Juan José, who had followed Luisa the whole way with his eyes. Eladio lifted both of his arms in the air in a victory gesture and Juan José did the same in response.

Eventually, Eladio shooed the couple away. "You are scaring away the customers," he teased. Go walk around the plaza. I can handle this stand by myself."

Manuel de Jesús did not wait until Sunday night to see Luisa again. He was there that very afternoon, to everyone's delight. Rosa, Domingo and Micaela arrived with Sebastiana, Francisco and baby Pilar. Petra and Juan José were there with baby Francisco. The whole family was reunited, with the exception of Sebastián, and it was a joy-filled evening.

In the midst of the eating and laughing and talking, Manuel de Jesús lowered his little buddy, Toño, from his lap, got up and held out his hand to Luisa. They walked hand in hand to stand under the mango tree at the edge of the *batey*.

"Have I told you in the last hour that I love you?" he asked.

At a shake of her head, he said, huskily, "I love you, Luisa Torres. I am looking forward to our wedding and to being together for the rest of our lives." He drew her close in a tender embrace.

"We can all see you!" announced Juanito in a sing-song voice.

Embarrassed, Luisa and Manuel de Jesús broke apart as the family started hooting and whistling. They looked at each other and both shrugged. Their arms went around each other again and this time their lips met in a sweet kiss, right there in front of everybody.

Glossary of Spanish Words and Phrases Used in This Book

¡A bailar, todos! – Everybody dance!

achiote – a spice made from the red seed of the annatto tree

adiós – goodbye

A falta de pan se come galletas – When you don't have bread you eat crackers.

amapola – a hibiscus-like flower

amigos – friends

A mojo con ají no se le paran las moscas encima – Flies don't land on spicy garlic sauce.

arroz con dulce – a traditional Puerto Rican rice pudding

arroz con gandules – rice with pigeon peas (a traditional Puerto Rican dish)

arroz con pollo – chicken with rice

asalto – a sneak attack or surprise visit of musicians and friends bringing an instant party to other friends late at night during the Christmas season

Así se hace – That's how it is done.

asopao de gallina – chicken stew

ay, bendito – oh, blessed; can be used as an expression of dismay or sympathy

¡Ay, Dios mío! – Oh, my God!

Ay, que linda – Oh, how pretty.

¡Ay, mi madre! – An expression of surprise such as "Oh, my!" or "For heaven's sake!"

bacalao – dried and salted cod

bailar – to dance

barrio – a district of a town

batey – a Taíno word for an open flat area

bendición – a blessing

bordonúa – a large, deep body bass guitar which is native to Puerto Rico *buen provecho* – bon appétit

buenas tardes – good afternoon

buenos días – good morning

café con leche – coffee with milk

caldero – a cauldron

 (la) Carretera del Café –Coffee Road

chicas – girls

claro/ claro que sí– of course

colador – a strainer

(el) Colorao – the red one; a nickname for a redheaded male

comadrona – midwife

(el) Cano – the white/gray hair; a nickname for a blond male

¿Cómo estás? –How are you?

¿Cómo has estado? – How have you been?

Como no – Of course.

como si nada – as if nothing had happened

¿Cómo se llama? – What is his/her/its name?

compai – slang for *compadre,* the godfather of your child or the parent of your godchild

Con permiso – Excuse me.

coquí – a tiny but loud frog endemic to Puerto Rico

cuarentena – quarantine

cuatro – a small guitar often shaped like a viola

cuñada – sister-in-law

De una boda sale otra - Out of one wedding comes another.

Dios la/lo bendiga – God bless her/him.

Dios te bendiga – God bless you.

domplines – fried dumplings

¿Dónde irá el buey que no are? – Where will the ox go and not plow?

Don/Doña – a title of respect used before a man or a woman's first name *el granito de café* – the little coffee bean

El tiempo dirá – Time will tell.

empanadillas – meat turnovers

En el nombre del Señor todopoderoso – In the name of the all-powerful Lord.

¿En qué les puedo servir? – How can I help you?

entren – come in (addressing more than one person)

¡Escucha! – Listen!

Escucha al pájaro carpintero – Listen to the woodpecker.

está bien – (he/she/it is…) all right

Está más perdido que un juey bizco – He is more lost than a cross-eyed crab.

Es tiempo – It's time.

¿Es una promesa? – Is it a promise?

Feliz Navidad – Merry Christmas

flamboyán – a flamboyant tree, also called royal poinciana

flan de coco – coconut custard

fricasé de pollo – chicken fricassee

gandules – pigeon peas

gazpacho de bacalao – codfish salad

Gracias – Thank you.

Gracias a Dios – Thank God.

guamá – a long bean-shaped pod with a sweet cottony interior that melts in your mouth

guanábana – soursop

guaracha – a lively genre of music/dance that originated in Cuba

hola – hello

hombre – man

igual/igualmente – same to you

jíbaro – a Puerto Rican small farmer or rural worker, generally of mountainous regions

La gatita tiene miedo – The kitty is afraid.

lágrima de montaña – tears of the mountain (moonshine rum)

la hija de – the daughter of

la misma – the same one

Las aguas siempre vuelven a su cauce – The water always returns to its channel.

laurel geo – a medium-sized flowering evergreen tree native to the Antilles

lechón asado – roast pork

Lo siento – I'm sorry.

(la) luna creciente – the waxing moon

(la) luna menguante – the waning moon

mal de ojo – evil eye

maduros – ripe, fried plantains

Mami – Mommy or Mom

Mamita – little mama, used as a term of endearment

masa – dough

Me alegro que estés aquí – I am glad that you are here.

Me das permiso? – May I have permission?

mi amor – my love

Mija/Mijo – my daughter/my son – used as a term of endearment

Mira quien está aquí - Look who is here.

mosquitero – a mosquito net that is hung from bedposts

Mucho gusto – Pleased to meet you.

(la) nena – the little girl

nogales – walnut trees

No hay mal que por bien no venga – Something good always comes out of bad things.

No importa – It doesn't matter.

No se puede tapar el cielo con la mano – You can't cover up the sky with your hand, meaning that the truth will eventually come out.

Nos vemos – See you.

novenaria/novenario – a person who leads the prayers and litany of a Catholic novena.

novio – boyfriend or fiancé

Nuestra Señora de la Guadalupe – Our Lady of Guadalupe, the Catholic cathedral in the Ponce plaza

ñame – yam

Padre – father; used in referring to or addressing a priest

padrino – godfather

pandero – a tambourine

Papá – Dad

Papi – Daddy or Dad

pan – bread

para endulzar – to sweeten up

Para nadar hay que tirarse al agua – To swim you have to jump in the water.

parranda – a Puerto Rican Christmastime social event featuring traditional music, food, drinks and dancing, typically moving the party from house to house *(la) Pascua Florida* - Easter

pasteles – a typical Puerto Rican food made with seasoned pork and other ingredients encased in a *masa* made of grated green plantains and taro roots, wrapped in banana leaves and boiled.

Piensa para hablar y no hables para pensar – Think before speaking and don't speak to think.

pitorro – Puerto Rican moonshine

plaza de mercado – farmer's market

pobrecita – poor thing

pollo guisado – stewed chicken

por favor – please

pretendiente – suitor

promesa – an oath or a vow taken to do/not do something in exchange for God's fulfillment of a personal request

púa – a pick

quédate – (you, informal) stay

¿Qué pasa? – What's wrong?

¿Qué pasó? – What happened?

¿Qué tienes? – What ails you?

¿Quieres bailar? – Do you want to dance?

recao – broadleaf coriander

ruiseñor – the Puerto Rican nightingale

salsa criolla – Creole sauce

Seguro es el pájaro en el nido – The bird is secure in its nest.

señora – a married woman

señorita – an unmarried woman; a young lady

Será cuando Dios quiera y si Dios quiere – It will be when God wills it and if God wills it.

Sí – yes

sobrina - niece

sofrito – a Caribbean sauce of tomatoes, onions, peppers, garlic, and herbs

Son pajitas que le caen a la leche – They are crumbs that fall in the milk - things of little importance.

súbete – come on up

tembleque – a smooth Puerto Rican coconut pudding that jiggles

¿Te traigo café o agua? – Shall I bring you coffee or water?

Te veo después – I will see you later.

Te ves bella – You look beautiful.

tía/tío – aunt/uncle

Tienes otra niña hermosa – You have another beautiful girl.

tiple – a stringed instrument of the guitar family that originated in Puerto Rico

tomen su tiempo – take your time

uy – ugh

Vámonos – Let's go.

vamos – we are going

Ven acá. – Come here.

Vete ayuda a tu papá – Go help your father.

vianda – an assortment of tubers such as yucca, taro, celery root, malanga, and yams

¿Vienes para la casa? – Are you coming to the house?

yagrumo – a tropical tree of the Cecropia genus

Ya Luisa se puede casar – Luisa can get married now.

Ya tú estás grande – You are already big.

yautía – taro root